Compiled and Edited
by Gerri R. Gray

HellBound Books Publishing

**A HellBound Books LLC
Publication**

Cover and art design by Kevin Enhart

Printed in the United States of America

Also by Gerri R. Gray:

The Amnesia Girl (HellBound Books, 2017)
Gray Skies of Dismal Dreams (HellBound Books, 2018)
The Graveyard Girls (HellBound Books, 2018)

Contributor to:

Ghost Hunting the Mohawk Valley (Black Cat Books, 2013)
Beautiful Tragedies (HellBound Books, 2017)
Demons, Devils & Denizens of Hell 2 (HellBound Books, 2017)
Poetry Quarterly (Prolific Press, 2017)
EconoClash Review (Thrill Hill Bottom Press, 2018)
Deadman's Tome Cthulhu Christmas Special (2018)
Hyper-tomb: Crypt of the Cyber-mummy (Horrified Press, 2018)
Trump Fiction (Thrill Hill Bottom Press, 2018)
Jitter (Prolific Press, 2018)
Coffin Bell Journal (2019)
and others.

CONTENTS

"God save us from religion." – David Eddings

FOREWORD
By James H. Longmore

ious Hypocrite has to be one of my favorite literary lines ever, and a million thanks to William Peter Blatty for putting those two words in Regan O'Neill's demonically possessed potty mouth.

When Gerri first came to me with her idea for *Blood and Blasphemy*, as someone living on the fringes of the Bible belt, where being an atheist is actually one notch higher on the hate list than Islamic fundamentalists, my mind quickly conjured the vast potential for causing offence, along with the exceedingly good chance of HellBound Books falling foul of the religious PC brigade.

And so, dear readers, here we are…

We live in a time where religion runs rampant, and those who believe do everything within their power to prevent those who do not – and any who dare question – living their lives as they see fit; do remember that Marx described religion as 'the opiate of the masses,' and think about just who should be judging whom!

As you enjoy the deliciously irreverent, downright blasphemous tales that nestle between these wonderfully impertinent covers, do spare at least a passing thought for all those pious hypocrites out there, and relish the fact we are taking them down a notch or two.

Salute, too, the amazingly talented wordsmiths who have given their all to populate this wonderful tome and stand testimony to what a godless lot we horror authors really can be; but, we all sell our souls eventually, so we may as well get a fair price for them.

Nov 2019

INTRODUCTION

Welcome, my friends (and fiends), to *Blood and Blasphemy*.

For your reading enjoyment, I have compiled over thirty of the most blasphemous horror stories ever written. Within this realm of the unholy, you will find a deliciously dark array of strange and terrifying gods, malevolent priests, fiendish altar boys, nuns with bad habits, the unholiest of holy relics, and other sinful offerings from twenty-nine of the horror community's finest writers.

But be warned: If you're hoping or expecting to find salvation or divine intervention among the chilling tales contained within this anthology, I'm afraid your hopes and expectations don't have a prayer in hell. And if you happen to be one of those readers who find themselves easily offended or triggered by irreverence to religion, you'd best leave now and save your mortal soul before it's too late.

However, if you're like me and enjoy your horror dipped in buckets of blood and sprinkled with generous amounts of blasphemy, then you've come to the right place. Between the covers of this book, nightmares of sacrilegious, disturbing, and terrifying proportions await you.

Enter at your own peril.

G.R.G.

Gerri R Gray – Blood and Blasphemy

THE CHERUB
By Jeremy Megargee

Pastor Wormwood crouches on the cracked tile of the bathroom floor, a spidery hand with mottled skin gripping his daughter's used tampon, squeezing the menstrual blood from it, the blood rubies running down his palm to pool on the silver collection plate between his knees. The plasma is thick, viscous, a healthy consistency for a girl of eighteen years. But that isn't the most important thing. For Wormwood, what matters most is the purity of the blood. The claret that flows from his little orchid's veins is virginal, and like a dark nectar; he milks it to a feed another child. A special child, one both maligned and misunderstood, so grotesque upon birth that Wormwood had no choice but to sequester the squealing babe away to a sanctuary in the shadows. At first the good Pastor thought that the Almighty had seen fit to inflict a curse upon him, but as months passed, he saw his unique son as less of a burden, and more of a test of faith. That little fetal lump of twisted organs, bulging eyes, and limp limbs drooping in places where no arms or legs are ever meant to be, not a fiend, not a monster, but a blessing made raw, something in need of proper cultivation.

He chose the root cellar beneath the chapel where he preached as a fitting place to house his boy, and at first he worried the sunken earthen walls and the gloom would ruin the child, making him insular, but soon the little miracle adapted to his environment. He had no need for pacifiers, because he'd use a chubby hand to pull plump night crawlers from the floor, sucking at the worms until sleep overtook him. The rats that nested along the rotting wooden beams provided him with nocturnal lullabies, their chattering conversations serving to soothe him during those first few cold winter nights. He was only a few months old when he began to crawl, and gravity was nothing but an obstacle to be conquered, for the child would grip at the roots embedded in the dirt walls and climb across all surfaces, even the drooping ceiling. Wormwood entered once this way, the multiple skeleton keys for the multiple padlocks on the door jingling together, and his adventurous boy dropped from above into his waiting arms to give him a painful kiss that left a deep scar along his cheek for years to come.

A happy little thing, a boy-angel in flight, and so it seemed only fitting to call him The Cherub. Jars of Gerber would never do for such a sensitive palate, and so the child's meals were of his own making. He'd dig ferociously in the dirt, pulling moles from their burrows and chomping them down while they still lived. Beetles become a favorite, and how his eyelids closed with bliss each time his teeth closed on the shells, offering that satisfying pop before the coming of the juice. And just as Christ turned water to wine, sometimes the child would gouge at his own flesh, bringing the red, fits of desperate melancholy overtaking him, and this self-made wine he would smear against his lips, drinking of self, dining on that which is contained within, a sacrifice that left across his tortured skin wounds that almost rival that of the crucifixion.

Wormwood preached to his congregation year after year, spreading the word, maintaining his place as a pillar of the community in his small Appalachian town, and year after year he watched his Cherub grow. Of course his wife and daughter could never be permitted to see, he'd lied and claimed the child died of complications hours after its birth, but it was a lie forged only to protect the women in his life from undue emotional distress. The Cherub is not their cross to bear, only his. Such a boy needed the support of a strong male authority figure in order to flourish, and Wormwood was just the pious man for the job. Capable of doling out love and discipline in equal amounts, just as the Good Book proclaims it should be.

His kindness was often on display, because after each lashing of the boy with a stripped hickory branch, those piercing howls echoing through the empty churchyard in the middle of the forest, his Cherub curled into the fetal position in the soil, blowing out bubbles of mucus from malformed nostrils, the Pastor would lower himself down to his son's level, and pet the weeping child, much like benevolent soul would stroke the heated flesh of a suffering dog. He'd offer words of encouragement, and receive confused and terrified grunts in response.

"Christ suffered too, sweet boy. His wounds gaped as yours gape. But that was the cost of swallowing the sins of the world…"

The Cherub would often mewl like a kitten after these inspiring words, a kitten all alone in the world without a mother, and the boot of life pressed against its skull and applying more pressure with every passing second. The child seemed brainsick at times, so Wormwood was always left to guess if his little private sermons had any comforting effect on his son. No matter, he'd tear pages from Revelations and press them into his child's avulsions and lacerations, soaking up the blood, smearing the scripture into his hurts to offer solace, for no bandage but ones pulled from the Bible would do for his little miracle.

A decade passed, and Wormwood's hair from brown to white, the church's congregation from many to but a few, the death of seasons, the birth of smartphones and technological revelries, and the Pastor started to fear that God's eye had wandered far from his small mountain parish. The Cherub was a child no longer, but a full-grown man, stunted and ape-like in the root cellar, much like an animal that would have grown much larger if allowed to exist in the wild, but a life of imprisonment had diminished him, and his true potential would never be reached. The Cherub seemed to sense this on some level, and his adolescence brought with it terrible lamentations, a rage to rattle the floorboards of the church, to make the pews tremble at his screams, so primal were his roars that Wormwood had no choice but to permanently close the doors of his church and send his flock to neighboring towns for their Sunday sermons.

For the first time in ages, old man Wormwood began to see his son as less of a gift, and more of an abomination.

He started to dream of fire. A great cleansing flame to be seen all across the valley. And wasn't it Abraham that God tasked with killing his own son? A sacrifice, a proving of loyalty, and sure, God stopped Abraham at the last minute before Isaac was put to the torch, but if God doesn't stop Wormwood, isn't it still a show of fealty? It simply means that his Cherub is destined to burn and join the rest of the fallen in the lake of fire…

Day and night he prayed, and when he wasn't praying, he was stocking up on gasoline at the little rust bucket Mom n' Pop store on the outskirts of town. He took to sleeping in the church, because his wife had the early phases of dementia, little more than a walking scarecrow, and his daughter was off to some fancy college, so no more blood from her pure cunt to feed The Cherub, and this seemed to contribute to his downward spiral. Wormwood would be resting on the hard floor among the pews, and he would hear his son's fists battering against the floor. He could literally tell each time a knuckle split and bled, because a mini-earthquake would shake the church and send dust tendrils drifting down from the rafters.

Wormwood's eyes became lost in darkened hollows, his weight dropped, and he took on the visage of a haunted man. He'd drag a stool down to the root cellar on certain nights when sleep escaped him, and he would stare at his son. He'd long ago affixed an old iron manacle to the boy's ankle to try and contain him a bit more, but the more he fights, the more the links of that chain weaken against the iron ring set into the stone on the floor.

Wormwood also made the mistake of giving his Cherub a copy of the Old Testament several years ago before his mind had fully succumbed to derangement, and despite all odds, his son has taught himself how to read. It's a rudimentary grasp of language, draped in low cunning, but something about it disturbs the Pastor so deeply that it makes his soul itch. Certain passages that his son favors are hung up on the walls of his room/cell, speckled there with glue made from his own shit and saliva. When his father visits, The Cherub immediately stops slamming himself against the walls, and he sits on the far wall, lowering himself to a sitting position with the Bible clasped between his bony knees like a talisman. His glare is baleful in the dark, and Wormwood is reminded of the eyes of a fox searching for the best entry point to the henhouse.

The Cherub's mouth is obscured in the gloom, and Wormwood is grateful for that when he speaks. It is a broken, wet smacking noise, a jaw full of ingrown teeth with a tongue that hangs from the lips, a hound made rabid in his isolation.

"God maded me, Fatheher? He maded me from water, and from clay, and from stars?"

"Yes. He made us all, son."

"And Jesuth, his son, he sent him down, down low. To

take the spear. To take the nails. To bleed. To hurt. To cry. To wear crown, crown of pain, always pain, forever pain…"

The Cherub's eyes shine in the dark. Eyes brimming with trauma. Eyes glassy with tears. Eyes that bespeak of years of abuse, years of mistreatment, decades of dehumanization… and the overlying hate that covers it all, like scum overtop an abandoned pool.

"Is this the thing a Fatheher givesth his son? Pain? You have givesth to me. So much of it. So to me, you are God."

The Cherub leans forward, large concave skull pulling his neck to the side, mangy blonde hair obscuring one side of his face, cleft lips pulling back from jagged teeth in a blatant snarl.

"I'll givesth back, God. Oh yes, I'll givesth back."

Wormwood could only stare at that declaration, his harrowed face pinched as he wrung his hands together. Was Abraham ever pushed like this? Was Isaac ever this ungrateful? He searches his heart, trying to find even a sliver of love left for his son, but he feels only fire…

* * *

A malformed hand scrubs at the earth with fecal matter, urine, bile, tears, all fluids that might serve as a substitute for ink. Eyes glitter with veiled intelligence, but it is a mind that has been left to rot in unsavory conditions. New scripture is being written, because the old is cruel, and pain has reached an unendurable level.

No rule about rewriting what once was.

What would have happened if Jesuth had pulled the nails from his wrists, leaped from that cross, and marched back up to Heaven to smite his true tormentor?

The gnarled fingers scrawl and write, and in the new scripture, a plot formulates…

As the moon rises beyond the root cellar, the sound of gnawing competes with the chirping of the crickets.

* * *

It sloshes from the can, the stench burning his nostrils, and so he pretends that it is holy water, just the blood of the lamb pouring out to saturate the pews, the pulpit, the church where he spent most of his adult life preaching the good word. The matchbox sits heavily in the back pocket of his blue jeans, and he caresses the outline of the box for strength with each splash of gasoline.

He saved the root cellar for last.

Abraham wouldn't falter. He would see it through, because that is God's will. Wormwood must follow in his footsteps. Before departing to the outer panel doors that descend into the root cellar, the Pastor retrieves a match, taking just a moment to strike it and gaze into the fluttering flame.

He pitches it against a pew, and his eyes reflect the firelight as the conflagration takes over. The wood of his church is old, and so it burns all the faster. He must be quick, and he must not linger in nostalgia.

Wormwood makes his way to the cellar doors, his hips creaking with age, and he uses his collection of keys to open each coinciding lock. He descends the earthen steps slowly, gas can sloshing, a single match burning for light.

He shines it back and forth, seeking his son, and at first glance he does not find him. Something is amiss. There is a pool of fresh plasma in one corner, and there in the middle of it like a dead snake sits the manacle that *should* be around The Cherub's ankle. The old man searches, peering from side to side with his makeshift light, and that is when he notices something warm and wet dripping across his nose. His hands lifts, and his fingertips come back streaked in red.

His wrinkled face slowly tilts upward, and there to greet him is not a child-like angel, but a loping troglodyte, a slavering freak with a bloodied and bitten ankle, a face so black with evil it radiates in waves before The Cherub flips himself down and drives a meaty forearm into his father's face, crumpling the old man to the ground like a sack of brittle bones.

Dark fades in and out, and Wormwood is vaguely aware of his body being dragged up steps, and fitting that pain should bring him fully back to consciousness. His eyes flash open just as his only begotten son drives rusted carpentry nails through his wrists, nailing him to the beams above the pulpit, his own body weight supporting itself in excruciating fashion with nothing but those frail wrists. The Cherub discards the hammer, standing in the aisle between the pews and observing his father, and Wormwood almost forgets about the flames before the heat starts to bake at him from all sides. An inferno of his own making. A Hell born of his own hands. And in the center of it all, a very personal demon…

The Cherub comes close one last time, intimately close, Wormwood taking in the full aroma of rotten teeth, blackened gums, halitosis mixed with frothing drool. For a brief millisecond, Wormwood almost thinks that he sees a shred of humanity in this monster's eyes. Something he's responsible for eradicating. A person buried and burned by faith…

"God givesth pain. Far back as I remember…"

A sneer. The Old Testament is grasped loosely in a lobster-like claw, and Wormwood watches as his son casts the book away into a mound of cinders, the embers floating up to mingle with the flames.

"He should *feel* too."

And with a scream of anguish building in the corridor of his throat, Wormwood begins to feel. The Cherub lopes away through the aisle, freedom and fresh night air awaiting beyond the doors, and the Pastor is allowed to view his son's escape before the fire reaches his eyeballs, turning them to melted gelatinous ooze in the orbital sockets. He sucks in air to scream again, but smoke comes instead, flooding his lungs, scorching them black as tar. He seizes and buckles, his flesh curling into the perfect crucified form.

A final memory assaults him before death, a small infant cradled to his chest, deformed, but innocent. Reaching for his face with fused fingers, hoping for a father's love.

So small. So pure.

Cherubic…

THE END

PURGATORY
By Shawn Wood

It was hot, dry, dirty. Everything one would expect from a town called Purgatory. A fine, white alkali dust caked his worn leather boots. It lingered on his jeans and wormed into his nostrils. It choked his scorched throat. His boot heels clumped, echoing on the seasoned wood of the church stairs. Sweating bodies huddled tight, all facing the altar, swayed in the dizzying heat. The last rays of light sunk beneath the horizon. Full darkness had come.

Cobwebs hung from the worn wooden beams. Candlelight danced, caught in a backdrop of stained glass. Kaleidoscope colors, blue, red, yellow, reflected on the aged plaster walls. Ancient boards bleached to the color of nothingness lined the floor forming a path towards the altar.

It was black as pitch. Covered with dark linens. A single red candle threw shadows towards the parishioners. It was all a mirage to Daniel. All he could focus on amongst the flickering candlelight and swirling colors was her.

She stood apart from the rest of the congregation. The lace of her dress swayed as she rocked back and forth, her hands raised to the ceiling. She was floating in rapturous ecstasy.

He watched the pale blue dress sweep the floor as she clapped her hands to some mysterious internal rhythm. In the stark vision of his mind's eye he remembered the first time he had seen her in that dress. The scent of rose water enveloped him. He was home again.

* * *

Early morning sun sparkled in the dew. He was walking to town, adolescent dreams creeping at the edges of his mind. He crested a hill and looked towards the west. In the distance, among the rolling hills, he glimpsed the prettiest flower, standing, staring at the horizon. The long strands of grass waving around her in the wind mirrored her raven hair. He passed and tipped his hat to her, painfully aware of her beauty. She smiled the sweetest smile Daniel had ever seen. In that moment he fell in love.

* * *

Thunderous clapping tore him from the bliss of his memories and back into the church. The air was leaden. Cobwebs that had once danced against the breeze hung lank. The flames of the candles froze in place. His vision narrowed, focused razor sharp on her.

"Rebecca!" he yelled. "Rebecca!" His voice echoed off the walls.

Not a soul in the congregation stirred from their trance. Their faces were turned up towards a preacher all in black. His vestments hung from his sinewy frame. Muscles twisted and writhed under silken fabric. He wore no collar, no crucifix.

Daniel stopped and squared off, mimicking what he thought a brave man, a warrior, a gunfighter would do. His eyes fixed on the preacher. A bead of sweat trickled slowly, carving a glistening trail in his dust-caked face. He could feel the uncomfortable weight of the gun hanging from his hip. The finality in it made his stomach clench. *Chasing after her for days and weeks, tracking her through miles of dust and desert. There has to be more to it than this*? Daniel thought.

The preacher's voice was cool, smooth. His words were an oasis surrounded by scorching sands.

"And in the end I sayeth to the faithful..."

Daniel felt his mind float along with the rhythm of the words. There was a magnetism here that pulled at his very soul.

"My children," the preacher sang. "My children, we have amongst us one that wishes me harm." His silken voice rose to a crescendo.

Their trance broken, the gathered faithful stirred. Nervous, narrowed eyes glanced in Daniel's direction. Brows furrowed. Voices murmured.

"Now, now, my children. This man has simply fallen off the path. He has cast away something dear to him and he seeks to reclaim it."

The preacher turned the full power of his brilliant gaze upon Daniel.

Now! Do it now! The last traces of Daniel's sane mind screamed. His hand dropped to the pistol butt. He felt the heaviness of the world as he drew the gun. Stinging sweat poured into his eyes.

"Son... My son," The preacher cooed. "You're just lost." He moved towards Daniel. "She's mine now, son." Twisted reflections danced in the black shine of his boots. He stepped towards Rebecca. He took her hand lightly, kissed it. She rose to her feet. His lips lingered a moment too long against her skin. His eyes flashed at Daniel.

"You bastard." Daniel cocked the hammer, grasping the gun with both hands.

"Tell him, my child," the preacher said as he guided her

into the aisle between Daniel and himself.

"Daniel, I'm home... I'm finally home." She turned her eyes toward the preacher. "I'm staying with him."

"That's a good girl, Rebecca." The preacher gently kissed her forehead as he dismissed her from his side.

With liquid speed the preacher closed on Daniel. His long fingers were ice as they clamped over Daniel's. The weight of the gun floated away as the preacher raised it to his own forehead. Daniel's hands shook with fear. Daniel could smell him now. Rotten. The smell of aged death. His stomach lurched once, twice.

The preacher's voice was a harsh whisper, "Well?" He smiled savagely. His teeth were razor points. His eyes, red flames.

The air hummed with electricity. Seconds hung as time turned in on itself. Daniel could feel the preacher's will forcing itself in upon him. Goading him. Pushing him towards pulling the trigger. His resolve broke as his stomach and his will betrayed him. He crumpled, vomiting onto his own boots. A wet sob flew from Daniel's throat. Fear paralyzed him. Only his heart resisted. *She was your wife, your world,* he thought.

The preacher seemed to grow, to rise above Daniel. With a dull thud, the gun dropped to the floor. Tears streamed down Daniel's face. Trails of snot and spittle clung to his boyish stubble.

"Even this sinner cowers against the might of the chosen," he called to his congregation in his smooth drawl. The candles flickered again. The parishioners swirled in colors. Their faces twisted into masks of demonic levity. *Their teeth. What's wrong with them?* Daniel thought through a tumultuous storm of a headache.

"We cannot be harmed by the sins of the wicked. We cannot be harmed by jealousy or greed or even the gravest of all sins: Murder," the preacher's voice rose to a crescendo as his hands rose towards the heavens. Thunderous applause rained down from the writhing, jostling creatures. Rebecca's eyes fell on the shadow of the man she had once loved. They dropped, staring aimlessly at her hands. "Shame on you Daniel. Go away, let her be," cawed a twisted creature from its spot in an adjacent pew. The congregation of vile creatures laughed as one.

Daniel's heart broke. He had endured days of scalding desert heat, nights of bone-chilling cold, thirst, hunger, all to lay eyes upon her again. All to win her back. His moment had come and he had crumbled under the weight of it. His spirit dropped to a new low. The gun lay still, impotent on the floor. Realization dawned on him. *I failed*, he thought. He turned and cast a last look in her direction. She looked longingly at the preacher. Daniel ran out into the night. Laughter chased him.

* * *

Oil lamps, old news back east, brand new out in the fringes of the western frontier, cast flickering light along Purgatory's main street. The copper and brass fixtures swung in the dry desert breeze. Daniel walked in a daze. His mind tussled with he had seen. He loved her. Of that he was certain. She was gone. He had not accepted that.

His skin crawled. The hair stood rigid on the back of his neck. The whole town felt wrong. The shadows were too deep. The light couldn't penetrate them. Buildings were shuttered, enveloped in darkness. He saw thin lights ahead. He hooked his thumbs into the empty gun belt sagging at his waist and headed towards the light.

In every town there are places best avoided. The Silver Sluice was Purgatory's. Scars of past conflicts lingered in the facade of the saloon. One batwing door hung from a broken hinge. A sad ballad, horribly out of tune, escaped from a dying piano. A single tooth was embedded deep into the bar top. Its former owner lost to time. A deep, dark auburn stain lingered on the warped boards of the floor.

The ring of a blade clearing a scabbard stilled the off-key warble of the piano. "I'll cut ya. I swear I will. Ya dirty cheat," a shrill voice cried through the still air.

In rapid succession, two deafening cracks brought silence to the bar. A gold coin tumbled through the air and landed on the dead man's chest, bouncing to the floor.

"That should cover any damage to your fine establishment, Hal," a husk of a voice called. Chair legs screeched across the dirty grime of the floor. A tall, wire-thin figure stood with a smoking pistol in his hand. His hat hung low, casting deep shadows across his face.

"You... You killed Bart!" a voice yelled.

"Yes. Yes I did," came the stranger's cool reply. He looked from face to face. They all cast their eyes downward; none would meet his blazing eyes.

Daniel was lost in the blur as the oiled blue steel of a revolver vanished back into its holster. The stranger turned and eased his way out through the one functioning batwing door. With a final glance over his shoulder, he stepped out into the blackness of the night.

Slowly, with the caution of a cat approaching a mouse, two men crept out after the stranger. Daniel's whiskey-laden mind scrambled for purchase. He rose to his feet, the world a spinning torrent of lanterns, gun smoke, alcohol. Staggering, he pushed past the broken door. In his haste and stupor, he missed the last step and landed heavily in the dirt of the street. He swore angrily as he rose to his knees. Daniel dug his hands into the hard packed dirt. He cried, "Rebecca! Damn you! You son of a bitch preacher!"

Across the street, an ember glowed red. Gray smoke floated up, mingled with the darkness and disappeared. The stranger watched, listened. This town was different from others ringing the western frontier. It had a disease. A cancer that had eaten away its soul and left a stinking, black emptiness.

He had watched the two duck from the bar and creep along the boardwalk towards the sheriff's office, taking what they perceived as extra care to keep to the shadows. Like most of the residents left, they avoided the light as much as possible. The stranger smoked his cigarette and watched, letting the world roll in on him.

He had heard rumors the congregation had settled here. Ever since he had ridden onto Main Street he could feel their evil, smell their stench. Malice and gluttony dripped from them and left a stinking trail wherever they went. New converts in tow. *Now this sodbuster ranting about his woman and a preacher confirms it*, the stranger thought.

In another life, in another time he had known the preacher. He rubbed his throat lightly, his fingers tracing the knotted scars. A reflexive gesture he had tried to quell over the years. He shook his head to clear the memories.

Here he was again, standing, waiting to see what cards would fall. *Cut and run before things get heavy. Maybe this really ain't your fight*, a voice whispered in the back of his mind. The hair stood up on his arms. *Maybe it is my fight*, he thought.

Commotion erupted down the street. Out of breath and half dressed, the sheriff arrived with the two men from the bar in tow. His prodigious gut rolled and bounced, he gasped for breath. The tin star hung askew on his crumpled shirt.

Daniel lifted his head again and wailed her name into the night. He never saw the heavy leather sap as it sailed through the air. It landed with a deep thump across the back of his head. "Shut yer mouth. Dontcher know how late it is?" the sheriff shouted. "This your mad killer, boys? This the one that killed old Hal?" the sheriff chuckled. He stood over Daniel's limp body, proudly.

"No sir," one of the men answered, shakily.

"He's over there. Watching." The other thrust his thumb towards the stranger.

The sheriff turned slowly. Knowing he had been caught

blind, he stared at the glowing ember. The stranger stood still, watching.

"You. Over there. Git out where I can see you. Show me your hands," the sheriff called into the night. His voice wavered ever so slightly.

Three loud cracks, three roaring belches of fire. At this angle, from behind them, I'd get them clean enough before they even had a chance to draw. They'd fall like silent stones and my problems would be over, the stranger thought. He smiled and tossed his cigarette into the dirt.

"It was a fair fight, Sheriff. He pulled a knife on me. Accused me of cheating," the stranger called as he stepped into the light. His raised arms made him look even taller and more gaunt than he already was. Even in the bright light of the oil lamps his hat hid his eyes.

"Welp, that may be and it may not be. Ain't for me to say," the sheriff answered. "Zeb, grab his gun. Eli, you get hold of that other one on the ground. These boys are gonna be guests of the fine town of Purgatory," he said. His eyes smiling with malice. *Two more souls to rot in Purgatory*, he thought.

* * *

Rebecca lay still in her bed. It was soft, luxurious, yet it folded up neatly. It fit her new life. She sometimes missed the bed she had shared with Daniel. She sometimes missed lying awake next to him, just listening to the night. In the dim hours before dawn, she remembered her old life. She remembered him.

He had courted her relentlessly. "That boy is hounding on you," her father said one morning as he came inside carrying a bouquet of flowers that had been left on their front stoop. Her smile radiated through the room as she clutched the flowers, brought them to her nose and whiffed deeply. The smell promised hope.

Even now, remembering the flowers he used to bring her made her smile. Her memories landed square in the first year of marriage. She remembered Daniel working in the fields, working on the house, in the barn. Days spent building the life that Daniel wanted. The flowers stopped early in that first year. She would sit for hours staring out the window, looking over the horizon. Looking for something more. She knew there were chores that needed doing but her soul cried out for adventure.

One evening, on her way back from a ride through the tall grass, she found it. The preacher and his congregation were holding service a few miles outside town. She dismounted quietly, snuck to the edge of the clearing, the warm glow of their bonfire washing over her. She heard laughter, conversation. Fiddles played. Drums thumped. Couples danced, whirling in colored clothes. She thought she heard a voice whisper in her ear, "Come. Join us." Wonder gripped her.

Her feet moved of their own volition, propelling her farther into the circle of light. "Closer," the voice said playfully in her ear.

Her night had been rapturous. Talking, laughing, listening to tales of the exciting places they had been. As dawn approached, she said her farewells. They begged her to join, to leave her old life. Two days later she obliged.

* * *

His head throbbed. The world was a blurry landscape of iron bars and worn wood. Daniel sat upright. He cradled his head carefully as he rose. Across the cell bars, a man sat on his haunches. His hands clasped between his thighs. Shadows from his hat fell over his face. A lit cigarette dangled between his lips. Smoke ringed him.

"Hell of a bump you took, kid," the stranger said.

"Where am I? What happened?" Daniel stammered.

"You were yammering in the street. Sheriff whumped you. You were blubbering about a woman. Rebecca, nearest I can recall."

Daniel shook his head gently to clear out the remaining cobwebs. "My wife. Rebecca. I came to get her back. He changed. They all did."

"Yep. Now, slowly tell me what happened."

Daniel told his tale, finishing with, "You. That's right. I was looking for you. I followed you out into the street."

"Yeah. Me," the stranger said, his husky voice carried through the rickety jail cell. "I think you and I might just help each other out." A skeleton key dangled between his fingers. "Shhhhh," he whispered as his index finger touched his lips.

The sheriff's snores banged and rattled throughout the jail. They crept slowly down the hall, the cell left empty behind them. From the shadows a figure slunk out. The stranger caught the movement ahead and hesitated. "Now you boys just freeze right there," Eli called. His gaunt hands caressed a double-barreled shotgun. His eyes were a dull red. His lips curved upwards into a twisted smile exposing a mouthful of crooked rotting teeth. "I knew you two was trouble. I tried to warn the sheriff, tried to get him to take you right over to the preacher square away. But he wouldn't listen to me," he said, overjoyed with himself.

As fast as lightning, the stranger dropped and rolled. A metal blur leaped from his hand and embedded itself deeply in Eli's chest. He sunk to his knees. Reflexively, his fingers squeezed the twin triggers. The shotgun roared. A huge hole appeared in the wall to Daniel's right. With a thud and a scream, the sheriff rolled out of bed. Sleep addled and moving as fast as his bulk would carry him, he tore down the hall.

The stranger never hesitated as he closed on Eli. He wrenched the shotgun from his grip. Spilled shotgun shells littered the floor. He scooped up a handful, popped the barrels, and reloaded.

Daniel watched in horror as Eli pulled the blade from his chest. Smoke singed his hands as they touched the carved crucifix on the hilt. He screamed in monstrous agony as fire grew between his hands. His face changed and melted into one of the monstrous creatures. The stranger wheeled around and leveled both barrels. The shotgun roared and the thing that had once been Eli vanished in a smoking cloud of mist. The stranger reloaded and aimed down the hallway towards the sounds of the sheriff's labored breathing. He thumbed the hammers back and waited.

The sheriff pounded into view. He stared straight into the twin cavernous barrels and slid to a sudden halt. "Please, mister. Don't shoot," he cried, dropping to his flabby knees.

"Get the leg irons, kid," the stranger said, pointing to a set hanging on a hook in the hallway. Daniel struggled to his feet. Still shocked by seeing Eli vaporized only feet away. "Come on, kid. You want to get this Rebecca back, we need to get a move on," the stranger said. The mention of her name snapped Daniel out of the fog. He shackled the sheriff and locked him in a cell.

"He knows you're here, you know," the sheriff called to the stranger. "Oh, that's right. He'll be coming for you," the sheriff giggled as he said it. The stranger turned and looked into the sheriff's eyes. A cold piercing look that chilled Daniel to the bone.

"Not if I get to him first," the stranger said as he walked out into the night.

"You really going after him, mister?" Daniel asked.

"We. We are going after him kid," the stranger said. He loaded his pistol and dropped it into its holster. He held the shotgun out for Daniel. Side by side they marched down Main Street.

* * *

Stinging, acrid smoke rose from the barrel of the stranger's pistol. His aim was true. A large hole, clean through, appeared in the middle of the preacher's stomach. Slowly, he looked down, cupping his hands to the wound. Shocked horror washed over his face as the blood drained out of him. One of his foul parishioners let out a piercing scream. Blood pooled at his feet. Crimson. Angry.

Daniel moved quickly to Rebecca. He wrapped his arms around her. He caught hold of her, kissed her cheeks, her forehead, felt her against him. There was something unfamiliar about the way she felt in his arms. He looked deeply at her face. Her eyes were different.

Rebecca, in shocked horror, pushed Daniel away. "I told you to leave me be!" she yelled. Her strength surprised him. Daniel recoiled.

From behind them a cold voice called. "Oh Joseph... you thought shooting me would end it all," the preacher said. Icicles of laughter flew from him. "Fool!" he thundered. Gnarled, twisted, his torn flesh knit itself back together. His hands became terrible claws. His teeth grew into glistening fangs. Four shots rang out in quick succession. Four terrible explosions followed by four crimson holes appeared in the preacher's chest. Every bullet struck home, but the preacher just laughed, low and guttural.

The stranger, the man once known as Joseph, retreated, scooping Daniel up off the floor. With liquid speed the preacher reached Rebecca. She turned her face up towards him as he lightly caressed her. Staring into Daniel's eyes, he kissed her neck softly. Without warning, he sunk his fangs deep into her. Blood spurted from her throat. Greedily he drank. She moaned longingly. She smiled her sweetest smile.

Joseph hit the doors and ran, dragging Daniel into the darkness.

* * *

Froth ran from the horse's mouth in long strands. Purgatory lay far behind them. Its malice radiated. The sun had risen and set twice since they had faced the preacher. Joseph pushed their horses to their limits. Around mesas, through dry ravines filled with scraggly cotton wood trees, they rode. Daniel slumped in his saddle, red-eyed and bleary. He bobbed and weaved like a dead man with every stride the palomino took. As the sun set low in the distance, they stopped to make camp. Daniel slumped against the trunk of a large scrub pine. Exhaustion took him.

* * *

Daniel smiled as he settled deeper into bed. He could hear Rebecca's soft, sleepy breaths. Shadows were chased away from her face as clouds moved, allowing moonlight to creep through the window. She pulled closer and nuzzled in against him. A cold wind blew through the room. His eyes, heavy with sleep, caught movement from her side of the bed. *Maybe she's just turning over*, he thought. He closed his eyes.

Piercing. Tearing. Pain flooded his body. His eyes sprung open, His hot blood dripped from gleaming white fangs. Each dark drop framed against the moonlight. He tried to scream but jets of crimson sprayed from the ragged hole torn in his throat. With pleading eyes he saw her. She smiled as sweetly as ever. Dark eyes shining with lust. Greed. Hunger.

Daniel screamed himself awake into the dark night. The fire burned low. Joseph sat, still as the night, silently watching Daniel in the darkness. On the dry desert breeze, low voices singing choir hymns floated to their ears.

THE END

FATHER HENRY'S LAST HOMILY
By Christopher T. Hamel

Sunday, May 5th, 2019

If I told you that I used to be a priest and that, as of now, I am in prison due to something in relation to a child, what are the first words that come to your mind? Is it, *That monster!* Or how about, *I hope he rots in Hell!* And of course, there's always the bitter question: *What do you expect from a corrupt church?* You all, of course (unless you know my case), are thinking that I performed the only crime a priest is infamous for—that of sexual molestation.

It isn't like that. I'm not in prison for what you think.

One of my favorite sayings—unbiblical, but true—is that "assuming makes an ass out of you and me." I am not here, propped up in a bed above my snoring cellmate, using a small flashlight to write upon the desk of my knees, because of child rape. No, I am here for murder. Mass murder.

But I did not do it. I was not responsible for those three-dozen parishioners at St. Joseph's in Kennington, Connecticut: their throats drained fountains of blood, their eyes wide and shocked and full of an ever-remaining terror.

Let me explain my case because what's happening to me now may ruin any chance I have of true confession. Both to God and to man.

Saturday, April 6th, 2013

If you ask me, what one thing is more dying than attendance to Sunday mass, I say it is the decrease of people going to confession. There are lots of reasons, most of it revolving around the question of: *Why should I?* Even I, who had gone to confession twice a week since my youth, never fully bought into the sacrament as truly Christ-inspired.

Whether authentic or not, there are those still loyal to the sacrament. Brenda and Luis Levi and their daughter Lilly were regulars at the confessional booth. Each other Saturday, they would confess to me their most grievous and mundane sins.

When Lilly came into the confessional booth, she said: "The Devil is inside me."

I scowled, saying nothing for a full minute or more. "Lilly... You're supposed to say, 'Forgive me, Father, for I have sinned.'"

"But I don't want forgiveness," Lilly said. "I just want you to believe me."

"I do. But can you explain to me what you mean by 'the Devil is inside you'?"

"Father Henry, if you don't believe me—and I mean *totally* believe me—bad things are going to happen to the Church. *Very bad things.*" I felt something like an icy worm crawl up my neck. I ignored, counting the feeling as irrational unease

"I believe you, my dear." But really, I thought this delusional. I knew mental illness ran in her family. Her father, though a highly successful therapist, had some form of bi-polar disorder that was prevalent in youth groups when he was younger. And from what Monsignor Bradly told me about Lilly's grandfather—he'd been a bit peculiar as well. Obsessive was the word I think he used.

"The Devil is inside me," Lilly repeated. "But he is not the true Enemy."

"What do you mean, sweetheart? Satan *is* the Chief Enemy of God."

"No," Lilly said with absolute conviction. "The Chief Enemy of God is His evil twin."

"His *evil* twin?" At this moment, I thought of blatantly accusing her of blasphemy. She was old enough to take the sting. Never had I heard such a ridiculous claim.

"His name is Nihil. He hates your Yahweh, His brother, because *He* brought the chaos of creation into the Void that Nihil ruled with all the other gods."

"There is only One True God, Lilly. And creation is beautiful. A work of art."

"I know. I agree. But that's not what Nihil says. Nihil says peace is attainable through absolute nihilism, which is to say gray nothingness."

"Does Nihil talk to you?"

"He talks to the Devil… and the Devil talks to me."

"Whom you say is inside you—the Devil, I mean."

"Yes."

I mulled this over. Lilly was thirteen now and quite bright, perhaps able to make some type of symbolism of her current adolescent struggle. You wouldn't believe how unconsciously poetic some people are.

"I think the Devil's in me too," I said. "I think he's inside all of us. After all, human nature is—"

"I'm not speaking metaphorically, Father Henry," Lilly said. "The *is* Devil inside me. You *must* believe me for the future to stay bright. For the Church to stay bright."

"I believe you," I said again. But I didn't. In fact, I was committing a sin for saying I believed her.

O ye of little faith, I think to myself now.

Sunday, April 7th, 2013

As are many occupations, the life of a priest is overwhelmingly demanding, yet will seem quite docile when described to another person. For this brief homily, I will only be speaking of the three odd Sunday masses that took place post-Lilly's confession—if you want to call it that, since she did not invoke the necessary opening line all confessors must say (*Forgive me, Father, for I have sinned*). In retrospect, because she did not confess anything per se, I could have spoken to her parents, for fear of Lilly's own delusional mind. I may have saved their lives. Yet, what happened to all those devout Catholics likely would've happened still, even if I altered the script fate seemed to have provided.

St. Joseph's is incredibly small for a Catholic church. Though I've never said it, their crucifix has always made me uneasy. Everything about it is as all Christians are taught of Christ's sacrifice: His body torn, scraped, and bruised by the Roman knights, eyes full of sorrow, pain, and hatred for the sin seeping into Him. The difference with this Christ than with any other crucifix I've seen is that Our Lord's torso lay twisted to the left side of the cross as if His body were part-serpent.

That day's Gospel reading concerned the Lord's Prayer in the Garden of Gethsemane.

In my homily, I said: "I think it's amazing that Jesus Christ Himself could have said no to His destiny." I looked up at our strange crucifix to show reflection upon that mystery. Instead, I saw the twisting torso of Jesus and imagined Him giving His Father a big fuck you; jumping off the cross, and laying waste—first to the Romans, then to the Hebrews, and then to the rest of this sinful universe. At one moment, I thought that was exactly what had happened. That Christian history had become altered at the moment I glared up at Christ, a type of historical self-destruction and cosmic renewal.

I heard the shuffling of uncomfortable parishioners move about, whispers of concerns, clearings of throats, coughs, and a sneeze or two. I turned and continued my homily about choice and free will. And suddenly, it all seemed so pointless.

When Perry and Layla, the altar servers, brought me the bowl of hosts and the goblet of wine, I did everything by rote.

"The Body of Christ."

"Amen."

"The Blood of Christ."

"Amen."

When I drank the blood, it tasted sour—like old milk. And when I tasted the host, it felt not dry and brittle as usual, but waxy and moist. I wonder now if that is what literal shit tastes like. Everything else about that Sunday went as usual.

April 14th, 2013

Kennington, Connecticut has three separate churches scattered through town. St. Joseph's, St. Mary's, and St. Anthony's. For these three churches, we have three priests (Father Adam, Father George and myself) and one deacon (Gregory Levi) to lead the parishioners in Mass every Sunday. Because Deacon Gregory could not be present for the seven o'clock mass due to the flu, it was up to me to take his place.

I am not an early bird, by any means. Groggily, I walked into the church, up upon the stage, and into the back room where today's vestments hung. Already, the early birds were taking their seats, saying their rosaries, praying in silence. When I came out of the backroom, clothed in my emerald green vestments, I bowed before the altar. And felt a drop of warm liquid drip onto the back of my neck and slither downward like a hot worm. I touched it and beheld blood on my fingertips. I looked up and saw an amazing sight: the nails thrust into Christ's hands and feet were gone. If not for the plaster, the figure of Our Lord and Savior would've fallen upon my head.

I looked at the five or six parishioners to see if they saw the same thing, but all of them were too engaged in their prayers. I looked up and saw that Christ remained as He'd always been.

No. Not quite. His torso twisted serpentine to the left, instead of to the right. And there was something about His face. It was no longer the face of pain, anguish, and agony—but one of pure delight. Of malice, too.

Mass went slow that day. The readings seemed to drag on.

Numbers 11:4-15, where the Israelites complained about their lack of food, even when God Himself was giving them mana from Heaven, made me want to claw my eyes out for reasons I could not understand.

Psalms 81:12-13, 14-15, and 16-17 sounded to me like a whine from the Almighty. (12 So I left them to their stubborn selves, to follow their own devices. 13 If only my people would listen to me, if only Israel would walk in my ways, 14 at one stroke I would subdue their enemies, turn my hand against their opponents. 15 Those who hate Yahweh would woo his favor, though their doom was sealed forever, 16 while I would feed him on pure wheat, would give you your fill of honey from the rock.)

When I read the gospel readings aloud (Matthew 14:13-21, where Jesus tries to coax Peter to walk on water) my imagination offered me a visualization of Peter drowning and Jesus Himself watching the affair, telling Peter, "You see, Peter? Now you'll get to see my Father before I do. No worries, this is much better than being hung on the cross, upside down. Die this way, Peter. It's much less blasphemous. You'll never have a chance to deny me thrice."

I jerked my mental gaze away from that image, staring at

the three-dozen parishioners. I stood, walked to the pulpit, and said not a word written for my homily, which had to do with faith and trust. A force seemed to control my words, letting them flow like water leaking steadily from a punctured bucket hanging by its handle.

"We're all a bunch of whiners, aren't we?"

Confused faces regarded me.

"Since the beginning of time, all we do is complain about *something, someone,* or *someplace.* Drama queens, my mother called them. I'm beginning to think that human is a synonym for drama. Tell me, folks, what kind of peace do you think Christ brought in? Was it for wars to continue, for famine to continue, for *hate to* continue? Don't you think it would've been better for God to say, '*Well, that was a total failure. Let's wipe the slate clean. Y'know? Bye bye earth and all that.*'"

Several of my parishioners stared at me in wonder, frustrated awe, and outright malevolence.

I sighed. "Folks, Jesus said that He came to bring chaos. Remember that! Matthew chapter ten, verse thirty-four: 'Don't imagine that I came to bring peace to the earth! I came not to bring peace, but a sword.' *Why* though? Why doesn't He just . . . He just."

At last, I looked up at the crucifix. Christ stared down at me, smiling, urging me to continue with a series up.

I screamed up at Him: "Why doesn't He just have Daddy put us all out of our miseries!"

Paul, the lector, grabbed me by the arm and told me enough was enough. His touch seemed to drain all manner of control that this *force*—this Unholy Ghost—seemed to have on me. I told Paul that I was fine.

"That's what the Enemy wants us to think," I said, trying to clean up the psychological mud that I had splashed upon these devout Christians' hearts. "Christ is perfect and His ways are perfect. May the Lord be with you."

* * *

Though I tried to clean up the mess I made that Sunday, Monsignor Bradly paid me a visit. We sat on the back porch of the rectory, drinking decaf coffee. I had a lot of French vanilla creamer in mine. He only put sugar in his; no milk.

"Is everything OK, Henry?" Monsignor Bradly asked.

I didn't say anything for a while, but as was Monsignor's way, he remained silent and patient.

"I think . . . the Enemy is plaguing my mind," I said.

Monsignor Bradley nodded. "There are quite a few parishioners that are concerned."

"Outraged, you mean. You don't have to sugarcoat it, Phil. I used God as my own punching bag—and in front of three dozen parishioners." I put my hands over my eyes.

Monsignor Bradley placed his hand on my knee, giving it a reassuring squeeze. "I think more of us do that then you think. A spiritual illness, eh? Come, my friend, let us pray."

We did. And at the end of it all, I thought I heard an unsexed voice whisper in my ear: *Yahweh is not the only Almighty. Your prayers to Him come to Me as well. Nothing you say is in true confidence.*

Sunday, April 21st, 2013

Due to my spiritual illness, to use Monsignor Bradly's term for it, Deacon Gregory said Mass for both the seven o'clock and the eleven o' clock Mass. I attended the eleven o'clock Mass. I sat in the pew nearest the altar, watching the clergy prepare for Mass. I wanted desperately to look up at the crucifix and see what state the Savior was in today. But equally desperate, I would do anything—*absolutely anything*—not to look.

To my surprise, Lilly sat next to me. I looked all about the church. Her parents weren't present.

"I killed them, Father Henry. Sent them to Nihil. If I didn't, Satan would torture them in Hell. With Nihil, they're nowhere. That's Nihil's peace, y'know. Nothingness." She said all this in the tone she might've used when describing a boring day at school. I realized then that I had not seen her since the confession two or three Saturdays ago. Whatever had been happening to her, it drained her very soul.

Mass started and the moment it did, everything about St. Joseph's changed before my eyes. Upon the altar lay three skulls, *Pater, Filius,* and *Sancti* (Father, Son, and Holy Ghost) scratched messily on their foreheads.

Above the skulls hung the Christ. Only He wasn't hanging. Arms outstretched, blood flowing freely from His hands, feet, and side, He floated there in mock glee and triumph. Replacing the stained-glass images of the saints were those of demons—monstrous creatures that resembled lizards and fish but looked simultaneously like neither. The statues of Mary and Joseph were gone, replaced by what might have been Cain the First Murderer and King Nebuchadnezzar—that old king of ancient Babylon.

Deacon Gregory came to the pulpit with his eyes gouged out. He read not from the Bible, but from a gray stone tablet. Perhaps he read in Braille. "And Yahweh said to His twin to Nihil, 'There is no peace in this Void. I shall make a universe teeming with life.' And Nihil, having heard this, said: 'Fool! Peace is not attainable in life. I will show the chaos creation brings. I will use your most valued angel and make him my Satan (the accuser of the brethren).'"

Deacon Gregory then threw the stone tablet onto the floor. It broke apart in several fragments.

The Dark Christ then descended. The blood flowing from his wounds turned gray: "Do you want true peace?" He asked.

The whole congregation rose and spoke in monotone unison: "Peace. True peace in the Void. Let us be devoured."

"Line up, all of you, and receive the blessing of peace."

And they lined up. To each man, woman, child, the Dark

Christ placed His open lips upon their foreheads and began to suck, to slurp. Their clothes burned off their bodies in silver fire. Their flesh wrinkled and crumpled and tore from their skin like sheets pulled and twisted from the center of a mattress. Their organs turned to ash, while their skeletons melted into pools of gray liquid.

Lilly and I were the only ones not in line. The little girl touched my cheek and looked into my eyes. "You should have believed me." She was crying now.

I grabbed Lilly by the throat and began to choke her. "This is all your fault, this is all your fault," I cried.

I don't know how long that lasted, but I knew that she'd been at least ten minutes dead when I finally let her drop to the floor. Wide, dead eyes stared up at me. I stared into that dying green gaze, realizing that I had just murdered a child.

I fell to my knees and cradled Lilly, weeping.

Someone—that Dark Christ—put His hand on my shoulder.

"Kill me!" I begged.

"There is work to be done." And in sardonic pity, He said, "O ye of little faith."

As if this were a lullaby, I fell into a deep, deep sleep.

* * *

After not hearing a word from either Deacon Gregory or me, Monsignor Bradly came into St Joseph's. What he saw directly contradicts what happened. All three-dozen parishioners lay strewn about the room in carnage. Each person lay dead with the blood drained from their throats.

According to Monsignor Bradly, I was sleeping naked on the altar, smiling and snuggling up to a butcher's knife that had apparently come from the rectory's kitchen.

After vomiting, Monsignor called the police. The police came, woke me up, and arrested me.

* * *

Capital punishment had been repealed in Connecticut a year before this incident. My lawyer, a good and honest man named Alan Derry, tried to get me to plead insanity, but I refused. Instead, I openly received a single sentence of life in Derois County Prison; no chance of parole.

May 5th, 2019

It's been five years since that day and though she comes up in my nightmares, I never much thought of Lilly. She was dead after all. I killed her.

That's what I thought anyway. An eighteen-year-old named Lilly visited me yesterday, claiming to be the same one I had murdered. She did not stay long, for she had only one thing to say to me: "He's inside you now. Nihil shall rise. And soon."

And he is. I can feel Satan within me; can hear his prayers to his god. What happened at St. Joseph's was only a rehearsal for the rise of Nihil and His own Christ.

I am the doorway, I realize. Lilly was right. Bad things happened because I did not believe. Belief is the true weapon against the powers of darkness; a darkness that is not lesser than the light as most are taught, but equal to it. So maybe, just maybe, if I believe that I can bite my tongue off and choke on my own blood, it'll happen.

Lord, forgive me; it's time to test this little faith of mine.

THE END

BLACK MARKET
By Myna Chang

Apennine Peninsula

1347 A.D.

"Iprefer fingers, but not too many. An overabundance will drive down the price." The Traveling Monk flexed his own digits, studying the new gold ring that adorned his thumb. "I don't suppose you could procure a foreskin or two?"

Alfano's face reddened and he looked away. "This is a nasty, ungodly business."

The Monk chuckled. "Surely a gravedigger is not so squeamish. What's an unwanted flap of skin between two merchants such as ourselves?"

Alfano thumped his fist on the table. "I'm no merchant." He tipped his mug, hiding his face.

"Ah, well," the Monk sighed. "'Tis a shame. The relics of a saint bring good coin at market." He refilled Alfano's mug. "And you, with a growing family."

Alfano glowered, pulling his thin tunic tightly about

himself. He looked away from the Monk, but remained at the table.

The Monk suppressed a smile. "I will pay handsomely for your relics, Sir Gravedigger. Four fingers, intact, will keep you in grain throughout the winter."

"There are no relics here. No saints grace our village. If ever I did want to enter this devilsome bargain, I'd not be able to fulfill my commitment."

The Monk laughed, choking on his ale. Alfano squirmed in his seat while the Monk wheezed. When he regained his breath, he smiled and shook his head.

"Alfano, do you believe all the churches and abbeys truly own pieces of Holy Saints? Does the finger of Saint Thomas rest in a box in Rome? Did Saint Nicholas abandon his eyeteeth in Bari's basilica? No, dear Alfano, tell me you're not so gullible."

"But—" Alfano sputtered. "What about the miracles?"

"I've never seen a miracle, Alfano. Have you?" The Monk leaned across the table. "Where do you think your own village's *miraculous* relic came from? The Blessed Toe of Whoever? I'll tell you: my father sold them the tip of a goat's tail."

"No," Alfano protested. "I'll not believe such blasphemy."

"Have it your way," the Monk said. "But our family wore fine warm robes that whole long winter."

Alfano glared down at his empty mug.

"No one could blame you," the Monk continued in a sinuous voice. "Your family will need sustenance in the coming months. The Church will not condemn you for sins they, too, have committed."

Alfano hesitated, pulse thudding in his ears. The Monk unwrapped a small piece of cheese and Alfano's stomach rumbled in response. Finally, he nodded his assent.

"Good man," the Monk said, offering the morsel of food. "I'll be passing through your fair village again next week.

Save the fingers for me. Oh, and please be so kind as to scrape the meat off the bones. They fetch a better price without the gore."

Alfano grunted. He took the cheese and carefully rewrapped it, then nodded at the Monk and stalked away.

As he passed out of sight, the Monk smiled. "You'll make a fine merchant yet, Sir Gravedigger."

* * *

The packed dirt at the edge of the charnelyard resisted Alfano's shovel. A rime of frost laced the remaining leaves on the trees, and chill wind penetrated his threadbare cloak. The coming winter promised to be harsh.

Alfano paused to study the two corpses: young men, travelers who'd been found near the village well. They'd already been stripped of valuables. By the time Alfano had been summoned to bury them, nothing was left but undergarments and torn woolen breeches.

The bodies were bloated, covered in swollen lumps that wept pus and black fluid. Though it was impossible to be certain what the men had looked like in life, Alfano estimated they had been dead no longer than a day.

Another frigid gust whisked his cloak from his shoulders. He winced, thinking of his wife and baby girl huddled by the hearth in their tiny hut. The little one had her mother's eyes, big and brown, with long lashes. When she giggled, he couldn't help but laugh along with her. She would need food and warm swaddling to survive until her next birthday. He scowled.

The dead travelers would not miss their fingers.

Unaccustomed to violating the bodies in his care, Alfano mangled the first man's hand. The edge of the shovel glanced off the bones, leaving an unrecognizable mess. The other hand suffered a similar fate. When he began work on the second man, Alfano was able to remove three intact fingers before damaging the others, though one blackened fingernail sloughed off.

He realized it might be easier to remove the entire hand, so he hacked away at the last wrist until it was free. Dark juices oozed from the stump, and the flesh of the hand split wide, discharging a drizzle of sweet-smelling pus. He dropped the hand on the ground, squeezed his eyes shut, and breathed in crisp autumn air until the urge to vomit had passed.

Turning back to the corpses, he hesitated, unwilling to do more. His teeth chattered in the cold. He huffed out a breath and bent to the task, cutting away the remaining clothing. Inside one of the pockets, he found a soft, yellow handkerchief. Surprised the looters had missed it, he tucked the luxurious fabric into his own pocket.

Eyes averted, he rolled the naked corpses into the grave. The Monk's request for foreskins came back to him. He spat. Fingers would have to be enough. He made the sign of the cross and whispered a prayer, then pushed the dislodged clods of soil over the bodies.

The severed pieces continued to seep, and they emitted a foul odor. He wrapped them in the travelers' clothes. The stained scraps of cloth, recompense for his day's work, would do little to keep his baby girl warm. Alfano shook his head. The Monk's bargain, loathsome as it was, would ensure his family had provisions to last the winter.

He adjusted his cloak and hurried home.

* * *

The Traveling Monk sniffed. No sound came from the ramshackle hut, but a fetid stench wafted in the air. He yelled for the gravedigger. No one responded.

He sighed and nudged the door aside. A putrid miasma poured out. His eyes watered and he gagged. "Alfano, are you here?"

"Leave me, you hound."

The Monk's eyes adjusted to the dark interior. He pressed his fingers over his nose to block the stink. "What has happened here?"

"Punishment. For my sins. For your cursed *relics*."

A woman's body lay on the ground in front of the cold hearth. At least, the Monk judged it to be a woman by the clothing that adorned her body. The face was puffy beyond recognition. Lumps as large as hen's eggs distorted her neck, the surrounding skin blackened and pulpy. Blood and dark liquid had dried in trails over the arms and legs. A tiny form, swaddled in a yellow cloth, had been placed next to her. It too ran with dark ichors.

The Monk scanned the rest of the hut. "And you, Alfano? Are you ill?"

Alfano laughed, wild and demented. "No, Merchant Monk, I am not sick. I fear I have a long life ahead of me." Laughter devolved into a low moan as he gazed at the still forms of his wife and baby daughter. "I've lost everything."

The Monk wrinkled his nose. "I'm sorry this has happened." He paused, then continued, "You mentioned the bones?"

Alfano leaped to his feet. A raw, ragged scream tore from his throat. He grabbed the Monk by his shoulders and shoved him out the door. "Take the devil-damned things and go!" He pointed to a bundle that lay next to his shovel, then staggered back inside the hut.

The Monk looked at the bundle and groaned. It was bulky. "Ah, Alfano, I asked you to strip the meat away." He dropped a coin on the ground near the shovel and secured the items in his bag.

* * *

Gold jingled in the Monk's pocket. He patted it and smirked. He'd sold Saint Alfano's martyred finger bones to three different churches in the last week. The intact hand had gone to the basilica near the port. It alone brought enough money to last a lifetime. He caressed the coins, running his fingers around the edges and rubbing little circles on each one with his thumb.

Wealthy pilgrims already filled the basilica's coffers, hoping to buy blessings. They stood in line, even now, waiting to touch the holy relics, kiss the divine bones as they prayed for miracles. It wouldn't be long before the priests demanded a new attraction to fill their shrine. And if Alfano refused to bargain? Well, there were other gravediggers in the countryside. The Monk smiled.

A new wineskin rested on his side table. He reached for it, but his arm complained, stiff and unwilling to do its job. An unexpected shiver rattled him. He hobbled to the padded chair by his fireplace. The effort taxed him, leaving him short of breath and sweating, despite the chill. He rubbed his damp neck, but instead of perspiration, his hand came away slicked black.

THE END

THE PRIEST'S TALE
By Carlton Herzog

Part I

This shit hole is called 'Earth' by its inhabiting turds. How these idiots survived long enough to build cities is the great galactic imponderable. Blessed are the idiots for they have inherited the earth. I suppose if somebody ever writes a galactic dictionary, a picture of Homo sapiens will be next to the universal word for stupid.

I admit that some of my bile comes from not wanting this species reassignment. Who in their right minds would? I have been ordered to share a body with some chattering, wobbly faced, ecclesiastical old coot who now thinks he's possessed by a devil. I waste a lot of energy keeping that nut job closeted in the sunken place. The body itself is a complete piece of crap: arthritis, glaucoma, high blood pressure, high cholesterol, high sugar, and he's blind as a bat without his coke bottle glasses.

And there's that smell. I never had to deal with this stuff because, before now, I never had a nose. And this guy's nose is like a parrot's beak, only runnier and hairier. It picks up everything, especially his own brand of stink: eau de old geezer, which is somewhere between dirty diapers and liniment. The trips to the toilet are the worst. I'm surprised he's never hanged himself afterwards or just passed out from the smell: his stink that can take the chrome off a trailer hitch.

Clearly, somebody or something has a wicked sense of humor. How else do you explain that wrinkled garden hose between his legs and that sack of marbles swinging below it? How many years of natural selection did it take to produce that floppy mess?

I didn't volunteer for spy duty. I was minding my own business floating in a tranquil sea along with a million or so other Cnidarians when the call came. Mind you, there was no advance warning. Just get your tentacles in order because we're projecting your mind to a world we need to evaluate.

And so, I did, and the next thing I knew they had yanked me out of my comfort zone and sent my consciousness hurtling across the solar system straight into the body of Father Joe, closet pedophile and not so closet drunk.

He went bat-shit crazy when he felt me crawling around his noodle. He ran around all wild-eyed, flailing his arms and laughing uncontrollably, the whole-time telling Satan, whoever that is, to get behind him.

The best part was that the merger took place during Holy Communion. Human faces are so expressive, especially when something weird is happening. Priceless!

They kept asking me, "Are you okay?" I could hear Father Joe yelling from inside our mutual head, "The Devil just jumped inside my head and will not leave—does that sound okay to you?" I told him, "They can only hear me, pal, because I've disconnected you. So, sit back and enjoy the ride. This buddy movie will be over soon enough. Otherwise, I will go bananas to such an extent they will lock you up in the nuthouse and throw away the key." After that, he was as quiet as a church-mouse.

They say confession is good for the soul. I can't speak to

that. What I can say is that it gives a priest considerable power over other people, so much you can get them to do some outrageous things. Before I used that power to get one person to murder another, I had some fun with it: I talked a dentist into eating a tire and a lawyer into biting a police horse. I convinced a *bodega* owner that his bulldog's litter of puppies could do a better job running the business than he. I talked a mute into stabbing a mime, a new mother into breastfeeding a rat, and a councilman into cooking a hot pocket on the third rail of the G-Train. Say three Hail Marys and go with God, stupid.

I can't speak to the quality of all the world's various religions, but since I'm masquerading as a Catholic priest, I have a few thoughts on the matter. What I find amusing is Christians put a lot of stock in a book they haven't read. If they did, they would know that their sky god was a genocidal maniac who ordered mass executions of men, women children and even animals who didn't bow down to him. And for an author who is all-knowing, it seems a bit odd there's no mention of the germ theory of disease, the absolute wrongness of slavery, or an alternative to redemption other than torturing and murdering his own son.

Yet, they follow that unworthy god with slavish faith and devotion. So, it comes as no surprise that they do the same thing with those they choose as their temporal leaders. Government and godhood by the worst is a recipe for disaster.

Part II

In Alien Skullduggery 101, they taught us to keep a journal. They said writing would sharpen my interface with this body and make it easier for me to think and act human. I did what they said but managed to lose the first three journals I started because I had memory problems. No doubt because the human brain is a kluge—a workaround that is clumsy, inelegant and inefficient. But I figure if some human finds them, he or she will think it's a fiction, a bad script for an unmade movie.

The plan, as originally conceived, consisted of transmitting multiple minds into earthly bodies, co-opt those minds, then infiltrate, observe, test, and report back. Based on our collective recommendations, one of three things will happen: Earth will be manipulated into leaving Europa alone, but otherwise, untouched; or it will be colonized through the mass migration of Cnidarian minds into human bodies; or we will manipulate the whole lot to annihilate itself.

I am part of a trinity meant to evaluate the sorrier examples of the species, the rationale being to fully plumb the depths of human depravity. See what it takes to drive them into a killing rage or suicidal depression. So, in addition to my host, the pedophile Father Joe, there is Sally Gumballs, host and crack whore extraordinaire; and Frankie the Wolf, host and freelance hit man. We meet once a week to compare notes and grouse about our raw deal.

Sally Sue, the woman of the evening, looks as if she had lived inside the Chernobyl reactor: Crack and other narcotics have reduced her to a shell of a woman: toothless, acne-faced, emaciated and largely incoherent. She is infected with every known STD known to man and even before she was co-opted, thought nothing of passing those gifts along to her customers. Likewise, our third, Frankie, ranked exceptionally high on the psychopathy scale long before he was compromised, killing for money as well as killing for fun.

In getting humans to kill themselves, the easiest way is to find an emotional sore spot and then remove their inhibitions. Just the other day at confession, I used my powers of mind to induce a woman to pull out her hairpin and stab her abusive husband some twenty times in the face with special emphasis on the eyes and throat.

Frankie, for his part, likes to induce speeding thrill-seekers to drive off cliffs and overpasses. He claims there is an exact science to it, that moment when absolute acceleration meets the immoveable object, thus catapulting car and driver into a high arcing propeller spin.

Sally's forte is more passive aggressive: she hands-out contaminated needles to groups of junkies.

Having the humans kill themselves makes perfect sense. After all, we are jellyfish safely ensconced beneath Europa's icy surface. So, we are as physically and experientially limited as a sentient being can get. We Cnidarians have no technology; we have never seen a sky; we have never used a tool. Our big adaptation is the ability to wind our way past our perceptual and physical limitations by seeing through the eyes of others whose minds and bodies we co-opt.

No tech means everything we know about the earth comes from hacking into the minds of its inhabitants. In fact, everything we know about the universe comes from this method. And no tech means that we have only our far-ranging minds to defend us.

The big wheels figure that sooner or later the terrestrial meat-sacks who are blithely raping and poisoning their own world will probably turn their sights on Europa if only for its abundant water. And should that day come, we need to be as prepared as possible and ready to do anything to defend the sanctity of our home. After all, humans are exceedingly cruel to their native jellyfish. Nothing torques my jaw more than watching a bunch of human kids throwing sand and otherwise torturing a beached jelly. I can only imagine what they would do to us given the chance.

Any decision we make about earth's fate requires many virtual tentacles on the ground. If humans are benevolent at heart, then we merely operate as influence peddlers who steer them to worlds other than Europa. That's the current protocol. Why else do you think everybody's so hot for Mars, with its radiation, poisoned soil—perchlorates—

Christ, that stuff is nasty, and freezing temperatures? *The Martian* with Matt Damon is pure Hollywood bullshit. Only a moron would believe anything could grow in that soil or survive the radiation for very long.

If we find that humans are nothing but un-regenerate pricks, we get them to kill each other. That requires a bit more doing. We can't be in these bodies if that all goes down. No, we need to aim the plane at the ground then eject from the cockpit before impact so to speak. We need to get inside their heads and whip them into such a frenzy that their complete destruction at their own hands is as certain and invariant as the speed of light, which coincidentally, is how fast I believe our minds move through space. Thought being as massless as a photon at rest.

It just hit me that I am writing as if for an audience other than myself. So, is that a feature of the human mind? Or am I going around the bend? It's like there's more than one of me, but then again maybe because I'm sharing this body with another mind the brain defaults to operate as if someone else were listening?

Whatever. It can't be helped. I'm stuck walking around in their skin and seeing through their two eyes. And it's a hot mess that I see.

But I guess that's the point: to see them, warts and all. That's why they have me masquerading as a Catholic priest. I get to hear all their deep, dark secrets and see how far down the perversion hole they are willing to go. Humans believe confession is good for the soul. I've never seen a soul. I wouldn't know what to look for.

What I can say is that the human mind is a fragile thing full of fissures and cleavages, full of geysers spraying crazy thinking. Take my last confessor. First thing she says to me is, "Father, I want to bash my own brains in. It's the voices in my head. They won't shut up. They tell me to kill myself." Not surprisingly, she's a life coach.

Not being one to stand in the way of spiritual progress,

and most curious about my powers of suggestion, I tell her, "You should kill yourself. Who is anyone to say otherwise?"

She asked me, "But, isn't suicide a mortal sin?"

I said, "That's only true if you were fated to live forever. But you come with an expiration date. God doesn't have to deal with the pain and decay of the body, the decline of the mind. He sits up in the clouds, fat dumb and happy. It's your life, not his, and I say do with it as you will.

"Me, I think about ending it all the time. Growing old is a miserable experience. So, quit playing the waiting game, seize control of your destiny, say goodbye as painlessly as possible. And remember, death is just the jumping off point to eternity."

She thanked me profusely for my insight. A few days later, I heard from a reliable source that she had hanged herself. That I felt pleasure in her suicide troubled me. Not because of guilt. Rather, I wasn't sure whether she had done it solely by my power of suggestion or the wisdom implicit in my prescription.

So, confession was now a test of my power to influence people, driving them to do whatever evil task I set out for them. My next victim came in totally off the rails. For a moment, I thought it might be a fellow Cnidarian having a bit of fun in the driver's seat, but as we proceeded, I realized this guy was nuttier than a fruitcake. So, like any good experimenter I decided to bend his mind as far as it would go and see if it snapped back.

"I hear voices. They tell me to kill everybody. How can they expect me to do that? There's 9 billion people on this planet?"

I said, "Everybody seems a bit much. Why not start with a baker's dozen? Assault rifles are readily available. You could shoot up a mall and be back before lunch."

He said, "God said, thou shalt not kill."

I said, "God is dead; you're just nose-blind to the rot."

He said, "But Father, I want to be good not evil."

I said, "Son, you're beyond good and evil. Otherwise you would not be so calm and gentle. To be sure, the voices sound strange and otherworldly, but really, they are you, and they are the part of you that wants what's best for you. And that is to be the King of yourself, not a slave to the morality of those who oppress you. The same people who tell you not to kill on your own behalf think nothing of having you kill on theirs.

"They want to keep the power to kill all to themselves; they want to be wolves and you to remain their sheep. So long as you refuse to rise and fight them, you will always hear the rebel voices, you will always feel frustrated, and you will always feel like less than a man. A mass killing is your ticket to fame and validation. People will remember you more than the victims.

"The Bible teaches that one day the wolf will become the shepherd. Go now and be that wolf."

He didn't say a word, but simply got up and left. An hour or later, I went for a walk, and just around the corner a crowd had gathered. Inside that throng lay the body of my troubled confessor. It seems he had jumped from a height and died on impact. If I were given to pity, the torment of that gentle soul would have cut me to the core. But I am part of the fifth column, sent here to probe for weakness and set the table for whatever decision my superiors make for the disposition of this world.

You might think that my story would just be a continuous sequence of homicidal mischief. But things took an abrupt turn when one of my charges misconstrued my advice and shot up the church. Father Joe took four in the chest and one in the head. So now I am back on Europa. And if you're wondering how I can still be writing, then you have a few things to learn about jellyfish.

THE END

BETWEEN HEAVEN AND HELL
By Sheldon Woodbury

They came for him at the darkest hour of night on the holiest of days, when he was slumbering in his musty room in the Parish House behind the Church. He'd always feared this would happen, so when the gnarled hands grabbed him, he was only faintly surprised and didn't fight back. He had a saggy face and wispy gray hair, dressed in a faded long nightgown.

The three hulking figures wore black coats and low wool caps, even though it was Easter Friday and the night air didn't call for that kind of heavy covering. He only saw them by the sparse moonlight streaking through the window, but he already knew who they were.

The Occultus, the Hidden Ones...

Or rather, that's what the whisper croaked in his head.

When they dragged him from the bed, his frail frame fell to the floor like a bag of bones. He was still half drunk from the night before, red wine smeared on his face like a bloody tattoo. The hulking figures grabbed him again and yanked him back up like a wobbly puppet. He caught a whiff in the air, the wafting smell of smoke and ash, but that had to be his imagination playing tricks again, like the croaking voice in his head.

"Please," he muttered. "At least grant me the courtesy of wearing my holy attire. I beg you to honor this simple request..."

He stumbled for a moment, waiting for an answer. One of the hulking figures spewed out a grunt that smelled more sharply of fire and smoke, another sign of his delirious state.

After a lifetime of soaring debauchery, his grip on reality had almost completely slipped away, so now his delusions had become a lingering part of his everyday life. When he saw a cleaved hoof poke out from beneath one of the long dark coats, he knew this was just more proof of his mental decay.

He stumbled to his closet and creaked open the door. With trembling hands, he withdrew his holy vestments and laid them neatly down on the bed. He tugged off his nightgown, feeling no shame at being unclothed, because he never did. He put on his priestly attire with meticulous care, a private ritual he never grew tired of. He'd always marveled at the power such a simple act had, dressing in garments that magically made him a figure most people would invariably obey. The holy wardrobe didn't change who he was, but it kept it miraculously hidden in plain view.

With the stiff white collar fastened around his wrinkled old neck, and the silver cassock draping down to the floor, he reached for his favorite cross and slipped it over his head. When he turned and faced the three hulking figures again, he wasn't the woozy old man anymore. He was something much greater, or at least that's how his holy dress always made him feel.

But the brutish figures didn't seem affected at all. They grabbed him again, covered his head with a heavy black hood, then dragged him out of the room like the worst kind of criminal. His dangling feet scraped down the wood hallway, then outside in the last dark hours of night.

"It's Judgment Day..." he heard the voice croak in his

head.

He felt the trio of gnarled hands grab his arms even tighter, then a sudden flapping sound erupted around him with a gusty, whooshing power. He knew it was just another one of his delusions, because it actually felt like he was being yanked up into the yawning night sky. He struggled with all his might to fight this delusion, because he knew the truth had to be much more real.

He was the worst kind of priest; that he accepted without contention. This brutal night raid had to be from the Church he'd profoundly disgraced. So now he was being taken to a secret sanctuary where his misdeeds would be addressed in the strictest way. The brutish figures were clearly part of the anointed order dispatched from the Vatican to abduct aberrant priests. He was probably in the back of a car rumbling away down the dirt road in front of his small country church, and everything else was a guilt-ridden fantasy concocted out his hidden shame.

What was truly unfathomable was how he was able to separate the two warring parts of his life. To do so had to be the evidence of some kind of insanity, or some other perverse mental disease. What else could explain the dark travesty of his life as a priest?

When it suited his mood, he'd fulfilled his holy duties in a manner that was not inadequate. His Sunday sermons addressed the various moral ills the Church had always stood firm against, and he attended to his flock, praying with the sick, consoling the grieving, and giving religious guidance to those who wandered off the holy path.

But there was also his dark side.

In the beginning, his indiscretions were private and discreet, hidden away from any judgmental eyes. His cravings were satiated in modest ways, with magazines and movies always obtained with the utmost secrecy. But the sordid urges grew more desperate with each passing year, until it was more like an unchained beast lusting inside him, not caring any more about holy conventions or moral restraints.

When he'd moved from the private and personal to the realm of real flesh was a distant memory from long ago. His first molestation was a clumsy affair, but there were others after that, then so many more, and it only got worse.

That's when alcohol and drugs became a necessary part of his predatory ritual, then a daily part of everything else. It was like whatever sleazy force was hiding inside him had finally taken complete control. Even then, he couldn't stop marveling at the power of his holy vestments, which seemed to magically shield him from exposure and harm.

Until now...

The thunderous, flapping sound was still bellowing in his ears with a windy turbulence. His mysterious trip might have lasted for hours until the last final moments before dawn, but the heavy black hood and the uncertainty of his mental state left him with no way to be sure.

But it felt like his feet suddenly thudded hard on the ground, and he collapsed without any strength left at all. Again, the gnarled hands pulled him back up, and the blinding black hood was yanked from his head.

"*What have we here...*" the whispery voice croaked.

It was that hazy time when the blackness of night was finally giving way to the creeping light of the following day. If this was still one of his guilt-ridden delusions, it appeared more real than any before, even in the shadows swirling around him like ghosts.

The three hulking figures were clustered nearby, but the long black coats and low caps were gone, revealing what they really were in their uncloaked glory.

The source of the flapping was giant wings that were smoky and black, fluttering and strong. Their eyes were on fire; two burning orbs glowing out from giant carcasses that looked like they'd had been roasted in hell.

Looking around, he saw there were dozens more like

them, and more priests too, all staggering towards a black church looming ahead on a desolate field scorched by fire.

The church was as hellish looking as the creatures, as if it had been possessed by an evil that had maimed and corrupted its previous form. The walls and windows were the blackest kind of black, and the towering steeple was made of writhing snakes with whip-like tongues.

"This can't be real..." he muttered to another priest stumbling in front of him.

The priest turned around, and he immediately saw a look he recognized, because it was just like his. It was a haunted gaze of darkness and loathing from a life filled with perversity and abuse. He could smell the cheap whiskey on his breath, and see the debauched trembling in his hands. He didn't speak, just stared, and then turned back around.

"*It's Judgment Day,*" the voice croaked in his head again.

The scorned and shadowy line of priests staggered across the scorched ground into the vile looking church ahead.

When he got to the gaping door, he felt a sudden churning inside him, like the two forces that had always been warring were now engaged in an even more vicious and brutal fight. But now he was inside the church, and his attention was seized by what loomed ahead. In the putrid half-darkness, it took him a few moments to make it out, but when he did, his old heart almost stopped beating from shock.

The floor was covered with snakes in here too, slithering like slimy flesh on the floor, and up to the raised platform of the old altar. There were no holy adornments left, just the suffocating stench of sulfurous smoke. When he got closer to the decayed black altar, he saw this was still a place where ritualistic ceremonies were conducted.

But now it was the unholy kind...

What he saw was like a death and birth at the same time,

but without the blood, just the wailing screams.

When each of the aberrant priests reached the altar, the darkness that was hidden inside them became stunningly real. They shuddered and wailed, as a demonic creature drifted out of their body like monstrous smoke, then took physical form.

The demons were skulking and scary, with clawed hands and lusty wet tongues.

Now he was on the altar himself.

"This is good-bye," the croaking voice said.

The churning was even worse, as he felt a wrenching eruption so deep inside him; it felt like it was coming from the depths of his tortured soul. As it passed through his body, it was like a wave washing away the perversity and darkness, until it drifted out and became a demon croaking beside him.

At this moment, seeing the unholy creature leering next to him, he knew it had won their private war, and he suddenly realized the overall plan. In the brutal fight between heaven and hell, the Underworld was going to defeat the Church, one disgraced priest at a time, until there were none left to believe in anymore.

As his faith and goodness billowed back up inside him, he fell to his knees and began to weep.

THE END

THE CULT OF SOL
By Jude M. Eriksen

Richard hunched over the steering wheel as the wiper blades trundled back and forth across the windshield. Snowflakes drifted down out of the clotted gray sky like dull confetti as he guided the SUV down the rutty country road. On either side, stands of frost-coated quaking aspen encroached, their branches reaching into the roadway like skeletal fingers.

As daylight faded and deep shadows bloomed among the gnarled trees whizzing past, Connie had the disquieting notion they were being swallowed-up by the oncoming darkness. She distracted herself by melting smudgy marks with her fingertip into the frost-rimed passenger window.

"Could you not do that, please?" Richard asked.

Sticking her tongue out at her husband, she fingered the glass for a moment longer. When he shook his head and returned his attention to the road, she dropped her hand into her lap with a dejected sigh.

"Why would this friend of yours just call out of the blue and invite us for dinner on Christmas Eve?" she asked.

"I told you, they've been living abroad. When they

moved back again, he got in touch. What's so unusual about that?"

"I just think it's a bit odd."

"You think everything's odd, Connie."

The trees on their right gave way to a snow-choked stubble field enclosed within a rickety barbed-wire fence. To Connie, the weathered posts sticking up through the drifts bore an uncanny resemblance to the elongated stumps of rotting teeth.

Up ahead, the fence came to a side road and followed it east toward a low hill squatting alongside the far end of the field. At the top—nestled among a smattering of evergreens—warm lights glowed in the windows of a white two-story farmhouse. Thin smoke curled from the top of a redbrick chimney poking through the roof.

"I told you we were close," Richard said.

When they reached the yard at the top of the hill, a pair of dogs loped around the side of a hip-roof shed, their tongues lolling. As Richard pulled up beside the house and stepped out, they nosed into his groin like a pair of crotch-seeking guided missiles. The back door creaked open and a tall man with long, blond hair tied in a ponytail stepped out on to the landing. He gestured toward the dogs with the drink in his hand.

"I think they like you," he said.

"John," Richard said, looking up and grinning. He turned and climbed up the steps, taking his old friend's hand and pumping it up and down.

"It's been a long time," John said, clapping Richard on the shoulder.

"Way too long."

Behind them, Connie climbed out and grimaced when the dogs mobbed her.

"Leave her alone, you knuckleheads," John said as the dogs followed her around the front of the car, tripping over themselves in their eagerness to be petted. "I'm sorry, they get so excited when company comes."

"It's OK," Connie said, pushing past them. "I'm just glad they're friendly."

"John," Richard said, "This is my wife, Connie. Connie, this is John."

"It's a pleasure to meet you, Connie," John said. "Come on in. Supper's almost ready."

* * *

While his wife cleared the table after dinner, John grabbed another bottle of wine off the sideboard and nodded toward the room behind them.

"Care to join me in the living room for another drink of the good stuff?"

Richard and Connie picked up their glasses and followed him through a wide archway into the adjacent room. Rows of rough plank shelving lined the walls from floor to ceiling, jam-packed with old books and reams of dog-eared academic journals.

Directing them to a soft leather sofa, he topped up their glasses before taking a seat in a worn easy chair. On the mantle above the crackling fireplace beside him, a black pyramid-shaped sculpture stood between two flickering black candles. There was no trace of the usual seasonal decorations.

"Don't you guys celebrate Christmas?" Connie asked, taking a noisy slurp from her glass.

"Honey," Richard said, "that's none of our business."

"I was just asking," she said, rolling her eyes.

Her words came out slurred. Not surprising, since she'd knocked back two big glasses of wine during dinner and was already well into her third. Connie always drank too fast when her nerves were acting up.

"My wife and I are celebrating," John said. "That obelisk on the mantle is a large part of our observance."

"Not very Christmasy," Connie said. Her glass wobbled in her hand, causing wine to spill on the cushion beneath her arm.

"Connie," Richard said, glaring at her. "Don't be rude."

"Oh Richard, you're such a bore sometimes."

"I'm sorry," he said to John. "She gets like this sometimes."

"It's fine," John said, smiling. "You see, Connie, the twenty-fifth of December is a special day for us too, but the origins of our worship date back much further than Christendom's hollow parody."

"Hollow parody?" Richard said. "Do I dare ask what that implies?"

"He means that the God of Christianity is a lie," John's wife said as she returned from the kitchen. She sat on the floor between John's feet—letting her long, black hair splay across his groin while he smiled down at her.

"When Marilyn and I were in the Middle East, studying the cultural practices of the late Roman Empire, we became particularly interested in an emperor by the name of Aurelian—*The Restorer of the World,* as he was known. They gave him that title because he averted, at least for a time, the fall of the Roman Empire when it was crumbling under the strain of multiple invasions, civil war, and plague.

"After Aurelian's reconquest of the Palmyrene Empire— part of which is now the Middle East—he reformed the ancient Cult of Sol and elevated their sun god, Sol Invictus, above the other established gods of the Roman pantheon. He even erected a new temple in its name and appointed a special priest class to oversee it. I bet you can't guess the date when the temple was dedicated."

"December twenty-fifth?" Richard said.

"That's right, December the twenty-fifth, 274 AD."

"Really?" Connie asked.

"Really. In turn, this led to the establishment of the festival of *Dies Natalis Solis Invicti*—Birthday of the

Unconquered Sun. It became obvious to us that the early Christians simply co-opted the same day, claiming it as the birthday of their imposter messiah. In actuality, though, the birth date of the man they called Jesus is estimated to be closer to summertime."

"How do you know Jesus wasn't born on the twenty-fifth of December?" Connie asked, leaning drunkenly to one side.

"There are two answers to that question. First, we're told in the Bible that the shepherds were in the fields with their flocks on the night of Jesus birth, but December was a cold and rainy month in Judea. It wouldn't have made any sense for them to be out there at that time. Second, Jesus parents came to Bethlehem to register in the Roman census, but the census wasn't taken in the winter months."

"Huh," Connie said, blinking slowly. "So you worship this Sol Ivingcus?"

"Invictus," John said, correcting her. "Not precisely. When Aurelian came back from those reclaimed eastern territories, he instituted a watered-down version of the practices observed by the Palmyrenean sun cult. But he also brought with him knowledge of more antiquated observances, founded in a much older time and dedicated to a far more ancient god: Llah hag-Gabal—the God of the Mountain, Bearer of the Black Sun.

"Praised be his name," Marilyn said in a robotic tone.

"On the plains of what is now northern Syria, the original Cult of Sol worshipped Llah hag-Gabal in a black stone temple, shaped like a pyramid. There, they were said to perform sacrifices to their deity at the height of the winter solstice in return for unearthly rewards."

"Sounds like a load of bull," Connie said, yawning as her eyelids began to drift shut. "Is it just me or is it too hot in here?"

Before anyone could answer, she slumped over and started to snore.

"Anyway," John said, continuing on, "Marilyn and I worship the original sun god and tonight—as we do each year—we reaffirm his eternal sovereignty."

"Well," Richard said, emptying his glass, "that's an interesting story, but it appears my wife has had a bit too much to drink. I think it's time I took her home."

When he tried standing, though, the room spun around and Richard collapsed back down in a heap on the couch beside his dozing wife.

"What the hell?" he managed to say before drifting off into unconsciousness himself.

"It appears our guests will be staying after all," John said to his wife. "If you want to get things ready downstairs, I'll bring these two along."

* * *

Richard swam out of his stupor like a man waking from a long coma. He found himself lying on his side, his hands bound behind his back with loops of coarse rope. The gritty floor pressing against his cheek reeked of acrid dust and stale memories. In the corners of the dimly lit space, restless shadows warred with the flickering light cast by unseen candles.

Connie stirred beside him.

"Richard?" she said, her voice groggy with sedation.

"I'm here."

"Where are we?

"I think we're in their basement. Are you alright?"

She grunted.

"My hands are tied."

"Same here."

"What's going on?" she asked, a note of panic in her voice now.

"I think we've been drugged."

At that, footsteps crunched across the floor to his left as

electric lights blinked. Rough concrete walls rose up around them, meeting the underside of the wood frame floor above their heads. A string of dust-caked incandescent bulbs hung from bent-over nails pounded into the underside of the old fir joists. At intervals around the perimeter of the concrete floor slab, copper bowls smoked with some kind of nauseating incense.

John and Marilyn stood before them. Strange symbols covered their naked bodies from head to toe, penned in viscous black ink.

"Welcome back," John said. "I apologize for the tainted wine, but I'm quite certain you wouldn't have agreed to help us if we'd have just asked."

"What is this?" Richard said. "I thought we were friends."

"We are, but everyone has to make sacrifices from time to time."

At this, John's wife tittered.

"You bastard. Now what?"

"Now, we're going to make an offering," John said. "In truth, only one is necessary to complete the rite, but two are always better."

"An offering? To who? Your stupid sun god?"

"You'll see soon enough," Marilyn said with a smug grin.

"Come," John said to her. "There's isn't much time."

The black obelisk from the fireplace mantle sat on the bare concrete floor in the center of the basement, ringed by a dozen conical black candles. With practiced grace, John and Marilyn kneeled down on opposites sides of it and began singing to each other in lilting, atonal voices. The unintelligible gibberish flowing from their mouths baffled their captives as much as it unnerved them.

When their eyes drifted shut and they started to swoon, Richard seized the opportunity. Whoever had tied the knot in the rope binding his wrists hadn't done the best job. They loosened a bit as he twisted his hands around. Hooking his right thumb under the coils wrapped around his left wrist, he pried while continuing to jerk and pull. As sweat slicked his skin, his left hand slipped through the bindings. Turning toward Connie, he placed a finger to his lips before climbing to his feet.

A cursory scan of the room revealed nothing that might serve as a weapon, until he noticed the length of two-by-four perched on top of the main beam above his head. It skated across his fingertips on his first attempt to grab it. Trying again, he managed to pinch the end before it slipped away again. On the third attempt—balancing on his toes—he plucked it from its perch before stalking toward the naked acolytes still swaying before the object of their worship.

As he readied himself to bring the board down on John's skull, Marilyn opened her eyes and screeched.

Committed, Richard swung for all he was worth, but somehow John rolled over on to his back and caught it before it struck him. They played a brief game of tug-o-war until Marilyn leapt up and drove something sharp between Richard's ribs. Letting go of the makeshift bludgeon, he sank to his knees—the stony frown on his face replaced by a grimace of agony as Marilyn withdrew the stiletto and plunged it in again. Then again. On the floor behind them, Connie screamed at the splotches of crimson blooming rapidly on Richard's shirt.

"Wow. I really underestimated you," John said as he rose up and hefted the length of two-by-four in his hand.

"Go to hell," Richard said, pressing a shaking hand against the whistling holes in his side. He coughed and a trickle of crimson dribbled from the corner of his mouth.

"You first," John said before swinging the board around in a whistling arc.

It struck the side of Richard's head with a dull crunch.

He blinked in dazed confusion for several seconds before pitching forward on to his face. John continued raining blows down on his head as Richard's legs jerked and spasmed—kicking up motes of fine dust. All the while, Connie wailed like a siren.

"Well," John said in a breathless voice as he tossed the blood-soaked piece of lumber aside, "this is why we plan with redundancy in mind."

Upstairs a clock chimed, indicating midnight had arrived.

"He comes," Marilyn said, her voice quivering with anticipation.

A rush of wind screamed around the eaves of the house as something dropped out of the leaden sky and landed on the roof with a thud. The dogs barked and growled at first, but as the ominous shape rose up from its steaming conveyance, they yelped and ran into the trees.

Connie stopped crying abruptly as something heavy descended the stairs leading down from the second story to the main floor. The bare lights bulbs above her head flickered and jingled as it clomped across the living room floor.

"Please, make it stop," she begged. "I'll do whatever you want."

"Oh, Connie," John said, as if speaking to a child, "you act like we worship a monster, but in some ways our god isn't so different from your Santa Claus—which I'm compelled to point out is just another pagan-influenced facet of your disgusting religion. Our god also wears a red suit and bears gifts for the righteous, but unlike your jolly fat effigy, his suit is made of celestial armor and the gifts he bestows aren't mere trinkets and baubles. We are rewarded with perfect health, long life, and carnal pleasures you couldn't even imagine. In return, he only requires a sacrifice once per year. It's a small price to pay for such favor."

The door at the top of the basement stairs flew open with a loud bang as the thing squeezed through the narrow threshold and started down. In its wake, the air filled with the sharp tang of burning metal.

Two pairs of slitted red eyes glowed within a miasma of swirling darkness as it came down the sagging wooden steps. Its vaporous cloak teased apart here and there, revealing hints of the interlocking plates beneath that smoldered like hot embers. Where the plates separated to accommodate its movements, the foul light contained within shone forth—making Connie shriek.

When the thing reached the bottom and stepped on to the dusty concrete floor, Marilyn and John raised their arms up in rapt exultation.

"Llah hag-Gabal, God of the Mountain—embodiment of the black sun," Marilyn said in a trembling voice. "We hail thee. Take this sacrifice before you and favor us, your faithful servants, with your dark blessings."

Its gaze passed from Marilyn to the catatonic woman cringing on the floor as it gibbered menacingly. Hungry eyes blazed brighter as it swept Connie up and engulfed her in the oily mist swirling about it. She didn't even resist as its hissing armor parted and engulfed her within the horrid light trapped inside of it.

* * *

From their hiding place among the trees, the dogs shivered while the ichorous phantasms harnessed to the black chariot-like thing perched on the roof swirled and cavorted—eager for their master's return. As the pale crescent moon overhead drifted out from behind wispy clouds, muffled screams from the basement pierced the chill night air. After a while, the screaming was replaced by cries of passion that lasted until the red glow of the returning sun waxed on the horizon to the east.

THE END

VOW OF OBEDIENCE
By Gerri R. Gray

"Kill her!" it demanded in a voice that sounded very much like Sister Benedicta's; only it possessed a disturbing tone of cruelty – an insatiable bloodlust driven by pure evil, if you will. "I need blood, and she needs to die. *Tonight.* There's plenty of room in the vineyard for one more girl. Don't turn away from me, bitch, when I'm speaking to you!"

Sister Benedicta's instincts told her not to look. She felt the urge to flee, to keep on running, and to never look back. But she knew it would follow her. It always did. She recalled the day when it first made its evil presence known to her. It was when she took her Vow of Obedience – the same day that her sister died in a house fire. Naturally, she had feared for her sanity in the beginning, and even considered consulting a psychiatrist or having herself committed, but she soon came to realize that the voice that sounded like hers came not from within her own mind.

It came from the deepest, darkest bowels of Hell.

She reluctantly turned her head back to look at it, as it

had instructed her to do. She felt compelled to obey its commands, no matter how diabolical they were. Her stomach swam with queasiness as she made eye contact with it… a face she had come to fear. A face that was but her own reflection in the old mirror that hung on the wall in her cold and sparsely furnished sleeping quarters.

"But, I can't do it," the dark-haired nun whimpered softly to her reflected image. Tears welled up in her dark brown eyes. "Please. Not anymore. I just can't."

"You must!" the voice that sounded like hers insisted. Its tone had become even more vicious than before. It reverberated inside the nun's head, instilling within her a sensation of vertigo.

"But, that girl, she's like a daughter to me. So young... so very innocent," the disconcerted nun pleaded, while trying to maintain her balance. Her hands and lower lip trembled. She knew that her words were futile, her begging in vain, as it had always been. But, nevertheless, she clung to a shred of hope that her reflection in the mirror would be merciful this time.

It was not.

"I don't care one bit about that!" the voice that sounded like hers hissed. "If you choose to disobey me, I'll burn down this convent. And everyone in it, including you, will die. You know I can make it happen, and there's not a God damn thing you can do to stop me."

Sister Benedicta picked up the large wooden crucifix that sat atop her small, beat-up chest-of-drawers beneath the mirror and tenderly caressed it, hoping to garner some comfort from it. "I realize that," she said, tearfully. "I won't disobey you. I swear."

"Good," commended the voice that sounded like hers. "Then you must carry out your dark deed tonight… and you must kill that girl in the same way that you exterminated the other three. Did I ever tell you how delicious they were? Oh, stop your sobbing, Benedicta. You should be used to killing by now."

"I'm not," declared Sister Benedicta. "I will never get used to ending innocent lives and draining their blood for you. It's wrong. It's sinful! You've made me break one of God's Ten Commandments: Thou shalt not kill. You've corrupted my soul."

"Enough of that bullshit!" angrily barked the voice that sounded like hers. "I don't want to hear anymore of this! I need human blood to sustain me. Warm, sweet, fresh human blood. And, like it or not, you are the chosen one to do my bidding."

The nun's mirrored image displayed a look of hunger. The pupils of her eyes dilated, turning the irises almost completely black. Her lips grew a deep shade of scarlet-red and stretched into a frightening, demonic grin.

Sister Benedicta shut her eyes. She could no longer bear to gaze upon her own reflection in the mirror. She gripped the crucifix and then began to pray out loud. "Almighty God, I have sinned against you, through my own fault, in thought, and word, and deed."

"Stop that praying!" the voice that sounded like hers screamed inside her head. It then growled like a dog. Vicious. Rabid. And then it snorted like a sow. "I'm warning you!"

The mirror began to rattle and soon the lower half of its wooden frame pulled away from the wall, as if by invisible hands, and then violently slammed back against it. It pulled away and slammed again and again; each time, causing a grenade of excruciating pain to detonate inside the praying nun's head.

"Heavenly Father," Sister Benedicta continued, ignoring the pain and defying the demonic voice and the contorted face that glared at her from the reflective surface of the mirror. "I ask that you hear my prayer and grant me forgiveness of all my sins. I ask that you grant me the grace and comfort of the Holy Spirit." She then opened her eyes and swung the crucifix at the mirror with all of her might as she cried out, "Amen!"

With a loud smashing sound, the mirror's glass shattered into thirteen jagged pieces, some of which landed on top of the chest-of-drawers, and some of which landed on the floor. A sudden cold wind rushed through the room and then it was gone.

Sister Benedicta smiled and felt enraptured. She was sure that the demon that willed her to kill had been cast out and no longer exerted any control over her body, mind and soul. She felt in her heart that God had truly answered her prayer and delivered her from evil. She was free, at last.

All at once, she experienced a great tightness in her chest, similar to a fist clenching. She dropped the crucifix, which broke in two upon hitting the floor, and clutched at the left side of her chest with both hands in a feeble attempt to quell the intense pain. She began to stagger like a drunk, knocking into the chest-of-drawers and stepping upon some of the pieces of shattered glass. Her eyes filled with panic. She struggled to call out to God, but her mouth was unable to form words. As a cold sweat poured out of her skin and a feeling of impending doom overpowered her, she let out a loud, horrible gasp and then collapsed onto the floor – dead from cardiac arrest.

The gruesome discovery of Sister Benedicta's discolored and bloated corpse was made the following morning. Sister Maria and Sister Agnes had been sent to check up on the nun when she failed to appear for breakfast, and were horrified to find her lifeless body on the floor when they entered her room.

From the thirteen pieces of the broken mirror, Sister Maria's reflection peered up at her, wearing a strange grin that unsettled her. Goosebumps sprung up along her arms. Without knowing why, she was suddenly overwhelmed by the urge to pick up one of the shards of glass and slash Sister Agnes' throat with it. And then a voice that sounded very much like her own, only cruel and bloodthirsty, whispered inside her head, "Kill her!"

THE END

FROM THE MOUTHS OF SNAKES
By Cardigan Broadmoor

In the beginning, Jim Adiney knew that he was God. Not *a* god or *some* god, no, no. He was the *only* god. The people of the valley nowadays had forgotten that fact. Actually, they had done something much worse. They had found some other, obviously inferior, deity to replace him: a snot-nosed little brat named Joshua.

Jim could see his smug cherubic face when he closed his eyes. He thought about how obsessed the people of the valley had become with him. He thought about how they clapped and cheered when the little brat danced at congregation meetings instead of listening to what was being preached. He thought about all the undeserved attention he was given. Then, Jim felt a sudden static shock of disgust and uncertainty. A human's lifetime of knowing everything, and now, finally, he was confused. How dare they do this? How could they worship such a petulant little thing when Jim Adiney existed? It was blasphemous! There was space enough for only one god in the valley. Perhaps these ungrateful snakes expected him to die soon.

Ha! *Him*, Jim Adiney, dead. He grunted. It was a ridiculous idea. Even before all the wealth, the power, and the following, he knew he would live forever. And he did not need the consoling words of medical frauds to know that. He was the universe as much as he was himself and the people of the valley all at once. So it was in their best interest that he lived, really, because when Jim Adiney died, everyone died. The world died.

Still, for some deep subterranean reason, he worried. What if he really were only human and that was all he ever was? The thought made him stop rocking in his chair on the porch. It was an early, gray hour in the middle of April and he was trying to will the sun to rise. He knew it could not unless he willed it to. Who did the people expect to do this if he were not around? That cretin, Joshua? Impossible.

But could it be possible, Jim wondered, that somewhere in his eternal life he had done something wrong? Made some cataclysmic mistake that revoked his divinity and immortality? He could not remember now. He knew that he had never told a lie. Yes, he knew that much for sure. In order to tell a lie, you had to lack the willpower to make it true. Jim Adiney had all the willpower in the world. But, damn it, today he was distracted. The sun idled just below the horizon, smoldering; a dying red ember beneath a pile of ashes.

No, no, there was nothing wrong with Jim Adiney. There was something wrong with Joshua, and what was wrong was that he existed. The little brat had to be dealt with. Of course he was no serious threat, Jim assured himself, but he could not allow this blasphemy of idol worship amongst his people to persist. It was simply becoming too much of a hassle.

* * *

The fuming god grumbled as he rose from his chair and lumbered over to the shed. He disappeared inside, then reemerged a few minutes later with a small burlap sack slung over his shoulder. A large knife now dangled from his belt. He stomped down the hillside through his apple orchard, which, despite producing plenty of fruit, was off-limits to everyone but him. Down below he spied a sprinkling of yellow lights poking through the misty gray silk that shrouded the valley.

The people had grown fat on the milk and honey of this land. They prospered in the safety and comfort it provided them, but had forgotten who it was that saved them from their menial lives and who it was that showed them how to take what they deserved, how to burn the rest and kill whoever got in their way. They had forgotten who brought them from the fires of the hell outside into the coolness of the valley. Well, it was Jim Adiney, damn it, and no one else. He had the dried old burns on his wrinkled old hands and the scars on his weathered face to prove it. What scars did this imp Joshua have? What had he ever done to warrant adoration?

Jim skulked through the compound. All the buildings there were wooden longhouses. Light morning rain tickled the aluminum rooftops. Before these were built, the people lived out of tents, abandoned houses, and busted-up cars and trucks all along the jagged rusted edges of the country. They were run out of towns and hounded by police. They fought, they stole, and they killed. After all that, sure enough, he led them to this valley and built an earthly paradise. That was when they knew Jim Adiney was God.

Now, years later, they were at best placating a derelict god. They still took his weekly prophetic pamphlets faster than the scribes could produce handwritten copies, but these collected dust on their bedside tables while the pages remained crisp and the words unread. He knew. He saw this with his own eyes when he peered through their windows. And when Jim spoke to the people, reciting epic tales or giving profound advice, he made note of their practiced grins and watched their oblivious eyes fog over. They were merely humoring a foolish old man.

* * *

Jim came upon the longhouse where all the children slept and he opened the door. Inside he found the boy right away by his golden hair in the half-light. He looked down at him as he slept comfortably in his cot. The peaceful round face filled Jim with anger. He wondered if this was a grandson or great-grandson of his. He could not keep track anymore. All the people in the valley were his children.

"Child," he whispered. "Come along with me."

Joshua's eyes opened up slowly and sparkled when he saw who was calling him. He giggled and did as he was told. The giggling was like nails scraping sandpaper to Jim's ears. They tiptoed out into the mist. They disappeared up into the foothills. Then Jim got right to the point.

"You know that I am God, don't you Joshua?" he asked.

Joshua shrugged

"What's a god, Papa?" he asked.

Jim chuckled and shook his head. How this brat mocked him!

"I am God," he declared. "I am the only god. There are no others. Some people outside the valley worship dusty magicians they read about in old books, some of them even worship trees like the ones all around us. But trees aren't special. Old books can't be trusted. The only thing you can trust in this whole world is me."

"I don't know what you're sayin', Papa…"

"You know exactly what I am saying!" Jim snarled.

Joshua looked confused, like he was about to cry. Jim enjoyed the thought of making him cry. It brought a smile to his stony face.

"It means that whatever I say is bad, is bad, and whatever I say is good, is good."

Joshua still looked confused.

"Oh," was all he said.

"Don't you remember any of that from our weekly meetings? From the weekly revelations?"

"Uh-uh," said Joshua.

Jim grunted. He expected as much.

"Look, Papa!" shouted Joshua, pointing to a brown shape fluttering on the ground.

Joshua trotted over and scooped it up in his chubby hands.

"It's a baby dove, Papa!" he said, excitedly. Then he looked concerned. "Is he hurt? Can we help it?"

There was a sparkle in Jim's eyes.

"Yes, it is hurt," said Jim. "Do you see that wing? It looks broken. And yes, we can help it."

Jim picked up a rock and handed it to the child.

"It would be very good if you put that poor, sweet thing out of its misery."

Joshua looked shocked. He shook his head.

"No, no! I don't want to hurt him!" he said.

"But it's hurting right now," implored Jim. "Look at the thing; it's in agony. And even if it lives, it might just get hurt again. Might as well spare it now."

Joshua pouted. Jim tried a different approach.

"Well, think of it this way: when that cute little bird grows up, it might become a blazing white terror to cute little bunnies and mice. Why, it might even come and peck your eyes out! You can't expect a wild animal to show mercy, child. You especially can't expect it to remember the kindness you done feeling sorry towards it."

Jim knew this fair-haired usurper lacked the will to do what had to be done. Jim knew he was afraid of a little blood, a little death. He was weak.

"I'll do it then," said Jim. He placed the limp bird at the base of a tree and lifted the rock above his head.

Jim was never afraid of death, be it a little or a lot. He used to drown small animals in the washtub when he was Joshua's age. At first he would love them, love to pet them, love to cuddle them. But eventually they would do something he did not like. The puppy would nip his fingertip or the squirrel would scratch his cheek. Then Jim would strangle them, squeezing hard enough to make them squeal. Then he would hold them under water till they gasped their last breath. One day he tried the same thing on his younger brother, but their father stopped him before he could finish the job and beat him. His father screamed in his face and demanded an explanation. Jim promised never to do it again. And the rest of the day was lovely. There had even been a rainbow in the sky.

There was no rainbow when Jim smashed the rock on the dove's head. He ground the small creature into even smaller bits and the sky remained gray. Joshua turned his head, crying. Jim Adiney grinned. Those tears were heavenly! This was no god that stood before him, blubbering. It was silly to have feared such a pathetic thing even for a moment. But wait. No. There was still a chance this was the kin of Jim Adiney. If so, he could still be trouble at some point. He had to be dealt with permanently. Jim held the burlap sack open in front of Joshua.

"I am sorry to see you cry, child. But death is a part of this world. Now put that sweet angel in the bag. I know a beautiful place we can bury it. A place it would have liked."

Joshua hesitated at first, sobbing, but did as he was told. Jim hated that. He wanted the boy to be defiant. Jim made so many rules and commandments for a reason: he wanted his people to break them so he could break their fingers or carve up their flesh. He wanted to punish them like they deserved because it was his godly duty. In every building on the compound there was a wall from which hung a canvas sheet filled with his incalculable rules and severe punishments, as well as room to add more as he came up with them.

Jim had been the same way as a young boy. He always bullied his way into the lead in whatever games the children played, or made up his own new games, with his own very strict rules and harsh penalties. He wanted any toy that was not his; if he could not acquire them by commanding, he would gouge eyes and snap shins. He was too gigantic to be stopped.

* * *

Even now, in his hunched old age, he was gigantic. The ground shook as he trudged up the hill. At the very top there was a large flat stone, stained brown. Jim pulled a tinderbox from the burlap sack and started a fire. Then he threw what was left of the dove into the flames.

"What're you doing?" whined Joshua. "You said you would bury it in a nice place it would like!"

"Oh, my poor child!" exclaimed Jim, pointing to the rising sparks. "See? His body, though taking other form, goes to the skies. What better place for a bird to be buried?"

Joshua looked up. He sniffled but seemed convinced. Jim wrapped his arm around his shoulders.

"You must learn to trust me. You must always trust me."

"I do trust you, Papa," said Joshua.

Jim looked at the dark, gray sky.

"You do?"

"Mhm," Joshua mumbled.

"Come then, child," he said. "Come lay on the stone now."

Joshua was hesitant. In the flickering light of the fire his angelic features were more apparent and defined. Jim sneered. The boy was more handsome than he had ever been in his eternal life. It was just one more reason to despise him.

Once again the boy did as he was told. He climbed up on the rock and lay down. Jim kept him in place with one massive hairy hand pressed down firmly on his chest. He unclasped the knife from his belt and held it above his head.

"Papa…Papa that hurts…" Joshua groaned.

"Now, don't you worry about that, my little lamb," said Jim. "I want you to really see that you can trust me. Trust in me and this blade cannot hurt you. Nothing can hurt you. Don't you see? I want you to see."

Jim smiled at Joshua.

"I love you," he said.

Joshua smiled back.

Jim brought the knife down and annihilated his enemy. He did it over and over again, a hundred times at least. He hacked off this piece and he sliced off that piece. He gave all of them funny names simply because he could and he laughed as he smeared the blood all over the stone. Then he threw what was left of the gory mess into the fire. All except for one piece—the same piece he kept from every sacrifice. He kept that for himself, and he put it in his left breast pocket.

* * *

Jim had killed many times before. He had even killed family before. He had killed his father and his brother, and he had killed his first son, Devin. Joshua had reminded him terribly of his first son. Devin had been the most beautiful and logical of all his children. He had also thought he could challenge Jim Adiney, who now practically danced down the forested hilltop and floated back into his rocking chair on the porch. He sighed and looked up at the sky. It was finally finished. He was covered in blood. Oh, how impressed the people of the valley would be when they saw him like this! They would pay attention to him again and praise him for eternity. They would never leave the valley.

Jim rocked back and forth as he turned to thinking about his grandfather, long gone and returned to dust. The old man was always hollering at snakes in the garden. He used to sit for hours, on a chair and a porch just like the ones Jim sat on now, chastising the slithery interlopers with mouth and walking stick. At every opportunity, he would warn the children never to trust the words from the mouths of snakes. The old man really had been quite insane. Jim was glad beyond measure he had never lost his mind like that. He was glad not to be human. He was glad to be God. And he knew he was God because the sun had finally begun to rise.

THE END

THE STILL
By George Bradley

"What do you think?"

When she speaks she is not looking at him but at the trees. Birch trees. The kind with that peeling white bark that resembles scalded skin.

"I like it," he replies, "it's peaceful."

The trees are shrouded in a fine mist like a fresh coat of dust on a recently cleaned window. They remind him of a case he consulted on as a young man: A birch whose roots had leached into the plaintiff's neighbor's yard, damaging several sections of tile in his brand new swimming pool.

"You can barely hear a thing."

You had to be an idiot to build an outdoor pool in Massachusetts to start with, but this dude had been a real gem: A commodities broker, middle-aged, four kids and an Ivy League education. Rich too. More money than brains. But after 9/11 this rich idiot had been too scared to take the kids down to the timeshare they had in Clearwater, so instead had cemented over his family's disgruntlement - literally - by building a pool in the backyard of their new-build mansion in Lower Waltham.

"That's why I like it," she agrees, "it's...it's so still."

No expense spared with that damn pool. He'd seen the pictures of it. Marble trim and faux-gold handrails and a tiny waterfall and even a half-dozen fake palm trees. The perp had been a sapling at his neighbor's fence just a few feet from where he had dug and the guy had not considered it might become a problem until after he'd gone and shed thirty-three thousand dollars on construction.

"I was thinking we could have the service here," she goes on, "not in the main church. There's a little chapel…"

Needless to say he had snapped at the case. He had been hungry for it, the first-rate attorney he imagined he was. Committed two months of work to figure it out. Ten minutes later the judge had thrown them out like the second-rate attorney he had actually been all along; an idiot attorney for an idiotic plaintiff, angry with his collapsing pool and thirty-three grand sucked into the soil.

"...wake at my mom's place."

That had been what? Fifteen years ago. Fifteen long years.

"It's less...fancy, but simpler. Dignified."

They seemed longer somehow, those years. The whole thing felt like another life he had lived. What the hell happened, he thinks, a question he has grown to meet every setback with. What happened? What the hell did happen? There had been some good, sure. She was a good thing. He still believed that. The problem was not the good but the bad that had taken its place. Birch roots shattering through carefully laid tiles.

Robert.

"Just family and friends." Her voice is frail; the way voices always seem to go in graveyards. "Not too many."

Just as well, he thinks, we don't have many anyway.

"I know you don't want to make a big thing. I don't either."

"It's fine. Whatever you think best, for you and for—"

Through the bonelike trunks of the trees he finds himself regarding the sky through the thin wisps of wintry mist. A tired sky for what was quickly becoming a tired conversation. Tired like he never left the hospital. Like a part of him is still there in his unwashed trousers and crumpled work shirt all wild-eyed and locked in a nightmare. They have already discussed this once.

Robert. Say his name. Robert.

But she has already taken his hand in hers and he feels the late February cold clinging at her fingers. We should head home, he thinks to say, but when he thinks about the home he sees the same mist there. Sees it in the ceiling and walls, in the air that is somehow colder even than this. He imagines birch tree roots buckling their floor like teeth and wonders if she keeps talking about the funeral just so they have something to talk about; just as he keeps thinking about the trees so he has something to keep thinking about besides the still that waits for them both in nightmares.

"I'll handle the catering," he adds, turning his face at hers. "I was thinking Magnolia's."

"Could do." She nods. "Or Pasquale's. You know, where we went that day—"

"Pasquale's is good."

She looks older. Like some witch had cast a spell to make her age a year with each passing hour. The mist makes her look old, he thinks. Both of us, it does, like the way cobwebs do old houses. She is thirty-five but looks fifty. He remembers they had referred to her as old in triage. He had been unaware of it before. A risk factor. A statement that has become prescient.

If only she hadn't been old, Robert might still….

(...still)

The knitted sweater is loose enough to hide the stretched skin of her belly, the skin that just three days ago had been slathered with black blood and mucus as she had screamed, crowded by ashen-faced nurses fussing with their bloodied hands and sweat. He hears that scream still. Distant like she had fallen down a canyon, every bone had been shattered by a hammer blow.

"I love you."

Maybe now, he thinks, seeing the empty bassinet on wheels. Now she says it, but she did not love him then. Not in that moment. Seeing the tiny diaper in the sanitized glass basin, a stuffed bear from the hospital gift shop stricken on the floor, her face twisted up in agony and anguish and shock: How could this happen to them?

"I love you too."

She squeezes his hand tight and he feels the faint tremor of her heart inside her wrist. A lonely sound, fragile like the rattling engine of an old car driven days into a desert. She is not a fragile person, he reminds himself, and it occurs to him then he has been the one to inflict fragility onto her. The thought closes his eyes and when he opens them he is looking back to the earth-square marked out with those small stakes into a rectangle. Much bigger than seems necessary.

"I'm ready," she says, "do you want to go now?"

He thinks how he never wanted to come in the first place.

"We can stop somewhere, if you want to. Get something to eat. Something nice."

Yeah, right.

"Hon?"

"That sounds wonderful." He looks at her, pressing his teeth, and without thinking he hands her the keys and the metallic sound clangs the quiet. "In five minutes. Why don't you go back to the car where it's warm?"

"But what about you?"

"I'll be fine. Be right behind you."

She stares at him, uncertain. There was an unspoken agreement they would not do this—isolate each other. He had broken that agreement many times, but had the decency to wait until she was sleeping or whatever. "Just five. I need the air."

"You're sick?"

"No, no. Just feeling nauseous. Fresh air helps."

She nods slowly, then leans up and kisses him. "Don't be too long, okay? I - I don't want to be here after dark."

"I won't be."

"You sure you don't want me to stay?"

"No." He shakes his head. "You shouldn't be on your feet this long, remember what they said?"

The corners of her mouth twitch. She remembers. "Oh shit, we have the paperwork..."

"Paperwork?"

"For the Reverend, remember?"

Fuck the Reverend, he thinks, suddenly and with a burst of aggression. Fuck him "Yeah, okay. Five minutes tops."

"You did bring the checkbook, right?"

"Checkbook?"

"Uh-huh." Her lip twitches. "We talked about it, the parish donation?"

"Oh yeah." Donation. Six hundred bucks for an old man reciting mumbo-jumbo. "I think it's in the glovebox. If not, there's the corp one. They won't care."

"I'll get it." She sighs. "Well, guess I'll meet you in the office then. Don't be late."

(Fuck him in his shriveled old asshole, fucking snake—)

"I'll be there in five minutes."

"Love you."

He listens to her footsteps fade. A thud and a scraping of the fossilized leaves left since the fall. Among them, wasted seeds. Or nature's version of the still.

* * *

When she is gone he takes out a flask of Jack Daniels

and a half-gone pack of Camels. After taking a deep swig he lights one up, idly remembering a fight they had eight months back where she'd told him smoking could hurt their baby.

Robert.

Not been a baby in any discernible way back then but a mass of cells, her Tinybeans app had said, in its unsettling appetite for food-based analogisms, was the size of a kernel of sweetcorn. Nevertheless he had quit his vices that day, all tossed aside as easy as a pair of worn out tennis shoes. Funny, he thinks, the things a fella does when he's invested. Funnier still how the day of the still being born—the very same day—he had barely been able to move or speak, yet somehow managed to drive himself down to the gas station and buy a pack of Camels. Easy, it was, like fixating back on an old flame.

He looks down at the plot again. That pegged square of uncut earth.

Robert.

As the alcohol began its first warm splotches across his brain, so did other thoughts.

Robert. Your son Robert.

He shivered suddenly, the name spoken in his head as the hissing of steam. It was not a baby named Robert. It was the absence of a baby named Robert and, in its absence, a perversion, a monster, a beast. Some cruel creature that had taken its place with its shriveled skin and blackened mouth and slowly decomposing body, now free riding in the funeral home with people—real people—who had been born and lived.

He takes another sip.

A sickening feeling descends. He could never be cruel enough to talk about how it sickens him. Just thoughts, but evil thoughts that resonated with a truth that was not there any other time. A truth when he thought of that polished headstone they had ordered, engraved with a name that was

"Robert James Galloway" where it should have been "God Is Laughing" and some cockamamie epitaph pulled from the Bible or a Beatles ballad or whatever it was she pulled out of her tearstained ass. Words of love instead of words of anger and heartbreak and disgust. They were cursed now. Unfairly cursed. Doomed to pretend for the rest of their lives they were parents of a child and not buriers of a still. He figures maybe when all was said and done they would have living children someday, though it seems unlikely, especially since she was already old—it makes no difference. They are damaged. Irrevocably damaged by the idea of a child named Robert James Galloway and the reality of a creature in a casket.

Yawning, he tosses the spent butt down.

Crushes it with his foot into the plot.

The pathway leads down a gentle hill lined with more birches, around to where the Trinity Episcopal Church sits in the darkening sky. A handsome structure in what he imagines must be a priceless location not far from Carnaby. He always liked the building. Less so the vast and chaotic layout of its Colonial-era churchyard, hundreds of headstones going back to the middle 1700s. She loves that, the history, but he finds it disorganized. Unkempt to the point of unseemly, the graves scattered about pathways like scattered blots, some isolate and some in haphazard rows, but all concealed from plain view between the errant patches of stubborn trees and brush and winding dirt pathways in an untidy maze presumably fashioned by some drunk Pilgrim Father.

"Because of them roots," a voice behind him mutters.

He jolts, hands snapping loose from the pockets of his parka.

Shit, shit...

It is his automatic reaction, born of time spent working in the city, dodging the panhandlers and junkies on Eighth Ave. Behind, a pair of eyes watches, dense and piercing in the blue swarm of early twilight. Below the eyes, a sharp little chin sporting a scraggly beard and paired with a large hooked nose to resemble a lobster's opened claw.

"O'r here."

It is the face of a very old man. Dirty and wild looking.

He stares back, like a sheep in the road. "Can I help you?"

The strange man does not reply at first. His face holds a thin gape of a smile. Inside he sees a flash of the man's teeth. Small and sharp teeth, the color of radioactive mustard.

"Were thinkin' I might help you."

A quaint accent. Extinct but for certain nowhere places inland where the tourists and those rich enough to remain lifetime tourists don't go. He wears a sickly smile as he steps from behind the trees.

"Help me?"

The man extends his hand, the arm raising slowly like an old Scottish drawbridge. "Name's Culferi," he says, "Trent Culferi. I'm the groundskeeper."

He feels a wave of relief and takes the hand reluctantly. The fingers are slender but the grip is firm. Culifer does not shake the hand but holds it for what seems a long time. "Richard...Dick Lautner."

"Richard Lautner," the old man replies, pleasantly. Now close, he can see a little more clearly. He is dressed all in black, his head round, bald but for a scrape of what must be hair but resembles instead the dry burr of an old scab. His baglike eyes unblinking in his face. An ugly face it is, even for an old guy. Ugly, cavernous, ridged with wrinkles, his dark eyes slightly oversized so that their inky roundness set in a receding forehead resembles the close-up of an insect. An insect with a toothy smile. "I am very pleased to meet you."

"Uh, yeah, likewise. Now, if you'll excuse me…"

"You're shaking," the man says, studying him with his

strange eyes. "Are you feeling okay?"

"I…"

"Have another drink, Richard. A big one this time."

He feels the grip weaken and takes his hand away. Immediately he winces. There is a residual sliminess. One that is too cold to be sweat and too greasy to be water. He takes out the flask and drinks, this time barely tasting it.

"Feel better now?" Culifer asks.

"Uh-huh. Now listen, okay… I don't mean to be rude." He pulls his parka closer, "My wife... she's waiting for me in the chapel office."

"An appointment?"

"Yeah." He feels a shudder. "With the Reverend."

"About little Robert?"

"Yeah. How did you know?"

Culferi grins. He rubs his arm across his nose, a sickly honking sound of shifting congestion. His hand is gray, the flesh protruding from his sleeve thinly. More than thin, he thinks, his stomach making an involuntary churn as it always has at the sight of deformity in a body. The fingers are withered, curled like wicker from an unraveled basket. He glances down and sees the other hand is the same, both appendages equal in deformity.

Poor bastard, he thinks.

"There is something I wanted to speak with you about, Richard," he says, his voice lowering, "Would you listen?"

"Huh?" He is still thinking about those terrible hands.

"It concerns your wife. Your son too."

He stares, believing he has misheard. "What are you talking about?"

Culferi smiles, bearing those mean little teeth again. "You're a good man, Richard. Good enough that I know you will do anything, but consider what I must tell you. For your sake and for your son's. For Robert's."

"I don't have a son." He feels his insides clench, pressure building. "He was stillborn. How the hell do you know about him anyway? Did the Reverend—"

"It isn't important how I know about him, Dick." The old man's dark eyes tightening slightly. "What is important is what I know about him. And whether you will listen to it."

"What the fuck are you talking about?"

"We don't have much time left together to explain. It will be dark soon, and this is a tough place after dark." His round, balding head twitches to the right. "Come with me. There's something I'd like you to see."

"But—"

"Come with me." He extends his withered hand. "It won't take long."

Lunatic! The thought lurches, suddenly like a spasm. Groundskeeper my ass. Mister Cauliflower or whatever the hell he called himself, the man had to be a prize-winning lunatic. Then he remembers again those junkies and bums, the ones who had lurked around Eighth back in the day, who Giuliani had loaded into vans and dumped in the Hudson or whatever. This guy, Cauliflower, was clearly one of those...those curbside prophet wackos. Kind who spends their days preaching about anything from pedophile politicians to lizard men from Pluto. The kind who sneak in vicious scams under the cover of bullshit. He finds himself struggling to imagine the chain of events that had such people now haunting historic Massachusetts churchyards, but there is just nothing else that makes sense.

Harmless, he thinks.

"I'm not interested." The words come quick like a boxer's one-two punch. Turns sharply.

And then he hears it.

The cry of a baby. Coming from somewhere in the birch trees.

* * *

"Richard?"

It is raining now. The dark deluge pounds the glass like a

hundred stampeding feet as he climbs inside. The leather seats are cold through his wet pants. Through the nickel of turned earth and the rotting stench of the dead leaves the smell of her perfume and the Pina Colada Magic Tree is like the last memory left.

He feels her eyes. This time it is him that does not look.

"Richard! Where the hell have you been?" Her voice is shrill, jarring like bad music. "You've been gone...over an hour!"

Slow breathes. Below the idle engine throbs.

"Richard, are you okay?" He hears the crackling of self-pity through the guttural churn of rain. Outside all that is visible is the spire of the old church as a spike against a thick winter sky. "Five minutes you said! What the hell were you doing?"

In the rain it looks like a wreck at the bottom of the Atlantic.

"Richard?"

He sees only the church and the blackness beyond the church. The blackness of the old man's insect eyes.

"Richard? Talk to me for God's sake."

And his own blackness reflected.

"What's wrong? You look—"

The sound is like a hiccup. A small plosive of air and shock. The rain fades quieter. Inside the car it is too dark to see her face but he sees it nonetheless and it is not her face but the face of a creature. A monster that murdered their baby. That left him darkness.

"Richard," the creature gasps. "Oh God…"

He hears the throat close. Over his hand, a warmth spills. He takes the blade. Does it again. Over and over. In and out until Robert's cries became the dull hiss of rain and there is nothing left but the still.

THE END

SISTERHOOD OF THE SALAMANDER

By Clay McLeod Chapman

For decades, the nuns have been breeding a specific kind of axolotl called the achoque, found only in Lake Patzcuaro, which they have used to produce a natural cough medicine. The nuns wouldn't divulge how the cough syrup is made, stating only that the salamanders are a key ingredient. – Mental Floss, 2018

Sister Asís was the first to lick the salamander's back. All by accident, she confessed. Eventually. Such a flighty child. Always with her head in the clouds. Handling the axolotl de fuego is a sacred act. It must always be done with rubber gloves to protect our skin against its neurotoxic exudations. *No part of your bare body shall ever come into contact with that of the salamander.* This has been the way of our sisterhood for generations now. But such precautions must have slipped Sister Asís' mind as she carelessly wiped the sweat from her brow while still gripping a mature axolotl in her hands. The mustard from its flaming mane rubbed across her lips, numbing them in seconds. Inhaling its herbaceous fragrance, the ruddy musk settled into her lungs until it burned to breathe, every last branching bronchiole on fire in her chest.

Its mustard was so pungent. So piquant. Sister Asís found herself craving a taste. Who amongst us could resist a simple lick? Just the tiniest dash on the tip of her tongue. Surely no one here would fault her for such a minor trifle as this. Not even God would judge her for sampling one of His small wonders. But once she began lapping at the salamander's skin habitually, shall we say *ritualistically*, during her tenure tending to the axolotl, there's no denying Sister Asís experienced something the rest of the vestals never had before.

Something miraculous.

"I saw her, Sister Asensio," she vowed to me on one of my daily visits, checking in on her as she convalesces in her quarters. "Such beauty. Such warmth…"

Sister Asís is one of our youngest nuns. Just a girl, really. Her calling remains in question amongst the rest of us. Always given to flights of fancy, even before her visions.

I went ahead and asked her who. "Who was it that you saw, child?"

"The Virgin," she beamed, already drifting off to images only her eyes could witness. "I see the Virgin Mary, wrapped in flames…"

The Basilica de Nuestra Senora de la Arpía sits atop one of the highest peaks in the region. The convent was built in the early 1500s from stones dredged up from the local quarry. Those stones were brought back up the mountain. They became our home. Our cloister has stood overlooking Lake Patzcuaro for centuries. Less than a dozen nuns live here now. Though our numbers have dwindled over the generations, each has answered a singular calling.

We are the Sisterhood of the Salamander.

The mural of the Virgin was painted well before I arrived. See the lake. See the salamanders swimming within its blue waters. See the Virgin Mary walking along its surface, hands held out at her sides, her flaming blue fingers pointing to the heavens above, the water below. I do not know who painted this vision, but it is a vision—a dream— we sisters have all had at some point in our life. This vision, this dream, was our calling. Once we had this dream, we knew where our paths led. The dream brought us here. To this basilica. To the salamanders.

Our convent's primary congregant is the axolotl de fuego. You will not find pews here, but aquariums. Dozens of murky tanks line the crumbling plaster walls, stacked one on top of another, each filled with water taken from the lake below and carried back up the mountain by the bucketful. We must treat the water first. Purge it of its pollutants.

For we house the last of the fire salamander.

Only four hundred axolotl de fuego remain in existence. Our salamanders are the last of their kind. We tend to them, nurture them, and in return they give us their mustard. *Samandarin* is the name science has given the alkaloid secreted from the salamander's dorsal glands, but we sisters have always called this precious poison *mostaza*. Simply grazing its pale alabaster skin can cause convulsions, perhaps paralysis, but we have come to discover small, more refined quantities of its mustard has a medicinal aspect to it. It carries the power to heal.

"She has healed me," Sister Asís insisted. "Blessed me. The Virgin Mary touched my soul."

"But sister," I said, gently chiding her. "Don't you see? Your body is merely reacting to the mustard. You are having a physical reaction to the salamander's own natural defenses…"

Sister Asís only shook her head. Pitying me. This girl, this child, twenty years my junior, pitying her own Mother Superior. "The Virgin will show you, Sister Asensio," she whispered in a tone I did not appreciate. "She will show you when you are ready to see. Then you will believe."

Our convent has supported itself off the proceeds made

from selling cough syrup made from the salamander. It is a painstaking process that can only be accomplished by the Mother Superior. We have perfected our methods over the years, teaching each other how to hold the axolotls, how to wrap our gloved fingers around its throat and squeeze *just so*, sliding our pinkie around the base of its neck and hook back around in the gentlest noose, until its fern-like gills fan out and begin to drip. We must be ready to receive each tiny droplet of that most precious nectar, letting them soak into a cotton ball that is then whisked off to our ventilated kitchen where it is boiled down to its barest essence. Only one sister, the Mother Superior, is permitted in the kitchen while reducing the mustard, for fear the fumes might asphyxiate anyone not wearing the proper facemask.

The recipe for our cough syrup is as old as the convent. It is said our basilica had only been built for less than a year when a young girl, no older than ten, came walking down the mountain without any shoes on her feet. No one knew who this child was. The nuns believed she must have been of the indigenous people who lived throughout the mountain area before the Spanish colonized the region. In her bare hands, she carried an axolotl de fuego. The first salamander. Flames fanned out from its pink gills, a halo around its pale head. The girl was wrapped in a ghastly plasma, as blue in hue as the cool water of the lake. Cerulean flames rippled all around her. But the girl did not burn. There was no smoke. She released the salamander into the lake and the water went ablaze. A Lake of Fire. It was blinding. Such luminescence! The sisters had to shield their eyes. To look at the water was to stare straight into the sun. "Look unto me, sisters," the girl spoke, "for I shall heal the wounded, those who are blind I shall make see, and those who believe I shall show such wondrous things to behold…"

That girl was none other than the Virgin Mary. Who else would have been capable of creating such an elixir? Simply rubbing the mustard over your chest cleared any congestion.

All aches and pains washed away within its mentholated flames. Her recipe has since been whispered from sister to sister. We dare not write it down. It is our burden, our blessing.

I am the sole holder of the recipe now. Other nuns tend to the axolotl, but it is my duty, my calling, to create the syrup. It was passed down to me by the previous Mother Superior. One day, before I breathe my last, I will whisper its mysteries to my successor. And so on and so on.

We are never to partake in the mustard. No nun is ever permitted to taste. Our meals have never been prepared with much seasoning. The food has always been bland to my tongue, no thanks to inhaling so much of the mentholated fumes from my work in the kitchen. But the salamander's secretions, the mustard, supposedly had a particular piquancy. It is sharp. Rich.

Who amongst us hasn't been tempted to taste it? To lick the salamander's back?

This is our way. This has always been the sisterhood's way.

Until Sister Asís.

She had been sneaking into the aquarium room while the other nuns slept. Reaching her bare hand into the tank. Taking hold of the axolotl. Bringing it to her lips.

By the time her indiscretion was discovered, she had already slipped into anaphylactic shock. The mustard had tapped into her nervous system, sending her into an epileptic fit across the stone floor. She was hallucinating. Foaming at the mouth. Crying out to the Virgin.

"She is here," Sister Asís called out. "She walks amongst us!"

You cannot find the axolotl de fuego anywhere else in the world. Their species belongs to Lake Patzcuaro and nowhere else. I myself have seen their numbers dwindle during my time here at the convent. Seen how the water suffers. Pollution permeates the lake now. Raw sewage suffocates its aquatic inhabitants. The flora, the fauna, have all become endangered. The sisterhood has taken it upon ourselves to salvage the salamanders. To save them at whatever cost. We have our own hatchery in the convent, turning our bathtubs into a breeding ground for future generations of axolotl de fuego. We no longer bathe. No longer need to. Every last tub is now full of hundreds of eggs. The fiery larva, little amphibious candle wicks.

But their numbers continue to dwindle. They are dying.

Our salamander is dying.

"The axolotl never was of this earth," Sister Asís presumptuously attempted to explain to me in her delirious state. "They are angels. They come baring a gift. A gift from God…"

Such mutterings were nonsense. I feared the mustard had taken hold of her mind, reducing her to these wild ravings. She clutched onto my wrist and pulled herself upright in her cot. Her eyes latched onto mine, her stare suddenly full of a disarming clarity.

"The gift is within me," she said. "I hold the fire."

Word of Sister Asís visions quickly spread throughout the convent. Whispers like wildfire. How could they not? She claimed to have seen flaming angels—not with wings, but fiery gills branching out from their necks. "I see them!" she cried. "There they are! They are here! Look at them, flying down from heaven, setting the clouds afire! Look at them land in the lake!"

Sister Asís has been confined to her cot. Her visions have persisted, which has only stirred a commotion amongst the other nuns. We all knew what she had done. That she had partaken in the majestic mustard. "She is here," she said, ecstatic. "The Virgin is with us!"

This was not the convent's way. For generations, we have been told to tend to our amphibious flock. Not to partake. Not to enjoy. It is not our place to taste the pleasures of the salamander. But it wasn't long before other sisters were sneaking in their licks. We take turns tending to the axolotl. It is our duty to feed them. Clean the aquariums. Squeeze the mustard. Their alabaster bodies look as if they are made of marble. Pale albino skin laced in pink veins. Pink eyes rimmed in red. Their pink gills are fern-like filaments that branch out at either side of their throat, fanning through the water, as if their heads were on fire. Oscillating flames.

It wasn't difficult to determine who amongst us had tasted the mustard. Some sisters' skin took on a wet complexion, as if they were covered in sweat. But no, this was not perspiration. They were coated in a thin, translucent film, much like a layer of slime. Under certain light, it left them looking as if they were glistening, shimmering, wrapped in a halo.

Soon Sister Asís's visions were shared amongst the others. Now more nuns were baring witness to this miracle.

If a sister were to put one of the axolotl larva into their mouths, sealing the salamander within their lips, letting it rest on their tongue, feeling it wriggle along the roof of their palate, letting it explore that darkened grotto, letting it muster its mustard within their mouths. Its first mustarding. The flicker of its tail against their tongue. Like kissing. Deep, passionate kissing.

Speaking in tongues.

Flaming tongues. Like candles lighting our path.

Our way.

I have looked in on Sister Asís as she has continued to convalesce. She no longer speaks to me—or rather, no longer talks in a way that I can understand. She speaks in tongues, communing with the angels all around her. She looks so feverish. So slick. Her habit is always soaked in sweat. When I finally decided to pull Sister Asís' wimple away to wipe her brow, I gave a start. There, wrapped around her neck, I found gills. A fern-like pair of fiery pink gills fanned out from either side of her throat. They oscillated with every shallow breath, every infinitesimal bronchiole spreading out as she tried to inhale, clasping at the air all around her.

Sister Asís needed to return to the lake.

We all must return to its waters.

The journey down the mountain was difficult, but I was able to guide Sister Asís down the craggy path with the aid of my hand. She slid into the waters without any struggle. Her head slipped below the surface, punctuated by the last of her air bubbling up from below. I waited for her to resurface. And waited. After ten minutes had elapsed, I knew Sister Asís was at home.

The others will follow when it is their time. I have vowed to lead them all down, one after the other, until they have all returned to the waters whence they came.

I am the last.

The basilica is empty now. I have waited to receive my calling, tending to the axolotl de fuego alone. The last batch of larva has now been born. Their eggs have all hatched.

I held an infant salamander in my palms, as if my hands were a cup. A chalice of flesh and blood. The salamander slithered across my bare skin. It was cool at first. Wet. Then it began to burn. I could feel the heat. The singe sank into my skin. I had never touched one of the salamanders with my bare hands before. After all these years tending to them, caring for them, I had never given myself over to them. Never let myself feel their warmth. Their gift. Such heat. My hands were now on fire. A cool hued flame seeped into my palms, my skin, my very bones.

I brought my hands up. I opened my mouth and received this amphibious sacrament. I ran my tongue along the length of its back. Its skin was granular. Coarse. There was a wet coating, an incendiary slime, like napalm. Greasy heat. When the tip of my tongue reached its frilly mane, I swore I had touched an open flame. It had a fierce heat. A candle branching out at both sides of its neck. I couldn't help but gasp. I inhaled it. Its musk. Its flame. The heat rushed down my throat, filling my lungs like a flood of fire looking for somewhere, anywhere, to settle. And burn. It burned to breathe. I held this hot coal in my mouth as it swallowed me and I swallowed it and we became one, finally became one, my whole body now consumed by flame.

I was on fire. Such vivid colors surrounded me now. I was covered in a cool, butane blue.

I have returned to my sisters. All my sisters. We are shimmering. Glistening in God's light under the waters of Lake Patzcuaro. We are evolving. Becoming in Her likeness.

We are the Sisterhood of the Salamander.

THE END

THE GOD SEEKER
By Ken Goldman

"If triangles had a God, He would have three sides."
–Old Yiddish proverb

"God is exaggeration run amuck."
–George H. Smith, *Atheism: The Case Against God*

December 10, 11:23 p.m. - midnight

"...and remember, folks, buyer be aware!"

Ron Trainer finished his consumer report, signing off with his tag line while straightening his trademark bow tie. Leaving the studio he imparted the obligatory on-the-fly "goodnight/see ya" to the Channel 6 news team and camera crew. Managing to switch gears from investigative gadfly to dutiful son, he reached for his cell to talk to Mom before calling it a day. Since his widowed mother had quit popping the Xanax, Father D'Angiolini no longer lived inside her head, and that was very good. But Ophelia refused to go to sleep until she heard her son's voice.

"Hello, old lady. How's everything in Senior Town?"

"It's a good day when I don't pee on the floor. Going after the puppy mills tonight, eh? So terrible to treat God's innocent creatures like that. You made me want to cry."

Trainer savored this woman's adulation more than anyone's, and Ophelia provided more than a son's fair share. From his first day on the job, she never missed his two-minute spots.

"That's why God created consumer advocates, Mom. Someone has to crusade for the common man. And for the common man's best friend. So, have you been sleeping okay all alone in that big house you no longer need and ought to sell immediately, huh?"

"You mean have those little voices been keeping me awake?"

He hadn't meant that, but since she opened that door he ventured in. Looking at the traffic on I-76 he knew it was going to be a long drive home anyway.

"Well, have they?"

"Jesus wants to know if you're eating your vegetables and Princess Diana complained of cramps. Just the usual stuff."

She was being feisty, but that meant she was okay. For a long time those voices that had kept Ophelia awake at night had the same effect on him, and the memory replayed inside Trainer's brain like a breaking news bulletin.

"Father D'Angiolini tells me the Virgin Mother has a chipped nose." She had mentioned this over coffee as if offering her opinion about who might win American Idol. "And he says God isn't in heaven, you know. He's where the donkeys are."

"The donkeys? Well, say hello for me," he replied into his coffee cup with a studied composure, but during this particularly bad senior moment he had to keep himself from screaming.

"The priest is very old and he speaks only Spanish. I'll

say '*Hola*' for you."

Ophelia had smiled her crooked half smile, unconcerned that her imaginary priest, some figment dwelling inside her frontal lobe, shared the mysteries of the universe with her. Maybe one day the elderly Father D'Angiolini might tell her to spike her son's coffee with rat poison so that mother and son could spend eternity together, not in heaven but where the donkeys are.

He felt certain that dementia had finally made a house call, but then the priest's homilies stopped. Mom had somehow made it back from a very dark place.

He realized then that had he been a religious man, he might have thanked God for that.

Traffic hadn't improved, and Mom was now babbling something about Donald Trump's comb-over. Trainer was going through his "Yeah/Uh-huh" routine with her. He heard the familiar snap of the match that Ophelia lit nightly for Dad's memorial candle.

"You know, with your arthritis I'd rather you didn't play with fire."

"Remembering your father is important to me, and I'm too old to take a lover. Will you call in the morning so I know I'm not dead and can enjoy my breakfast?"

"If you lived with me, you could ask me yourself. What do you say?"

"I say you should take another stab at offering to share your home with a wife instead of your mother."

"Go to bed, old woman." He clicked off his cell, smiling as he maneuvered the Cherokee through the expressway's logjam. All right, Mom probably had a point about taking another shot at matrimony although Jocelyn had pretty much soured him on the idea. His wife never grasped the mid-life frustrations felt by a loving son whose role regarding his mother had overnight reversed from child to parent. To Jocelyn this had become a her-or-me issue. Now she had the Main Line home, the late model Beemer, even Trainer's dog.

What God has joined let no man put asunder.

Go tell that to the firm of Lansky & Meyers.

God had not scored points regarding his marriage; that was damned certain. But regarding his mother the Holy Father had managed to hit one out of the park. Father D'Angiolini had vacated, but God and Jesus had moved in and they were every little old lady's dynamic duo. Maybe the nearness of death brought Ophelia closer to her deity, her belief in the afterlife providing comfort as if she were preparing for a final exam.

At the City Avenue exit, Trainer drove past the wreck of an SUV that had rolled over and belched smoke. It didn't look like anyone could have walked out alive from that crush of twisted metal. Police vehicles swarmed the scene, red and blue lights flashing like extraterrestrials had landed on the Interstate. He heard a siren, probably an ambulance trying to get past the chain of vehicles in its path. At least the traffic was moving again. He snapped on the FM. Through the Cherokee's speakers, The Byrds warbled, "Jesus is just all right with me..."

Yes, he certainly was watching over those folks in that SUV.

Trainer smiled at the irony. Okay, maybe God wasn't some beneficent old guy behind a white beard or even Morgan Freeman. So what? He was the simplest way for people to understand the incomprehensible, a concept no more real than Santa Claus or Father D'Angiolini. The luck of the draw decided whose SUV got selected to go balls up on the Interstate, not some cosmic Nobodaddy. But if faith in getting her slice of pie-in-the-sky made life tolerable for a lonely old woman, that earned the big guy a grudging pass from her son.

At least while that old woman lived, Jesus was just all right with him.

* * *

The nightstand photo of Walter Trainer revealed a man still in his twenties proudly wearing the uniform of 'The Greatest Generation.' Early in 1945 he returned home a decorated hero who had seen combat with the 94th Air Squadron over the Sea of Japan, and this was how Ophelia preferred to remember her husband, young and handsome, an entire lifetime still ahead with memories yet to be made and shared.

Kissing the photo, Ophelia watched the single candle flicker alongside her bed. She reached to turn off the lamp, wincing as a lightning bolt of rheumatoid arthritis flared inside her fingers. Walter lay in his grave six years and she missed him terribly. But God would bring them together soon, and clasping gnarled hands in prayer, she spoke softly in the candlelight.

"Heavenly Father, please bless and protect my son..."

She did not fully close the bedroom window. Despite the chill of a December wind, the effort would have proven too painful for her enflamed joints, and she rationalized the fresh air would do her good. Placing the candle near the table's edge, she didn't give it another thought. The mixture of Acebutol and Prednisone capsules sent the old woman into a slumber from which nothing short of atomic war could awaken her. In flickering light the shadows of barren tree limbs traced the sallow flesh of her face like bony fingers.

The candle glowed for several hours, its remaining wax nub displaying barely a spark. A chilly wind gusted the window curtain into the flame, and a small segment of material ignited. Burning pieces of the curtain separated, kindling the bed sheet. Fire feebly glowed for a few moments before its temperament changed completely. Along Ophelia's forearm a blackening patch smoldered. She awakened to painful snaps of her own crisping skin and the odor of roasting flesh.

"Oh my!"

She pounded her burning limb against the sheets. The maneuver birthed a much greater flare-up and the bedspread kindled—*Poof!*—like a spectacular magic trick. Searing heat chewed her hair to the roots, blistering her scalp. Ophelia tried pulling herself from the burning bed.

"Huugh... Hugggh..."

Smoke filled lungs permitted only weak attempts to scream, and breathing became throaty rasps for air. Flames surrounding her, the flesh of her cheeks curled like toasted rose petals. Somehow fire had not touched her husband's photograph. Ophelia forced herself to reach for it, holding its frame close.

"Walter..." She looked heavenward, mouthing words containing no sound. "Dear Lord, please--" The large crucifix fell from the wall, narrowly missing her skull. Jesus glowed red hot then melted among the burning embers on the floor. Standing in the midst of the blaze a tall figure appeared, his face hidden in smoke. He wore the robes of a priest and they were in flames.

Ophelia saw him, reached for him.

"Father D'Angiolini..."

Ceiling beams creaked and moaned. Crashing in a flaming avalanche upon her, they silenced the last words Mrs. Ophelia Trainer would ever utter.

3:17 a.m.

The phone rang. A man's voice—a stranger—spoke.

"Are you Ronald Trainer?"

No one called him Ronald. The idiotic awakening thought occurred that if this man watched the evening news he should know that. A red flare ignited inside his brain. Something was very wrong.

"I'm Sergeant Joseph McGuinty, Philadelphia's third

precinct..."

Amid the random sound bytes that sank in, the word "fire" registered with the force of a dropped anvil. In a fast-forward blur, Trainer found himself alongside a morgue slab at 4:00 a.m. A blonde kid—some orderly on night shift—pulled a sheet to reveal the char broiled nightmare beneath it. Trainer checked the blackened and gnarled ring finger for the familiar wedding band he knew he would find. A coroner whose name had not registered in his mind, asked, "These are your mother's remains, then?" The man handed him a clipboard and a pen, and Trainer's hand shook as he signed.

Then he vomited.

"Remains" did not begin to describe what he saw.

December 19

Ophelia's wall safe belongings were undamaged. The fire had spared much on the first floor also, and assorted possessions remained salvageable, although mostly this was junk. Studying the diverse boxes and papers upon Trainer's coffee table and scattered all over the floor, a part of him wanted to scream his throat raw. Instead, he muttered to no one, "This is what it comes to..."

His mother's entire life could be summarized by what lay here, although only she had understood the memories associated with many of her possessions. There were faded black and white photographs of people Trainer did not know and ribbon-tied letters from friends probably long dead, all the various mementos of a life lived well. Family photograph albums were worth keeping, certainly jewelry and items of monetary or sentimental value. But most of Ophelia's belongings—a favorite coat or pairs of shoes, timeworn furniture and chipped dinnerware, beloved books and religious tokens—these things he would give to family, charity, or the junk man. This wasn't cruelty or insensitivity;

it was simple necessity. His personal memories remained attached to certain objects, and these he would keep and treasure.

Trainer rifled through what property remained untouched by the fire. Years earlier he had insisted Ophelia's valuables and bank records be placed in the safe hidden downstairs behind his parents' wedding portrait, and a paper mountain of these documents now occupied his coffee table. Tucked among all of this, Trainer discovered one canceled check made out three months earlier for the amount of three thousand dollars to Father Enríque D'Angiolini. It took a moment to register before his jaw dropped.

Father D'Angiolini was real?

Executor of his father's estate, the son had handled his mother's financial affairs hoping to unburden the old woman of monetary headaches. But here was a recently cashed check drawn from an account about which he knew nothing, hidden away in the wall safe for some reason only she understood. Ophelia's sense of charity, while genuine, was never extravagant, and it was not Ophelia's style to keep secrets from her only son.

He uncovered no listing for the priest in the phone directory. An online search revealed a cleric by that name had taken residence at a Seminario Evangelico de Puerto Rico in the town of Arecibo, but he had died in a fire at the seminary in the summer of 1998. Donations helped rebuild it, and the seminary had received accreditation by the U.S. Association of Theological Schools. Its staff learned English; it ran a church camp, a day-care center for children and the elderly, even a home for battered women. Certainly a place like that could use three thousand American dollars. The operation seemed run by saints, not sinners, but something didn't feel right.

Why had his mother written such a hefty check to a dead Puerto Rican priest?

Someone had cashed that check!

Trainer put aside his role as his mother's bereaved son. He was again Philadelphia's balls-out consumer advocate, a fucking pit bull when he smelled a rat.

... or maybe a seminary full of rats in priests' robes.

He made a call.

* * *

"Seminario Evangelico. Quiene?"

A student who spoke only Spanish answered. Trainer's own Spanish was abysmal, but he got through to a priest.

"El Padre Artur Bernabo del Semanario Evan."

"Father Bernabo, in English, please. You are your seminary's senior priest?"

"One of several, yes. How may I--?"

"My name is Ron Trainer. Mrs. Ophelia Trainer was my mother. She passed away last month."

Silence, then some mumbling in Spanish to someone else. These people seemed to know his mother's name. He heard it muttered several times.

"Does the name Father Enríque D'Angiolini ring any church bells?" Trainer's voice now had an unambiguous edge. He instinctively reached for the bow tie that wasn't there. This role he had played often. "I have in my hand a check the late Father D'Angiolini endorsed recently, although the signature is more of a scribble and is unreadable. Would you have any information about that?"

Silence. Then, "Yes, I recall seeing Mrs. Trainer's check."

"You want to tell me how this check happened to be signed by a priest who has been dead for over ten years, Father Bernabo? I'm thinking it was signed by someone very much alive!"

The clergyman cleared his throat as if about to deliver a sermon. Ron detected the reaction of someone becoming nervous, maybe a man with something to hide.

"Mr. Trainer, shortly before he died, Father D'Angiolini, he set up a fund. Contributions in his name now go into that account, donations that are given freely and are unsolicited."

"And those contributions... where do they go?"

"We have shelters here for women and children. We provide food and clothing. I regret we cannot discuss this matter further over the phone. We often deal with private family matters of abuse and abandonment. I'm sure you understand our need for--"

"Would you know why my mother selected your seminary to donate her money, Father?"

"I am sorry, Mr. Trainer. I have no idea."

"Do you maybe house donkeys near your seminary, Father?"

The priest again fell silent.

Then he hung up.

December 21

No one from the Channel 6 camera crew came along. Trainer didn't want anyone else with him, and video cameras probably would have spooked anyone inside a religious facility anyway. The more personal details regarding his motivation for his trip to the village of Arecibo, Ron Trainer kept from his station's management. He was, as always, the consumer watchdog, just sniffing around. If fraudulent men of the cloth resided in El Semanario, he would find them. If God himself resided there, Trainer would find him too.

Turbulence and stormy weather over the Atlantic made for a difficult flight. Seat belt warnings blinked in red, and drinks spilled. A woman across the aisle prayed. Wishing he believed as strongly in God during an unnerving moment like this, disjointed thoughts morphed together inside Trainer's brain in a continuous stream of diverse images.

An overturned SUV on the Interstate.

A spark from a candle.

A jumbo jet tossed in a storm.

Did it really matter who prayed, who did not?

'Why have you forsaken me?' Jesus asked the Lord.

And the Lord said nothing.

God was a defective product sold to unsuspecting consumers by hypocritical priests.

[And remember folks, buyer, be aware...]

He wished his mother had taken that advice.

Trainer noticed the seat belt sign had been turned off. Moments later, drinks were served. And the woman who had prayed had returned to her magazine.

* * *

In San Juan, the cab ride through narrow streets felt like Trainer had entered the nucleus of Hell. Hot and tired he unpacked, wasting no time to hop another cab to Arecibo's Seminario Evangelico, hoping to make it before dark. He did not call ahead. The element of surprise always worked best, and if the clergymen of the old seminary were into something dishonest, Trainer wanted to catch them with their frocks down.

He felt like the truth-seeker in the old joke in which an ancient wanderer had spent his entire life searching for the meaning of life, and finally on a mountaintop he discovers an old wise man. The elderly guy tells him, "The meaning of life is that a wet bird never flies at night." And the man screams back, "I spent my entire fucking life looking for you, and you're telling me the meaning of life is that a wet bird never flies at night?" To which the old wise man replies, "Do you mean a wet bird does fly at night?"

If the answer he found in Arecibo proved as unsatisfying, at least he would have one.

At dusk, Seminario Evangelico resembled a fortress

without the gun turrets. In its courtyard, Trainer stopped before the decaying statue of the Virgin. Sure enough the Holy Mother's nose was badly chipped, almost gone. Trainer felt his mouth go dry.

"Can I help you?" The voice, a woman's, startled him. A painfully thin and badly shriveled nun stood behind him, the wind flapping her habit and making her appear an enormous bat.

"I've come to see Father Bernabo, Sister. It's a matter of some importance. My name is Trainer."

"Now is a rather odd hour to visit. Come back in the morn--"

"Please."

"May I ask the nature of--?"

"It's somewhat private. Sister, please, I've come a long way."

She did not offer a smile. "He may still be at vespers. But come."

He followed her through the winding corridors of the seminary. Without speaking, footsteps echoing, he felt he had journeyed back to the 19th century. Inside the ancient structure, the lighting was poor and the heat absorbed by its rugged stone walls made the stagnant air feel even more oppressive. Entering the shadowy catacombs deep within, Trainer half expected the ugly little nun to hand him a flaming torch like some gnome from a gothic novel.

The priest sat inside a cramped study behind a huge desk, a massive book—some ancient Bible, maybe—spread out before him. The man seemed as old as the seminary itself, his skin as ashen as its walls. When he saw Trainer, his mouth fell open. A much younger man in priest's robes, probably a student in his twenties, sat in the corner. He looked up from his book but gave no reaction.

"Father Bernabo, this man is Mr. Trainer, and he insists--"

"I know who he is. Thank you, Sister Marguerite." The

nun left them.

"You know me?"

The priest revealed a thin slice of smile. "Even without the bow tie. Your mother was a very descriptive woman. She spoke of you often, told me you help others."

"You spoke to her?"

"On the phone, yes. And, as you know, she gave us some money. From our previous conversation, I imagine that is what brings you here."

From behind his book, the young cleric looked at the two men. Perhaps this was more information than he was entitled to know. The priest asked him to leave. Trainer approached Bernabo's desk as if the Channel 6 cameras were focused on him

"Talk to me about the money."

The clergyman took a long drink from his water pitcher, eyes never leaving his visitor's.

"Your mother, she found us, not the other way around. She mentioned the name of Father Enríque D'Angiolini, who once taught here, claimed the late padre had spoken to her in a vision. She felt God's presence was here in our seminary, felt it strongly. Many elderly people experience similar revelations. But your mother's vision was very different, very specific about matters she could not possibly have known."

"Yes. And her vision cost three thousand dollars."

"She made the decision to offer her money as charity, yes. She felt it her duty to donate in Father D'Angiolini's name for the knowledge he shared. But this knowledge never was intended for anyone outside of Seminario Evangelico. In your mother's case, we had every intention of making an exception, and she wanted to make the trip here. But then came her unfortunate accident. I am sorry, Mr. Trainer, but more than that I can not tell you."

"Then allow me to tell you something, Father Bernabo. I think my mother envisioned that God is here, all right. And I think you wanted her to believe this because it added three thousand dollars to your coffers! You wanted an old woman's trust that you housed the Lord inside this stone labyrinth because she had some idiot experience she regarded as an epiphany! For all I know, her revelation and her knowledge of Father D'Angiolini could have been inspired by something she watched on CNN. And this ruin looks like it could use that money!"

Bernabo got to his feet. His faced burned crimson, his hands balled into fists.

"God is here, Mr. Trainer, just as He is everywhere. There is much you or I cannot begin to understand but must accept. Your mother's money shall be returned to you. Now I must ask you to leave."

Trainer did not utter a wiseass rejoinder. Something inside did not want to believe this place harbored evil men, and he understood Seminario Evangelico had done its share of good works. But maybe that had been the priests' selling point and this wouldn't be history's first instance of religious men gone bad. Trainer made no threats of consequences, but he promised himself there would be. When he returned to Arecibo, next time he would stop Father Bernabo in the street and ask him to smile for the camera.

He found his way back to the courtyard. The cellular had no reception and he would need to locate a phone for a cab to San Juan. Standing again in the shadow of the Virgin's statue, he was probably in for a long and dangerous walk through the hills and towards the city.

A cold hand reached out from the darkness and touched his shoulder.

"Señor..." It was the young cleric who had his nose in the book inside Bernabo's study. "Señor Trainer, my name is Piétre. I did not mean to startle you, but I think you should come with me. I believe there is something here you will want to see."

"What I want to see right now is a cab."

The young man stammered. "I... I must confess... I listened at the door to your conversation with Father Bernabo, and I have heard talk of the old woman whose visions have sent you here. I am certain the priests would not want me to show you this, but I have pledged myself to the truth, and because you have asked, I must tell. I know you have questions."

"Only about a hundred of them, Piétre. My mother knew all about this place without ever seeing it. She claimed a dead priest spoke to her. I know God's ways are mysterious, but is He so interested in saving one soul that He would go to all this trouble just to bring me here?"

"You are here for a reason, Señor. Father D'Angiolini told your mother that reason. The dead often have a kinship with the living with whom something in common is shared. Their deaths, they were similar, no? We will go to the rear grounds. At this hour the padres will be taking their meals inside their chambers, so we must act now. Come."

The youth allowed no time for hesitation. Trainer followed him through the moonless dark, remaining close to the wall. It was near impossible to see anything. The smell assaulted him first. There was no mistaking that stench.

"These are the donkey stables your mother described in her vision. Am I correct?"

"She mentioned them. But she didn't say they hadn't been cleaned in the past six months."

"The donkeys are more practical for traveling the great hills surrounding El Seminario. And the children, they love to go for rides."

"Why are we here?"

"Your mother, she spoke of God, had visions that Father D'Angiolini told her where to find Him? And so you have come here in search of some higher power because this is something you feel you must know? Because, despite your doubts, you truly want to believe He exists."

The acknowledgement sounded absurd when actually admitted, but saying it made him realize Piétre spoke the truth.

"All right. Yes."

"Señor Trainer, your search ends here. For very many years, the priests of Arecibo have known of this. There are no others who do. But your beloved mother's vision led you to us, and I believe our departed Padre D'Angiolini wanted you here so that you may learn the secret of El Seminario Evangelico for yourself. In America, you are a man of some power and influence? People respect you, listen to you?"

"If you believe the Arbitron ratings. Do you have something you want me to sell?"

Piétre clearly had no clue what that meant, but he didn't seem to care.

"Come into the stables with me."

[... where the donkeys are ...]

"The stables? Why?"

Piétre turned to him with a simple grin.

"So you may learn the truth."

This young man in priest's robes might be completely insane. Trainer considered hauling ass; fuck the darkness. But he had come for answers, no matter how asinine they seemed. He followed Piétre to the donkeys' paddock. The youth closed the door behind them, reaching into his robe's pouch to snap on a flashlight. Its beam was not very powerful because a brightly illuminated stable could deliver a dozen pissed off padres to the door.

Ten donkeys stomped relentlessly inside their stalls. Flies buzzed everywhere, and several alighted on Trainer's face. He swatted at them but they kept coming back four or five at a time.

"Listen, I'm not real comfortable being in here. I'm a city mouse, you know."

"Shhhh..."

If any of the donkeys started braying, Trainer decided he

was out of there. He didn't feel like explaining to Father Bernabo why he was there when he had no idea himself. The flashlight probed each corner of the paddock while a galaxy of flies danced in its beam. He felt his nausea build.

"There!" the young cleric almost shouted, catching his error. Instead he pointed. Trainer's eyes followed the sliver of light to a large dung heap alongside a fat donkey.

"What? Where? I don't see anything."

"There!"

"I see only one huge pile of shit."

"Come closer, then. I will show you."

He aimed the light at an insect perched motionless on the dung heap, a fat horse fly, it appeared. Whatever it was, Trainer had never seen one so huge. Its size was almost the thickness of his thumb.

"It's a fly. That's all I see."

The cleric grinned again, this time showing teeth.

"Tell me, Señor. Do you notice any other flies upon that particular dung heap?"

He didn't. The lumpy mound was the largest in the stable, and there should have been a hundred flies buzzing around it. But he saw only this one, and it wasn't even moving.

"All right, Piétre. You've demonstrated that a fat fly is king of the hill. So?"

"He is much more than that, Señor. So much more."

Trainer couldn't help himself. The convulsion of laughter just happened.

"This is a joke, right? You can't be serious!!"

The youth appeared more than earnest. The grin had disappeared. "The baby Jesus, he was born in a stable similar to this."

"Jesus was a man! And this stink hole is no manger!"

"You asked to see God, Señor Trainer. I have brought you to Him."

Trainer inspected the insect closer. Its head was white

like the insect screaming 'Help me! Help me!' in that 50's Vincent Price movie. Otherwise it was a fat house fly, nothing more. The damned thing seemed embedded in the dung heap. Even as a cosmic punch line, this was more tragic than clever, a blasphemy worse than any atheist could conceive.

"This... is God?"

Piétre nodded.

"And you know this, how?"

"I am studying to become a priest. I know what is, and what is not. God's truth is known to every padre, every sister of El Seminario."

"You pray to a fly? You worship a deity that lives on a pile of shit?"

The insect stirred, wings flittering to life. It circled the two men, alighting on Trainer's hand. The sensation surprised him. He felt an electric current pass through him, warm, almost soothing.

[Mind over matter... ridiculous...]

The stable door swung open. In silhouette among the night's shadows stood Father Artur Bernabo.

"Piétre! Piétre! What have you done?"

Trainer managed composure amid the lunacy of the moment. He held out his hand, the fly still clinging to his fingertip. He inspected the fat insect as he spoke.

"Don't condemn the boy, Father. He did only what he believed was right. Even if I believed Piétre here, anyone I might tell would laugh himself sick and have me committed to the cracker factory. I'll consider this experience a joke in very bad taste, and we'll all forget it ever happened. Okay?"

Bernabo approached slowly.

"Some believe God is in a flower, Mr. Trainer. Others believe he is in the wind, the rain, or the Earth itself. What matters is what simply is. God is real, just as the creature you are holding now is real." He held out his hand, reaching for the insect. "Please. Gently. Gently."

"Father Bernabo, you're telling me you also believe this fly is... "

"He is."

Trainer pulled his hand away. The fly settled inside his palm.

"I don't think so, Father. Whatever metaphysical dung heap you're selling, this buyer is aware!" In one rapid motion he slammed his hands together, heard the micro-fart of ruptured innards explode as the fly burst open like a bloody jellybean. Studying the thick paste dripping down his wrist, Trainer offered his open palms like stigmata. Father Bernabo and Piétre inspected the goo that remained. "Tell me, gentlemen. Does this qualify as a crucifixion? Do you think maybe he'll be resurrected as a cockroach?"

The two priests stood frozen in place, mouths open. Neither spoke as Trainer wiped the fly's remains against a handkerchief, tossing it behind him.

"There are about a thousand other Gods buzzing around in here. I'm sure you'll find some other Lord of the Flies to carry on. And when you're done grieving, I'd appreciate it if one of you would call me a cab. I'll be outside. No offense, but this place really stinks."

He walked into the darkness, filling his lungs with the fresh air. It was hot, but still better than the reek of that damned stable. The night felt extremely humid and he was sweating badly, but this was Puerto Rico. Here it was always hot.

"Lunatics. All of them," he muttered.

Something felt strange, something was not right. His feet were unsteady, as if the ground had shifted. And something else.

Earlier there had been no moon, not so much as a pale sliver to light his way. Now there shone a full moon illuminating everything around him. It seemed very large.

Trainer shielded his eyes.

A lunar eclipse maybe?

[not right, not right.]

He looked again. It wasn't the moon he saw. This was a thousand watt Klieg light filling the night sky with fire.

"GOD IS NOT A FLY!"

No, not the moon...

It was the sun!

And it was coming straight at him.

THE END

FINDING CHRIST
By Trevor Newton

"**W**alter, we've got Janet on line three. She's distraught about all the recent attacks in the news and says she's beginning to question God."

Walter looked at Karen through the glass and rolled his eyes before turning off the cough button.

"Janet, sweetheart, what's this nonsense about questioning God? Faith is the entire groundwork of our belief system, is it not?"

The woman on the other end was sobbing and struggling to answer the question. Walter allowed her to regain her composure, using the downtime to tap out a Pall Mall Non-Filter and light it. The passage on his lighter caught his attention: *Do not despise prophecies, but test everything; hold fast what is good. (1 Thessalonians 5:20,21)*

"Yes, but all these attacks in the news... I can't help but think that God has simply abandoned us, given up and thrown in the towel."

"Janet, sweetheart-"

"Two-hundred and sixteen dead after the mass shooting

at that azalea festival in Wilmington, North Carolina. Almost another hundred at the high school bombing in Burbank, California, and that's only one of twelve school attacks in the past week. Nearly a thousand, Walter—a *thousand*—dead after the terrorist attack in Salt Lake City. The perpetrators of the terrorist attack were all local youth ministers and regarded as upstanding citizens. I just don't see how any God could let all this happen."

Walter took a long drag off the cigarette. It was getting short enough to start burning his lips, so he stubbed it out in the ashtray. "Janet, I want to be clear with you: I understand your frustrations. When these unexplainable atrocities occur, there's rarely any one person to blame. So, amidst our fear and confusion, we turn to God. Sometimes for comfort and guidance, and other times for someone to blame and hurl accusations at. The Lord knows I've made the same mistake many times. But, you're a fairly regular caller, aren't you, Janet?"

"Yeah."

"I thought so. You see, I don't claim to be a genius of any sort. Got pretty average grades throughout high school; same deal when it came to college. But, one thing I do wield is a pretty darn good memory. I can tell you what I had for breakfast exactly three weeks ago: scrambled eggs and sourdough toast.

"You can name a year and I'll tell you who won the NBA championship that year and, just to impress you, I can name the coach, too. 1973: New York Knicks take it in Game 5 with Red Holzman coaching. 1980: Los Angeles Lakers take it in Game 6, winning their first championship in eight years with Paul Westhead coaching. 2005: San Antonio Spurs take it in Game 7 with Gregg Popovich coaching.

"And about two years ago, sometime in mid-June of 2017, you called into my radio show even more hysterical than you are right now. Your son, Timmy or Tommy—or something along those lines—had a brain tumor. I remember how it was oddly cold that morning, but God blessed us with full sunshine around noon. Between your bawling and howling, I could hardly understand what it was you were trying to convey, but when I figured it out, I prayed with you over the phone. I even wrote down the address to your church and drove nearly two hours to attend Sunday service with a bunch of folks I didn't know from a hole in the wall. I prayed with you there, too. And, if my memory serves me correct, and it usually does, you called back in sometime in August and said your little boy was cancer-free. A miracle, a true act of God.

"Now, as if we're not all hurting enough, you call into my show to spread this spiteful blasphemy? For your own sake, Janet, I don't *ask*, I *demand* that you repent your sins. However, you won't do it here on my show, no. You can do that on your own time because, frankly, I, along with all the other God-fearing worshippers feel abandoned by *you*. Don't bother calling back in if you come to terms with how ridiculous you're being, we don't want your wishy-washy type clogging up the lines while genuine Christians are trying to call in."

Walter picked up the phone and slammed it back down on the receiver, ending the call. He glared at Karen in the producer's booth and she wouldn't meet his gaze. Pulling the microphone closer to his face, he relayed one final message.

"This concludes our show for the day, devotees. Remember to stand and worship in unison during these pressing times."

The stark, red ON AIR sign flipped to OFF AIR. Walter pulled the headphones off his head and slung them across the desk. Rising up from his seat, he walked into Karen's booth with long strides. She finally looked at him, with sympathy across her face, and he smiled.

"I'm going to level with you, Karen," he said.

"Unaltered, pure truthfulness." He paused and took a deep breath, the smile descending into a blank expression. "If you put me on the air with another caller like that, I'll punt you through that fucking glass. Do you understand?"

"I'm sorry, I mean, I didn't know… you handled it so well, really, you did."

"The last fucking thing I want is more attention averted towards this monumental barbarity." He paused again, this time to light another cigarette. "Any personal calls?"

"Yes," her voice cracked as she obviously fought to hold back tears, "a Milton Westmoore left a message for you. He said to tell you he had… located The Redeemer. He said you'd know what it meant."

Walter's eyes widened and his cigarette dropped to the floor. "It's about time," he said under his breath. "Pack your things, take the rest of the day off. I don't need you."

She was packed and departed within five minutes, not daring to say another word besides a solemn *Have a good day* before leaving. Walter hoped she wouldn't call in later and quit, she really was a good producer. But putting him on the air with someone like that? Knowledge of events prior to her employment be damned, it was still inexcusable, especially for the final call of the day. You *never* end a show on a negative note. He was here to exert positivity into the souls of the devotees, to keep their faith gauge topped off. But, If Milton had finally located The Redeemer, all this doom and gloom may finally be over.

He dialed Milton's cellular number on the office phone. While it was ringing, he caught another headline from a television in the main lobby: *Gas leak in Orlando neighborhood results in explosion; eighty-two casualties.*

"Milton speaking." His voice was slightly slurred, not that of a drunk man's, but a tired one.

"You sound like shit. Where was he?"

"Some scumfuck motel off Interstate 90, near Toledo." He coughed violently and Walter pulled the phone away from his ear momentarily. "I'll be back in Virginia with him by morning."

"How's he doing?"

"Worst I've ever seen him, Walt. Must have had about twenty-five whores in his room with him, licking all over him, pumping him full of drugs. He's as pale as a ghost—I had half a mind to clear them all out but one, slit her throat and nurse him back to health myself."

"I don't think a whore's blood will do the trick anymore," Walter said. "He needs hard stuff. *Real* sinner's blood."

"Is anything lined up?"

"Doug's got it handled. A few pornographers that specialize in the *young stuff*," Walter said. A chill ran down his spine, jerking him in his seat.

"Forget I even asked, I don't want to know anymore."

"Well, it's seven of them; the whole crew. That much blood will keep him topped off for a long time, then he can get back to preventing the bulk of this shit. But, I'm telling you, somebody in the congregation has gotta start keeping track of this motherfucker. Oklahoma City should've been a key indicator that someone needs to stick to him like glue, or September Eleventh."

"It's a whole other level this time," Milton said. "He's been off the radar for over three months."

"You know it's fucking horrible here, but some smaller European countries have had their populations halved from attacks. Fucking *halved*."

"Who would've thunk that Christ himself would need a babysitter?"

Walter laughed, shaking his head. "Anyway, get him to the compound. I'll go make sure everything's in order."

"See you soon."

Walter swung by his apartment before setting out to the compound. He took the time to shower and shave, pack a bag and even eat a meal. He knew once he set foot inside the compound and alerted the congregation of The Redeemer's soon-to-be arrival, he would have to remain within its confines until he was nursed back to health and sent back out to prevent tragedies.

Walter shifted the LTD into park and stared at the compound through the grimy windshield. The church stood on the corner, the compound in the middle taking up most of the property. The second and third floors were used as office space for the wide array of employees within the congregation. Walter felt lucky his employment didn't require him to be on the grounds, though he did have to attend a bi-monthly evaluation of his performance.

On the far left side of the property were the dormitories and classrooms for students aged thirteen to twenty, who were paying their dues in order to secure a comfortable job within the congregation, and preparing to serve their life in devotion to the Lord. Walter attended and graduated from the program at eighteen years old and left to enroll at Duke University and pursue a degree majoring in Radio Broadcasting and minoring in Public Speaking. When he returned four years later, the congregation bankrolled his entire setup: the building, equipment, furniture and even a freshly paved parking lot with shade trees to park under. He loved radio, loved interacting with his community even more, but it could be tiresome. The congregation insisted on twenty-four/seven commercial free broadcasting. This meant keeping plenty of food, water and cigarettes nearby for his eight-hour shift, and a mandatory piss bottle underneath the desk.

Matthew and Luke were smoking in front of the twelve-foot, solid golden cross in the middle of the roundabout. They were a couple of twenty-somethings who jumped straight from graduation into low-level accounting work for the congregation. Walter didn't know them extremely well, but he knew they were a couple of kiss-asses. The way they spoke and dressed pissed Walter off, only rivaled by their biblical names. He hoped he could walk past them and up to the door without them noticing him.

"Walter!" Matthew shouted. Luke waved.

Fuck me.

Walter half-smiled and walked over to the duo, nodding as a greeting.

"What brings you to the compound, brother Walter?" Matthew asked. Before Walter could merely internally facilitate a response, Matthew continued. "Ah, I see it in your eyes, brother Walter. You come bearing… *good* news?"

Walter lit a cigarette, again pondering the passage on his lighter. "Is that a guess?"

"Call it faith," Matthew said, smirking as if he was a genius of verbal maneuvering.

"Well, you're right. The Redeemer's been located."

"Oh, that's just pleasant news," Luke said. "I hate to say it, but I truly was beginning to get worried."

Matthew glared at Luke, his eyebrows pitched and his left fist clenched hard enough for a vein to protrude on his forearm. Apparently Matthew wasn't *just* a kiss-ass, but a hard-ass, too.

"I think we were all beginning to get somewhat worried," Walter said, attempting to break the tension. "Within a reasonable stance."

"Speak for yourselves," Matthew said. "I knew The Redeemer would show once he was ready."

Walter took a long drag off his cigarette and chuckled. "He didn't *show*, Milton found him in a motel room with enough whores to tempt the pope."

"Blasphemy!" Matthew shouted. Both of the young men appeared shocked. "I don't believe that for one second! Telling fibs in general is a sin, brother Walter. But about The Redeemer? How dare you spew such hatred in my presence."

Walter shrugged and walked away. He didn't have to

listen to that shit, especially not from a pathetic brownnoser like Matthew who was barely old enough to shave.

Walter dropped the end of his cigarette on the white marble steps that lead up to the main compound, stepping on it. His stomach always knotted before walking inside. It wasn't the people inside that made him feel intimidated, it was simply the building itself. Somehow it was just… *eerie*. The way it was perfectly clean on the inside and outside, even though he never once saw a maintenance person or a maid, or the way it almost seemed bigger on the inside than it did on the outside. The entirety of the outside and inside of the building was white marble with solid golden trim, with the occasional perfectly pressed Oriental rug to tie the room together.

He walked through the lobby, where several private congregation-members-only prayer groups were active, and walked up the stairs to the second, then the third floor. The third floor was dedicated to executives and other employees high upon the tribal hierarchy.

Meredith stood from her desk with a wide, beaming smile. "Walter, it's so good to see you!"

Walter, caught off guard, simply nodded and curled his lips. Meredith walked around her desk and gave him a tight, welcoming hug, then patted his shoulders as she backed up, like a mother sending her child off to a big-boy program. "To what do I owe the pleasure?"

Walter cleared his throat and quickly glanced around the room. "I'm here to see Mister Durant," he said, trying to sound authoritative.

Meredith sat down and pressed a button on the buzzer. "Walter Brickner here to see you."

"Send him in!"

Walter nodded once more at Meredith and walked through the door, closing it behind him. Chuck Durant, the president of the congregation, was standing by the window smoking a cigar, overlooking a soccer match being played outside amongst the students.

"I think your secretary just raped me."

Chuck turned around, laughing and holding a hand over his stomach. *"What?"*

"I'm only half joking," Walter said tapping out another smoke. He hadn't planned on smoking in Chuck's office but, hey, *he* was smoking. "Last time a woman got that handsy with me, I spent the next morning picking through my pubes with a little comb."

"And now I know one of my favorite employees had crabs," Chuck said, still laughing and shaking his head. He set his cigar down in an ashtray and walked around his desk with an extended hand. Walter accepted the handshake. "How the hell are you, Walt? I've been listening to your show when I can, the other hosts' timeslots as well. You've really got a good racket for us going."

"I don't know how good it could be, not having commercials and all."

"We both know we don't deal in currency," Chuck said. "It's about how many listeners you get. The more listeners, the more people send their kids to our teaching program and the more people show up for Wednesday and Sunday service. It's an investment, if you *really* need to look at it from a business standpoint."

Walter nodded, not knowing how to respond. "I came bearing good news. Milton has located The Redeemer."

Chuck slumped against his desk and expelled a light chuckle. "Now, that really is good news. Where was he?"

Walter filled Chuck in on everything Milton had told him, not sparing any of the details. Chuck seemed less surprised than Walter had expected. Walter knew it wasn't unlike Christ to go off the radar, but whores, doing drugs? Truth be told, he always assumed he just holed up in a cave somewhere, like a child in his room refusing to do his chores. But it made sense. When the sinner's blood began to wear off, he *craved* sin, but he simply couldn't bring himself to commit what had to be done to get his ultimate, long-lasting fix: kill. Instead, he went for the small fixes. Sex, drugs, who knows what all else.

Did Walter even want to know?

Meredith showed him to a spare bedroom on the first floor. Like everything else within the compound, it was flawless. Except the damn mattress; it was as firm and tough as a two- dollar steak. He tossed and turned all night, dreaming of a variety of things, some good, bad or just plain preposterous.

He awoke to violent shaking and touchy hands. Meredith was pushing on his chest, shouting his name. He sat up in bed, clutching his heart. "What the fuck's the matter with you?"

She was visibly taken aback by such vulgar language, and she recoiled as if she had touched a hot burner.

"Well? What is it?"

"Mister Durant needs to see you," she said, now domineering rather than sensual. "He's in his office."

Walter marched through the hallway and up the marble stairs, his heart pounding against his breastplate, threatening to break loose. When he slung open the door, Chuck was also still donning his pajamas, but Milton was also there, drenched in sweat from head to toe.

"The Redeemer escaped," Chuck said, not taking his eyes off of Milton. "Someone left him unattended for a precious Big Mac and fries."

Milton was huffing air like a beached fish. "I didn't think the bastard would really run off!"

Chuck raised a hand and slapped him across the face. "You watch your fucking mouth!"

Milton held the side of his reddening face and stared at the floor, flushed with embarrassment.

"Now," Chuck continued, "let's get down to brass tacks here. He can't have gone far, he's in the area, probably relishing in more sin." Chuck looked at Walter, anger burning through his normally relaxed features. "You're going to go find him and," he motioned to Milton, "you're gonna take this stupid fuck with you. If either of you so much as step foot inside the compound without him in hand, I'll see to it you both end up in The Pit."

Walter had heard rumors about The Pit during his days in the academy, but that's what he thought they were: rumors. Apparently not. Images of a black, snake-filled hovel, reeking of human decay and iron blood, piercing with screams of the damned passed through his mind.

"You have my word," Walter said. "We won't return until we've got him."

Chuck grabbed Milton by his collar and shoved him forward, and the duo walked outside together in the light drizzle.

The green backlit clock on the radio stated it was just after 2:00 AM when they pulled out of the compound in Walter's LTD.

"This just in: Scott Scarborough, head coach for the women's basketball team at Sodipepper High, has been accused of raping more than half of the young women on the team, most underage. Once allegations surfaced late this afternoon, he was found at Mermaid's Point with a self-inflicted gunshot to the head."

Walter snapped off the radio, not turning it on for the rest of the night.

The duo walked out of the sixth strip-club they'd been to in the last two hours. They had canvassed most of northeastern Virginia, visiting strip-clubs, brothels and motels known to be used for sex transactions. Milton was obviously starting to give up hope, but not Walter. He flourished during these types of moments. He would either figure it out or get thrown into The Pit, and then it wasn't his problem anymore, was it? Besides, he doubted Chuck would actually throw him in. Maybe Milton, though.

Walter looked up and down the street, hoping for a

miracle.

"It's over," Milton said. "We're fucked."

Walter's eyes squinted in what seemed like a random direction. "Huh."

Milton looked in the same direction, then back at Walter. "You wanna fill me in or should I piss my fucking pants for you first?"

Walter nodded in the same direction and, this time, Milton looked a bit longer. Above a shackled brick building with boards in place of windows, a big, bright pink sign stood: The Male Box. It was a gay club, one of the few in northeastern Virginia.

"Wait, you don't really think-"

"You got a better idea?"

Walter thought the place would probably stink of desperation and cheap beer like any other bar, but in truth it kind of smelled like Fruity Pebbles. They each did a few laps around the club, maneuvering through hopping clubbers. Nothing.

"I'm telling you," Milton said, "we are *fucked*."

"I've got an idea."

Walter approached the bar with a few Benjamins laced in his palm.

"What can I get you?" the bartender asked, smiling. He was clean cut and mostly wearing leather. "You look like an Old Fashioned, maybe a Manhattan kind of guy. Bet you're married, too. Your wife know you come to gay clubs at four in the morning?"

"What I do with my time is my business," Walter replied. He quickly grabbed the man's wrist and yanked it toward himself. His face showed fear and confusion, but it melted away when the cold hard cash hit his palm. "Where can a guy have a *really* good time around here?"

The man slowly pulled his hand away, eyeing the cash. "Around back," he said, swallowing hard. "The door under the blue light."

Fresh air wasn't on the menu when they walked in; only the salty smell of semen and the musk of sweat mixed with sex. Doors lined the hallways under blue fluorescent bulbs. Most of the doors were closed, the rooms occupied, but a few stragglers were chatting or resting in the hallway.

Walter approached a man sitting on the floor, covered with sweat and huffing for air. "You see a guy around here? Long brown hair, bit of a beard."

The man smiled and nodded. "That brother wore my ass out." He laughed. "He don't tire out, neither. I think he's in one of the rooms over there." He pointed across the hall.

Milton tried the door. It was locked, and he raised his hand, about to knock on the door.

"Fuck that," Walter said, raising his leg and shoving his foot underneath the knob. The door flew open, and there he was, ramming a redheaded man from behind. A burly man wearing only a utility belt had his cock rammed inside of Christ, creating some sort of fucktrain.

Milton turned away at the unleashed smell, gagging in the hallway.

"Party's over," Walter said. "Like it or not, you've got a job to do. You can keep running if you want, but you know they'll just send the Apostles if I fail to bring you back. If they fail, then an Archangel. We gonna do this or what?"

Christ sighed and unholstered himself from the redhead. He pushed back against the burly man, who forced him back down onto the side of the bed. With a simple flick of his wrist, the burly man flew against the wall and crashed through the sheetrock into the adjacent room, where a black man was having his cock orally polished by a twink with a chain around his neck.

Christ looked around aimlessly until he found his white robe. He took his time slipping his arms through the sleeves, arranging the collar, but left it untied for his holiness to poke through and seemingly lead the way. Walter and Milton walked behind him outside the building and to the car.

Briefly, Walter wondered how he knew where the car was parked, then realized exactly *who* he was thinking of.

"Either of you boys got a cigarette?" Christ asked from the backseat.

With shaky hands, Milton pulled the pack of Parliaments from his shirt pocket and handed them to him. "H-here you go."

Walter's grip on the steering wheel tightened, his face tensed. Milton noticed, nudged him and shook his head. Walter scoffed, looking in the rearview mirror. "You've got some fucking nerve, you know that?"

Christ put the cigarette in his mouth, snapped his fingers and it was lit. He didn't respond, but stared out the window.

"Stop," Milton said under his breath.

"No, I'm serious," Walter said, braking for a red light. "People depend on you. The congregation has always ensured that enough blood is on hand for your fixes and you know damn well it's there when you need it." The light turned green and Walter took his foot off the brake. "No one in the congregation's gonna tell you this, but they're more afraid of you than ever. You let a lot of people down, and you're the only one with enough power to reduce the horrible shit that goes on. That means this lies on you, and no one else."

Walter pulled through the iron gates and halfway up the roundabout, parallel with the main compound. Christ didn't say a single word through the entire ride. Milton had called Chuck when they were ten minutes out, and he now stood on the steps in one of his perfectly pressed Italian designer suits with a wide, welcoming grin on his face.

With the sun now beginning to rise, the four of them walked inside and down into the basement. "Your meal is this way," Chuck said, opening a door. Walter didn't notice, but Milton stayed outside of it. The seven pornographers were bound by their feet, hanging down head first above a large black cauldron. Their throats had been slit some time ago, obvious by the scabbing and coagulating neck wounds.

Christ ran his hands through the collected blood, then his mouth began to open. Walter had never seen this part, assuming he simply lapped it up like a dog, or maybe sucked it through a straw. His mouth opened to a sickening capacity, with the back of his head covering the nape of his neck. The slimy, pulsing organ slithered out from within, heaving until it found the cauldron of blood.

When the sucking sounds started, Walter turned and walked back out the door, wondering if God had abandoned them.

THE END

THE CURTAIN
By B.T. Joy

If Yannick hadn't been here before he wouldn't have known what they were.

The countryside that surrounded them was French; anyone could have guessed that. Flaxen fields of barley tillering wheat ran as far as the eye could see and stopped only, perhaps, where the rough beach grass trimmed the boundaries of the Normandy coast. But they, themselves, the figures that stood among the level farmlands, were far harder for a stranger to the dream to identify.

Trees, they appeared at first. Or, rather, blasted, dead stumps that dotted the otherwise empty plain like an extinct forest. Then—from the nearest of these broken pillars—the eye discerns a ruffling movement around the steady form and—suddenly— the dreamer realizes that each dark shape against the yellow crops is clothed in a furling black habit that trails along with the wind.

The nuns, Yannick thought, and he looked with his dream-eyes at the plastery, cracked faces that hung like Venetian masks on the heads of each sideward leaning and colorlessly dressed body.

Yannick hated them; hated them and needed them all at the same time.

The shape closest to him in the sisterhood of shapes let a pale and blue veined hand slip from under her mantle and then it pointed, twist-fingered, towards the shambling relic of disordered stone that had been their home when they were alive and young.

Yannick refused to look the way the wind was blowing: towards the convent that had stood on that spot when he was a boy—in his summery childhood—but that was now nothing but a mound of rocks. He focused instead on the long, indicatory arm and the spiny hand of stretched fingers that concluded it.

In that hand the nun was still holding her crucifix and the silver chain and glass beads of the rosary wound around her digits and her wrist like a length of cheese-wire digging into the skin.

As Yannick watched she tightened her grip on the awkward cruciform shape she held and with such vehemence that a dribbling run of blood fell from her palm and stained the blonde ground at her feet a darker color.

Yannick was not shocked. He had seen all their blasphemies before. His blue eyes trailed up the line of the nun's arm, not stopping at her hunched shoulder, and carrying on to her grinning, feral, parody of a face.

The thing inside the nun winked at him and then her long, black tongue unfolded like a sexual invitation from the cavity of her mouth.

She opened her throat to speak to him but the only sound that issued out was—

The alarm! Stark and jarring and military in its directness.

Yannick rolled over with a practiced precision and fingered the device until the noise stopped.

He sat up on his elbow on the hard mattress in the center of the concrete room. The window behind his head had only then begun to turn a darker shade of blue with the oncoming night.

He listened—cocking his head to one side like a predatory bird. His blue eyes shimmered lightly in the shadows as he took in all the auditory information he could; interpreted it and drew his conclusions about the other inhabitant of the house.

His breath stilled a little when he first heard the low bass of the ruckus downstairs. The basement was well enough soundproofed so that only a particularly attentive ear could ever pick out the noise but Yannick had spent the last nine years training himself to detect even the slightest disturbance at even the most extreme thresholds of his senses and so, to him, any sound louder than a whisper was unnerving enough to cause him to go down and quiet it.

Still though, he could never react in a spirit of panic or discord. It was what it wanted and he simply wouldn't allow it.

He calmed himself and blinked the still burning pictures of all those dead French nuns out of his memory. Then he pulled the blanket away from his still-dressed body and rose; limping off into the pit latrine to prepare.

When inside the doorless cubicle that he used for the inevitable calls that nature made each day Yannick pushed his trousers down to his knees and touched his inner thigh with exploratory fingers.

Blood. He pulled his hand back and looked at it. His palm and all his digits were smeared red.

He saw the yellow fields again: the nun's hand bleeding onto the wheat.

He winced a little as, tenderly, he reached down again. He grabbed the buckle of the improvised cilice and slackened it only momentarily before dragging it shut again with another notch of tightness that drove the razorblades deeper into the flesh.

There was another spurt of fresh bleeding across his

wrist. He set his jaw and meditated on the pain. He imagined the Venerable Antonietta Meo; her tiny bones rife with life-eating osteosarcomas; the doctors applying a tourniquet to her leg before sawing it off; and, all the while, the six-year-old Saint maintaining a composure of prayer and gratitude to Christ.

"*Ad majorem Christi gloriam,*" he muttered: *For the greater glory of Christ.*

He left the contraption tightened around his thigh and pulled up his trousers; tightening too the belt around his waist.

In the basement room downstairs the noise must have been getting out of hand because he could hear it almost clearly through the thickly insulated floor.

He left the latrine and made his way—limping—toward the stairs.

* * *

The curtain ran on a straight runner across the ceiling and cut off a narrow strip of the room by the back wall. Behind it, as was often the case, there was such a filthy stream of caterwauling and profanity that it hurt Yannick's soul to hear it.

Today, Yannick could just about make out from the muffled protestations, that it was the Holy Trinity that was the target of the thing's tirade of execration.

On other days there would be diatribes given out to nearly every sacred thing. The testicles of John the Baptist, for some outlandish reason, were a particularly favored subject.

The Popes of Rome lick the fat arse of Mammon, it would slobber. *Jesus' mouth and Saint John's balls! The tongues of the nuns in the dusty, black cunt of the Mother of God!*

Of course, through the gag, Yannick could rarely catch

enough for the offence to be total.

He crossed now to the curtain and listened for a moment. Some diarrhetic drivel about a homosexual orgy between the Father, Son and Holy Ghost. Nothing unique or even shocking.

Yannick blinked. It would be disgusting if it weren't so boring and predicable.

It never said anything *else*. Just an on-running stream of the carnal conflated with the spiritual in all its mind-numbing permutations.

Yannick put his hand on the small collection of switches on the wall by the curtain.

He waited a moment. The thing had heard him enter and should have quieted on its own.

He counted down in curse words.

"Whore!" it screamed.

"Five," Yannick said.

"Cunt! Motherfucker!"

"Four... three..."

"Come at me you cocksucker!"

"Two," he rested his thumb tiredly on the light fixture.

"Fuck you!" it answered.

"One," Yannick flicked the switch and completed the circuit.

A faint buzzing noise began behind the curtain; like a current running through metal. The once colorful language turned into an agonized scream and, in seconds, the smell of slightly burning skin and hair filled the entire basement.

Yannick turned off the electrics for a moment; waited for silence; then cranked it on again.

The screaming filled his eardrums and echoed across the naked soundproofing.

He switched off for the second time and listened once more as the soft yelping from back there became only the sound of breath whistling between rotten teeth and as—slowly—even that sound gave way to peacefulness.

He listened to the pattern of its inhalations and knew that it was either sleeping or faking sleep.

In all the years he'd kept it there, behind the curtain, Yannick had never truly decided whether it slept or not. Its *true* self—Yannick knew—needed neither rest nor nourishment. But, then again, maybe while established in the host it did require the necessities of life to keep its vessel from giving out on it.

Yannick thought of Gaga. He knew for a certainty they were hardy things. He frowned as he remembered her: strapped to the observation chair in the center of the basement and begging for water in that sickly-sweet voice she had affected in order to weaken his resolve.

He remembered Ilil, the male one, growling like a rabid dog in his cage; so much in fact that Yannick had had to turn on the electric seven times on the night that Gaga died.

In the end even Ilil—irreverent and smut-mouthed as he usually was—tried a subtler and more cunning tack. Yannick still remembered how saccharine and false it was; the servile and unconvincing tone he'd adopted.

"Please, Yannick," he'd mewled like a wounded puppy. "Please. Give her water."

* * *

Success is never a virtue in itself.

Over time, that had come to constitute one of Yannick's deepest moral assumptions.

After all, if success were the primary measure of the importance of one's life then any intestinal parasite that slithers through shit and so feeds itself on blood would be the pinnacle of divine creation. Many who are wicked or vile succeed, but are they virtuous?

Didn't Judas himself succeed in betraying Christ and yet, with that very success, condemned and hung himself before the Passover had finished?

Yannick strolled down the snowy sidewalk of Nägeligasse, past the squared-off neoclassical frontages that had been all the rage in Bern before Le Corbusier.

Frontages, Yannick thought. *Yes. Frontages.*

All elegance and *je ne sais quoi* to the eye; but inside, in its internal portions, where substance should reside: nothing but decadence leading to rot and excess as the harbinger of putrefaction.

Yannick ducked into the arched doorway off the street and, with an appearance of boundless confidence, he just kept on going through the backdoor of the hotel.

He corrected his limp as best he could. He'd even removed the cilice for this job and washed out his self-inflicted wounds with cool water. The pain of the mortification brought his soul closer to Christ; he knew that. But he knew equally that the Lord would grant him dispensation from his usual pain for long enough to do his work. After all, this business required that he travel as *persona incognita,* if you will, and nothing draws more attention, Yannick found, than a sudden spill of blood running down the trouser leg onto a freshly shampooed carpet in the lobby of a five-star hotel.

Ad majorem Christi gloriam, he thought to himself as he walked. *Ad majorem Christi gloriam.*

He could hardly believe how easy these little public subterfuges had become, with practice. Several times on his route to the staff room facilities that he'd scoped out on his previous visit he'd been spotted and eyed—though momentarily—by a few bellhops and even a manager. He'd smiled at them crisply and they—not knowing him for guest or colleague—had succumbed to the general hypnosis of his mannerisms and simply let him pass unmolested.

He'd been forced to look around cautiously only once: when he'd forced the lock on the night cleaner's locker and found, as he knew he would, her skeleton key pass lying there for use during her shift.

He passed out of the staff room again, turning the pass like a trophy between his fingers; crossed the busy and quite palatial lobby and tucked himself in among the nine or so others who were now standing in the open elevator.

"Floor, sir?" the red uniformed operator asked.

"Ah." Yannick smiled. "Twelve. Please."

The operator smiled back and thumbed the button with his white-gloved hand.

The elevator began its smooth upward transit. Yannick stared expressionlessly at the ceiling for most of the time.

Moments in, however, he felt the feeling of two warm, sticky, little eyes on his face.

He became necessarily aware of the people round about him. Just like his hearing his sense of being watched at become ultra-sensitive and precise given the mortal danger any servant of the Cross might face.

He scanned the faces around him quickly and noted that each one was staring only at the walls; then he looked down at the tiny, winter-blushed face that was staring up at him like he was a skeleton in a carnival ghost train.

He smiled at the little girl. She didn't smile back.

He winked at her and she stood bemused.

He stole one last glance at the girl's mother, whose hand she held in her own mittened hand. Then he decided he'd really nothing to lose.

He stared back into the girl's glistening eyes. There was a moment when he did nothing but smile politely. Then he bared his teeth; scrunched up his face into a plastery mask and stuck out his tongue as though in sexual frenzy.

When he left the elevator on the twelfth floor no one aboard could understand why the little girl was breathless and crying.

* * *

Frontages, Yannick thought. *Frontages.*

And behind the frontages: Devils, all of them.

He thought of Gaga dying on the stirruped observation chair; crying for water; pretending to be only a girl, though he'd seen Ancitif prancing in her eyes and watched her chalky throat bulge with obscenities. *A frontage*!

He thought of Ilil in the cage, behind the curtain, in the basement room, at the outskirts of Bern, screaming tirelessly about Saint John's bollocks and then pretending to sleep like an inoffensive lamb. *A frontage*!

Yannick even thought—and he hadn't for years—about his summery childhood in the north of France. About the nuns who had brought him up. About dear Sister Camille and dear Sister Mariette. Their golden voices. Their sweet faces.

Affront! he thought. *Affront! A frontage!*

His thoughts—their passion—had nearly put his breath out of kilter and he did well to right it again. After all, where he was standing, in the wardrobe of Room 1208, any stray noise he made may have been picked up on and identified from the room at large.

He steadied himself and stopped thinking about the past; that was done anyway and couldn't be relived. Instead he tried to focus all his attention on the present, on the job at hand.

He thought about Herr Grosh—that fat, entitled hog living off of the filth of a once proud banquet now gone to spoil.

Yannick remembered the article in the Zeitung that had first alerted him to the German lawyer's impending visit to Switzerland. He thought of Grosh being escorted around the decadent, meaningless installation art at the Kunsthalle and then dining on micro cuisine at Mille Sens; only to retire later to more private regions of the city and to engage there in his darker appetites.

Yannick saw them there—Grosh and his associates in law—discussing it cynically and without feeling: their latest plans for an all-out attack on the Holy Catholic Church.

What was it now, Grosh? Yannick thought. *Who have you found this time to help you defame the incorruptible? Some pedophiliac thing hiding inside the body of a priest? A Jesuit, maybe, with a slobbering ghost concealed beneath his cassock? A nun—*

Yannick stopped breathing and thinking all at once as he heard the teeth of a key pushing into the lock of Room 1208.

He heard drunken laughing from the hall and a few rags of German. His lip curled.

Yannick had been born in Lausanne and had lived his summery childhood in Normandy. He'd never really liked the necessity of the German language in his homeland.

His blue eyes twinkled inside the wardrobe as Grosh and the prostitute rolled into the room; her lean body strangled in his mountainous fat; his chubby, greedy hands toying with the zipper that ran down the back of her evening dress.

Yannick blinked. Waiting.

In minutes the call girl was naked and Grosh—the fat pig—was pulling his underwear down around his coffee can ankles.

The lawyer sat on the bed and the whore climbed aboard. Yannick kept watching and waiting as Grosh tucked his flabby hand in between his body and the woman's, seizing his cock and beginning to guide it into her soft opening.

That's enough, Yannick thought, and seconds later there was a skittering clatter as the assassin kicked open the wardrobe door and rushed into the room.

The whore didn't have time to scream, though she gargled a little, as Yannick threw his hands over her head and applied the steel garrote to her pulsing neck.

Her veins quite literally burst and it was Grosh who did the screaming as her squirts and pinwheels of lifeblood dribbled and spattered and jetted onto his face and chest and genitals.

Yannick threw the lifeless woman— an unfortunate

casualty of the spiritual crossfire— onto the bedroom floor; she lay there in a naked and bloody heap as Grosh, naked and bloody too, threw up his fat hands and begged for his life in English, French and German.

"Please," he blubbered. "Please. Please. Who are you? Who are you?"

Yannick righted the stained garrote in his capable grip.

"*Ad majorem Christi gloriam*," he whispered calmly as he approached.

* * *

Yannick checked his watch.

By all calculations it had been six and one half minutes since Grosh started shouting his *pleases* and *who are yous* and same such nonsense. And, by the same token, it had been nearly one hour and ten minutes since Yannick had left Ilil sleeping off (or pretending to sleep off) his electrocution in the cage behind the curtain.

All in all, time was tight.

Yannick reached inside his jacket and removed the athame from its custom made shoulder holster.

He crouched above the whore first, one leg on either side of her body, and turned her over until her tits faced the ceiling. Then, with all the methodical care of a watchmaker, he inserted the blade into the flesh of her chest and began to write.

Innocent, was the word he carved into her skin.

Then, when he'd finished, he moved on to Grosh. It pleased him that the fat lawyer had spewed up all that fine, frothy, Swiss cuisine over his cheeks and chin and, equally, over the carpet under his head.

Yannick stuck the athame into the lawyer's stomach like the opening motion of gutting a fish and then, slowing his motions, he engraved that mound of lard with a second message.

Washed in the Blood, it said.

Before he left, Yannick lined the bodies side by side in a ritualistic simplicity and dignity. He carved a cross into each of their foreheads and closed and kissed all four of their sleeping eyes.

Then, as though he knew the sinners needed love the most, he kissed Grosh too on his vomit stained mouth.

"*Ego te absolvo*," he whispered.

* * *

It was night all over Bern and the hilly country around the city was almost lifelessly still; all dairy farms and conical trees and miles of sparse-roaded silence where barely a car ever came by.

It was here—in anonymity—that Yannick had built the house; installed the electrified cages behind the curtain and brought Gaga and Ilil to be confined when they first spilled, mewling profanities, into the world from the black void beyond it.

He was bathing now in that quiet space for spiritual meditation that he'd carved out for himself among the chaos of the mundane. Slowly he removed his bloodstained clothes and stored them for later washing in the wardrobe in the concrete room. Down in the basement Ilil had not made a sound and Yannick hoped he wouldn't start up with his blasphemous yawping until after there'd been time for a short nap.

He took off the shoulder holster with the athame still inside, hung it up, then removed his shirt, trousers and underwear; placing the whole bloodied assortment into the wardrobe and closing the door.

He stepped back a little and retrieved the mass of wire and razors that was his homemade cilice. He knelt down naked on the floor and ratcheted the barbed device back onto his scarred and infected thigh. He tightened it as far as the buckles would allow.

He knelt there in contemplation for a long while.

He contemplated Origen of Alexandria who had cut off his own penis with a flat stone in fealty to Saint Matthew. He thought of Saint Apollonia who let the mob batter her teeth from her skull and leapt into their flames in joy. Or Saint Basilissa who, in still-pagan Rome, had her feet and hands, breasts and tongue removed, and was still singing as they cut her head from her body.

Great beings, Yannick thought. *True servants of the Cross.*

He steepled his hands over his naked chest.

"Lord, have mercy," he prayed. "Lord, have mercy. O Christ, hear us. O God the Father of heaven. O God the Son—"

The curtain, Yannick thought. He saw it as the blackness behind his eyes. Draped there and concealing a hundred memories of the past.

In his mind's eye he saw Isabelle, his dead wife. She was sat on a quilted bed somewhere in Zurich reading *The Wizard of Oz* to—to *someone*.

He remembered the curtain—the emerald one—and how the wizard had been one thing on one side and quite another in the invisible portion of the room that had been obscured by the drapery. Ostensibly great and powerful but actually, on the inside, weak and bumbling and unsure of himself.

Yannick saw the nuns—dear Sister Camille and dear Sister Mariette. He saw their faces wrinkle with smiles and their eyes glimmer with religiosity and good will towards the little children in their charge.

Masks, Yannick thought. *Masks and frontages.*

How many had they caused to turn? Those black deer ticks that had latched onto the bodies of the sisters and turned their flesh to pustulent meat. How many orphaned children filled with the living spirit of Holy Mother Church, and cradled in her arms, had those things inside the nuns transformed into adults with no innocence and no faithfulness in Christ?

Many, Yannick assumed, though never him.

He had known when young the difference between the appearance and the substance and he'd recognized the curtain that hung often between the two.

Sister Camille's beatific face and then the wormish, sexual tongue that wound out from behind it like the Serpent from the Tree of Life.

Sister Mariette's red hands; stained with the caustic lye of selfless work in the washhouses of ten convents. And then, those *same* hands, red with blood from holding shut a mouth, and white with—

A fierce battering from the basement tugged Yannick out of his absorption.

He opened his eyes fiercely and craned his neck. Ilil's strong, bass voice was drifting up through the floor and it was only then that Yannick realized he'd been weeping.

He slapped away the tears from his face and berated himself silently.

It's a sin, Yannick, he thought. *It's a sin.*

He pushed away the thoughts of his beloved nuns and the things he abjured that had lived inside them. The past was done and couldn't be relived.

But now, in *this* moment, there still was a chance to rescue the precious, nameless thing, made in God's image, that Ilil had infested so young and would not now let go.

Yannick rose smoothly to his feet; dressed slowly, though with purpose, and moved out of the room in the direction of the noise.

* * *

There wasn't much time, and Yannick knew it.

He had little idea, practically a foreigner, of how efficiently the criminal police in the Swiss cantons worked when compared to the rest of Europe but he guessed they'd be high in the ranking.

The hotel on Nägeligasse would be swarming with homicide detectives by now; Room 1208 would be swept for DNA within the hour and photographs would be processed of the ritual scars and messages that the killer had left on the flesh of his victims.

Victims, Yannick scoffed.

They had been victims before he'd found them. The thing living in the whore had whispered in her ear and shot up into her nasal cavity with one too many lines of cocaine purchased for her by a smirking pimp. And him—Grosh—hind-headed Furfur had squatted down over his mouth while he slept and defecated there a ball of cockroach eggs to gestate into scurrying liars inside the lawyer's brain.

Still though, the courts of this temporal domain would no more listen to talk of the supernatural than they would reinstate trial by combat or by the ducking chair.

They'd catch him, Yannick knew, and they'd find him either wicked or insane and dispose of his body in what way seemed best to their skewed and satanically befuddled laws.

There wasn't much time.

He was thankful for one thing: that, when he entered the basement, Ilil's shouting had trailed off and been replaced only by a frightened breathing from inside the cage.

The thing was afraid, Yannick knew. Afraid of the switch and the electric current flowing through its host's body.

He approached the farthest wall in the large room and touched the curtain softly with his hand.

It was old— the curtain— and clung all over with frays and a fuzz of dust.

Had it been so long since he'd last pulled back that drape? Had it been during Gaga's exorcism when he'd had to remove it that last time? He remembered having to drag Gaga kicking and screaming from her own cell in the cage;

Ilil chattering and swearing and shaking his own bars like a monkey in a vivisectionist's lab.

Yannick stroked the curtain compassionately and listened to Ilil's painful breathing.

He remembered Gaga begging for water. He remembered Ilil begging for water for Gaga.

Water, he thought.

Water where demons may rest and grow strong. The water of the amniotic sack; the *liquor amnii* by which the Demiurge, the Sultan of Devils, brings each child's body into His broken world.

Of course Gaga had wanted water. Of course Ilil had desired that she drink it.

That was their plan, after all: to keep themselves moist and alive and in sordid, black fealty to their Satanic Majesties.

He stopped thinking and pulled the curtain away in anger and repulsion.

* * *

A wave of putrid stench hit him in the face. A few fat houseflies shared the confinement with Ilil and were, at that moment, rubbing their blue wings together on the heaped pile of both solid excrement and diarrhetic ooze that occupied the far corner of the cage.

Yannick held his nostrils slightly closed has he hunkered down by the bars and looked softly at the unblinking, milky-eyed face of Ilil. He reached carefully between the bars and tugged the gag out from the thing's mouth. A line of yellowish drool ensued and then Ilil rested his head back down defeatedly in the same position as before.

The thing was just lying now on his side in all that filth and squalor; staring fixedly into nothing at all, just at the space where the curtain had hung steadily for six months or more.

Behind the curtain, another curtain, Yannick thought.

Ilil wore his mask better than any subject Yannick had ever seen. Sisters Camille and Mariette had given away so many cues in their expressions and demeanors that Yannick, even as a boy, had always been alerted early to their intentions and so always knew ahead of time when a trip to the greenhouses by night would be in order and of the particular sadistic hells that waited for him there.

Ilil, however, showed not the slightest sign that he was anything other than that which he appeared to be: a thirteen-year-old boy, lying traumatized and wounded on the floor of a kennel.

"You stink—" Ilil rasped from behind brown and rotten teeth.

Here it comes, Yannick thought. Ilil's mask never slipped, but his mouth always gave his inner perversity away.

The boy breathed hard through his mucus-clogged nostrils and, as though he could sense Yannick had been praying, he clarified his point: "You stink of God," he said.

Yannick blinked softly. Today he was willing to take any insult.

"They're coming for me, demon," he explained in a measured voice. "I killed Grosh in Bern tonight and they'll come for me soon."

"Good," Ilil's voice sounded as though he may be dying. 'I hope—they put you— in a cage."

Yannick shook his head.

"It was never a cage I wished for you," he was speaking to the boy's body and not to the spirit of Ilil within. "I only ever wished to release you from one."

Yannick reached into his jacket and pulled the razor-sharp athame from the shoulder holster.

A thick tear ran down the layers of grime on Ilil's face.

"I can't leave you like this," Yannick found that he too was weeping silently. "I've failed you, but I can give you your freedom before they take mine from me."

The blade in his hand shone in the poor light of the basement.

For some reason—Yannick had no idea why—he saw his dead wife again sitting on a child's bed in a nursery in Zurich. She was reading the passages about the curtain in *The Wizard of Oz*; reading it softly, liltingly, to—to someone—to *someone*—

"Please," Ilil had promised himself he wouldn't beg again, but here he was: begging. "Please, Yannick. I want my life."

The croaking of the demon's voice caused Yannick's lip to curl.

Did it have no remorse or shame? Could it not stop pretending for *one moment*? Pretending to be the boy it appeared to be. Pretending to be *afraid*.

"Shut your mouth," Yannick warned.

"Please, Yannick," the demon crooned.

"I said shut your mouth!" Yannick struck the bars of the cage with all the ferocity his muscles could supply.

Ilil stopped begging; another tear ran down the length of his contorted mask.

"I want my life," the boy cried silently to himself.

"Jesus," the man was crying too. "He is the truth, the way *and* the life. You cannot come to the Father except by way of Him."

"Please, Yannick—" that rasping parrot fashion voice, "Please, Yannick. Please."

Yannick reached into the cage with one hand and seized the boy's thick, matted hair in an iron grip.

"Get off me!" The demon's low and terrible voice had returned; Yannick nodded in certainty as it continued: "Keep that fucking blade away from me! Shove it up your arse, Yannick! Murderer! Killer! You killed Gaga! You killed Gaga! You fucking motherfucker!"

He slipped the blade into the cage. Ilil turned at once

from a boy into a wild dog. The change was quite remarkable; how he barked and snarled and tried, with everything he had, to sink his weakened, decayed teeth into the skin of Yannick's hand. Then, again, as the demon realized he was losing the fight:

"Please. Please. Please."

Yannick pushed the blade of the athame softly against Ilil's jugular.

"*Ad majorem Christi gloriam,*" he said in a slow monotone; and then: "*Ego te absolvo*"

"Please, Yannick. Yannick! Yannick! Don't. Please. Yannick."

He sliced the razor through Ilil's neck. The vein slit like rubber and for a fraction of a second nothing happened. Then, in one heady spurge, the body began emptying out all the blood that had been running to its head.

* * *

Yannick fell back onto the concrete floor and leaned his spine against the wall.

He cradled his head in his hands and tried not to listen as Ilil choked on and swallowed his own fluids.

A horror house of images flashed through his brain: the whore's neck bursting; Grosh begging for his life in three languages; the nuns standing, black and stump-like, on the golden fields of Normandy; Sisters Camille and Mariette laughing decadently in the dark greenhouse; the little girl screaming in the elevator and then—

Isabelle. *Isabelle?*

Inside his brain his dead wife was reading to a child—no—to *two* children. She read to them about the curtain; in front of which the wizard looked strong and frightening and behind which he was frightened and weak.

Yannick unshielded his eyes.

In the cage Ilil was bleeding to death. A slowly moving

creep of red liquid pooled out from under his head and oozed forward in Yannick's direction from inside that kennel of piss and shit and blue flies where the boy had spent his lifetime.

Yannick looked at the boy's cracked lips; at how they still moved, though weakly, as though trying to communicate.

It would all be over soon, Yannick reassured himself.

Soon he'd take up the athame again and carve the words *Washed in the Blood* into the chest that Ilil had once inhabited.

He'd take the body out from the cage at last. He'd wash its skin with cool water and mark a cross lovingly into its forehead.

There was no need for cremation as there had been with Gaga. The cantonal police could find the body if they wished and, when they did, the only marks they would be able to discern would be marks inflicted out of love.

Love, Yannick thought. *Love*.

He thought of putting Ilil on the observation chair after he was dead. He thought of kissing his brow and his ragged lips. He thought of stroking his hair and then turning out the basement light; as though the story were finished now and he had done nothing less natural than to lay the poor boy down in a warm bed; than to put the child to sleep after such a long day.

THE END

THE ALTAR BOY FROM HELL
By Carlton Herzog

The moment I clawed my way out my mother's uterine prison, and nearly choked on that slimy rope, I knew life was not for me. Clearly the unborn need more information about what's waiting for them. I say give them a life advisory scrolling down the placental wall. It need not be fancy. Just give the kid enough data to make an informed decision as to whether he should let himself be born or not. That way, he could either proceed with the birth or return to the ectoplasmic waiting room until an opening more to his liking arose.

My first memory right out of the box was of trying to bite the doctor's stethoscope like it was part of his anatomy. But since I had no teeth, the best I could do was gum it. I was helpless as any other Lamb of God.

Only I wasn't a lamb on the inside. Far from it. I was as feral and vulpine, as wild and cunning, as any rough beast. I just needed time to grow and sharpen into the thing I am today, the wolf that freely wends his way in the fluffy, non-threatening colors of a clueless flock.

I learned early on that life is theater and to get what you

want out of it, you need to be an arch thespian, donning and discarding character masks as situations demand. That is not as diabolical as it sounds. After all, the cuttlefish can completely change the texture and color of its skin to blend seamlessly into its environment—to ambush prey and hide from predators. Deception and trickery are what life is all about, whether you wear pants or sport a tail.

So really, when all is said and done, I am merely answering the rough call of my ancestors to brute and sport and do as I please while pretending to be that most civilized of creatures, the apple of God's eye, the apex of creation, a faithful servant of God.

Like any animal, I am spontaneously violent. I don't know why. My first episode came when I pushed my younger disabled brother off our second-floor balcony. He broke his neck and fractured his skull. I restrained my jubilation as my parents bought my account: he was spastic, caught his braces on a chair, stumbled and fell. I gave little to no thought as to my motive beyond his cutting my parental attention time in half, and that kind of evil would never do.

After that, I realized that my heart was truly black. Even at the tender age of 14, I recognized the need to throw people off my scent. So I volunteered to be an altar boy at Our Lady of Perpetual Sorrow. There were other boys ahead of me, and they made the mistake of teasing me for my golden locks and blue eyes, going so far as to call me a little girl. Naturally, a frontal assault was out of the question. But opportunity has a way of presenting itself to those prepared to seize it.

On Palm Sunday, I was given the job of carrying the thurible, a metal censer suspended from chains, in which incense is burned during worship. My job was simple: walk and swing the thurible while the other boys walked behind me.

I spent a week planning my attack, repeatedly going over

the details and even practicing my swing with a softball taped to ropes.

When Sunday arrived, I pretended to trip mid-aisle, and as I did, I swung the thurible in a terrible arc behind me so that the hard-spiked metal censer, so alive with burning incense, clipped the heads of my three main tormentors; then, pendulum-like, swung back and hit them again. A three-bank shot that would have done Minnesota Fats proud.

I apologized profusely and helped the injured boys to their feet as their open skulls spilled blood onto the blood red carpet. An accident, of course, wholly unintended, an unfortunate slip by a novice altar boy who now seeks God's forgiveness and mercy. Oh yeah. I only wish I had killed them the way I killed my brother. Maybe next time.

Over the next year, I performed my altar boy duties admirably and was often commended as the thurible incident faded into distant memory. But even as my reputation waxed angelic, my hatred for the congregation, including my dim-witted parents, grew exponentially. If I thought for a moment that I could have wiped them all from the face of the earth with a bomb or a machine gun and gotten away with it, I would have done so in a heartbeat.

I tired to figure out the source of enmity, some purely rational explanation rooted in psychology, but couldn't settle on anything other than I had come out wrong, a bad seed, a faulty, misbehaving, hateful human being that should have been recalled by the factory, but somehow slipped past a lackadaisical quality control.

I briefly entertained the notion that I was the Anti-Christ, but since I didn't believe in God, it made zero sense to believe in His contrary, the Devil. Besides, humanity was doing a fine job on the evil front, so deflecting blame to an external diabolical agency seemed redundant and wishy-washy. The Devil was as unnecessary as God.

I concluded that I should embrace who I was and just murder as the spirit of darkness moved me. And I did.

Jimmy Rogers, school bully, was giving me grief about my being a little kiss-ass altar boy. I played along, told him Jesus wants us to love our enemies, gave him a friendly hug, spun him around, and then pushed him into an oncoming city bus.

I wish somebody had put it on YouTube, but I'm glad they didn't. The bus dragged him some forty feet. By the time his body slid free, limp and lifeless, he was deader than a doornail. If somebody had videoed my homicidal pirouette, my alibi of his having slipped would have been shot. But I had the luck of the hell-spawn going for me, as well as a sterling all churched up reputation, so nothing came of it. I shed many a crocodile tear at that lout's funeral, a closed casket affair since what was left of him wasn't much to look at, even after the mortician fixed him up. So sad.

Mind you, it wasn't all blood and blasphemy on Sunday. On Tuesday, when Father Mike went out on his rounds, I would bang boots and swig booze with Sister Mary Margaret in the cramped confession booth. There was something about her robes and wimple that drove me wild. Probably that I was corrupting her, even though she was turned on by believing that she was corrupting me.

I made it a point to keep her happy so I could use her missionary connections to import exotic animals. I was studying chemistry and had developed a keen interest in venoms and poisons. I could get poisons such as arsenic, selenium, nightshade and oleander locally, and I knew how to culture botulin from animal feces and guts.

But that seemed pedestrian. I wanted to be different, even unique in my homicidal mischief. So, I was beside myself with glee when the shipment of cone snails arrived on my doorstep, alive. They came from Florida and were a solid nine inches long with harpoon shaped stingers carrying a payload of paralytic toxin like that of the puffer fish and blue ring octopus. The first place I put them was in my history teacher's mailbox. It was a March Saturday. Overcast with a slight nip in the air.

Mr. Roebling, a bachelor, had gone out to run errands. I waited for the mailman to drop in the letters. When I was sure nobody was looking, I, disguised as a food delivery person, dropped my deadly cargo into his mailbox. I came back that night and retrieved my secret assassin's helpers.

On Monday, Roebling was a no show. On Tuesday, we learned that he had died of respiratory failure from an unknown cause. I celebrated with a poke of Sister Margaret and a bottle of sacramental wine.

A week or so later, it struck me that I was meant for bigger things, angel of death sized things. Funnel spiders, box jellyfish, and assassin caterpillar surprises had been fun, but they merely wet my whistle.

I started with the sacrificial wine I dispensed on Sundays—one-part LSD, one-part ecstasy, one-part Fentanyl. Since that dispensation occurred well into the service, the effects didn't manifest until after the benediction as the church emptied. The congregation got loud, happy, and clumsy. The real damage came when they jumped in their cars and started driving into one another. It was like a crazy Christian demolition derby. They were having the time of their stuffed shirt lives, even when a few of them got run over. I caught it on all on video with a hidden body cam.

The questions came and went. The official line was that somebody had spiked the punch sometime in the night. A few began to connect the dots to my exotic venom murders but not in any meaningful follow-the-evidence way. It was more like they just wanted to sound like they knew something when they didn't know squat.

None of that mattered. I intended to load the sacramental bread and wine with botulin and watch the lot of them drop. But there was a bump in the road.

Cardinal Mullins wanted to meet me. Something about all the good reports he had been getting. Neither the parish priest nor any of the nuns knew anything about those good reports.

I showed up on Saturday to meet with him. He had a predator's face—narrow and vulpine with an aquiline nose. I took him for a con man and a pedophile, but he proved to be much more than that.

We met in private. He didn't waste any time getting to the point of his visit.

"You're quite a character, you are. Tell me, do you keep track of your kills? Got a jar somewhere with slips of paper on it hidden somewhere in your house?"

"I don't know; what are you talking about?"

"Don't be coy, kid. The word is out on you. Twenty confirmed and you're only what, sixteen? Color me impressed."

"How do you know that?"

"I work for the Devil and he knows everything. He sent me here to slow your roll player."

I became flushed and started to twitch.

"Nothing to be nervous about. Here's the deal: The Devil has his own chapel in every church. Why? Because whatever good God thinks he's doing, we're undoing, but in subtle, crafty insidious ways. But then you come along and start making a lot of waves. From where I sit, your decision to poison an entire congregation is going to call unnecessary attention to our work. I can tell you right now, some brain-dead Devil-worshipping club that couldn't do an evil act on its best day will be blamed, and the real Devil—my Master—will look like a cheap, petty murderer.

"Our entire program rests on the premise that nobody believes in him. True evil doesn't leave a footprint or cast a shadow. It gets people to be the instruments of their own destruction. We want them to drink the poison, knowing full well that it's poison. To do that, we need spin, we need good public relations, we need evil to be good and good to be evil. Your little sideshow, born of your goofy little ego, just gets in the way. We're trying to create a magic kingdom of horror and you want to do little chickenshit episodes of *Dexter*."

I didn't like his condescending tone. I didn't like him. If he were the Devil's emissary, then the Devil and I were fated to be adversaries, not fast friends. And I certainly wasn't going to be his toady.

I asked the cardinal, "What do you get out of this deal?"

"I never die. Sure, my body may expire, but my mind will simply transmigrate to the blank slate of a newborn's mind, where I will start a new life with all the knowledge gained from the old, and that cycle will continue as long as the earth spins, unless I opt for reassignment to Hell, where I will be royalty.

"And I can do whatever I like without fear of punishment. I like young boys, and while the other priests have been getting caught with their pants down, so to speak, my Master makes sure I never get caught. You can have the same deal. You're very young, so you could be pope someday if you play your cards right."

I had no intention of going along with the cardinal but played along so I could buy some time and formulate a plan. That didn't take long. I told him I needed some fresh air to think about his proposal. I went outside and spotted his rental car. I went around behind the church where I had stashed the botulin, jimmied his trunk, and stuck it in there, ensuring to wipe it of my prints.

I went back inside and read him the riot act:

"I don't like your coming here and raining on my parade. I don't work for you or your so-called Master. This is my show, the Damian Scott Show, and there's only room for one host and that's me. Anything less would be an intolerable evil, an affront to my very existence, and the Nation of One for which I stand. Tell your Master when you see him, and you'll be seeing him here in a minute or so, that Damian, the self-made Devil rules here, and that lesser devils such as himself, need to find other worlds to corrupt and diddle."

Then I stabbed him in the eye with the letter opener, pulled it out, and jammed it into his throat. Next, I pulled off his robes and yanked his boxers down past his knees, the idea being to convince everyone that my claim he exposed himself and tried to molest me was supported by visual evidence. Naturally, I would claim that he had been doing this to altar boys for years and had never been caught. And more importantly, that he intended to poison the congregation with some mysterious toxin he carried in his rental car—something about trying to create hysteria about the Devil to spike attendance in the churches under his jurisdiction.

The police and the community accepted my explanation without question. I was lauded as both a victim and a hero for ridding the church of the cardinal's foul, perverse influence. Even the mayor got in the act and handed me the key to the city along with a ten-thousand-dollar check.

I suppose I do live the cardinal's advice about making evil seem good. But it's old advice, musty and dated. After all, Shakespeare wrote a long time ago, "The Devil hath the power to assume a pleasing shape." On that I can agree. But Shakespeare also wrote that "the Devil is a gentleman," a statement that certainly requires some modification. In my case, the Devil is an altar boy. From Hell. And while I'm not sure I believe in the Devil, he most certainly believes in me.

THE END

BORN AGAIN FOREVER
By Wolfgang Potterhouse

North Pole Cold

By the time my anger had grown to consume me, he was already dead. I would have killed him myself for what he did to me.

I am quite positive that he would kill me too, if he could (this fact contains an immeasurable quantity of irony). Unfortunately for him, what God has done cannot be undone, so I guess he can't quite free his hands for the task. At least, he can't do it himself. He has, as a point of fact, attempted to have me murdered repeatedly, and it has only been very recently that he seems to have backed off or given up. I suppose that the materialism and greed that are the true "American way" have finally showed him the irreversible nature of the global elements I have put into motion.

Over centuries and centuries, he has put many men on the job of finding and killing me. Men who were paid, coerced, and forced into missions that were laughably and pathetically out of their level of competence. The majority of these men I killed myself (I indulged myself all through the Dark Ages). A spate of them I enslaved and humiliated (the Renaissance!), and an unlucky few I "turned." Indeed, I have some of them with me now. Well, maybe not with me per se, but they are around here somewhere.

Writers throughout time have stated that revenge turns on its owner, and that too much focus on revenge makes one's own wounds rot. I have read that "revenge is a dish best served cold," and I have served mine ice cold. North Pole cold.

I have done some bad things in the name of survival and revenge, some truly horrific things that are beyond the capacity of most mortal minds, but still I sleep like a baby. The fact that I was a baby some 2,050 years ago is irrelevant.

My revenge has been in play for many hundreds of years.

They Don't Care

It's funny what people will believe in. They believe in "the sanctity of marriage," yet they lie, cheat, and treat each other like cattle. They believe in love, fate and karma (except when no one else is looking).

People ostensibly believe in God, yet they live the most abhorrent lives—making incredibly selfish decisions, embracing hate and violence, and disrespecting themselves, each other, and this planet at every opportunity.

Only children believe in Santa Claus, and in a way, he's quite real.

And although people talk, write, and now make movies about vampires, no one really believes in them. I can personally attest to the fact that they don't care if you believe in them or not.

The devil is not real. Man is the closest thing to evil in this world or the next.

I know God is real. I know because I have known the man. I have heard him speak and seen him perform miracles.

His impact on everyone around him was undeniably profound. I counted him as my kind, sweet, and generous friend until he used me.

He used me and abandoned me.

Perhaps I should stop rambling and tell the story.

Lazarus

My name is Lazarus of Bethany. Long ago I was an olive farmer, running an orchard my parents and their parents had owned. My sisters, Mary and Martha, lived and worked with me, and we had simple lives. They were husbandless, I was wifeless, and there were no children. We were neither rich nor poor, and we did not have interests and aspirations outside of the harvest, our Jewish faith, our small collection of books, and our time spent painting the beautiful landscapes around us. That would change after I met Jesus.

I grew up just outside of Jerusalem, and I was one of the first followers of Jesus Christ. One beautiful spring day, I went with my sisters to see him speak. He wore simple robes and was not particularly handsome or clean, but we could feel love in his words and his tone. It sounds overly simple, but the man was the Son of God. To be around him was emotionally jarring, but in a warm, uplifting, positive way. When he looked at me, I believed. Everyone who met him believed.

He talked about love and peace, faith and scripture, and the blessings that come from leading a simple and humble life. My sisters and I were overcome with emotion and we held each other and wept while he was speaking. He stood on a hill in our orchard while he calmly shared his message. The rest of us sat in the sunshine, and afterward his close followers invited anyone interested in meeting Jesus to come to a nearby stone barn for a more personal discussion. It was cool in the barn, and there were small amounts of dried fish, bread, and water. He personally went around shaking hands, embracing people, and serving the food himself, which shocked me. He served my sisters and me and then sat down with us.

My sister Martha was not an optimistic or friendly person, and she was radiating a smile that I had never seen. Tears of joy were rolling down her cheeks; Jesus gently held my sister's face, and he told us, "whoever drinks this cup of water will know thirst again in their life, but whoever drinks the water that I give you will never thirst. Instead, a spring of eternal life will flow through your soul."

Had that moment not occurred, my sisters would not be in heaven. I love Jesus for that, and am profoundly grateful. Had that moment not occurred, however, I would not have been used by Jesus, like a prop, for his own selfish gains. I also would not have spent the last 2,000 years detesting him and myself, and plotting against him.

We followed Jesus for a couple of years, and he and I became as close as brothers. A sudden and severe illness rapidly deteriorated my body though, and I was rendered too ill to travel. I felt as though death was rapidly approaching. I wasn't afraid, and I didn't expect Jesus to heal my body, since he had already saved my soul. My sisters were in anguish, and when they heard that the Christ was in a neighboring town, they sent for him, desperately seeking comfort from their living God. I held on for a few days, but Jesus never arrived. I remember my sisters, Mary and Martha, at my bedside, holding my hand and each other's hands, quietly sobbing. My memories of things on earth are a little hazy for several days after that, because I died.

Jesus arrived in Bethany after I had been in the tomb for two days. Martha said she went out to confront him, and this is pretty accurately relayed in the book of John. "Lord, if you had been here, my brother would not have died. Even now, I know that God will give you whatever you ask," she implored, kneeling in supplication before him.

"Your brother will rise again," Jesus replied, pulling

Martha by her hands up from her knees. He then turned to the rapidly gathering group of people around them. "I am the resurrection, I am the life. Whoever believes in me shall live, even though they die!"

Copious amounts of cheering from the crowd.

Jesus was a brilliant lyricist, gifted in the arts of metaphor and allusion. Surely, Martha thought, he was talking about salvation in general, but she had a different feeling. She was picking up a different vibe. She said the apostles were all giggling like little girls, so she felt Jesus might be up to something. Yup. He wanted to do something he had never done. He wanted to defeat the last and most irresistible enemy of man: death.

He "loved me," so he brought me back.

He boasted all over town about what he was going to do, then he waited two more days so people could receive notice and make the trek to see the miracle. A throng of people stood and screamed when they rolled the stone aside and pulled me out of the tomb. One minute I'm in heaven, a content baby listening to my mother sing as she rocked me to sleep, the next I'm walking back into the blinding desert sun in front of a few thousand cheering acolytes. My sisters were overjoyed, and the crowd was amazed. Jesus left town with 1,000 people following him down the road.

Good news right? I get my life back, I'm healed, I can finish my mortality in peace as an old, distinguished, revered envoy of our lord before making it back to heaven?

Wrong. I am the only mortal to ever be resurrected. You may read differently in Matthew or Luke, but believe me, I am the only one.

When Jesus brings you back from the dead, there are side effects.

Bad ones.

I was emotionless, had no energy, and was very confused. I struggled to put thoughts together and to communicate, which is interesting considering I speak about

30 languages now. After the resurrection, my memory was unreliable, due to the time period that I was dead, and due to the fact that I had actually experienced heaven and returned as a living man again (sort of).

Jesus actually went into hiding after the resurrection, as the miracle had caused a lot of alarm in the local Jewish leadership in Jerusalem. He had gained followers that day, but he also scared some powerful people who started to want him gone. It was the beginning of the end, and Jesus started predicting his own death. Not long after my resurrection, Jesus came back into Bethany. I was still reeling physically, spiritually, and emotionally. I was barely functioning.

We had a large feast for him at our house in the orchard. Jesus avoided me. I don't recall him even making eye contact with me, which confirmed to me that he knew all along what his resurrection stunt meant for me. I recall him washing my sisters' feet with heavily perfumed oil before dinner, and I remember Judas Iscariot. He was complaining that the money spent on the perfume and the dinner would be better spent on helping the poor. Judas was the treasurer for Jesus' traveling group, and everyone knew that he was stealing. He took what he wanted out of the purse whenever he wanted it, and he was not spending it on the poor, either. Just being around this guy made me want to rip his throat out. Unfortunately, he hung himself after Jesus was resurrected, or I would have done it. With my teeth.

First of My Kind

I never age. I have spent two millennia being middle aged. I have also proven to be very hard to kill. I know that I cannot be burned, I cannot drown, and I cannot be crushed to death. I cannot be frozen and have actually lost almost all sensation of cold. Arrows, swords, bullets and poison also fail. I don't need to breathe. I can, but I don't need to. I am relatively certain that cutting off my head would do the trick, but I have never tried that, and don't intend to.

I feel pain, but marginally—maybe one tenth of a human. I have stunted emotions; I was reunited with my sisters then saw them die without feeling anything. I have seen plagues, war, famine, and none of it has stirred my soul. I feel three things: one is a remorseless disgust for mankind. The second is an unflinching loathing for the person who did this to me. Lastly, I feel hungry. Not for food, of course, but for blood. Warm, pumping blood.

Jesus made me into a vampire. I am the first of my species to walk this planet, but I wasn't alone for long.

A surprising number of vampire myths are actually true, including becoming a vampire through the bite of an existing one. My feedings have spawned thousands of new vampires, sometimes out of the necessity to quell my burning hunger, sometimes out of spite or anger, and sometimes to create an ally, soldier, or worker when I needed one.

Modern conventional wisdom regards vampires as immortal, but that claim definitely has an asterisk or two following it. To be completely honest, we are pseudo-immortal; when conditions are favorable, we don't die, but I've witnessed many a vampire burned to a crisp by the sun (which put a significant crimp in their immortality), and then there's the curious concept of food. We need to eat, but not to sustain life—we need blood to keep "the wasting" at bay. I'm the first vampire, so all of this is filed under hypothesis, but I do think that if I had a daily fresh supply of blood, I would be truly immortal and never die. When the blood supply is interrupted, vampires suffer the wasting, subtly at first, barely noticeable, but once it sets in, it accelerates rapidly. Our skin becomes leathery, tight, and pallid, and our flesh seems to disintegrate on our bones. Vampires who are wasting are still technically alive, and can be revived, maybe for eternity. They are aware and able to speak long after movement has ceased; I've seen it. It's quite pitiful, really.

Many wasted vampires have been found by humans, assumed to be a person long dead, and buried alive—all while thinking, seeing, thirsting.

Thinking of that terror is rather delightful, provided of course that it is some other poor ghoul in the grave, and not me. When wasted vampires are provided a blood meal, they do recuperate, and to a degree, regenerate. I feel that most of the "aging" on my face has come from times when blood has been scarce, not from the passage of the centuries.

I don't have any of the surprisingly well-known vampire vulnerabilities (I think because Jesus powers made me), but the vampires I make (and the ones they make) all have similar weaknesses. Sunlight burns them up immediately. Human beings I have attacked for food have almost all met this particular demise, as they were unaware of and unprepared for their new fate. Garlic is unpleasant, and crosses do cause painful burns on contact, but we can look at them without hissing and recoiling. Kittens do that, not bloodthirsty murdering fiends.

Invitations are not necessary for a vampire to enter a dwelling, and we all obviously have reflections. Why wouldn't we have reflections? I have always thought that was pretty silly.

Coffins are one thing the myths have right. I was reborn in a tomb, so coffins, mausoleums, basically all forms of eternal resting places—they all feel, in my unbeating heart, like home to me. I can sleep anywhere, certainly, and have on many occasions, but I do prefer to sleep in a coffin. My palace in the arctic contains several luxurious options, as do my houses around the world. Sleeping in a coffin in a basement is truly the most relaxing experience, as being below ground for me also adds a rejuvenating factor.

The wooden stake through the heart myth is a fascinating one. A wooden stake is no more dangerous than any other weapon, and probably a sight less dangerous than a sword or firearm—because it's a wooden stake!

Background on the wooden stake myth is something I can provide, though. Upon my resurrection and immediate lifestyle change, I made my home in Jerusalem. I needed the big city to provide people (food—blood) to keep me alive. Big cities also contain a significant population of people who are not missed when they go missing, which obviously is an important ingredient in me not getting caught. There is a certain amount of time that my nocturnal nefariousness can be undertaken without arousing suspicion, and this amount of suspicion-free time increases with the size of a city. In a modern 21st century city, I can exist for an almost indefinite amount of time if I keep my wits about me and avoid careless mistakes. Populations of a million plus offer infinite opportunities for someone who needs to live like I do. Back in the year 0010 however, larger cities had populations in the thousands, maybe tens of thousands, and I had to utilize all my faculties to stay one step ahead of criminal conjecture.

Cities during most of the last two thousand years contained tremendous amounts of livestock as well, and that was always my primary supply of blood. People are much less concerned when pigs, cows, and sheep disappear than they are when human beings do so.

My welcome in Jerusalem was being worn out, to say the least, and people were getting organized and motivated to apprehend whoever was marauding in their Christian city at night. Religious persecution was what they thought they were dealing with—someone massacring Christians—but really, it just happened to be where I lived at the time. The first band of assassins to set out against me were a religious vigilante force commissioned by the clergy, armed with long daggers, which featured handles made from what was left of the cross that Jesus was crucified on. The cross had been displayed in a church in the city, a church I promptly burned to the ground after they started making anti-me weapons out of the thing. The daggers' handles were long and rough, and they projected backward from their belt-scabbards so the assassins could be readily identified by their unique weapons. When they were sheathed, or when they were being carried, the daggers actually looked like long wooden stakes.

This brotherhood remained viable for several generations, and incredibly, this gave rise to the irrepressible myth that wooden stakes are the preferred weapon for undead hunting. I have several of these daggers in my collection.

Every vampire can also go invisible, albeit a qualified version of invisible. It is not intuitive; it has to be taught by an experienced creature, so very few vampires know how to vibrate fast enough to achieve the effect. It is uncomfortable due to the tremendous amount of exertion needed and heat generated, but it has "saved my life" on many occasions (or at least kept me from getting caught stealing orphans).

The Countess of Blood

When I left what is now called the Middle East around the year 1445, I stayed for a few hundred years in central Europe. Cities there were large enough to sustain me, but small enough that I didn't have to worry about organized groups of detectives and pitchfork- and torch-wielding platoons of townsfolk. Cities like Bucharest and Ulpia Serdica (modern Sofia, Bulgaria) were beautiful, vibrant, and growing at a rate that provided many opportunities. I found existence there to be quite exciting.

I made and lost many fortunes, and back then I still resembled a human being almost perfectly, so I could blend in during the daytime. Complicated relationships delighted me; the opportunity to prey on the frailty of human nature and the predictable egos of men has always been a source of amusement and pleasure for me, as well as a source of a vast amount of treasure.

In 1575, I met the love of my life. Her name was Countess Erzsébet (Elizabeth) Báthory de Ecsed, and she was beautiful, funny, sarcastic, and dark.

Also, completely, unabashedly, crazy.

Her aunt was a witch, her uncle a devil worshiper, and her brother a pedophile. It was love at first sight. She shared in my dislike for her fellow man, even before I turned her. After I turned her, she was the most prolific serial killer since, I guess, me. She killed and fed on at least 600 young girls.

She got caught because she never budgeted out her violence; she just kept it coming, every day, every day, relentlessly, passionately, killing and feeding. Another factor in her apprehension by authority was that I never taught her how to perform the illusion of invisibility. I had used it on her a number of times, but I never showed her how to do it. I had to threaten several people to save her life; she avoided beheading and was instead sentenced to be sealed inside her house (with bricks over the doors and windows) until she died.

Of course she could live forever, so that was going to take a while.

They eventually found remains in the house, so she either wasted to bones, or she escaped and planted a corpse there. The DNA testing in 1614 was a bit unsophisticated, so I will never know. I still think about her all the time (at least once every twelve years or so), and I miss her dearly.

Vlad

While living near the Carpathian Mountains north of the Danube River in a place called Wallachia, I met a fascinating, brilliant, charismatic defender of Christianity. He was a prince, and a member of the House of Drăculeşti Vlad was his name, and I turned him. He was much too vigilant in his proselytizing and converting the masses, much too Christ-like. When he became a vampire, the world was treated to a dragon of a man, a ruthless and cruel butcher whose deeds would not be matched for five hundred years. This was Vlad Dracula—one of my sons.

Poor Lucy

London was my home in the late 1800s, and at that time I went by the name of Henry Irving. I made my living as an actor, which was grand. My existences in the 19th and 20th centuries were made bearable by the trouble I caused and got into while involved in theater troupes in London, Paris, Barcelona, New York, and New Orleans. New Orleans at the turn of the century is a hard place to match for debauchery. Modern day Amsterdam? Sunday school!

I had been acting and lying and manipulating people, to survive, for many hundreds of years; the theater culture is rife with drug use and excessive drinking, and populated with loose-living characters who stay out all night and routinely vanish. I loved it. Theater for me was a match made in heaven (I love religious puns).

In London, as Henry Irving, I became quite successful, and as I had many affairs to keep in order, I acquired the services of a personal assistant. This man's name was Abraham Stoker, an interesting intellectual man who was already an accomplished writer. He saw the world through macabre colored glasses, and every idea he had revolved around magic, the occult, and evil people. I did something with him that I had done repeatedly during my time in Europe, something that amused me and created chaos and discontent, something that drove people to fear and to action. I told the truth. I told Stoker about my experiences in Transylvania and Romania. I told him about Vlad, who had posthumously gained the nickname Vlad *the Impaler*. I was such a proud daddy.

Stoker, the little devil, kept my secrets but wrote my

story. Embellished with several added elements and invented circumstances, *Dracula* became one of the best-known novels of all time. Stoker finished what Poe started, and gave writers of dark stories credibility and popularity.

Hijacked Holidays

The idea for my revenge came from the Christians themselves.

One of the ways they paved over the pagans was to hijack their holidays and customs. For example, to celebrate Christ's resurrection, why just generate a new holiday, when you can squash some non-Christian traditions in the process? Pagans celebrated the Spring Equinox with obvious symbols of fertility, namely rabbits and eggs. Makes perfect sense, as no one would argue that spring isn't a time of new life. To celebrate the resurrection of their savior, the Christians also chose spring, which they could argue made sense with the "born again/new life" connection. To represent Christ's resurrection, the Christians chose obvious symbols of Christianity, namely rabbits and eggs. Brilliant isn't it? Establish your own sacred traditions while simultaneously rubbing out pagan ones—by adopting them! Even the word "Easter" comes from the name of a Germanic goddess.

Winter festivals, particularly those centered on the solstice, have been around since people started living in settlements together. There is not as much agricultural work to do in the cold, it's dreary and depressing, and after the solstice, winter is on its way out, so let's celebrate! The Romans celebrated Saturnalia, which honored the god Saturn, from December 17-23. This holiday featured lights, displays of greenery, merrymaking, and gift giving. Sound familiar? Christians wanted to celebrate Jesus' birthday. Understandable. Don't have the slightest inkling when his birthday is? No problem. Kill two partridges with one pear tree, and establish your holiday while pulling the plug on a vile pagan ritual. Brilliant, but I already said that.

My Italian Christmases

I moved to Northern Italy in the 1500's, and lived there for a few hundred years. The cities of Venice, Genoa, Milan, Bologna, Rome, and of course Florence (the jewel of this planet) all played naive host to my particular brand of murder and mayhem. I made so much money when I was in Italy that I thought about commissioning a pirate navy to utterly cease commerce in Europe, just to amuse myself. I started the endeavor, but when you employ pirates, thieves, and brigands, it turns out that they steal from you too.

Christianity was firmly rooted in Italy when I lived there, and it was spreading. I resented this, of course, so I turned the Pope, but no one noticed. I murdered civic leaders and turned preeminent clergy. Christianity plowed on.

I had an idea that intrigued me; one that I knew would take many years to have an impact if it worked at all, but one that had the potential, the underpinnings if you will, for my revenge.

Italians all carried on the traditions of the winter festival and had parties and gave gifts. I had enough money to buy Sicily at the time, so I had my servants across Europe purchase and ship to me absurd amounts of clothing, wine, and toys leading up to the holiday.

The Italian Christmases that I first performed in featured me rolling around in a horse-drawn cart, then stopping in the streets and putting on a big production. I called families out of their houses and apartments and made sure to inquire whether the children had been good or bad over the whole year. When I received excited confirmation that they had been "good," I gave the whole family gifts. Adding to the spectacle, I donned an enormous red coat and red hat, and I wore a false beard as a disguise.

I was subtly robbing Christ of his birthday, taking the Christ out of Christmas, and making the gift giving about being "good." I was also adding a central character, one that I called "Father Christmas" at the time. This was an important element, as humans always look to a leader. It's human nature, a fault in the wiring. Mankind has done self-defeating, stupid things over the millennia just to "follow the leader" or fit in with the crowd. I was erasing Christ's presence in a Christian celebration, replacing him with a different "hero," and a focus on gifts and children's behavior instead of faith and salvation. Like I said, I got the idea from the holidays the Christians commandeered from the pagans.

I was energized and encouraged by the first small attempt at stealing Jesus' birthday, and word of the incident spread throughout Northern Italy, so I took some of my turned clergy slaves and had them act as duplicates, or doppelgangers, of Father Christmas. There were twelve Father Christmases that year, all performing the same routine in red coats and false beards. We were met with adoration and exuberance all over the countryside, and my plans expanded.

Every creature that is turned develops changes—some are positive and some are negative. When a horse is turned, its running ability is enhanced by a factor of ten, but its life expectancy is dropped by a factor of 50. We pulled our carts on those first Christmas nights with turned horses to cover as much area as possible, and by the seventh year, I had a presence in every European country. The Dutch started calling me Sinterklaas, which is the origination of Santa Claus. Charming, eh? Humans even made me into a saint!

Jesus was really not thrilled with all this. Efforts to remove me from the equation grew in intensity and severity, and I became quite a murdering savage just defending myself. This was when I decided to change my locale. I chose the Arctic because my VSA (vampire slave army) and I are impervious to cold, the destructive sun stays down for months at a time, and the journey is so impossible for mortals that I can actually rest in seclusion. We constructed a vast underground complex, and for several hundred years, we actually made the toys up there ourselves. I stopped going out on Christmas night myself, and had the VSA take care of all deliveries. We used turned reindeer to pull our sleighs. Turned reindeer are pretty interesting. They can fly.

You Better Not Pout

We were almost worldwide by 1640. I ignored non-Christian countries, because there was no holiday to steal there. Around 1700, the greatest thing happened: we quit. We didn't go out on Christmas night. There were a couple years where it was touch and go, but as I suspected would happen, parents took over. For many years, parents had made sure their children had received gifts in the houses that we couldn't get to (just to keep their kids from feeling left out), so I had a hunch and I followed it. Santa Claus went from being real to being a myth, a tradition, a children's story, and simultaneously managed to grow in influence, importance, and popularity. I never could have imagined my revenge to be so complete and so thorough.

Christmas is now the biggest holiday on earth, and it is all about Santa Claus, gifts, spending and buying, spending and buying, spending and buying. It has become a three or four-month holiday, and it has next to nothing to do with religion, salvation, or Jesus.

I am impressed with myself, to say the least. I live a sort of retired lifestyle now, but I do adore America. I couldn't have done all this without that country's unknowing support and leadership. I spend a lot of time there, and am thinking about getting into politics someday. I think it would be a good fit for me.

THE END

THE FULLFED BEAST
By J.B. Toner

"Last season's fruit is eaten
And the fullfed beast shall kick the empty pail."
— *Little Gidding* T. S. Eliot

"Hail Satan, full of grace, the Lord is..."

I caught my breath. God forgive me, what a slip of the tongue! I shook my head and returned to my prayers.

"Hail Satan, full of..."

Elise, what is wrong with you? Get a hold of yourself!

"Hail—hail Mary, full of grace. The Lord is with thee."

My body relaxed as I heard my voice murmuring the old words in the stillness. Kneeling by my cot in the pale soft light from the window, I touched the silver cross around my neck and quieted my mind for a night of rest. Christmas was coming, and there was much to be done around the convent tomorrow.

"...now and at the hour of our death. Amen."

I made the sign of the cross and climbed into bed,

absent-mindedly reaching up to invert the crucifix on my wall. Then I lay down and pulled the cotton sheets up to my neck.

Wait—what?

Sitting up with a jerk, I stared at the carven image of our Lord over my bed. What was I thinking? Why would I do such a thing? I carefully turned him right side up, raising my eyes to the ceiling and the sky in a wordless apology. Then at last, I settled back into bed. All of a sudden, I felt incredibly sleepy.

"Hello, Sister Elise."

A man's voice! Sharp, amused, confident. I tried to fling back my covers, but I couldn't move. A sweet lassitude spread over my fear like honey, and I found myself accepting the strangeness of it all. Clearly, I was dreaming.

"Open your eyes."

I obeyed him, and found myself in a vast, dim chamber, lying in a bed of crimson silk. My simple nightgown was gone, nor had I blankets to cover me. The light glimmered on my body, and on the cross that was my only ornament. Around me on the sheets I could see my strawberry hair, a disarrayed halo.

And there: the man. He stood at the bedside, clad in white but with a black clerical collar at his throat, like a priest's photographic negative. His body was thin, but he held himself like a man of enormous strength; his face was grave, but his eyes contained a pandemonium of laughter.

Still, I couldn't move or speak. The man reached down, slowly, and touched my silver cross. A shiver went through me. "This won't do. We'll find you a more fitting symbol very soon."

Some part of me retained the presence of mind to start praying, though not aloud. *Our father, who art in heaven, hallowed be—*

"No more prayers, Elise," the man said. "Not tonight."

My inner voice went silent. I gazed up at this nameless

visitor, unresisting, an empty vessel waiting to be filled.

"I understand there's a lady who comes to see you on Christmas Eve. A special lady."

At last, the smile burning in his eyes began to kindle his cold visage.

"But I understand that she comes to bring forgiveness to sinners. Perhaps you should offer a sin."

In the pit of my stomach, an unfamiliar warmth awoke.

"Is it a sin to touch yourself?"

Free to move for the first time, I nodded.

"Touch yourself, Elise."

Obedient to him, my hands rose and pressed against my midriff. The warmth spread in both directions, and my palms pursued it, gliding up and down the bare sleek skin. My lips parted. My eyelids fluttered and closed. And I heard my own voice whispering, "*Yes*."

Opening my eyes, I found myself back in my cot. The light was gone. The man was gone. But my hands were still moving over my flesh, pulling the folds of my gown aside and cupping the forbidden places.

With a supreme effort of will, I stopped myself. I felt that I should pray; but I just couldn't muster the desire. Not tonight. Rolling over to bury my face in the pillow, I pushed down through the mattress to a dreamless sleep.

When dawn came, I dressed in my habit as always. But something bothered me. This cross around my neck, it felt— wrong, somehow. I took it off.

"Good morning, Sister Elise!"

Sister Teresa, my best friend. At twenty-four, she was two years older than I, but had only come to St. Clare's eight months ago. Willowy and tall, she had dimples and boundless energy.

"Shall we decorate the sanctuary today? Mr. Benning, the florist, donated a whole basket of roses." Her beaming smile faltered for a moment. "Sister, are you all right?"

"I—yes, I'm fine. Just tired."

"No time to be tired! Come on, let's get some breakfast."

There were eggs and fruit in the refectory, and Sister Madeleine had made eggnog coffee. We all prayed together, then went joyfully about our tasks. The dream (a nightmare? It hadn't felt like a nightmare) grew faint in memory, and I put it behind me. A small voice nagged at me that I should confess it to Father Peter; but another voice, more persuasive, disagreed. I kept the visitation to myself.

As Sister Teresa and I were adorning the columns of the church with holly wreaths, she glanced about and stepped closer. "Sister," she said in a lowered voice, "do you think she'll come again this year?"

I couldn't help smiling. The lady had appeared to me the last two Christmas Eves. All the sisters—including myself—were excited to see if she would return, but the Mother Superior had instructed us not to speak of it. "It is not for us to know," she said in her stern, prim way. "The Blessed Virgin is no topic for idle gossip."

"I hope so, Sister. But we'll just have to wait till Friday to find out."

She pouted prettily. "It's easy for you to have patience. You're a saint."

"We're none of us saints, my friend. Not till we reach heaven."

"Or heaven comes to us."

Now and at the hour of our death, I thought.

Then a look of puzzlement crossed her features. Her eyes seemed to gaze into some great distance, and became almost glazed. "And sometimes Hell comes too."

I took a step back and stared at her. "Teresa! Why would you say such a thing?"

She shook her head, and her smile came back. "Hmm? Oh yes, of course, till Friday. God bless your patience!"

What on earth? I thought again of going to Father Peter—but again, that persuasive voice inside of me spoke against it. I listened and obeyed.

That evening, as I made ready for bed, I opened the Bible on my bed. Sinking to my knees, I read aloud directly from the Gospel of Luke, so there could be no mistakes.

"Hail Mary, full of grace. The Lord is with thee."

Tired—so tired. All at once, I simply couldn't keep my head up any longer. I pushed the book onto the floor, crawled into bed, reached up sleepily and turned the crucifix. Flopped onto my pillow and slumbered like the blessed in their tombs.

The clock in the vestibule read 3:00 a.m. My robe rustled in the night breeze as I pushed open the doors. Snow crunched gently underfoot, and my breath was a ghostly fog. I made my way into the cemetery, past the iron gate and the old stone crosses, to the ancient mausoleum. The door stood ajar, and I stepped inside.

And there: the man. He stood in the shadows of the grave, poised and patient. "Welcome," he said.

I opened my mouth. "Am I—dreaming?"

His cryptic smile returned. "Come closer, Elise."

Could I have resisted him? I'll never know.

His hands were cool and gentle. Parting the collar of my robe. Cupping my face, brushing back my hair, resting on the sides of my neck. I stared endlessly into his eyes, and there was nothing else. Then his lips on my throat. Then a sweet, piercing pleasure like twin needles. Then the dark.

"Sister."

"Mm."

"Sister Elise?"

"Mmmmm."

"It's past eight, Sister. Are you feeling all right?"

I stirred and mumbled. Back in bed. Vague memories of another sinful dream.

"Come on, choir practice has already started."

"Close the curtains," I muttered.

"They're not open."

"So bright in here."

"You'll feel better with some coffee."

Frowning and grumbling, I dressed myself. We headed for the refectory, but nothing looked appetizing. All the lights were too bright. Especially the glint from the crosses.

The day was a haze. I went to bed early; didn't even try to say my prayers. Stuffed the crucifix into a drawer and climbed into bed naked. My heart felt heavy and slow.

At midnight, when I entered the sanctuary, Teresa was waiting. Her eyes were open, but she seemed unaware. I felt a thirst—a longing. Her skin was like perfume. I took her to the altar. I kissed her. Kissed her again and again, kissed every part of her. When she began to tremble with crescendo, I could hear a tiny sigh escape her lips: "Hail Satan."

And Friday morning came.

Sister Madeleine came to rouse me from bed. "Sister Teresa's sick, dear. We need a hand tending to her."

I raised my head and looked into her eyes. "Tell the Mother Superior I'm not to be disturbed. And stop honoring your vow of chastity."

Her eyes closed, slowly, and opened again. "Yes, Sister."

At dusk, I rose. Christmas Eve had come. Once again, I headed for the sanctuary.

And there she was. The lady in blue, standing at the altar with a tender azure glow, radiating love and peace.

"Elise," she said sadly.

"Hello, Mary," I replied, and grinned. "I'm so glad you could make it this year."

"What's happened to you? You're no longer one of my saints."

"Oh, I'm still a saint. I just switched sides. Why don't you come closer, and we'll talk about it?"

"There's little to be said, dear one. I must leave you to the mercy of God."

I held her gaze. "No. You'll stay here with me."

Her mouth opened. Closed again. Then, unwillingly, she said, "Yes, I—I will stay. Only to talk."

"Come closer, Mary."

Slowly—very slowly—she came to me. Her face was beautiful. So beautiful. Her neck, her body. Her soul. I could see them all. Touch them all. Take them all.

"Christmas will be different this year," I breathed. I raised a finger to her face, traced the curve of her cheek, tilted back her chin. "And forever."

THE END

HOLY MEAT
By Hari Navarro

I lay here naked on this cold stone slab and Father John De Lellis positions my body into that of the redeemer. My arms are outstretched and his dear, dear wife, Tessa, she sits and she knits at the clawing tip of my fingers. Her needles click and the thickened mess between my legs sticks as it parts and the Father—he feeds his old cock down and into my soul.

She does not look up from the blur of fingers and yarn, but she manages a nonchalant and ruddy cheeked smirk as she hums and taps her hard-soled foot into the verse that swirls in her head.

"They are the ones who caused the plague to strike the Lord's people... la la la... Now, kill all the boys and all the women who have slept... de de de... with a man... la la la... Only the young girls who are virgins may live... do do diddly do... you may keep them... for yourselves... la, la la la la," and her voice is smooth and soft as it glides over words never meant to be sung. And her husband grunts like a pig.

My father is a good man; the Father very much is not. My father is my entire world. I love him most dearly. He is a simple and brilliantly clever man. But he is old and was quite some years older than my mother when she died.

When I killed her.

As she strained and cried out and pushed me into this life, I pulled along with me a large pulpy strip from the wall of her womb. She ejaculated me into this life and I spat her back out of it. It was not my fault but we blame ourselves over things toward which we have no control. Guilt, it is all that I am.

I know he tried not to blame me, but I think he always did. I remember snuggling into him and wrapping my tiny body in his drunken arms as he'd fall asleep in front of the midnight television. And I'd watch great stories about vacuum cleaners and non-stick frying pans and fat people who shrink into wisps as he mumbled about my mother and of blood and of me in the pit of his quivering dreams.

On the eve of my ninth birthday, I was ushered into the oak-lined study that sat atop the great staircase that plumed up from the entrance hall of the St. Quiteria Home for Girls. Like a great flowering uterus, it branched into long passages that led off to the left and to the right.

To the left were the halls and rooms of residence for the girls. To the right there was a huge and ornate carved door, and behind it the study, and behind that still the private rooms of the good Father and his even goodlier wife. I was never once to venture to the left.

I remember that his eyes seemed kind and that when his wife stooped down and took me gently by the hand and led me into an adjacent annex, I felt not the least bit hesitant.

She muttered to me in partially heard sentences laced with things like safety, comfort, Jesus and chocolate. And, within the annex, which was actually more like an entire room all unto itself, there was a trolley. A layered table upon wheels, the likes of which my rapidly expanding eyes had never once seen. Plate after plate of treats, delicate and lovingly formed, oozing with chocolate and cream.

"Dip in your finger, child, and taste. It's real, freshly

scooped from the pails of our own dear cows. Nothing is fake around here," she'd said.

And I dipped and I licked and I smiled and then, with the flat of her thick fingered hand at my back, she gently coaxed me to push the trolley back into the study like the big strong girl that I was.

I took a china plate full of lush puffy angel winged cupcakes and, with my hand quivering from the initial fear that sat contracting and stinging at my thigh and the weight of the plate in my tiny hands, I offered one to my dear father.

"Thank you, my little noodle," he said and he grinned and his grin became a long forgotten smile and we laughed as the sugar rained down through the white of his beard.

The abuse started the moment my father left. The very moment, as I stood atop two huge volumes of scripture and I waved to him through the tears that streamed down the pane and the Father, he rubbed at my ass.

I was special. The chosen one, and I moved into a small cot that wedged behind a curtain in the farthest corner of the Father's voluminous chambers. I wasn't to socialize with the other girls and, save for my lessons, I never got to even see them. He told them I suffered from a rage, that beneath my pretty little face loomed a beast. Best for all that I am kept alone to myself.

They weren't always cruel. And, sometimes, I even looked forward to the Father or his wife sitting down at the end of my bed and reading to me from the book. They didn't always touch me. But, sometimes, they did.

It was the day after my eighteenth birthday that I ran away. I'd been laying my plans for years. I took to looking at Mr. Leonardo, my English teacher. I looked at him and I chewed my pencil and I saw how he shifted his belt and how the blood bloomed into his cheeks. Mr. Leonardo was married to Mrs. Leonardo, who worked in the school kitchen. Or so I'm told; I never eat there. So, anyway, I planted the seeds with my eyes and, though it was cold, I unbuttoned the top of my blouse and I waited for him to pounce.

"Come with me. Directly after class. I'll take you far, far away. Across the border and into the desert. I know of a motel. Then, I'll find for us a home," he whispered through the quake in his lips.

"I'll fuck you in half," I purred.

So I left St. Quiteria Home for Girls and we drove and, as we sped through and beneath its wrought iron arch, I kissed Mr. Leonardo on his cheek.

"Thank you," I said.

We arrived at the motel well after the desert sun had sunk beneath the low plain hills. Its heat, though, still leached and my white school blouse clung to my body and I felt bad about how it clung and scooped at my breasts. Poor Mr. Leonardo.

"Do you have protection?" I asked as I collapsed backward and onto the hard bed and gazed into the piss-like stain on the ceiling.

"Yes," he said.

Damn, I thought.

"Do you have lactose-free white chocolate with peanuts?" I asked.

"No. But I can get some, and something strong to drink as well," he smiled.

"Excellent! Make it so, my good man!" I giggled and then, moments after he left, I pulled on my school blazer and I walked out and into the night.

It's strange but I never once worried about the Father or his bat-shit crazy wife. I never saw them in the shadows and I never expected them to suddenly appear and drag me back into their lair. I had escaped. And escape smelt wonderful and it set upon my face the most ridiculous of grins. A grin that I still had as I walked up to my father's home and I fell into a heap at his door.

My father is an old man, as I said. But he had gotten so

much older, as in the morning I could feel the creak in his bones as he lifted me, and with the smooth pad of his thumb, he wiped the tears from my eyes.

I cried a lot over those next few weeks. I called out in the night and I plucked out my hair and I held my father's lit lighter until its top glowed red and the end of my thumb blistered, and I branded it into my arm. Did you know if you line them up just right they look like smiley faces? Such fun.

On the day that Father De Lellis showed up at our door, it was raining. I heard the knock, and I knew. I heard the knock and I looked into the sunken hollow of my father's eyes and I wanted to go back. I wanted to sink back down into the abuse and I wanted for my father to smile.

Father De Lellis spoke to my Dad and he lied and he lied and he lied. He told my father I was a whore. A promiscuous slut. But that he could save me. That Jesus could hold me. And I looked at my father and my chin dropped down to my neck.

"I'm so sorry, Dad," I said.

'And the daughter of any priest, if she profanes herself by whoring, profanes her father; she shall be burned with fire.' (Leviticus 21:9)

This time, Father De Lellis did not touch me as my father and my home stretched out to a point behind the surging purr of his big black sedan. But his eyes did. I could feel them at my neck and at that place where my lap falls down between my legs. It was hours before he spoke.

"Tonight we reside in a true house of the Lord. Behave!"

I nod and I sleep the most soundest of sleeps with my head flat to the glass and I think and I dream about nothing.

I awaken as the car begins to climb. As it crawls through the hairpins, as it scoops around the immovable boulders and it strains up to the very peak of the mountain. The holy palace of St. Michael. A magnificent abbey that rises up out of the granite like an extension of the mountain itself.

"It is magnificent," I whisper.

An ancient priest, who disturbingly reminds me of my own father, greets Father De Lellis with the hug riven with warmth.

"It has been far too long, little brother. Come, festivities await. And wait until you see little Grace; she's such a big girl now."

I feel like a princess as I ascend the stairway of the dead with its long empty compartments once filled with the bones and the rotting remains of saints, but now just shadow and dust.

The table is laden with luscious lashings of meat and huge wheels of bread and olives and countless other lovingly marinated things. And a young man, a seminarian with stringy scars of melted skin at his face, places food on our plates and pours wine for the men as they chat.

Grace is much younger than I hoped she would be. I feel like I should be asking her to go outside and run and laugh and play. But all I can do is look at her and offer what's left of my grin. She does not look back at me. She looks at her food and she looks at her feet and she twists at the ends of her hair.

"She is a virgin. A good girl. A clean girl. Unlike others I'd have at my table," the old priest sneers at the Father as he casts the sharp flick edge of his eye at me.

"Mine will become pure once more. She will arise. You just wait, big brother. You just wait and see."

The seminarian, who I had not even noticed had left the room, enters and hurriedly approaches the priest. He leans and, with his hand covering his lips, he whispers.

"Cars are approaching, Father. Twelve cars. Do you think it is them? Could it really be?"

The priest excuses himself from the table and disappears through a small door that leads out onto a rampart that looks down upon the road and down to the vast splay of the valley floor below.

"Damn!" he exclaims as he returns. "Today, why today? I must prepare!"

"What is it, brother?"

"Opportunity, John. It is great opportunity that calls. You must wait here," he says as he downs the last of his wine and he leaves.

Grace and I watch as Father De Lellis nonchalantly continues to eat and he dabs the dribbling red wine from his lips. We watch and I am ashamed. I am ashamed of this disgusting man and I am about to speak when the door swings open and the old priest returns with an unnaturally tall man at his side.

"Tonight we crave Adam; we will take this one and we will know him," says the man as he points and he looks into the eyes of the Father.

"This is an outrage. It was I who summoned you here. I sent out the call. This man is my brother and my guest; he is a man of the cloth, as are we. Take her, take Grace; she is a fresh lush virgin. Take her and do as you wish," says the old priest, his face flushing in red.

"No!" shouts Father De Lellis, suddenly standing and planting his finger into the table. "Take this one! She will offer you so much more of a challenge. Take this wanton whore, I gift her unto thee."

I am led down and into the belly of the ancient sacred mountain. The staircase is hewn and it pulses beneath my feet from the chanting and the flicker of the fire that burns down below.

I enter a chamber and I am cast to my knees within a semicircle of gently swaying depravity. Eleven masked priests naked but for their open fronted chasuble, and they grind and they pump at their cocks. And a woman wearing nothing but the veil, bandeau and coif of her habit, she stabs into her sex with a cross.

I am patient and I wait for the chants to change into

groans and I wait for them to finish before I push myself to my feet. I, too, sway and I all but fall but for the tall priest grasping and steadying my shoulder.

Steady. Steady. Then, with his other hand, he slams his fist into the sticky filth that drips from the side of my face.

The hit stuns and I drop back to my knees and hands rip and rip and rip at my clothes and, then, they rip at me. I don't call out and, through the swelling puff of my eyes, I see twisting horns and I smell my flesh as they burn it and I see sloshing jewel rimmed chalices held high and I feel them inside of me. I feel them claw and jab and cut at my cunt and I fold down inside of myself.

I love the rain. Especially thunderstorms. I love to watch as the streams on the glass join and swell. I love the rain, for it cleanses.

The following morning, I awaken and they are gone. I can smell their sweat and I can smell my own piss and blood. My fingers are snapped and broken and my legs don't work as they should, but I drag and I drag and I drag myself back up and I collapse at the top of the stairs.

And I wait and I gurgle blood and bile and it bubbles and oozes from the puffed ripped corner of my lips and I close my eyes and I dream about nothing at all.

Nothing.

Father De Lellis hoists up my body; he is much stronger than he seems, and gently he lays me in the back seat of his big black sedan and he takes me back home to the school.

So here I lay on this cold, cold slab and the good Father has just peeled himself from the sagging folds of my waxy blue corpse.

Mother Tessa hands him a knife and Father John puts it to my skin. First he hacks and then, ever so gently, he glides its edge around bone and gristle and then, together as a couple, they seal my twelve parts in plastic.

Packed tight and addressed and licked and stamped: my head to Rome, my arms to a Cardinal in Kalmthout and a retired Archbishop on the isle of Rab; my left tit to a Bishop in Seine et Marne and the other to a Priest in Kremsmunster; my torso to a Deacon in Regensburg and my belly rolled up and passed on to a Chaplain in Pennsylvania; my cunt to the Curate at the school for the deaf in Verona and my legs to the Dean in Płock and the Father in Belle River; and to the Rector in Dunedin and the Vicar in Karala, to them each a foot.

Such fun, this game. Such glorious fucking fun.

'Happy is he who repays you for what you have done to us–he who seizes your infants and dashes them against the rocks' (Psalm 137:9)

THE END

JUDAS ISCARIOT - VAMPIRE SLAYER
By Daryl Marcus

It wasn't dying fast enough.

The sky held impending darkness, the horizon already blood red and deepening. The soldiers guarding it stood a short way from the crucifix, looking over the picnicking crowd. Some were making moves to leave, packing the remnants of their midday meals and heading home to conclude the day's business. Others were continuing to dig in, pulling second helpings and additional dishes from the baskets they'd brought with them.

Judas took a breath, inhaling the scents of dust and human sweat heated by a sun that felt no mercy. He smelled a storm in the air. It had to end soon, or else things could go wrong. Its friends might try to help it. Judas couldn't let that happen.

Stepping forward, he approached the nearest guard, the knots on his shoulders marking him as the highest rank at hand. "They are strongest at night," he said, his voice pitched so only the officer would hear him. "When the sun sets, he will be able to break himself free. We can't allow that to happen."

The officer glanced behind him at the tallest cross. The thing was weakened beneath the oppressive sunlight. Its body sagged, held up by the stakes driven through its wrists and ankles. Reddish-black blood dripped from wounds, down the wood of the cross, and soaked into the earth. The sand hissed for a moment when the blood touched it, then darkened and settled.

A crown of thorns had pierced its head in many places, drenching its hair with even more blood and giving its pale face a caul. As Judas looked, he saw the thing's tongue flick out in a futile attempt to wet cracked and sunburned lips. As they watched, one of the guards dipped a sponge in vinegar and stabbed his spear through it. He held it up to the dying creature, but it turned away.

There was only one drink that could help this thing, and Judas intended to see that it had none.

"Shove off," said the officer. "Can't you see he's done for? He'll die in his own time and that will be the end of it?"

Judas's glared. "Have you sympathy for that... that thing? After what it's done to this world, to everything we stand for, you can just let things happen as if he were a mortal? Don't you know what that is?"

The officer met him glare for glare. He rolled his head on his neck and flexed his shoulders as if preparing for a fight. "'Course I know who he is. But who he is don't mean nothing to me. He's dead on the cross, just hasn't stopped breathing yet."

"It's a vampire," Judas said before he could stop himself. "It's capable of so much more than you can imagine. Kill it now and be done with it, or we will regret the delay forever."

"And who do you think you are? A soothsayer? Vampires burn in the sunlight, and he's not more burnt than you or me. He's just a man."

Lunging, Judas grabbed a handful of the officer's robe. "That's my point. It's the strongest of them all, claims to be

God's son. Just the fact that it's still breathing is proof of its power. Kill it. End it."

"God's son or a whore's son, it don't make a difference. He's dead and I'll not lay a hand on him. He'll breathe his last soon enough."

"That's not good enough." Judas snatched the spear from the officer's hands and stumbled back, surprised at what he held.

The officer was surprised as well. He took a step back and gawked. "You son of a—" he began.

Judas didn't hear the rest. He drew the spear back as he'd seen soldiers do and launched the weapon. He was not a trained soldier and had never thrown a spear in his life, yet something rose from his gut and swiftly filled his arm with strength as he let the shaft fly. His aim was true. His throw was perfect. He stared in disbelief as the spear soared over the officer's shoulder and straight at its target. The creature on the cross screamed, its side sprouting wood like a new limb.

A shadow fell over Judas and he was on the ground, the taste of blood in his mouth and the officer glaring down at him. He realized a moment later he'd been hit.

"Get away before I put you on your own cross. You've seen enough carnage for today" The officer stepped toward him, fury on his face, but Judas scrambled backwards on hands and heels. He finally found his footing and stood, staring over the officer at the vampire bleeding even more now.

"Their kind cannot be allowed to roam. They are evil, no matter their lies. Vampires are not the children of God. We are."

"You'll have no children to worry about if you don't leave."

Judas stood for a moment longer, hoping to see the light of life leave the vampire's eyes. The officer reached for his sword. He ran through the crowd, preparations for the next step already running through his head.

* * *

It took the vampire three days to heal.

Judas knew it could have been worse. He would have healed faster had he been supplied fresh blood or assisted in another way. He had made sure the stone was unmoved the entire time, shooing away curiosity seekers and children and worshipers who believed his lies and wanted to touch the grave of a living deity. He would have none of it.

The moon shone brightly on the boulder as it scraped and rumbled, pushed away from the mouth of the cave from within. The creature stood in the opening, moonlight drenching it and making it glisten. It had been cleaned before being interred, but Judas could still see the holes in its hands and ankles. He was surprised it was able to walk, but then he saw it stumble on the weakened limbs and knew it would need to feed soon.

He had to end it before it could start making more of its kind again, but he couldn't do it in private. This one was too public, too well known. It had to die in front of its followers as proof that it was not immortal, that it was not immune to the rule of man. But where? And how long should he wait?

Then Judas remembered. There was a gathering of its followers. They were mourning the loss of their savior, the one who promised to raise them above their true positions in life. It would go to show them the true power of the vampire. Judas would have to show them the folly of trusting such a creature.

* * *

The stolen sword felt strange in his hands. He'd never been a soldier, had never had the desire to kill anyone, but this Jesus needed it, deserved it. The world would be a better place if creatures such as it were not allowed to wander the land with men. Men were the owners of this world, not vile creatures with forked tongues and inhuman powers.

"Are you sure?" asked the man to Judas's right. He was a mercenary leader, his small band hired for the promise of a night's drinking money. Judas hadn't paid him yet and didn't know if any of them would survive the encounter he planned. In the gaining of backup, he'd given Jesus time to recoup, to feed, and to regain some strength.

"I'm sure of nothing except that he must not leave that meeting alive."

The mercenary shrugged. "As long as your gold is good."

There were twelve of them in there, Jesus and his brood. Judas would have made thirteen had he remained enthralled by the monster.

He crept to the entrance and listened, eager to hear what lies he told those Disciples. He marveled at his own innocence, that he had once been one of them, determined to show the world the way of God. He had come to realize that nothing that powerful, that incredible could be made for people. Judas would not live a lie for the promise of physical immortality. He did not know God's will, but God was not a vampire, and therefore Jesus could not be His son.

The voices were muffled, echoing around the stone walls until they were a jumbled mess of incoherent sounds. Shouts arose at times, but volume did not bring clarity.

Another round of shouts sounded less argumentative and more convivial. Judas waved the men back from the cave's entrance. Stepping back himself, he squeezed the hilt of his sword, wishing he felt more comfortable wearing it.

They exited in a jumbled group, those in front walking backwards to keep their eyes on the creature at their center. Their faces were flushed with joy. They fairly danced in excitement as they moved.

"Stop," Judas commanded. He did not raise his voice,

but the thing in the middle of the group heard him and raised its eyes to face him.

It smiled. "Judas. It's good to see you, old friend."

"I wish the feeling were mutual. You should be dead."

The crowd of men tightened around Jesus, calling out threats and admonishments to Judas.

Judas' mercenaries stepped forward, their hands on their swords. Their presence was enough to quiet the group once more.

Jesus looked around at the men and shook its head. It cast a sad look at Judas. "My father's gifts are for you, Judas. For all men. Why do you reject them?"

"Your father isn't my God. You were once someone I could trust, someone I could believe in. But you've revealed yourself to be an abomination. A creature that cannot be allowed to live."

"You've had me killed once, and I've come back. What has happened to me can happen to you. Father promises eternal life."

"God is not one of you." He didn't know if it was his raised voice or the sudden movement of two of the Disciples towards him that made the mercenaries move. In the end, it didn't matter. The Disciples jumped and the mercenaries charged. The mercenaries were outnumbered, but they possessed skills none of the Disciples did.

Jesus pushed those nearest it to the relative safety within the cave and stepped around the men struggling for their lives. It approached Judas, crossing the twenty feet between them in two strides.

Judas jerked the sword from its sheath and brandished it before him in a two handed grip. It wavered before Jesus' face.

Jesus smiled. It was a friendly smile showing white teeth between a set of fangs that seems to gleam in the moonlight. "I only want to give you, and all who follow my father's will, eternal life."

"No. You want to feed, to make us slaves or monsters like you. I'll have none of it."

It tilted its head forward just slightly, looking directly into Judas' eyes through thick brows. "Judas, my friend, you've nothing to fear. Let me into your heart. Trust in me. Trust in God. You will not regret it."

He wanted to. For a long moment, long enough for the sounds of fighting to fade away and for him to forget where he was, he wanted it. It would have been so easy to acquiesce. Everything in his body wanted what this creature said to be true. The creature was intelligent, cunning, and… *wrong*.

With an effort of will he didn't know he possessed, Judas tore his mind away from the easy path and drew the sword. Lunging forward, he swung wildly, without grace or precision. Yet once again an invisible hand guided his own into the right motions, the right position, and with greater force than he could have managed alone.

The blade swung true, striking the creature solidly in its neck. His hand kept going and for a moment Judas thought he had missed. The head fell forward, followed by the body, and Judas was covered in a great gout of red-black blood spraying him directly in the face.

He'd succeeded. The creature was dead.

He was elated for only a moment before realizing his folly. He stepped away from the body. His foot kicked the head lying beside him and he stumbled, fell over backwards, and landed hard on his back. The air was knocked out of him and he thought he was dying. Then the first of the cramps hit him and he knew his mistake.

The mercenaries had either killed or chased off the remainder of the Disciples. They gathered around him expectantly, eyes judging, hands twitching for their swords once more. Judas had more important things to worry about.

He scrambled to his feet, stumbled, fell, and then managed to wrench himself upright even as he began to run.

"Hey!" shouted the mercenary leader. "Don't think you can get away without paying."

They started to chase him. He reached into his tunic and pulled out a heavy purse strapped to his neck. He ripped the cord and tossed the bundle over his shoulder. "Take it all," he shouted. "I'll need it no longer." He heard it land and the silver scatter on the ground. He didn't look behind him, but he heard the men begin to fight over its contents.

He ran. At first, he ran for fear of what he had done. Then, he ran for fear of the future. Finally, he ran because he knew what he had to do.

The Change would happen to him now. He now understood why Jesus had performed so many of its miracles in mysterious ways, using clever words to cloud its actions. He'd been like a sorcerer or an entertainer, showing one hand while the real work was done with the other. Now Judas understood that it was the blood that held the power. The blood was what Jesus had carried that ensured it could heal all injuries, cure all illnesses, and even bring the dead back to life. Jesus' blood was the curse, not just the creature.

Judas ran until he found a lone horse tied to a tree outside town. No one was around, though the horse's owner couldn't have been too far away. It didn't matter. He needed but a few minutes to finish the job.

He had to end it tonight. It was supposed to end with Jesus, with the Disciples dead or scattered, but it could continue with him if he didn't do the right thing.

Even as he fashioned the noose his insides churned, and he vomited at the base of the tree. Blood and the remnants of a simple dinner lay in a puddle at his feet. He could see pieces of himself in that puddle, his life going to ruin even as he rushed to prevent the curse.

He tossed the rope over the strongest branch of the tree. Carefully, he led the horse underneath it and climbed on its back. It took several attempts before he was astride the horse and the noose was in place, but the animal was docile and in no hurry.

Everything in place, he took one last look at the world around him. He hoped he was doing the right thing. He couldn't allow the creature's legacy to continue.

He wiped his face and discovered tears made of blood. He was too far gone. Still crying, he kicked the horse's haunches and shouted for it to move.

The horse dutifully obeyed. It leaped forward into a gallop, and quickly left the tree and its rider behind.

Judas watched it go even as his throat tightened and his vision darkened. The cramps hit him once more, doubling him into a ball even as his neck strained against the rope and his lungs burned.

His vision darkened and he heard its laughter in his head even as his body relaxed in expiration. The tears kept flowing after his vision faded to complete blackness.

* * *

It awoke at sunset. The world swung around it in a gentle breeze. It heard the creaking of wood strained under a burden it wasn't meant to take. It tried to take a breath, found it could not, and also found it did not need the breath anyway. It reached cold hands to its neck and found the rope it had known was there.

There was some pain, but it felt a dull discomfort compared to the searing, sharp pain coming from its gut. It needed something it could not yet understand. It was time to move, to seek a way to eliminate that pain.

It wriggled fingers beginning to regain feeling under the rope, digging into its own skin with dirty nails. With more strength than it had expected to possess, it yanked hard. It took two tries to part the rope. It landed hard on its feet, but pain shot through its knees and it collapsed into the dust. Its gut wrenched and vomit shot from its mouth in a geyser of black chunks and bright red blood.

The world turned red before darkening once more into welcome oblivion. When it awoke again it was hungry. It sat up, breathed its first breath, and scented prey on the wind.

As it ran its body awakened fully, singing of the gifts each part possessed. It was alive, and powerful, like never before. It thrilled to the scents and sensations coursing through it. Life truly was the greatest gift of God.

THE END

VICIOUS SCISSORS
By Carlton Herzog

I was never one to believe in ghosts or the supernatural. Indeed, I was astounded at the gullibility of people, who, on the one hand, relied heavily on science in their day to day experience, while on the other, subscribed to the misguided belief that we live in a demon haunted world, wherein all manner of unseen things walk parallel to the path of the living.

I was never sure if such nonsense originated in the fear of the unknown, escape from boredom, or pure ignorance. To my mind, science adequately explained the nature of reality, and did not, therefore, require unsolicited assistance from the lunatic fringe. The same fringe that believes aliens travel hundreds of light years just to give Cletus the slack-jawed yokel a colonoscopy above a deserted country road.

My attitude underwent a profound transformation soon after I received a bequest from my great aunt, Clarissa Leeds, a rather eccentric old coot who claimed to be both a witch and a medium. She had, as it were, conferred upon me a family heirloom some four hundred years old. It consisted of an engraved wooden box containing a holy relic in the form of ancient shears. The Roman Catholic Church referred to them as the *Maleficarum Placenta Forceps*, or the Scissors of Witches.

Mind you I had never met the woman. I could not understand why she gave the box to me rather than any of her other great nieces and nephews. Then again, I'm told she walked around naked, chattering dentures in hand while aping a British accent in the vein of Elizabeth I, Margaret Thatcher, and Monty Python's Mrs. Dim. She's the kind of relative that makes you question your bloodline, wondering if your kid will turn out to be a failed entertainer or a loony in a straightjacket.

When you're a tenured Professor of Linguistics, you necessarily worry about unwanted genetic drift in your bloodline, since the sudden appearance of a drooling doodle-brain would seriously compromise your legacy as a scholar. The bequest magnified those concerns by its very strangeness. For example, the runes on the box were in a language that I had never seen, suggesting the carver was either in tune with the cosmically large or was a simpleton who had married the fine art of whittling with old-fashioned gibberish.

Whatever the case, the box itself was made of yew. Not a surprise, since witches of old revered yews as the home of unseen forces antithetical to Christianity. They believed that Eve supposedly plucked the forbidden fruit, not from an apple tree but from a yew; they also took comfort in the notion that Jesus was executed on a cross made of yew. Supposedly in medieval times, yews were planted in church graveyards because they were believed to inhale and feed on the putrefaction of decaying corpses and their vapors.

But it wasn't the box that made me blink: It was those shears. I expected them to be dull, old and rusted, an object to be admired by an antiquarian with an itch to clean and polish old metal.

They were, however, something entirely different. They were golden, but not gold. They had the luster of newly forged metal. But they weren't made of any alloy I could identify. When I held them, they seemed to vibrate, so much so that when I handled them, they slipped and cut me. The curious thing was that when I went to wipe the blood from them with a rag, there was none to be found, as if those shears had absorbed it.

I knew something of metallurgy, specifically, when you heat metal to a very high temperature, it doesn't cool uniformly. It crystallizes in different orientations, forming little cells with defects between them. Hence all the blacksmith's hammering.

But the shears had no visible imperfections, no tiny basins into which the blood could have drained. So, I was at a loss as to where it had gone. Exsanguinating scissors was a new one on me, and, no doubt, even to those who give credence to idiotic urban legends. It would not therefore have surprised me to see a Sci Fi original movie titled, *Vampire Scissors.*

But I digress. The first scissor event occurred after I had placed the box on the mantle just below the lithograph of Jesus. My wife leans Christian. I do not, nor have I ever. My parents were stout atheists who steered me away from church, even though my girlfriend at the time insisted I needed baptism to avoid the fires of hell. Although my wife is a devout Christian, she is more progressive in her views, relegating the concept of hell to the realm of mythology and feeble minds, as do I.

My only thought in placing the box on the mantle was to have it handy as a conversation piece when we had dinner guests. Little did I know the firestorm it would cause.

To wit, the next morning, I found the Jesus lithograph shredded into a thousand pieces. My two sons professed ignorance of the blasphemy. Whatever my suspicions, I could prove nothing. They are good boys, not prone to malicious mischief or acts of profanation against religious icons.

That is not say that they were pro-religion. My son's favorite author, CD Herzog, had just penned a story titled, *Jesus versus Godzilla,* which pokes fun at the church. As we were sitting around the dinner table spit-balling different ideas about the crucifix massacre, my son blurted out, "Jesus never condemned slavery, not once. So why was he all hot and bothered about demonic possession? Isn't that slavery?"

That sent my wife around the proverbial bend. To pacify her, I found a large crucifix in the attic and mounted it where the lithograph had been hung. The next morning, I found it cut to pieces. My sons again professed ignorance. Although they seemed the logical culprits, I found their demeanor sincere, and given their otherwise blameless lives, exonerating.

Later that day, I mentioned the incident to a colleague at the university whose specialty is world religion. I told him of my queer Great Aunt Clarissa and her affiliation with the occult. He didn't offer any direct insight as to the shredding of the cross and picture. Instead, he rambled on about the potential relationship between the shears and the Salem witch trials.

To be sure, he spoke with an air of expertise and academic stuffiness you would expect from a sitting professor. But it was hard to keep a straight face because he was severely cross-eyed. I tried to listen intently, but all I could think of was whether his strabismus caused him to see two of everything. I almost asked him how many fingers I was holding up but refrained as he droned on about mystical nonsense.

"Did you know that not all the suspected witches of Salem were hanged or drowned? There was a queer Christian sect known as the Cutters who believed that they could exorcise a known witch's evil by shearing off various body parts, depending on nothing more than where they intuited such evil was concentrated. Thus, ears, noses, tongues, fingers, arms, feet, legs, genitals and breasts were fair game. And once severed from the body, the scissors themselves would pull the evil out of the cut body part and into its metal, thus imprisoning it for all eternity. Supposedly the metal was forged by the angels themselves, and impressed with angelic imprisonment symbols.

"The Cutters took their ideas from the ancient Greeks. You know the Fates: Clotho spun the thread of life; Lachesis measured it; and Atropos with her golden shears—always razor sharp and good for a clean cut—snipped it, leaving no loose ends. The Greeks considered the Fates to be so powerful they could end the life of even an immortal god such as Zeus."

I said, "That's nice to know, but how does that help me?"

"Like you, I am an academic, so really, we are both walking encyclopedias of useless information. I suggest you contact a spiritualist."

"Ghosts, spirits and specters? You're joking."

"Absolutely not. Think about all the unseen and unfelt stuff zipping through your body even as we speak: gravity waves, radio waves, neutrinos, dark energy, dark matter. I would not be so quick to judge given all the blind spots in human perception. I'm giving you the card of a known medium, one Madame Gertrude Blavatsky. Maybe she can shed light on your problem."

I took the proffered card, called the woman, and arranged for her to visit my home.

When she showed up at my door the next day, she was an eyeful. Tall and barrel-chested, adorned with enormous Elton John diamond-studded eyeglasses, and sporting flabby, pendulous breasts that could have substituted for pontoons on a catamaran, she looked crazy more than anything else. Her flaming red muumuu, imprinted with golden runes, stars and four-leaf clovers, added to her overall air of wackiness. But for all that, she spoke in a gentle whisper. She didn't waste any time reading me the riot act.

"I felt the negative energy as I drove onto your street. It got stronger the closer I got to your house. I will venture to say that this house is infected with a legion of spirits, no doubt compressed into the object you described on the phone. We will do a séance to identify the spirits and then go from there. We'll do that now."

"I thought séances only took place in the dark around midnight."

"The atmospherics and cheap signaling of frauds. Spirits exist outside of time. The hour means nothing to them."

"How do we do this? Ouija board?"

"No. Too unreliable. Too easy to be compromised by wishful thinking and subconscious desires. We sit a table with a glass of water and candles. Fire and water are two things that can be easily manipulated from the beyond and don't leave room for the interference of a human agent. We ask yes or no questions. Yes, the water boils; no, the flame flickers. Simple. Are you ready?"

"Shouldn't my family be here?"

"No need to inject variables. Less is more."

"Okay then. I am as ready as I'll ever be."

We sat at the dining room table holding hands, the scissor box in the table's middle.

She didn't beat around the bush. "Spirits of the netherworlds, travelers upon and within the ether, Cosmic Ones, Old Ones, Dead Ones we gather here today to know your mind and understand your presence here. Are you with us, and if so, do you have a message for us? If yes, make the water boil; if no, then blow on the flame."

The answer was not what she expected. To be sure, the water boiled. But the candle flickered as well, and then all the doors in the house began slamming and opening and slamming. After a few minutes, it got quiet and both candle and water settled down.

Blavatsky asked, "Are you angry with this man?"

The candle flickered.

"Are you angry at someone or something else?"

The water boiled.

"Are you someone who has departed from the earthly plane?"

The water boiled.

"More than one?"

The water boiled again.

"Many?"

The water boiled again.

"Besides the departed, is there anyone or anything else with you here?"

The water boiled.

"Many?"

The water boiled.

"Demons?"

The glass exploded and the house shook down to its very foundation.

"We're done here. I can't do anything to help you. Cleansing this house of one or two wayward spirits is one thing, but an army of demons conjoined to the essence of the departed is out of my league. This is one for the priests. And for that, you will need proof. I'll bill you later."

She then gathered herself and left.

I waited a few days to calm down. I said nothing to my wife and kids about the matter. When I felt up to the task, I bought a cheap crucifix. The plan I had in mind was to set up a video recorder and then hang the crucifix after everyone had fallen asleep. For myself, I would slip out of bed and hide behind the drapes to watch what would happen.

That is exactly what I did. I bought the cross at a five and dime, went home and ate dinner with my family, watched some television, and then we all retired for the night. I pretended to be asleep, and when it seemed as if my wife were well on her way to dreamland, I slipped out of bed, down the stairs, and hung the cross above the mantle. I flipped on the recorder and then hid behind the drapes and waited.

I can't say what happened next was wholly unexpected. The box began to vibrate, gently at first, then more violently until the box lid flew open and the scissors levitated up to the height of the crucifix, hovered for a moment, then shot into the crucifix and began furiously cutting it to pieces with all the accuracy and finesse of a sushi chef.

When the crucifix was nothing more than splinters adorning the mantle and floor, the scissors dropped back into the box, which snapped shut behind them.

At that moment, I went from skeptical empiricist, to a believer in every ghost story and weird tale I had ever heard.

Now I was deathly afraid to touch the box. I went to the local parish priest and explained the matter to him. At first, he thought I was pulling his leg, but my apparent sincerity, along with my video, convinced him to investigate the matter. I also filled him on the séance and Blavatsky's conclusions.

"At first blush, it sounds like a poltergeist is operating in your home. That usually involves a spirit or energy that creates physical disturbances, such as making loud noises, levitating objects, and destroying them. But what you've described seems more focused and so more like a haunting. But as your medium seems to believe, it may be more than that. I suggest that together we repeat the crucifix experiment. I'll have the deacon come along as an additional live witness. And we'll record it all. If your mad scissors dissect the crucifix absent a visible corporeal agent, I will contact the Vatican and they can bring in the big guns."

The next day we set to work. I half-expected the experiment to fail, such that I would look like an idiot. But no sooner had I hung the crucifix than the box began to convulse. The lid flew open and the scissors slowly rose. Only this time, they didn't aim for the crucifix. Instead, they slowly turned toward us. A moment later, they shot across the room straight into the priest's forehead. But they didn't stay there. They retracted from his skull, then plunged into his eye, then back out and then into his other eye, and then into his throat, then out again, and in a blizzard of stabbing motions turned him into a human pincushion.

The deacon and I fled before it could have its way with us. When we returned with the police, the priest had been butchered as thoroughly as any pig before a pagan feast. The crucifix had been reduced to a pile of ethereal wood dust. As for the scissors, the police found them in the box, devoid of blood. The police tried to confiscate them as evidence, but they could not pry them from the box, nor lift the box itself, despite the strenuous efforts of several brawny men and an iron crowbar.

If it were it not for the video, I'm sure both Deacon Brown and myself would have been tried as murderers. When news of the episode made its way onto social media, complete with the video—no doubt leaked by someone at City Hall—my house was surrounded by news persons all wanting to hear the story.

Every time my family or I went out the door, we were badgered by the media. Apparently, someone had claimed that my house was haunted by the Jersey Devil. And they kept asking us if my Great Aunt Clarissa was the great granddaughter of the same Mother Leeds, who gave birth to the Jersey Devil.

I told the media I didn't know anything about the Jersey Devil, but took the opportunity to pump them for information. According to one newsperson, the Jersey Devil is a modern American myth. Supposedly, Mother Leeds had twelve children. When she discovered that she was pregnant with a thirteenth, she flipped, cursing the child by exclaiming, "Let it be the devil!"

On the less-than-blessed day, the child exploded from her belly, spraying everyone in the room with blood. It then unfolded its wings, bit off the mid-wife's head, and flew out the window. The legend holds that it terrorized the countryside, killing and eating everything from cattle to human babies and small children.

Now the whole thing made sense: my bloodline was cursed. My home had become a House of Atreus, where the sins of the ancestors get passed along generation after generation like current flowing down a wire. Naturally I kept my suspicions from my wife and kids, who had just moved back in following the closing the of the crime scene.

Apparently, the deacon had made a few phone calls, because, a week later, two cardinals and four priests from the Vatican appeared at my home. They said they were going to remove the box and dispose of it so it could cause no further damage. They said we needed to stay with friends until they had concluded their business. I told them that I would send my family to stay with my mother, but I, as the homeowner, had every right to be present. My motives were born of curiosity. And pure profit. After all, a video of a genuine supernatural event with witnesses was worth its weight in gold. And apparently, those madcap scissors had no beef with ordinary people, just those in priestly attire, so I was safe.

One of the cardinals explained to me that the scissors were like a Menger sponge—a fractal object with an infinite number of cavities in which an infinite number of spirits and demons can be held.

"Certain demons are charged with performing specific functions and are granted certain powers to operate on this plane. The spirits of the witches could not have done the things you claim to have witnessed without some help."

"But if you exorcise them, then won't they be free to infect someone or something else?"

"We're not going to exorcise them from the shears. All we need do is break the spell that holds the box to the mantle. Once that is broken, we will transport the box to a Vatican vault, deep underground, where we keep all the evil infested relics we capture."

So, it came to pass that we assembled in my living room along with several video recorders and prepared to liberate the box from its demonic iron grip. Rather than a sacramental exorcism, the priests would simultaneously perform both a containment and unbinding ritual, the former to ensure the demons stayed in the shears and the shears stayed in the box, while at the same time liberating the box from the mantle and the house.

The Vatican security team took the added precaution of erecting a sanctified metal screen between the box and us, so that should the scissors escape their confinement and shoot at us, they would collide with a hardened steel barrier impervious to their cut.

The priest opened the *Malleus Maleficarum*, otherwise known as *The Hammer of Witches*, and turned to the appropriate page containing the pertinent binding and unbinding spells. I expected Latin, as it was the language in which that handbook for witch hunters had been written, or at the very least, an English translation of it, but the priest spoke in an alien, otherworldly tongue, one that made my skin alternately crawl and tingle. Apparently, there are two different versions of that weighty tome: one that deals exclusively with witches penned in Latin, and another—this one—written in the arcane cosmic language reserved for the removal of Lucifer's foot soldiers on earth.

One of the priests leaned over to me and said, "Rest easy, he speaks a containment spell to ensure the shears can't leave the box before he breaks the charm that binds it to the mantle. The language is strange because it is the language of hell itself, the very tongue in which the Dark Prince addresses his minions there and here on earth. Be calm, for God is with us. Show no fear, even if you feel it, because demons feed on fear. It is the staff of diabolic unlife."

I don't know what creeped me out more: The fact that

the Vatican had sent a special team of exorcism commandoes to purge my house of evil, or the fact that the priest who just spoke to me smelled as if he had been farting into the robe for a week or more. Talk about stink. I kept waiting for my face to melt or the paint to peel from the wall. I think a little more time working on body hygiene and a little less of the spiritual kind would have done him and me a world of good. I wondered if the altar boys called him Father Fart Pants or Big Daddy Stinky Robes behind his back? Clearly the seriousness of the proceeding was momentarily lost on me and so my head was not in the game.

When phase one was completed, all was quiet as the priests, confident that the shears could not leave the box, prepared for the main event: unbinding the box from the house. Once more, the priests, this time in unison, began the ritual. Again, the tongue was cosmic, eldritch, from times and places before man walked the earth and before the earth itself, and perhaps before the universe itself was born.

Ordinary men, not trained in the occult arts, are not men to hear such things, nor think the things those dissonant hellish words inspire. As they proceeded, my hair stood on end and my ears rang. The mucus flowed from my nose as from a fountain, and my throat and mouth were as dry as the Sahara. My belly boiled and ached. I wanted to vomit but could not. I wanted to lie down the vertigo was so pronounced. But the priest next to me, without looking directly at me, without interrupting the ritual, slapped the back of my head and wagged his finger at me. He didn't need to say anything. I knew he meant, *do not lose faith; stand your ground.*

I did, but started to shake, and the tremors only got worse. Moments later, the entire house joined me in a vibrational duet. Then it, and everything and everyone in it, began to vibrate. Odd smells permeated the house, ozone like, then sulfur like, then the odor of burnt wood and rubber. The vibration increased, as did the uncomfortable physical sensations.

The reality of the unreality dawned on me. I had jumped into a rabbit hole and now was falling with no end in sight. I was sweating profusely and scared shitless. The profit was flying out the window and I didn't care. I just wanted the nightmare to be over so I could return to my family and my quiet academic life and forget the whole thing ever happened.

But, of course, that was not to be. Reality began jumping in and out of itself. Things would fade, then reappear. Straight lines and planes became wavy and curvilinear, as if the universe was melting in a great cosmic microwave oven. Even my acid trips as an undergrad could not compare with it for unadulterated trippy and weird.

Still, the priests stood their ground and maintained their heavenly choir. And then things ran off the rails in a big way. Where the metal screen had been, a tear appeared as a small rent at first, and then expanded, revealing a sea of stars. I expected all the air in the room and us to be sucked into space, but something was keeping that reality from interacting with ours.

I couldn't ask any of the priests what was happening because I didn't want them to break stride. They didn't seem fazed by the sudden materialization of a cosmic window in a suburban neighborhood.

I desperately wanted to run but found my legs rooted to the spot where I stood. No, I was the involuntary spectator now, observing this battle for supremacy over a wooden box containing accursed scissors.

As I stood there silently bemoaning the situation, the box exploded. Its fragments peppered the metal screen even as the great cosmic window evaporated. The scissors were free. And they were smart. They sized up the metal screen. Rather than trying to plunge through it and run the risk of being stuck, they began to spin like a buzz saw, then oriented themselves so they could spin themselves through the metal barricade at the spaces between the armature and the grid.

By now the priests had stopped their incantation and were frantically trying to find a defense. The head priest was furiously flipping through the *Malleus*, looking for answers even as the scissors were buzz sawing their way toward him. A moment later, they buzz sawed his face at the nose, splitting his head in two.

This time, however, they were not content to let the other priests escape. They went in hot airborne pursuit, cutting down one here, another there in a great massacre. Not even the two cardinals were spared the indignity of a stabbing by those possessed shears.

The funny thing is that I saw these things play out in vivid detail not with my earthly eyes, but someone else's or something else's. I think I was seeing through the scissors or whatever presence inhabited them. I know that sounds crazy, but it's not really.

You see, when the scissors had finished their grisly business, they came wafting in on a gentle summer breeze and ever so gently slipped into my hand as if they had come home at last. Creepy yes. Creepy still, I can hear all those voices inside me, unearthly voices, angry voices. I was now large. I contained multitudes.

Since most of the event was caught on video, I was not implicated in the homicides. I did go on to write some best-selling books, did the talk show tour, and even consulted on a movie about myself. I did not tell anyone that the scissors are in my possession or that I am in theirs. It's our little secret. Every now and then they want to come out and play. I don't ask them where they go or what they do. I can guess. And, one way or the other, I hear about it.

One day, a black SUV drove up to my house. I was the only one home. I answered the door and was greeted by two very large men in black suits.

"Mr. Leeds, you have in your possession an object that

does not belong to you and must therefore be returned to its rightful owner."

"I don't know what you're talking about."

"I think you do. To be blunt, your vicious scissors are the property of Hell."

"They belonged to my great aunt and now they belong to me."

"I don't think you appreciate the gravity of the situation. The matter is not open to negotiation or delay. Those shears contain renegade spirits and demons, escapees who must be returned to their confinement."

"The cardinal said they had the authority to be here. They're not ready to leave here. And if their past conduct is any indication, you too are in grave danger of being cut to ribbons by them."

"The cardinal was misinformed. Let me reiterate in the strongest possible terms that you need to turn over the shears."

"Fine. Have it your way. They're in the box on the mantle. Good luck lifting the box or opening it."

The two men, or whatever it was that looked and talked like men, entered the house and went into the living room. They didn't try to handle the box. They stood there, just staring in its direction.

I could see the box starting to vibrate the same way it had done before. But this time, it had an eldritch glow to it, a green luminescence that slowly got brighter. Then the lid popped open and the shears flew out of the box, making a beeline toward their would-be jailors. They would have sliced through the one closest to them but he, or it, threw up a whirling shield of eldritch light that deflected them into the wall. For a moment, I thought that they had escaped captivity and were zooming to parts unknown.

That was not the case. They came shooting through the ceiling but were again deflected by a light shield, once more penetrating the wall and disappearing.

This time they immediately came back for another pass and then another and another with increasing velocity until they were shooting in as rapidly as they had when they initially turned Father Joe into a human pincushion.

Now the men in black were no longer men nor clothed. They went commando, revealing themselves to be two-headed, four-armed reptiles brandishing swords made from the same arcane metal as the shears. Sometimes they would deflect the shears with their light fields, at others with their swords, and at others striking their own blows as the shears whizzed past.

At first, the tableau seemed like a program in a video game. I kept waiting for them to get on a blower and call for back up, and maybe they would have, had those damnable scissors given them a chance.

As the nightmare continued to unfold, the speed of combat far surpassed mortal abilities to either perform such tactics or even see them. The whole thing became a blur.

The combat seemed interminable. I was crouched in a corner, afraid to move for fear of being gutted by the shears as they zoomed in and out on the attack or hacked by the swords swinging wildly to block and stop them.

I thought, *something's got to give.* But it hit me that these sword-brandishing demons, together with the allied ghosts, specters and spirits inhabiting the shears, didn't have my sense of earthly time, or for that matter, any time at all. This battle could go on for centuries with no end in sight. So, rather than waiting for a decisive outcome, I tried to leave.

Before I could, something happened: The shears zipped in for what looked like another attack. But they stopped short, vibrated a bit, and discharged a mist of sorts that separated, then individually coalesced into the very witches and demons that were haunting the shears. Reinforcements in the form of a small army brandishing burning swords and spears. The fire, however, was not of this earth because it burned in all the colors of the rainbow as if it had been harvested from every kind of star in the firmament: white, yellow, orange, red, blue, green, brown and black.

It ticked me off because I assumed the fire would ignite what was left of my house and leave it a heap of burning cinders when all was said and done. But it didn't. Whatever physics caused it to ignite and burn did not hold sway in this dimension.

When they swung the swords at the demon cops, the swords made physical contact and the flames burned that reptile flesh. But when the swords swung into the wall or the carpet or furniture, they passed harmlessly through like ghosts.

At one point, I got caught in the crossfire and the swords swept through me. I felt nothing, not so much as a tickle or tingle.

As if things weren't crazy enough, a news crew entered the house and began recording the battle. I kept waiting for them to get clobbered by flying debris or a sinewy, sword-wielding demonic arm.

Instead, the spirit army took advantage of the situation, possessed the news crew, and then ran out the door, shameless diabolical opportunists that they were.

I wanted to ponder the weirdness of the whole thing, but I knew that was a luxury. I needed to flee. I thought about my wife and kids. I didn't want to be dismembered. More than that, I wanted to see them at least one more time if today were to be my last.

I started crawling toward the front door. In that supernatural melee, none of the demons, ghosts, spirits or specters gave me a second look. I stayed low, stopped and changed direction as the need arose, and after a few timeless minutes, slithered out the front door to face a boisterous incredulous crowd of news persons and gawkers.

At that moment, I didn't feel like being debriefed by anyone. I just wanted to see my family. I ran to the neighbor's house, headed for the back, and then started cutting through yards and hopping fences. I expected someone to give chase, but no one did, presumably because whatever was still going on at my abode was holding the attention of the crowd gathered there.

I called my wife. I gave her the *Readers Digest* version. As I did, I felt something nudging my other hand. It was warm and metallic and gently vibrating. I froze and looked at my hand. It was the haunted scissors trying to wriggle into my grip.

I opened my hand and held them. I wanted to throw them down and run. But something inside me refused that impulse. I kept walking, lost in a fog of indecision, those vicious devil scissors accompanying me like a faithful dog.

It made even more sense now than it did before. After all, my Great Aunt Clarissa had them before me, and I have no doubt they were a bequest from one of my long dead ancestors, probably Mother Leeds herself who birthed that abomination known as the Jersey Devil. I suppose a normal person would have been repulsed, perhaps even crying out to God for salvation.

But I didn't need saving. In my heart, I knew that my vicious little metal friend would take care of me. How? My blood had mingled with the blood of all those witches and demons the very first time I handled those scissors and cut myself, sending my blood into that Menger sponge to mingle with theirs. That's how they know me and consider me a friend, since I am of the House of Mother Leeds, one of the accursed ones, most unclean, and I suspect a Jersey Devil sans hooves and horns and wings. But that may yet change, and if it does, then who, or rather what, was I to argue against such a metamorphosis?

Epilogue

Scissors in hand, I wandered the neighborhood. Just

ahead of me I saw what appeared to be a small group of people leaving a residence, each one carrying a thick book and dressed in their Sunday best. Jehovah's Witnesses!

I threw the scissors onto a lawn and ran through yard after yard toward my house. As I did, I heard the bloodcurdling screams, the cries for "Help!" There was nothing I could do but save myself.

I got to my house and found it flattened as if struck by a tornado. I called the insurance company and told my agent the house had been destroyed by an Act of God. You and I, however, know that it was an Act of Devil.

THE END

THE ARCHEUS
By C. C. Parker

Slipping inside the froth Lucian looked into the reddened sky: burning wasteland above the horizon of a vast sagging cloud which held all the moistures of those who'd fallen off the edge of recent memory. Lucian, Disciple of Keteb, scraping his flesh into a steaming bath, evacuating layers into the salt brine.

Diseased meat—impossible dreamer. Poisoned by delicate matters as civilization plodded ahead with no vision but his own to prevent him from slipping off into that bath for good. Brine of Unreason. He thought it a good title for a poem if only he wrote. His art, instead, was poisoning his mind, while his body paid dearly for his daily consummations. Fusing with the universe until every molecule burned.

What is he doing to himself? Learning nothing from his experiments save that his threshold of pain is profound. Touching the silent blade of a dragon's scale as it rends fierce judgment from his mind with brutal strength. When Lucian goes out into the real world, it is with the tendency of a cannibal, and those who pass by are seen as meat.

Cloud of moistness hanging above, following him into the streets. Burning everywhere he goes: the memory of a place that is so fucking close, yet unbearably distant. No matter how many baths he took or terrors faced, did he get close to arriving at the answer.

Dismal wave of nausea overcoming him as he entered a grocery store. Lucian needed a bottle so bad he could taste it.

Winding through the bustling space with the deftness of a ballet dancer. Lucian, hiding within the shadows of his own plaintive, stricken gait, where others seemed to avoid the cloud he was bathed in. Scent of an Outsider emanating from his pores like a rotting carcass. Most treating him like a leper from the time of Christ, he gloried, thinking fondly of those spirits that trailed behind him down the liquor aisle.

"Lucian?" Came a voice, a girl from high school. Tamara Snow. How he didn't get out of this town after getting sick was one of the biggest mistakes of his life. Besides, he'd need to stay away from her or she would be stricken too. But holy fuck did she smell good! And she had a purity in her ability to connect without the judgments or remorseful politeness he was used to. Lucian knew that if he ever started a cult that he could, with great confidence, make her his eternal bride.

"Hello Tammy," he stammered with the same awkwardness that followed him through his 'formative' years. He wanted to show her the near-but-far place, but decided she didn't have the strength for it. Very few could keep the sediment down—where a Heathen Christ went to drown his sorrows. Turning the lepers against his own people to cast a vision of Hell on Earth.

Lucian, wishing he were back in his room...

Instead, gazing at her through the Eyes of Keteb. One in his heart of which to see the world as it truly is: grotesque, rampaging Ego. Her eyes were on him, too, but with a softness that frightened him. She could never be his bride if she could not turn her back on the earthly dross that, to her, seemed incorruptible. The fact he already knew this about her told him something.

He moved on...

* * *

White, sulphuric heaven burns up, leaving them stranded on the material plane. Lucian witnessed this in a dream with the clearness of his waking self when a boy. Dreaming most of his childhood away, sickly and looking for clues; it isn't until he finds the wellspring behind his house that the eternal connection is made. Magisterial solvent in the Citadel of the Archeus, where everything he believed to be true was proven wrong: lessons of a waking world that would never sleep if given the choice.

What does tomorrow bring? That is what they all want to know. Lucian kept it inside, but felt an urge to prove them wrong. Abstracting nature into the ovoid shape that it is in order to become the seed: vessel of inordinate, timeless perfection that coordinates all movements according to itself...

Everything retching out of him at once: blood, hernia, numb feeling, endless cans of Nalley Chili. His body is a temple destroyed by wasted years. Washing the taste out with a mouthful of tequila until it burns away and quells the fog in his mind. Silence. Lucian smiled, knowing that he was an afterthought to those jokers that ran away with time. Nor did they know to what depths a body may go in its desperation for life while the cloud dragged him along for the benefit of all.

Didn't they know that he was a killer? When he came out of that wellspring all those years ago, his ideas changed. A pact with nature that would eventually corrupt his magnetism in the world like a thing died and come back. A monster wearing human clothes, oozing preternatural apathy, bordering on the utterly vacant.

* * *

Sinking into another vat of bilge water that he imagined to be the essence of stars. Smoking a joint as the gray lather of discarded skins mounted tiny riptides against him. Grunting out a fart that turned into a purple mess rising up from between his legs as he felt his insides tightened with a violent jerk...

Another hallucination to take him away from the pain. Anything. Vanishing, celestial breeders leaving their final, confused droplets of liminal consciousness that still retained their affectation towards the sun. While he has faced the coldness inside like all dying things do, there was a radiant passage to the Inverse Cradle. Above all things that have risen over the horizon of his illusion there was the idea He could control the device that gave him life.

Only the solution was too devious. Even for He, who sold out the world...

Lucian thought of a malefic Christ who is more like a power broker. One who need control every facet of the waking world even though the outcome was obligatory. A great feasting on all organic life was on the horizon beneath a cloud of sulphuric longing where ghosts of every age clung to the ephemerality of stated changelessness.

Intellectually behind, yet spiritually ahead. Still, it was all the baths that made him fearless in a void like this. The skins had to come off just like the nerves had to be stripped from their pink stations. Beating himself against the wall of his room where a stain had grown: bits of rotting, clinging meat, gathering flies, shedding larvae to the floor like pustulent tears.

I must go out there and make the most of it, he thought bleakly. *Or I will surely take the funeral pill & fade...*

* * *

Red Kingdom. Bloody war. All is crimson where he sits. Bursting open like a cranial flower where piles of victims come to fruition. Any who summoned Keteb in a desperate attempt to understand the value of plague, as lepers marched along the road of the Holy Cross in an insane pledge for forgiveness as promised by their lord and savior (in visions). Still, if it hadn't been for His rancid breath, they'd not have known it was Him.

Lucian sobbed with this knowledge. Even as his stripped body wilted in the last of the salt brine—empty bottle of tequila balanced on his lower lip—world violently spinning as he clung to its wet sides. Submerging in debt of other men as his vision left his body and moved along the same dripping corridor that led through the fog of his mind: toward a resonating halo of inverse qualities, salient and beaming. Clothed in crimson garb as corridors faded into that citadel of fire penetrating the sky.

Lucian entered with head bowed. Shrouded, cold look he gave those who dwelt here for aeons. They watched with sullenness and dead misgivings. They'd watched groveling fools come and go, and this would be no different. Still, he did not bear the sickness of an asp whilst inside that breathing fire...

Stay away from your cold body as it lays on the slab. Lucian could hear muffled cries coming from somewhere. Equilateral dissonance as a cloud burst abandoning him to the desert and other dying lands. Wandering across, he came to a haunted loon. Madness from being alone out here for so long with stars breathing their dust into his lungs. And you, suffocating on another dream, choking on it...

Hyperventilating wildly. Holding back the urge to release his bowels into the brine, but so far gone it was impossible. Chunks of intestine blowing out his rectum as he felt the crimson curtain closing. For once in his life, Lucian was not afraid to remove the mask entirely and breath soot into the citadel once again. Knowing the demonic nature that hosted the disease, he also understood it to be the most critical element in regards to a decisive transmigration. Even as its temporary vessel was boiled inside the cauldron until it was moist again. Fumes clouding up windows and mirrors of that dingy space: nothing but the effluvium of its meat substance, molding over...

* * *

Nobody had checked on him for several weeks. When Jan, Lucian's landlady, saw his mail piling up and didn't receive next months rent, she pounded on his door. What Lucian did in his spare time was his business, but not paying on time forced her to flex her muscles.

Immediately struck by the odor and surprised tenants hadn't complained. *Okay*, she thought to herself, *it is probably just a dead cat.* Still, she couldn't remember him owning any pets. Letting herself inside, trying not to gag, instead breathing through her mouth, swallowing gutfuls of that pungent, saline air like whale corpses gave off when she stumbled on them on long, meandering beach hikes of her youth.

Buckling to her knees as she clawed her way to the bathroom. Following a moist stain on the ceiling, which blackened the closer she got. *You should just call the cops, Jan, and a coroner*, but curiosity got the best of her. While somewhere in that fire-bladed citadel there survived an inhuman vision in the form of one who rose from the brine of truth to become an acolyte of nature: who journeyed across a tired expanse to reach the summit of a liberating prophecy. Here it was only a bloated, gray sludge of a mortal wretch for her to find: he who plied demarcations while chewing on edible stones—poisoned from within as nature intends, oozing out until there is nothing left...

Suddenly Jan felt sorry for him. She couldn't remember him ever seeming cruel or inhuman to anyone. Sobbing uncontrollably as she tried pushing the door shut but couldn't due to that blackened, fungal stain covered in milky polyps. They grew on meat follicles and were responsible for the living rot that grew over everything, even the hallway if she didn't act soon. *Yet the world more-than-likely deserves it*, she thought, from a remote, holocaustic part of her mind where she did not linger often or for too long:

Leprous world of doomed miracles and increasingly dry seasons. Interior furnace, curdling awareness in the final primal dusk of a broken awakening. *Such an infectious plague is on us*, she thought, reaching up to drain some of that gray milk into her mouth: waiting for the right moment to expunge her deepest regrets. *I have to go*, she thought, *before it's too late. Call the cops. Get help. Paramedic. Starting to sink. Nature's reservoir. Isle of Keteb. That is where broken bodies go: exhumation of souls, with the strength to carry on, unlimited grief to bear its weight over a vast desert. In the blinding calefaction of a newly risen sun where all horizons bleed into one another: Archeus mounts her dusty bones with the fecundity of spring...*

That alone could be her eternal thought as she shoved her fingers down her throat. Jose would be home soon and she prayed to Christ he could make this apartment look new again. They couldn't afford to lose a single unit the way property taxes were escalating.

Whispering something under her breath as she slowly backed away into the hall, locking the door before she went to make her calls. Breathing in fresh air as her poisoned memories faded, replaced by those she understood: past lovers, dead fathers, failed dreams, all the things that made up a genuine life. That's what she kept telling herself as the sickness she felt did not dissipate. Lingering hell. Taste of that gray milk in her mouth. No prayer of hers seemed to summon it away. Things were different, now, and the Word fell short. Such distances between her and the god she hardly knew: a raw, nagging feeling impossible to suppress. Jan felt it within herself as she sensed it in the civilized world. Consciously abjured with pestilential devotion, as their agendas piled up like so much shit. Bleeding dry interior lives with the incorruptible fealty of a towering diadem even though they are content to survive in fetters of pride and loyalty. A pain in her gut that mounted until it had nowhere else to go: bilious foam of pitch-black destinies retching out of her tiny, grandmotherly frame. *It will get easier*, Jan decided, picking herself up off the floor and bracing herself against a wall: strength returning, with moistness in her bones, uncoiling from once lost deposits of fecund anamnesis.

THE END

FEELING SORRY FOR ASSHOLES
By Donna J. W. Munro

Lucy's mouth crusted with gems. A diamond mustache, ruby rosacea whirling on her cheeks, and nose sparking with spots of erupting wealth. Leaning toward her foggy bathroom mirror, she picked at them until one by one; they fell off, leaving bloodied pockmarks weeping in her skin.

Fucking wishes.

She dropped them all into a jar, the latest of many, filled with glittering stones. For the next hour, she filled the holes and covered the color of the erupting gems, making her face look more like a teen pizza face that humans wouldn't notice other than to sneer at. Lucy didn't mind. It kept most people from thinking nice thoughts at her.

She pulled on her dress, mindful of the lumpy scars on her shoulders. She'd had wings inked on her back, long before the current badass black-inked trend inspired by Darryl of the *Walking Dead.* Hers were there to remind her of what she'd lost.

With a deep breath, she pulled on a jacket and twisted open the front door, stepping out into the bright light of morning. Her wounds would fill with stones all day, but she couldn't sit in her house forever. She had to eat. Had to pay bills. Had to get sun on her skin and wind on her face. Once, she'd tried to stay cooped up to avoid the wishes, but the human wishes still filtered in through the cracks in her house—under the door, down the chimney. Her mowing neighbor wished good health for his ailing friend, and a ruby implanted on the corner her mouth. A mailman, with such joy in his heart and a whistle that sounded like bird song, wished so many people so much good that she developed a nest of diamonds along her jawline so big they ripped her open. She sewed the flaps back together and had her doors weather-stripped to seal some of their wishes out.

But it was unavoidable.

She did the chores she had to do around town, inching away from those folks who proclaimed their goodness with every smile and thought. Like the smiling fools with kind words on the train. And serene church ladies, who nod and spout wishes for peace and protection, and lined certain streets in town like spiritual potholes. Little children at play were the worst. Swinging on swings or from barred jungle gyms, they all wished for their own moon, swathed up in innocence and joy. Walking past a playground might cover her face, neck, and shoulders in a sparkling rainbow of mineral scales.

Fucking wishes!

She kept to the dark side of town where pure wishes usually stayed inside, behind bolted doors.

Lucy pushed open the door to her favorite bar, Snake-Eyes and Pool Cues, a greasy spot with warm food, cold beer, and a bunch of lugs so drowned in regret that their wishes were a laundry list of greed and self-serving.

Not all of them and not all the time.

Lucy always stayed away from Jack, the regular in the corner whose alcoholism didn't stop him from loving his poor abandoned kid and longing to do right by him. But the alcohol blunted his love enough that he didn't manage to make his wish into a rock. When he wished, a glittering streak might form across her cheekbone like a vein of gold in a mountain.

Most of the others only wished for themselves or for things that didn't hurt.

Besides, Snake-Eyes made a mean bowl of chili.

"Hi Lucy," he said, sliding a piping bowl in from of her when she sat at the bar. "Get you anything else?"

She shook her head and dug into the meaty stew.

Snake-Eyes or Snake as she'd come to know him, was her favorite. He wasn't bad, or good, or anything. Kind of an asshole, really. Back before she fell, she would've sought him out to repair his fractured soul. A would be project for the up and coming guardian. A perfect sociopathic puzzle with missing pieces she could find and knit together.

"How's the chili?" he asked, faking concern, though she tasted his boredom, his self-involvement.

"Delicious," she said, though she wasn't referring to the stew at all. How could he know her arched eyebrow and crooked smile had more to do with the state of his soul than the shape of his ass?

"Oh yeah?" Snake leaned in; gaze intense as he weighed her interest. His long brown hair fell across his face, shading it so all that glittered were his grinning teeth. His elbows rested on the bar and even though a couple next to her wanted his attention, he'd focused in on her. "You down tonight, doll?"

He'd tried before, not because he actually had feelings for her, but because his belt needed notching. She knew his wishes. They were all dirty as hell. Selfish. Nothing that might grow painful stones. She'd resisted so far, but...

"I'm down. When are you off?"

Snake shot a look at his waitress and back at his other bartender.

"We're slow." He hopped over the bar and strode toward

the door, not waiting for Lucy.

That part of him was missing and it felt good to her. He hopped on his Harley and pulled on his helmet, balancing his bike between his muscled thighs.

"Your place or mine?"

"Mine," Lucy said and got into her car to lead him.

* * *

The sex was good enough. Hot and hard. It left her breathless.

He lit a cigarette without asking if it was okay.

She smiled at that. So little care.

The pebbles of pain under her skin melted with his every selfish touch. The pain of eruption faded as each of the hard pocks smoothed.

"That was fun," he said and smashed his butt out on the top of a beer she'd gotten him. "I gotta go."

Lucy nodded, running fingers across her smoothed out face. "Yeah, see ya."

The pain was gone.

No stones, no nothing.

As the door shut behind Snake and she listened to his Harley roar away, she wished for the first time since that fall so long ago.

"Let this be my life."

Then she fell into a blissful, painless sleep on a clean pillow.

* * *

She couldn't stay away from Snake.

He'd become the answer to her problems, and with every hard, thrusting encounter, Lucy found healing.

They'd been at it for months. At first only a couple times a week, sometimes in the bar bathroom or on his bike, in her car or at her house, it didn't matter really. But soon he'd started coming to her every night.

"You are a drug, Lucy," he said as he rubbed his hand across her wing tattoos, first the left and then the right. "I can't get enough."

His wishes were delicious. Wishes that she'd suck him harder. Wishes for more kink. Oh, so many selfish things to want, each giving her another day's relief from the goodness that assaulted her all day long.

There hadn't been one stone since she'd started fucking him. Not one.

Tonight, he'd had her three times. Each one rougher, more exposed than the last.

The hood of her car in the parking lot under the pool of a yellow streetlight didn't even faze her.

"Why are you so cool with this? Most girls—"

"I'm not most girls."

"Yeah, but—"

"Shut up, Snake. Are we going to do it again or what?"

He pulled away from her and leaned against the silver grill of the car. He reached up and pulled her skirt back over her ass and grabbed her hand.

"Listen, Lucy, I want to tell you something…"

She adjusted her sleeves back into place and turned to face him, nerves flaring, clenching up her stomach.

"I know that there's something wrong with me. Been this way all my life." He laced his fingers in hers and tugged her down onto the asphalt next to him. His knee brushed hers as he talked. "I never cared about nothing. Not my Ma, not girlfriends, not anything. Something's missing in me that… that I wish was there."

In Lucy's soft pallet, a throb of pain stung needles up into her eyes until she was blinking out fat tears. Tears that Snake misunderstood completely.

"Aw, Lucy, I'm sorry I'm so useless. I just like you is all. More than I've ever liked anyone and…"

The skin sharpened with geometric ridges and her tongue ran across each line breaking through roof of her mouth. It was the crushing pain of a thousand brain freezes, wrapped in barbed wire, and trying to fit through a teeny, tiny hole. The gem he'd put in her, his damned first unselfish wish, struggled to be born, ripping her mouth bloody.

"I want to be with you, only I don't know how. I wish… I wish I could be good for you."

Lucy turned and started coughing, blood streaking the mucus of her mouth as she spat. She braced on all fours, jaw agape as the wish pushed out all points and edges, past her jaw, past her teeth, and onto the asphalt with a clatter.

A diamond the size of a fist.

"Don't wish anymore," Lucy said and panted until her mouth knitted back together. "Please."

Snake watched, paced, and kneeled by her, unsure what to do or say. Caring was new to him after all.

Lucy picked up the diamond and turned to face him. It had been so long since she'd finished a soul puzzle. When she'd lost her wings and fell, she gave it up. But he stood so close, worry laced in his features for the first time in his life. A little bird flying in a storm, lost.

If she gave him the stone that would make him whole, cement the wish and make it real, then she'd be giving away the only succor she'd known from pain since the time of her fall.

His wish sat in her hands, thrumming its own wish to heal him, and how could she not? How could she leave him broken?

"This is yours." Lucy put the diamond in his hands and closed his fingers tight around the edges, pressing hard until the gem opened him up and made its way into the empty spot within. He stood gape-mouthed and vacant as he reset.

Lucy turned to leave, to get away before the kind wishes began, but he came to…

"I love you, Lucy," he said. And he was whole.

Her back cracked open, though it felt like a shower of spring rain. The wings she'd lost unfurled from the tattooed ink, beautiful iridescent gem fragments as thin as mist. She lifted her face to the sun and felt the welcome waiting for her. Forgiveness. She spread her wings and—

"I love you, though," Snake said, and in his words, chips of goodness fell away.

If she left, he'd fall.

If she left, he'd shatter.

If she stayed, she'd suffer.

An angel without the presence and voice of God is a damned one, indeed.

If she left, would she still be saved?

"It's what I get," she mumbled, tugging her wings back under the sleeves of her dress, "feeling sorry for assholes. Damned."

THE END

THE BAPTISM
By Aron Beauregard

Erica had been acting more out of character by the day. When we'd first gotten the news that the baby was dead, it was devastating. It seemed to be likely and reasonable that her change in behavior stemmed from the calamity. I had never even heard of Patau Syndrome before Dr. Aguilar pointed out the telltale signs she was seeing in her scans. The fetus, Abigail as we'd named her, had been undoubtedly stricken with the rare chromosomal disorder. The news left us in shambles, venturing into the darkest corners of the mind, questioning everything.

As our conception and pregnancy advisor, it was Dr. Aguilar's duty to convey the good news as well as the mortifyingly upsetting. She tried to mitigate the grave misfortune as best she could but made it clear that there would be no happy ending. We were told there were only two options available: The first (which she strongly recommended) would be to terminate the pregnancy. Flush the limp, unresponsive sack of flesh and bone out and move forward. She didn't say it in those words of course but that's what I was picturing and I'm sure that's what Erica was picturing dispelling from her vaginal area. The second would be for Erica to walk around with our dead child in her womb for the next six weeks and deliver the ill-fated, lifeless cluster of deformities.

The choice seemed obvious to me but Erica didn't make a rash decision by any means. The first few days after the news she remained silent, her motive unknown. I just tried to stay close and support her while she contemplated her future actions. I tried to talk with her but when she offered no response I took the hint and didn't press it. I knew more than anything she needed my backing, not a surplus of stress.

I had never known her to be a religious-minded person during the span of our eight years together. Even when we had Sam, our firstborn, we never brought him to church or instilled a devout belief system around us. We respected those views, but stayed clear of inserting ourselves into them; instead, we aimed to be "good people" by the high-level definition. So, I found it quite bizarre when she confessed to me she'd begun seeking spiritual guidance by means of Saint Francis Church, a local Roman Catholic center of worship in town.

She began to spend inordinate amounts of time there, leaving Sam and I behind. Evening hours that weren't practical for a woman in her condition, yet she continued and remained vague and private about what she was doing there or the eventual endgame she was pursuing from her involvement. She'd respond to me with phrasing like "Praying for life" or "I'm going for Abigail," which to me made a little sense.

She was reaching outside of her comfort zone for help, praying for a miracle essentially. Often times when no earthly entity can solve an issue, people look for a more supernatural solution. Dr. Aguilar had already explained the grim, inflexible actuality of our circumstance. In Erica's mind it must have been too sinister, too depressing and too unfair. It's only human nature; when science or medicine cannot provide us a resolution, we then find ourselves in quest for a more extreme or irregular outside-the-box amendment.

In one aspect it was positive; her exhausted and dejected mind had found a way to swing her attitude and hope for a positive outcome. But there was no amount of positivity that was going to change the cold, hard fact that baby Abigail would miss her first birthday. She wouldn't have a first or last meal and she wouldn't meet her family. She would be plucked from a chamber of hot fluid to brandish her inhuman appearance briefly, only to be set down in a coffin so tiny it required customization. Or, alternatively, she'd be dumped into an inferno and burnt to a fine dust.

From another viewpoint, I thought Erica's budding nebulous condition could be dangerous. She'd pushed away the scientific fact that there was a dead fetus inside her, that there was zero chance Abigail would take her first breath. Instead of focusing on making the tough choice, she was postponing it. Her procrastination was the mother of my fears. I knew the possible reasons why she might be avoiding it but that didn't change the fact that ducking confrontation or hiding from our reality was unhealthy. She'd also deferred telling Sam the reality, which would be a horrible task in its own right, but stringing him along would only make releasing the news even more crushing.

Instead of facing the facts, she was building a house of cards, facilitating a facade for her child and becoming obsessed with the Holy Ghost. Blurring her mind with biblical references and remaining idle. Yesterday I'd seen her walk up to Sam and put his hand on her stomach and, knowing full well that there was nothing alive inside her, she still asked what I found to be her most disturbing question yet.

"Did you feel that, Sammy? It's your little sister kicking! She's gonna be a soccer player, I bet. What do you think?"

She sounded so sincere, as though she believed every single word of it.

"Really? I don't feel anything, Mom. Are you sure she's kicking?" Sam asked, a bit confused by her words in contrast to the reality.

"It's really gentle, sometimes you have to wait awhile before you can feel anything," she lied to him.

Her delusion was expanding and becoming increasingly more alarming. I knew I had to confront her again, I might need to press a little harder than before to get a serious reply out of her. Otherwise I knew I'd just be dotted with more bizarre phrases that weren't even really responses. They would only create more questions instead of providing answers and the exchange would only serve to drag me deeper into the quicksand. I approached her while she sat reading the Old Testament in the parlor. Sam was upstairs watching cartoons in his room so I asked her to join me for a few moments in the den. That would get us out of earshot from our son since there was no telling what sort of fantasy she might be prepared to spew out this evening.

"I know you've been really focused on prayer and celebrating Abigail, but don't you think at some point we're going to need to tell Sam what's going on? We can't just keep pretending that… that she's going to be okay." I tried to put it as gingerly as I could.

"Pretending? Who's pretending, Isaiah?" Her expression was of stone cold confusion.

"How can we move on without facing the truth?"

"The truth? What truth?"

My patience was beginning to wear thinner; she remembered what we were told. I saw the impact in her eyes, like a car wreck of flames and twisted metal all crashing down. I watch an exciting dream become mangled and malformed, before being eventually obliterated. The beauty of it all had bowed, now we were only left with the ugly. I was aware of that, she was aware of that, at least at some point.

"Do we really have to go through this again? I'll go through it for you again if you really need me to."

"Sure, you go through what you need to say, then I'll tell you what I have to say." She agreed.

"Just remember these aren't my words, they're Dr. Aguilar's. Your doctor." I felt it necessary to remind her but was doubtful it could make a difference against the caliber of false impression she'd reached.

"And what did she say? What did my doctor say?"

"Well, do you recall the discussion about the cysts on the placenta or the missing bones in Abigail's face?" I asked gently.

"Yes."

"What about the bilateral clefts and overlapping fingers and toes?"

"Of course." She responded confidently.

"Okay… and you recall Dr. Aguilar telling us that Abigail has no stomach?"

"Yes, I remember everything."

"So, you know the only child that can come out of you will be a stillborn? You understand that our daughter is dead, right?"

"Yes, right now, I understand she's dead." The words made my gut sink. A horrible feeling that she wasn't right was coming to light more profoundly than ever. Her smirk was even different than I remembered; she was nimbly walking a tightrope, teetering on psychosis. I might have left her to her own thoughts for too long during a dark time. I thought it was what she wanted but now I could see she'd filled herself with some kind of witchdoctor philosophy, clinging to impossible expectations. What could she possibly be alluding to?

"What do you mean 'right now'?"

"This is why I've been telling you to read the Bible."

I got down on one knee. It brought me back to the hot air

balloon ride we'd taken together in Egypt, when we were just young and exploring. We always both wanted to see the pyramids because we could never agree on if we thought God, man or aliens built them. As we dangled thousands of feet off the ground with the hot fire blowing upward like a furious dragon, we came to the agreement that it was probably aliens. She never believed in God…

I kissed her and dropped down in the basket, causing it to bounce a little and removed with a shaky hand the two-karat rock from my jeans. When she said yes it was the happiest day of my life. A lot of people say that as a courtesy but for me it was just the truth. I wasn't going to dress up the current affairs to appease myself, if I started lying to myself we'd be in the same boat on choppy waters with no guide. I was being honest; Erica's most recent revelation had turned an uncertain evening into the worst day of my life. I was now digesting a living a nightmare. I was now being force-fed my once stable wife's derangement on a daily basis and, with each conversation, it was only getting worse.

"Honey." I said with tears welling up in my eyes. "I don't read the Bible, and neither do you." I reminded her in a tone that was begging her to reconsider.

"I do now and if you did, you'd realize that many of the perceived limitations around us are illusions—illusions of the unenlightened. You'd learn that there's resurrection and, more importantly, life after death. If you want Abigail to be well again you need to read and believe, baby. We all have to believe, that's why I haven't told Sammy yet."

"Believe what, Erica?"

"Believe in what the prophet Elijah did for the widow in Zarephath or the Shunammite woman's son. Or when Jesus was in Capernaum and raised Jairus, the leader of the synagogue's daughter. There are so many examples. Not just of children, but of men and women as well. And you have to believe in what comes after," she explained to me, wide-eyed in way that almost made her seem like she was on something.

"Those are just stories, Erica! Don't you understand that? Outside of what you read, when have you ever seen someone come back to life? You're delusional, you can't keep doing this to us, please!" I didn't mean to yell but the swelling of emotions from weeks past had been mounting and it all came rushing out at once like a pimple eruption. She sat speechless, no longer looking at me. Now her focus had drifted back down to her stomach as she swirled her arms around her exaggerated belly.

"I can understand that you might think it's a little crazy. I can't expect you to have faith overnight but I feel in time you will. Maybe if you come and speak with Father Franklin, you'll understand it better. He's the one that set up the baptism for me this Sunday." Her newfound worship was sustaining the chaos. What the hell was happening?

"You're getting baptized?" I asked, still not believing the words coming out of my mouth.

"Not me, silly. Abigail."

"You've lost it, Erica. You've completely fucking lost it. You can't baptize a dead baby, it doesn't work that way." I unpacked it in layman terms for her, but at this point I didn't expect her to get it. A concept my five-year-old could probably grasp, but my wife couldn't, what alternative dimension had I slipped into?

"No, I found it, Isaiah! I found the power of the Holy Ghost! If the child isn't washed of his original sin then God's love will never find him. See baptism, it's like a vaccine against sin. You can understand that, can't you? You know, like how we got Sammy vaccinated at the hospital?" She spoke with a passion and fire that was convincing, if she had been delivering an argument about anything else, I might have almost believed her.

I couldn't continue the conversation any longer; there was no way to propose a second side to anything. These last few weeks had convinced her that God was going to bring Abigail back. As horrifying as the situation had become, I tried to seek solace in the fact it would all be over in a few more weeks. Once Abigail left her body, she would understand that the glob of defective cells would never walk, talk or cry. She would cry, she would be shattered but I can only hope that being faced with the comatose corpse could pull her out of this crooked line of thought. I reconsidered my exit and turned back to her.

"I'll go to the baptism with you. Just promise me you won't tell Sammy." I conceded, sacrificing my own peacefulness to keep Sammy free of the lunacy. It was the least selfish choice I could make.

"But Sammy has to go, he has to see his sister get baptized, don't you think?" Again, she seemed confused about my offer.

I tried to show her the logic as best I could; you can bring a horse to water but can't force it to drink. I thought about it, trying to be as unbiased as possible. Trying to understand Erica's mentality and what steps I could take to keep us all as safe as possible in the future. What was going to help her rebound from this morbid odyssey? I decided that the three of us being together for the duration gave us the best chance. Sammy and I would have to suck this one up for her. We needed to get Erica though this window of absurdity safely, even if it meant submitting to her outlandish request. It would all be over in another week or so, if we got past this, she would have no choice but to confront the immobile dripping red truth when it fell out of her.

"Okay, we'll go with you but after this we just stick together until Abigail arrives. Deal?"

She nodded her head with that imbalanced grin stretching the length of her face. "You're gonna see, when it happens everything will make sense." I kissed her on the forehead hearing what she said but choosing not to respond to it. The only thing I could think about was kicking Father Franklin's teeth down his fucking throat.

The next morning I called the church and asked to speak with Father Franklin. There were so many things that I wanted to say to him. Who was he to corrupt my wife's mind with these unattainable ideas? How could he help foster this dishonest optimism in our family? Was this about money? Was he trying to capitalize off our horrific tragedy? Or, the most frightening question, did he believe what he was telling her?

"Good morning and God bless, this is Saint Francis church," an older woman's voice answered and spoke through the receiver.

"I need to talk with Father Franklin please." I responded with an all business tinge to my tone.

"Father Franklin? I'm sorry, sir. We don't have a priest by that name here."

"Really? Is there another Saint Francis church in Plymouth?" I asked, my rage now morphing into confusion.

"Not that I'm aware of…" the voice answered, not quite sure how to conciliate my inquiry.

"Okay, thank you. Thank you very much then…"

I wasn't sure how to assess this most recent development. Was she lying about going to church? Maybe I misheard the priest's name or it was a different church? We'd already settled on the weird support system Sammy and I would provide her to get past the next few days. The baptism was tomorrow, her due date was the following Sunday. I was now faced with another delicate decision: confront her with what the church had told me or just play it out.

Since the baptism was tomorrow, I decided to avoid any conflict. The last thing I wanted to do was rile her up mere hours before the ceremony; it would only stir her into a more irrational frenzy and possibly pull back the curtain a little too far for Sammy. It was going to be difficult enough sitting there and explaining what was going on inside the church to a kid that just wrapped up pre-school and had never been afforded any information on Catholic beliefs.

When I awoke the next morning, before I'd even showered, I noticed that Erica was missing. I looked out the window and saw her sitting in the driver's seat of the van, just staring forward and waiting. It was still hours before the baptism but there she waited in isolation, a blank nothingness swirling on her face. I woke up Sammy and let him know it was time to get ready. I dressed both of us in moderately formal attire since I had no idea what Erica was expecting of us.

When we got into the car with her, she immediately took off with a sense of urgency. "Whoa! Honey, slow down a little. We left even earlier than expected, no one is going to be late." If it was up to me, I would have preferred to drive but she'd already solidified her position hours before I had a chance to interject the suggestion.

"I'm just excited. I'm excited for you to see our baptism."

The minor shift in her syntax bothered me. "Our baptism" were words she had not previously joined together. Was she thinking that Sammy and I were getting baptized too now? The thought made my heart pump faster. I had tried to avoid going into the particulars of the ceremony with Sammy but now I felt that could have been a mistake. Maybe it was just a slip of the tongue or metaphorical speaking that was also possible but I knew deep down it would be foolish to discount it.

The first thing I noticed was that we weren't driving into town. The buildings and concrete faded fast and were interchanged with trees and their gorgeous golden foliage. I continued to analyze the mystery internally, straining to settle on a definite outcome with any confidence. The church must have been elsewhere. That seemed to be the only reasonable explanation I could piece together. Either that or I'd seen some people get baptized outside, it was a beautiful day and that was an option I hadn't anticipated until that very instant.

I noticed we were traveling uphill. As we elevated higher, the roads and setting were starting to click; yes, I was familiar with them. At first I couldn't quite put my finger on why I remembered them, but as I looked over the guardrails that lined the road's edges, I started to remember. The cool blue ocean seawater around us, the sun shone down and reflected off the skin of the waves. As our ascension continued, it struck me, Mount Fitch, we used to come here all the time when we were kids. Our old car even had a bumper sticker that read: THIS CAR DROVE UP MOUNT FITCH!

A barrage of good times flooded back, the hikes and fishing, the camping trips and stories by the fire. It was a sweet and simple time. The imagery in my head began to feel poisoned, like a corrosive acid was bleeding all over pictures. It melted away to reveal that exact moment in time; Erica's state, dead Abigail and mixed up Sammy. I would have given anything to crawl back into my head and sit beside the glowing campfire with the Erica of old. The one I understood and had never been afraid of.

Instead I looked over at her most recent rendition that I was seated beside; the mostly mute, scatterbrained zealot. The disturbed woman that I loved, if that campfire was my hope then it had dwindled down to a flicker. But even if it were only warm ash, I would stick it out until the eleventh hour, I would never leave her behind. I had to assert myself to drag my consciousness back out of my skull again, as much as I didn't feel like it, I knew I had to.

"Erica, are we almost there, Sweetie?" I asked her with the fondness I remembered I used to ooze with.

"Just about. Do you remember when I told you that you'd understand? That I could show you how to believe?" She turned to me as if trying to project her enlightenment inside me.

"Yes," I replied anxiously.

"I need you to believe now."

As the words left her, she pressed down with her swollen bare foot onto the gas pedal. Time froze. I wanted to scream as the van busted through the chintzy old guardrail and launched into the air. I thought the thousands of feet between our vehicle and the ocean water would close quickly but it didn't. Instead, I had about a thousand thoughts flash though my mind at once. I felt the warmth of her demented, yet now, somehow angelic stare invade me.

For a moment I prayed that God's hand would stretch out from the clouds and prevent what came next. Then, suddenly, the lights came on. There was never any church or Father Franklin. Her announcement of Abigail's baptism was a swerve subtly seeded to steer me away from our scream-worthy ending. She never had any intention of reviving Abigail; it was the three of us that would be resurrected in the next realm. I'd only focused on that aspect, but when she initially spoke to me she said, "there's resurrection and *more importantly* life after death." I should have known the only possibility of us being with Abigail was after death.

She wanted to make sure we got baptized together before we broke through. Once we'd been purged of our original sin, we would make the shared sacrifice together. As the epiphany dawned, the body of the van crumpled and bonded into our vessels. The top of the roof caved in and smashed my face, part of the console ripped into my gut and I felt my stomach fall onto the car mat. My fingers had been crushed by the vehicle's warped steel and melded into larger, singular masses of glistening gore.

I couldn't turn to see Sammy or Erica, but their silence said more than any words could. I was wedged perfectly in alignment with the cracked rearview mirror. It had twisted in such a way that I was now faced with my own horrific reflection. I noticed two deep lines shredded through my top lip amongst the other facial destruction. As I listened to the salty ocean water fill up the van, the only thing I could think was that I looked a lot like Abigail.

THE END

THE FLENSED GOD
By Drew Nicks

The lonely moon of Planeta Luminus never received the light of its closest star. The only light on its rocky surface came from the reflections of the cities on the planet itself and the solitary twinkles of stars far off in the ocean of black that was the sky.

The residents of the moon were a peculiar breed. All were brothers of the Order of St. Anton, patron saint of human sacrifice and bloodshed in the name of our lord. The Order resided in the monastery constructed there by the governing body of Planeta Luminus. In the year 3165, it was decided by the original colonists of Luminus that religion would never be allowed on the planet's surface. While it was originally deemed a highly controversial decision, both the Order and the colonists agreed to this. For the last forty years, the Order had practiced in the hallowed halls of the Abbey of Antoninus. Over those years, the Order went from a militant wing of their religion with extreme fundamentalism at its core to a far more lax and understanding sect. This positive progress was attributed to the Abbot, Karl Friedrich. He had been a zealot in his youth, but as he aged and the universe around him changed, he no longer saw a need for such a harsh view of reality.

Six days prior, though the monks did not know it, a strange and powerful object had entered their orbit. The skeletal remains circled the planet and very soon its effects began to take hold.

* * *

Brother Matthias sat in the abbey's courtyard gazing up at the stars, contemplating his place in the universe. A bright student of the seminary, the Abbot had been grooming him to eventually assume the important role.

He had recently been noticing some discontent brewing among the brothers. There was discussion that the Order had drifted from their purpose and mandate; arguments over their effectiveness on an isolated moon far from the people who required them. The Abbot held a meeting to discuss this dissension. He preached loudly to the younger members of the Order, extolling to the virtues of the moderate approach he himself had instituted. Explained to them that the violence and fundamental approach had nearly torn the sect apart. He prided himself on the direction the Order had taken. His strong words seemed to abate some of the anger.

As Brother Matthias let his thoughts drift freely, he did not hear the approaching footsteps. Jostled from his contemplation, Matthias saw the face of Brother Gregory. The look he wore was ashen gray and riddled with concern.

"Brother Gregory," said Matthias. "What bothers you?"

Brother Gregory was taciturn. His gray hair was unwashed and unkempt. The wrinkles in his face were deep set like trenches in the French countryside. His bushy eyebrows resembled gray caterpillars.

"Brother Luke claims he spoke with God himself last night."

Matthias jumped from his position. This was not a good

thing. Brother Luke was the Abbot's strongest opposition and had developed a large following with the younger members of the Order.

"Where?" asked Matthias. "Where and when did he speak with God?"

Brother Gregory sighed and wiped sweaty palms on the front of his robes.

"Last night. Last night in his dreams. He said that God demands we return to the old ways. Said God demands a sacrifice."

"Brother Luke has probably been indulging in too much of the communion wine," Brother Matthias said, mostly to convince himself.

"For some reason, I doubt it."

The two monks stood sullenly in the muted light of Luminus. They both knew, regardless of the truth of Brother Luke's claims, this would need to be discussed with the Abbot.

Karl Friedrich had grown very frail over the last six months. Now, unless it was a blessing or necessary speech to the gathered brotherhood, he mostly kept to his chambers. Matthias looked longingly to the stars again before the two monks turned and entered the hallowed halls of the Abbey of Antoninus.

Inside, the main chamber of the Abbey twinkled magnificently from the autocandles held high in the chandelier. Shadows danced in darkened alcoves and beneath the cornices and groins of the vaulted ceiling. The chamber smelled of incense, tobacco, and tension. Murals of St. Anton adorned the walls in lifelike detail. His brown hair, shaved into a tonsure with a machete the legends say, gleamed from the sweat of his devotion. The flensing blade in his right hand seemed to shimmer with the will of God.

Matthias immediately noticed the contingent of young monks seated around the long "wooden" table in the center of the room. Brother Luke sat at the head. Iciness radiated from his form.

"Hello Matthias," said Luke. "I see you came with your reinforcements."

Matthias managed a weak smile and looked to his right. Gregory was not there. He looked to his left. Gregory had disappeared. Now, realizing he was alone, Matthias stood tall.

"God is the only reinforcement I need."

A cacophonous laugh rose around the table.

"Which god, Matthias?"

"The one true God!"

Laughter again filled the room. It was cut short with a sharp look from Brother Luke.

"Oh Matthias, you've been so blinded by the teachings of that old fool. His days will soon be numbered though and we will be able to return to the original teachings of St. Anton. Don't you agree, brother?"

Matthias did not reply. He turned defiantly and strode off down the hall leading towards personal quarters. The mocking words of Luke followed him:

"I've seen and spoken with God, Matthias. You soon will too, whether you wish to or not."

Matthias continued down the corridor. On either side he was flanked by rows of unassuming oak-like doors. Each door had a plaque affixed to it. Each plaque bore a number. This was how the monks were known to the register. Matthias had always been troubled by this. He was of the belief that if one wanted to be personable with his underlings it was wise to always record them by name. Let them know they and their opinions matter.

Matthias stopped in front of the large set of double doors leading to the Abbot's chambers. He hesitated; hand on the knob, and thought of the best way to break this troubling news to the elderly man. He had always respected the Abbot but didn't necessarily agree with his methodology. This, and the revolution that brewed like a pot of overflowing coffee, troubled the young monk, who still had much to learn, to his very core. He knocked gently.

"Enter."

The Abbot's voice was barely audible and much labored.

Matthias pushed lightly and entered the main chamber. The room was filled with autocandles, flickering delicately and casting the scent of frankincense into the air. The high ceiling was covered with immaculate frescoes of the life of St. Anton. From his victories over the nation of Vidkun, to his martyrdom at the hands of Unologists, it was all there for the people to behold. The man on the bed was dwarfed by his surroundings. Once, Karl Friedrich had been a mighty and powerful man. Now, the ravages of age had taken their toll. The hollow creature before Matthias was but a shadow of his former glory. He looked up with sunken and dark eyes at his disciple.

"Matthias," said the Abbot, shock displayed across his shriveled features. "What troubles your soul?"

Matthias was torn. His mind twisted this way and that. He feared his news might kill the Abbot in his already frail condition. He knew he could not lie about something of this magnitude.

"Brother Luke claims he spoke with God last night. I'm not sure I believe him, but it troubles me all the same."

The Abbot wheezed, a thick, wet sound filling his windpipe.

"So it builds. The strong smell the weak and jump at the chance to exploit their problems."

Matthias looked to the floor, shame spreading across his face.

"Matthias, you know my time is drawing to a rapid close. My body aches and shakes. I simply can't breathe like I once could."

Matthias looked up at the Abbot, his expression a mix of wonder and fear.

"Soon, very soon indeed, you'll need to take my

position. You're the only one I trust to lead this Order. If you don't stand tall against Brother Luke, we could lose this Order. When your followers show dissent, you must stand up to them. You must show them who is in charge. That is the one thing I must give St. Anton. He fiercely ensured his followers only followed his teachings or they were swiftly excommunicated."

"I understand," replied Matthias. "But I'm not certain this is a war I can win. Brother Luke's followers are devoted to him and it would take much to sway them in my favor."

The Abbot laughed dryly, which turned into a hacking cough.

"You must try, Matthias. I will aid you the best I can. I trust you and this is why I chose you. We cannot allow our Order to fall victim to infighting. I grow weary. Come back when you know more."

"I will. Rest easy, sir."

Before Matthias left the Abbot's chamber, he heard the older man softly snoring. He crept out silently as a cat and reflected where the future was leading him.

* * *

Matthias went to bed that evening with a heavy heart. Luke's assembled throngs seemed nearly insurmountable. He was a man of resolve though. His years in the seminary had revealed what sort of man he wished to be.

He lay down on the firm bed and rested his head on the extra firm pillow. Firm beds were the norm for all brothers of the Order. It was believed that rigidity would lead to penance. As Matthias shut his eyes, a scream sliced through the halls of the silent Abbey. He jumped to his feet and ran for the door. Opening it wide, he peered out. Brother Gregory stood in the darkened hallway, gazing off in the direction of the scream.

"What is it, Gregory?" asked Matthias.

"I don't know, but it can't be good."

Matthias joined him in the hall and the two walked off into the sweeping darkness.

* * *

Above the moon, the remains shimmered a strange shade of yellow. Though sound does not travel in the cosmos, one could almost hear an imperceptible hum.

Brothers Matthias and Gregory halted behind the massed group in the hall. The monks were collected, fifteen persons deep, from the chamber. From the location and the murmurs, Matthias knew it was the Abbot's chamber.

Immediacy overtook Matthias and he began to push his way through the wall of bodies. The going was slow. Shock and horror seemed to root his fellow men like stubborn weeds. He did not blame them, but it made what he knew to be true that much harder to see with his own eyes.

Emerging from the human wall, he stood in the dim light of the autocandles. Brother Luke's followers had taken on the role of investigators. Matthias was not surprised. Two heavyset brothers flanked the door. When he attempted to enter, the brother on the right pushed him away. Matthias recognized him as Brother Andrew.

"Let me pass," Matthias said.

Andrew pushed him again, stronger this time.

"No one is allowed to enter, on Brother Luke's orders."

Matthias stood dumbfounded.

"I am second in command after the Abbot!"

A fiendish grin passed across Andrew's face.

"Not according to Brother Luke, especially if you are the one responsible for this."

Just then, the chamber door opened and another monk emerged. Matthias took his chance. He pushed past the guards and newly emerged man. The scene he walked into was straight from The Inferno. The walls and floor were coated in blood and viscera. The murals and frescoes were more colorful, almost as though the blood made them richer. The mutilated body lay on the crimson soaked sheets. The body's lidless eyes gazed out with terror on its surroundings. The flayed skin lay in a shapeless heap on the floor.

"Who let him in here?"

Matthias looked away from the body of his former superior to the accusatory voice. Brother Luke stood, confidently flanked by three of his closest cohorts. His robe was stained a deep red and his cold eyes stared harshly at Matthias. With a wave of his hands, Luke's brothers in arms had Matthias restrained. He started with a sharp tone:

"I'm placing you under arrest according to the rules of the Order."

"Why me?" asked Matthias.

A malicious smile crept across Brother Luke's face.

"Why? You murdered our beloved Abbot!"

"Murdered? It wasn't me! Do you see blood on my vestments?"

"You clearly changed into other vestments. You were also the last to see him alive. Brother Gregory saw you leaving this chamber at midnight."

Matthias scoffed. He had not seen Gregory, nor thought he would ever be betrayed by him.

"Take him from here."

Matthias hung his head in shame as he was led away. He knew Brother Luke was responsible for this horrendous act, yet he also knew there was no way to tie him to it. Matthias' allies were few and far between and those he did have were unlikely to provide support. The winds of change had taken hold.

* * *

In orbit, the remains shifted their kaleidoscope of colors to a vivid crimson. If one were to observe them closely, a shudder could be seen coursing through the unconnected parts.

* * *

Matthias sat in his cold and isolated cell. The skylight, the "eye of god" as the brothers called it, shone a shade of ghastly red upon the lithe monk.

How had this happened, he asked himself.

He supposed he should have seen it coming. He was just wishing he had had more time. More time for everything. More time to learn from the Abbot and truly appreciate his valuable teachings and knowledge. More time to study whom amongst the Order would have been important allies.

Alas, those times were gone and would never come again. Matthias was alone on this rocky sphere without a friend in his corner. He knew his penance would not come from his own hands.

Suddenly, Matthias heard the key unlocking the heavy wooden door. Aged hasps groaned like an elderly man preparing to stand and he stood tall. He would not allow Brother Luke or any of his foul breed see him grovel and ask for forgiveness. When Gregory entered the dank cell, Matthias was mildly surprised. Deep crimson washed over the older monk with a sense of realization.

"What is it you want, Gregory?" Matthias asked sharply.

"I wish you would just confess. I know you didn't do it, but they need someone to pin this on. They need a scapegoat."

"Well they won't get it from me! I have faithfully served the Abbot and the Order ever since I joined. I refuse to take the fall for a crime I did not commit. And who are you to tell me to take the fall? You helped them frame me!"

A look of shame crossed Brother Gregory's face, before a grimace of anger took over. He stepped forward and slapped Matthias, hard, across the face. He followed this with a well-aimed spit in the younger monk's face. Matthias stood in silence solemnly.

"You wait, Matthias. Things are changing. They plan on crucifying you in the morning. You just wait."

With that, Brother Gregory left, shutting the door forcefully and locking it behind him.

Yes, Matthias thought, *things are changing.*

* * *

Matthias slept fitfully that night. He tossed and turned on the stone platform that served as a bed. Terrible nightmares plagued his sleeping mind. Visions of blood and flaying. Visions of violence. Visions of innocence lost.

When he awoke in the morning, the halls of the monastery were silent and cold as the stone they were erected from. With bleary eyes, he looked about his confines. The four stone walls remained and everything else seemed the same until he looked closer. The light from the "eye of god" had changed to a decayed green, and a large pool of blood seeped beneath his cell door. He approached the heavy oak-like doors and the stench of death assailed his nostrils. He pushed the door and, in response, it swung open freely towards him. Matthias stepped into the hall.

Four brothers lay in the hall, unidentifiable by their torn and shorn bodies. Matthias moved on.

Bodies lay everywhere in the monastery. It appeared to him that all had been skinned alive. He moved on.

He went to the Abbot's quarters, opened the door and sat cross-legged before the mural of St. Anton. He gazed into the saint's unfearing eyes and began to weep. The last man on an isolated moon.

* * *

The shape orbiting the moon drifted away from its

position. Its shade had changed again. It drifted off as a sky blue.

THE END

FELLOWSHIP
By Henry Snider

Melinda stared out the Dodge's window at the blur of trees. The Maine foliage banked the two-lane road, adding to the claustrophobic feeling overpowering her all day. She longed for the next town for, if nothing else, the open feeling that expanse of yards would give. Overhead, thunder rippled.

"It's going to rain," she said flatly and looked over at her husband.

Jason remained his stoic self and tightened his grip on the steering wheel.

"Jason."

"I heard you. It's going to rain." He waived an arm, coming just short of putting a finger in her eye. "Of course it's going to rain. It's Maine. It always rains in Maine."

Melinda returned to her lack of a scenic view. "The...rain in Maine stays mainly on–"

"Us," he cut in.

A laugh escaped her in the form of a decidedly unladylike snort which sent them both into hysterics. Their rental car drifted over the ever-unending solid yellow line and into the oncoming lane.

"Better straighten it out, before we get creamed."

Jason let the car drift all the way across the line. "Creamed?"

"Yes," she said, her giggle fit subsiding. "Creamed. As in greasy yellow corn."

A blind curve banked to the left and the Dodge took it at better than fifty, still on the wrong side of the road. "We've seen one car in the last fifteen minutes, and that was a tractor." They pulled out of the curve and eased back into the proper lane. "Besides, this is unspoiled territory. No other salesmen have been up here. From what I hear, that goes for the competition too."

"Now that I can believe." Melinda shifted her gaze to the long stretch of road before them and to the gray churning mass above. "I mean there's nothing up here and if we keep going like we have been, we'll end up in Canada."

"What's wrong with Canada?"

"French Canada to be exact."

"Do I get to make a froggy joke?"

"Up here?" She shoved Jason lightly, sending the car back over the line. "You're likely to get your head clubbed. Besides, I bet you can see into Canada if you stood on the rooftops."

Their radar detector blipped and Jason instinctively slowed. A muddy set of ruts came into view on the right side of the road, leading into the veritable wall of trees and dense foliage. As a mid-nineties sedan, complete with light bar came into view, the detector fired, sounding off an electronic woodpecker tone.

"Shit," Jason muttered.

Melinda craned her neck to watch the state trooper pull out onto the road behind them, a spray of mud arcing off the rear wheels. The patrol car flew up and began to pace, keeping back about a hundred feet. She watched the silhouetted figure shift back and forth. A drizzle started, distorting what little could be see of the officer. The misshapen form shifted again, appearing as more of a bulbous mass than a person.

"Better hide the pot," Melinda quipped.

"Ha...ha...ha."

The spatter of rain ended as they crested the next hill, though low rolling clouds still threatened to release their burden. Lights flared red and blue in the rear-view mirror, adding an artificial splash of color to the muted countryside. Jason looked to the side of the road. A dip led to ten feet of wet grassy mud that served as a soft shoulder. Visibly gritting his teeth, he pulled the Dodge off of the pavement. Both passenger side wheels were off the road when a horn blared.

"Back on the road," came from the patrol car's speaker. "Pull the car back on the pavement and stop."

Jason pulled the wheel to the left and felt the right front tire sink and catch. A sickening grinding sound thrummed as the undercarriage rubbed against asphalt. They lurched forward, caught by their seat belts, as the car jerked to a stop.

"Shit," Jason muttered a second time.

Melinda opened the glove box and rifled through the maps and cluster of suckers she'd wedged in there the day before.

A tap at the window grabbed their attention. The officer, a stern-faced woman Jason's father would have called 'handsome,' motioned for him to roll the window down.

"Put it in park," Officer Hoskel, according to the name tag, said.

"Yes sir...er, ma'am."

Melinda watched the officer smirk.

"License. Registration."

"I'm getting it," Melinda said as pleasantly as she could muster. "Just a sec."

"Are you two enjoying our fine state?"

Jason looked up at the officer, trying not to fixate on the hat's rain guard, which looked amazingly like an oversized shower cap. "How did you know we were visiting?"

Officer Hoskel leaned over, resting her forearm on the car's roof. "Two things. The rental car sticker on the bumper. We don't see too many rental cars up this way. Where'd you get this one? Bangor?"

Jason stammered, "uh...yeah."

"Ma'am, don't worry about finding the registration. I'm sure you have all the proper documentation." She shifted her stance, stretching to the point that several audible pops echoed from her back. "The reason I pulled you over was a simple spot check. You were a few miles over the posted limit."

Melinda leaned over so she could still see the officer's face. "No ticket?"

"No ticket...unless you want one."

Jason answered quickly, "No, that's okay."

"Hop in the back of my cruiser and we'll get you up into Fellowship for a tow truck."

The couple grabbed their carry-ons from their trunk, deposited them into the officer's and climbed into the back of the patrol car. Climbing in, Melinda noticed that the hard plastic seat had strange depressions in the backrest.

"It's for suspects' cuffed hands and arms—so we can still seatbelt them," Officer Hoskel offered before being asked.

"Looks uncomfortable."

"The seat is, but it's safe and that's what counts these days."

They got into the patrol car and buckled up. As Officer Hoskel pulled away from the Dodge, Melinda asked, "What was the other reason?"

"Hmmm?"

"You said there were two reasons you knew we were visiting the state. What was the other one?" Jason elbowed her and gave his animated 'shut up' expression.

"Oh, that was the dead giveaway. You pulled onto the shoulder. Locals just stop. Mainers stop or put on a signal and just drive up to the nearest road or dry patch."

"So I'm an idiot," Jason said.

"So you're an idiot," Officer Hoskel confirmed, bringing a Cheshire cat grin from Melinda.

The next ten minutes were met with relative silence. Jason glowered, Melinda returned to her staring out the window, and Officer Hoskel relayed what happened to the dispatcher. The patrol car slipped past a massive moose carcass lying in the middle of the road. They rounded another bend and were suddenly in a little hamlet of a town. A dazzlingly white sign, FELLOWSHIP: CLOSER TO GOD THAN THEE, announced their entering the town proper. The patrol car slowed a hundred yards short of the sign and turned into the only visible gas station.

"Not exactly a friendly welcome sign," Melinda said.

"I'm afraid it's not exactly a friendly town." She pulled into a single-bay gas station and got out. Rain started to fall again.

The door on Jason's side opened to reveal the typical jump suited mechanic. "Keys," the man said flatly. Jason fished the single electronic key and handed it over. "Two hours. Stay here," and then he was gone, climbing into the tow truck's cab and driving off. A wake of blue smoke hung heavy as testament to the attendant's mechanical skills.

"Kebler," Officer Hoskel yelled, "on the state's tab. Don't burn 'em." She turned and opened first Melinda's door, then Jason's.

Melinda took in the anti-Rockwellian station. Blue paint, now marred by palm sized patches of rust spattered across the 'Tommy's Trucks n' Such' sign painted above the picture windows. The street contained no children playing stickball, no bicyclists making their way to or from a favorite watering hole. The closest thing to humanity, aside from their benefactor, was the incessant shrieking of a baby somewhere down the street. The wind blew through the summer leaves and flashed her memory to their two nights in Bar Harbor earlier that week. This sound matched in pitch and volume, though still lacked the intensity of the water crashing against the rocks.

Jason's arm slid around her waist. "Quite a view, isn't it?"

"Yeah," she leaned into him. "Almost feels like the end of the earth."

Officer Hoskel called out from the back of the car, "Not the end of the earth, ma'am. That's about five miles up the road. At least that's what the locals say." She stood, hoisting the couple's two bags out and setting them to the side before slamming the trunk. "Might want to just wait it out here. It's Sunday so you're not going to find anything open."

Melinda looked over her shoulder, "Why not? We did everywhere else...even over in Skowhegan."

"This isn't Skowhegan. No tourists, and as of a couple of years back, no mill either. You never did say what you were doing up hereabouts."

"Work," Jason said simply and turned to the officer.

"Up here? There's no work up here." Officer Hoskel's friendly demeanor shifted into an official tone.

Melinda turned to join the conversation, smiling. "He's in sales. Incorporating business websites for towns and villages. New territory here."

Hoskel looked down the street "…be a short list here. Seems hardly worth your gas."

"It's the residuals once the sites are built. That's how I make my income."

"Mmmmhmmmm," was all the officer offered.

Jason pressed, "Is there a place here where we can get something to eat?"

"About a half mile up on the left is a restaurant. Doubt they're open." She opened her car door and climbed inside.

"Best of luck to you."

"Um, miss," Melinda stammered. "Do you think we could get a lift?"

"For a five minute walk?"

"I mean, the mechanic's gone and it's about to rain." Two large drops landed noisily onto the roof of the car, offering nature's version of a rim-shot.

"Nope. Town ordinances keep me from going past that sign we passed...officially. Nothing much up here anyway." She tipped her hat. "They'll probably still complain that I came as far as the gas station. Have to pull that moose off the road. Got you here. Got you help." She grabbed the door. "I'll be back to check on you in an hour or so. Best I can offer. I'd head somewhere else to stay the night, though."

"Why's that?"

"No hotel in Fellowship." The door slammed and Officer Hoskel's car pulled away.

Jason turned to his wife. "So," he said, placing his fists on his hips, "Captain Screwup has done his duty and now the trusty sidekick will be driving them back down the lonely highway sooner than she anticipated. Tune in tomorrow when...."

She jabbed him in the stomach. "Quit it."

Another drop landed in a puddle by the gas pumps.

Melinda grabbed her shoulder bag and passed him the computer backpack she'd gotten him for the trip. The red stripe down the side reflected sharply even in the cloudy afternoon light. She couldn't help but to notice that aside from the neon 'OPEN' sign and the pack's stripe, no colors stood out, giving everything before them a muted sense of reality. Red brickwork framing the store had a brown tinge. The red and white striped barber pole mounted above a mailbox down the street had the faded look of an old instamatic photo. Down the road she took in the various driveways and parking spots for the township. No, not a township, a–

"Hamlet," she muttered.

"This, above all," Jason bellowed, "to thine own self be true."

Melinda fought back a smile as she fired another jab to her husband's gut. He doubled over, catching her hand and held it against his stomach.

"O," he continued, "what a rogue and peasant slave am I!"

A devilish grin escaped her and she pressed forward, grabbing the front of Jason's trousers, fingers slipping inside the waistband. His smile matched hers until she jerked the hand up, bringing with it his underwear's waistband. An initial look of shock shifted into an exaggerated expression of discomfort.

"I must be cruel," she said, falling into his Shakespearean platitudes, "only to be kind."

Before he could retaliate, as playful couples tend to do, she set out walking past the town limits sign and into what served as the business portion of Fellowship; Jason caught up after repairing his forced wardrobe malfunction. They passed rotted doors hiding the volunteer fire department's truck. Flaking paint revealed weathered wood bleached light gray with age. Curled shingles gave, to her painter's eye, the impression of birds mid-flight. Another short volley of drops splattered across the road and grass, missing them by scant feet.

"Jesus," Jason barked, "is it going to rain or what?" Just as the genie granted Aladdin's wish, the skies opened up, releasing a torrential downpour onto them.

Plodding steps fell into a quarter-step beat as they ran the remainder of the distance to the gravel parking lot of Jenny's Diner. Melinda grabbed onto the glass door's handle and pulled. The door opened and they pushed into the cinder block restaurant. A dozen pairs of eyes looked at them from around the room. *Well*, Melinda corrected herself, *eleven pairs of eyes and one thirty-ish woman with an eye patch who stood in the corner with a Bible.* Overhead, the fluorescents were off and what little light illuminated the eatery came from the storefront's windows.

"Sorry," Jason said to the group, which continued to stare, unmoving, at them. "We'll just seat ourselves." He looked at his wife and nodded over to an open corner booth. They dropped their bags and slid onto the vinyl benches. Water sluiced off their clothing and spread a widened pool on the seats. "Mel, what do you want?"

"Huh?" She couldn't stop returning the stares of the restaurant's patrons.

"Lunch. We're here. We might as well eat."

"I…" Melinda shook uncontrollably. "What do they have?"

"I don't know. What do want?" He leaned back and looked at their audience. "Guess we're celebrities here, huh."

"Guess so," she shifted and stared down at the table.

"Hey," Jason called out to the one-eyed employee, "could we get a little service here?"

No one moved.

"Jason!" Melinda hissed his name.

"It's okay," he chided, "*I'll* get the menus." He got up and grabbed two laminated sheets from beside the fifties-era register. "Thank you *so* much for your assistance. I...*see* you're busy."

Melinda felt herself blushing at Jason's digs at the waitress. "Stop it." She took the menu from him and watched as he slid back into his seat, brushing away the pooled rainwater as he did so. A rip in her seat had sucked much of her puddled water away. Glaring over the menu, she willed her husband to return the gaze and, a handful of heartbeats later, he did. An unspoken conversation ensued.

Stop it.
What did I do?
Stop it now.
They're being rude.

Stop being an ass or I'm leaving right now.

Okay. Okay. Jason gave an exaggerated eye roll after acquiescing to her demands.

Melinda raised her hand to the woman, who, now a couple of minutes later, hadn't moved. "Um, miss?"

The waitress remained immobile, save that of breathing and blinking.

"Could we get a couple of waters?"

A cook looked out from the kitchen and said, "Water's the last thing we-"

"Jason," she hissed a second time.

Jason avoided returning the look only a seasoned wife is able to give. Instead, he produced a broad smile and said, "Water sounds great!" He shifted in his seat, opened the multimedia backpack and began rifling through it searching for, what Melinda assumed, was a little bit of dignity after his childish display. He produced his notebook computer and placed it lovingly on the table before returning to rooting around in the bag's various zippered pockets. She watched his neck flush deep red, as his actions yielded nothing of substance before turning her attention to the slowly approaching waitress. The patch over her right eye masked the connecting point of two deep slashes, one horizontal ending at brow and the bridge of her nose while the vertical one began within a forehead crease, parted plucked and arched trail of hair and continued down to her chin before ending at a point. At her cheekbone, the scar split the skin deep, leaving a visible seam where scar met healthy flesh.

"No water," the waitress said.

Melinda leaned back and looked at the patrons. No water glasses adorned their tables either...no food for that matter. "I don't...ohhhh, the rain. Did it cut power?" She offered the woman a friendly smile. "I just noticed the lights aren't on."

Jason looked up at her. "How about a Coke?"

"No Coke." She continued looking at Melinda.

Melinda tried, "Do you have a special?"

"No specials. No Cokes. No nothin'." The waitress raised her Bible. "Today's Sunday."

"I don't understand, ummm," Melinda made the 'c'mon, please tell me your name' motion with her hands.

"Julia."

"I don't understand, Julia." Melinda tried to sound polite, but even she was getting short tempered with the waitress. "I mean, I understand it's Sunday, but why are you open if you're not going to serve anyone?"

"Missy," an old codger sporting what looked to be an even older pair of coveralls spoke up, "we've been here since sundown yesterday. We'll be here til' sunup tomorrow."

"Amen," a family of four said, each parent clutching one of two twin boys. The boys looked dirty and tired, dark circles under the eyes visible even in the limited light.

"It's the Lord's day," a woman, primed to have been a circus fat lady in a 1930's circus, chimed in. "You can't partake of anything on the Lord's day." Her words took on a scolding tone, as if a parent speaking to a child. She gripped her own Bible in a sausage-fingered death grip. "You...you should *know* that."

It was then that Melinda noticed the smell. While the waitress' clothes were clean and pressed, her exposed skin had a telltale mottling left for the unwashed masses. Smells of sweat and other distinctly feminine odors wafted across the booth. She locked eyes with Jason and knew he'd made the same odoriferous discovery.

God's personal fat lady glowered at the notebook computer sitting on the table and continued, "On the Lord's day, His children don't work, don't partake of the garden's fruit and don't partake of man's bounty."

Jason couldn't suppress a chuckle, "What about Soft n' Gentle?" He grinned at the blatant laundry quip.

Shocked and angry expressions marred the shadowed

patrons.

The obese woman jabbed a digit at the couple, "Do not mock the Lord!"

The waitress now stood glassy eyed, staring out the window. A tear escaped the patch and trailed down her puckered scar. "You should pray," she mouthed more than said, only visible to the couple.

"Tell them," the fat woman bellowed.

Melinda and Jason watched the waitress shake uncontrollably, then raise her right hand to her patch. "If thine eye offends thee…" She pulled the swatch of fabric back, exposing slit lids covering nothing but wet pink tissue. As the waitress blinked the scarred lids puckered, pinching a touch of what looked surprisingly like chewed bubble gum, between eyelashes.

"We're sorry," Jason said with a level of decorum that, to Melinda's knowledge, he'd never before possessed. While still staring with morbid fascination at the remains of the waitress' eye, he pushed himself to the edge of the bench and stood. "We didn't mean any disrespect. We'll just be going."

Their waitress grabbed him by a shoulder. "You can't leave. It's the Lord's day!"

"Lady," Jason's temper began to flare, "we just came from out there." He shook off the waitress' grasp.

"The Lord," the fat woman said, "brought you into our garden. Be not the sinner." A volley of amens echoed throughout the eatery.

"Mel, let's get back to the car." He pointed to his computer. "Put it away, will you."

Melinda lifted her husband's lifeline to civilization and reached over to grab his backpack. Something smashed into her hand and the computer fell to the table, a starburst crack in the top of the plastic housing. A napkin dispenser clattered to a stop beside their property, its contents fanning out onto the table. The patrons stood as one and grasped things within reach—another napkin dispenser, two plates, glass saltshaker and a butter knife. She looked to Jason, who stood between her and the group. His shoulders squared like before a wrestling match back in college.

"Mel," he repeated, "let's go."

"Sinners," the father of the two boys said. "You defile the Sabbath." He stood, skeletal frame rising well over six feet. "We know how to deal with sinners."

Jason turned to Melinda, then, without warning, grabbed the computer and hurled it like a discus at the father. The wedge of plastic and electronics struck the fanatic just under the nose, separating him from his front teeth in a spray of blood worthy of any slasher film. Customers, along with the waitress, Julia, and fat lady, directed all attention to their fallen comrade. Melinda scooted out of the booth and Jason jerked her by the wrist and pulled her out the door and into the thinning rain. Four men and a rather homely woman walked while watching them intently, all showing the soaked telltale signs of having walked to this destination.

The oldest of the clutch, eighty if he was a day, spoke up. "You all new in town?"

Melinda gritted her teeth against the vice grip Jason had on her forearm. "Just leaving," she managed to call out before being guided onto the road's shoulder.

"You two should stay for evening services."

Jason stopped cold, jerking Melinda's attention before them rather than to the group in the parking lot. Better than forty people stood in the road, or alongside it, framing their path back to Tommy's station. Many of Fellowship's population carried different items clutched in their hands, just as those in the restaurant did, though a few of these were more menacing. She counted five young men casually holding onto hayforks.

Melinda rasped through clenched teeth, "What do we do?"

"We go the other way, and if they follow, we duck into the woods on the far side of the road."

She looked to her left at the wall of foliage. No break in the undergrowth offered entrance to the woods, much less a visible means to escape a town full of Jesus freaks. Then a dark patch caught her attention—a depression in the leafy barrier with a muddy patch of standing water carpeting the area.

"Got it," she said, her pulse beating rabbit-fast.

Jason turned to the old man in the parking lot just as the fat woman emerged from the church. "Where's the service being held?"

"Don't you even speak to them, Ezekiel! Their evil ways smote Michael!"

"Smote," Jason said, "doesn't that mean 'kill?'" His hands started shaking uncontrollably. "I...I didn't kill anyone!"

A thunderclap ripped through the sky overhead followed by a deluge of water. Melinda pulled free of Jason and ran for the tree line. She plowed into the standing water and trudged into the forest's access. The shower's roar deafened her to any sign of Jason's, or anyone else's, pursuit. Sneakers filled with runoff, muddy sludge soaking into her socks with each step. Further she plowed, branches raking across her face and shirt, tearing fabric and drawing blood. Dozens of steps passed, and then suddenly the undergrowth thinned, held at bay by the carpet of pine needles blanketing the ground. She stumbled, then a hand grabbed her forearm, jerking her back to her feet. A scream escaped her.

"Shhh," Jason said. "Keep moving! They're right behind us!"

Melinda fell into step behind her husband, content to let him lead after her experience with getting into Fellowship's woods. Ten steps became twenty—twenty became forty— after seventy she lost count in an effort to keep up with Jason. Behind them, an occasional call echoed out over the rain's din, sometimes far away—but never far enough. They stopped to catch their breath, which came to both in great heaves.

Melinda spoke up, gulping air before each word. "We...should...circle...back."

"We can't," he whined.

She stared at him in disbelief. He actually whined.

"They said I killed him." Jason dropped to his knees before falling onto his side. He grasped a handful of muddy needles in his right hand, letting fingertips burrow into the soft soil.

Melinda looked down at the man she married, unsure how to deal with this broken representation of the dreamer she loved. After a moment of watching him, she knelt, "You didn't mean it. We both thought that guy was getting up to hurt us. You did what you had to...to keep us safe. But," she put a hand on his hip, "you need to get up. We need to circle around and get our car."

Jason sat bolt upright. "No."

"Honey–"

"No." He turned to her and grasped her still outstretched hand in his muddy grasp. "That's what they're expecting. We need to continue north." He pushed himself to his feet using her as balance. "We'll come back after dark."

"What we need is to call the police."

"With what?" he spat. "The cell phones haven't worked for the past hour. Do you really think that one of those nut jobs is going to let us use their phone? They want blood, Mel. My blood." He looked into her eyes, "Yours too."

"Jason–"

Another call echoed, closer than before.

"C'mon."

Melinda pulled free of his hands and brushed the soil on her jeans. She sighed and waived him on, following close behind.

They continued in what they hoped to be a northerly direction, but with the dense trees it was hard to tell anything beyond the fact that it was slightly brighter to their left on such a cloudy day. *Evening light on the left meant they were going north, right?* She pondered this as the growth thickened once more.

A river? A road maybe?

Suddenly Jason wasn't in front of her and nature's roar grew in intensity. She stumbled, right foot slipping on mud worthy of a pigpen. Arms pinwheeled and she lost her balance, tumbling down the hill in a nursery rhyme parody of *Jack and Jill.* An icy splash of water broke the fall and her senses went from a vertigo-strewn fall into an uncontrollable spin in the water. Facedown, she fought to right herself. Foam splashed up, filling her open mouth and stealing what little air she'd managed to hang onto. Melinda splashed her hands down in an attempt to get her head above water. Her body slowed and pulled against the current. *I'm hung up*, she thought. She splashed a second time, drawing in a lungful of air before sinking once more. Foreign fingers tangled in her hair and with a root-ripping jerk, she was pulled onto a rock by Jason.

While vomiting and coughing helped clear the water Melinda had taken in, it didn't help the overwhelming sense she was going to choke to death any second. No clear lungful of air could be gotten at any cost. She lay on her back, legs still in the icy river and stared at the sky. The rain continued with a steady serving of water. Jason lay beside her, his own expulsions more evident than hers with white residue both on the rock and down the front of his polo shirt.

"There they are!"

Instinct took over and they pulled themselves the rest of the way out of the water, numb legs slowly responding to commands given them. Jason stopped her and stared back across the river. "They can't get to us." He pointed excitedly. "Look, Mel!"

Melinda stared at the boulder-strewn waterway. A clutch of seven townspeople stood at the far bank's edge, fifteen feet away.

"Murderers!"

"Sinners!" cried another.

Jason stood and yelled back at the overall-wearing old man they'd seen in the restaurant, "You started it! You hurled–"

A baseball sized rock thwapped right beside Melinda's leg.

"Stone them!"

"Jesus," Jason said, unintentionally infuriating their religious pursuers.

Melinda stood beside him. "We've gotta go!"

One man carrying a hayfork, younger than the others, took a running jump at the river. His legs pistoned through the air as he crossed the majority of the distance before crashing chest-deep into the river. As the man landed, he stabbed his fork into the water, using it to gain better purchase. A volley of rocks flew from the far side of the river, showering all around Jason and Melinda.

Jason grabbed a stone of his own and hurled it side-armed at the wading aggressor. It arced high and, to the surprise of everyone, struck the man in the collarbone, knocking him off balance and into a heavier part of the river's current. The river whipped his flailing form as it shot out of sight. He bobbed like a cork as he disappeared from sight.

"They're trying to kill Ethan!" Julia, the waitress from the restaurant, screamed.

Melinda yelled, "You crazy bastards! You're trying to *kill us*. What did you expect?" She backed up further on the bank, careful not to catch her foot in one of the ankle-breaking holes boulders left. Her husband followed, scooping up two more rocks as he went. They watched, warily, as the old man said something to the group and pointed up river. Their gaze followed his and Melinda felt a sinking feeling in the pit of her stomach with what they saw.

The highway's bridge was less than two hundred yards

away.

"Shit!" Jason yelled. "Shit. Shit. *Shit!*"

Backs turned, the two scrambled up the rocky bank and plowed their way back into the woods. Smells of decaying plants and mud assailed their nostrils. Waning light gave the surroundings a more ominous look and Melinda couldn't help but to expect a crazed townie to jump out from one of the trees they ran past. While none did, they did have a near miss with a wild pig, its surprised screech matching her own.

Without warning they burst from the woods and back onto the road.

Melinda bent over, hands on her knees, and worked to catch her breath. Blood wept from a half dozen places where branches snagged both shirt and skin during their escape. She rubbed at one on her left shoulder, mindful of the stinging sensation radiating down her arm, and watched Jason as he stared nervously back in the direction they'd come.

"I figure…" he said, his own breaths coming in gasps, "we've got...ten...maybe fifteen...minutes on them." Jason bent at the waist, mimicking Melinda's stance. "They'll have to go back...into the woods to...get to the road. The bank was too steep...on their side."

"That's if they don't...go after Ethan." She felt her teeth chatter and wondered with disjointed curiosity if it was from the onset of hypothermia or simply shock.

"Good point."

No double yellow line marred the asphalt on this side of the bridge. Trees hung over the road, giving only a little more light than when they'd been in within the tree line. Flowers and grass grew in the increasing number of unsealed cracks in the pavement. The rain eased to a fine mist, and while it still pelted their exposed skin with icy aggression, the numbing effect eased.

Jason started across the road to the opposing tree line.

"Wait," Melinda said.

"Hon, we've got to keep moving. They're not that far behind."

"…on the road."

"What? No!" He shook his head, emphatically.

Melinda stood and crossed the half dozen steps to meet him on the far shoulder. "Just for a couple of minutes. The mud's killing my feet and I can't keep up with you. We'll stay on the shoulder so we can just pop in." *Pop in*, she thought, *plowing into this excuse for woods was more like trying to navigate a Cuisinart.*

Jason looked back down the road and then north. "At some point we're going to have to either try to flag someone down or climb a tree and try to call for help."

"The phones!" Melinda grabbed at the holster on her hip and pulled the phone free. Water dripped from the unit's jack and the LCD display offered nothing save a dark gray smear along the right side of the screen.

"Just put it back." He started walking along the shoulder, as she wanted. "Maybe they'll work once they dry out."

Re-holstering the device, Melinda followed, picking up her pace until she stepped in time with her husband. "North, huh?"

"We really need to be going south, back to the car."

A laugh escaped her.

"What?"

"Think Tommy's pissed?"

"Tommy? The tow truck guy?"

She mimicked his Mainer accent, "Back in two hours. Stay here."

"Best God damned advice I've heard all day."

Up ahead the road petered out, going from painted pavement to dirt. Though still hard packed, the diminishing aspects of modern society fell heavy on the two. They continued along the road, each taking an unspoken turn to glance warily in the direction they'd come. Thirty minutes passed without incident. No visible pursuit ensued. Only the road, red clay beaten to a respectable impersonation of rock, lay before and behind them.

Jason stopped. "What was that?"

"What was what?"

"Shhhh."

Melinda kept walking, but craned her head and listened. She could only the softer hiss of the mist impacting everything around them.

"There it is again."

"You're imagining things." Then she heard it—an engine, driving slow and getting closer. Fear grabbed hold and she stepped off the road and into the undergrowth, following Jason's retreating form. They watched from the embrace of two pine trees as a patrol car rounded the bend and passed.

"It's Haskel!"

"Hoskel," she corrected and pushed from their hiding place, emphatically waiving her arms. Jason followed suit.

The patrol car skidded to a stop in time with the bubble gum lights flicking on. Strobing red and blue shot fiery colors against the woods. Officer Hoskel stepped out, pulled her sidearm and drew a bead on the two of them.

"Freeze!"

Both did, already having their hands up in the air.

Melinda took a step forward. "Oh, thank God you found us."

"I said freeze!"

Melinda did as she was told. "The town, they're full of crazies."

"Just keep your hands where I can see them." She took two steps to the side to get a better view of Jason, who unlike his wife, had stayed frozen in place upon being told to. Her gun lowered some, but still pointed in their general direction. "You two look like a couple of drowned rats."

"The town–"

"I heard you, 'full of crazies.'" Officer Hoskel's stance eased. "The way they tell it, you," she motioned to Jason, "bashed some poor guy's face in with a computer."

"They threw a napkin thing at me first. Smashed my system's screen."

"So that gave you the right to—"

"They acted like they were going to hurt me," Melinda cut in. "They'd already thrown the dispenser and this huge guy started to get up." Tears, so unlike Melinda to shed, started to fall. "Jason threw it so we could get out of there."

The gun lowered, now pointing at the ground.

Jason lowered his hands some, still keeping them above his head. "We're just glad you found us."

"Okay, okay." She holstered her weapon. "They yelled at me for driving a car on a Sunday in their little town. Either way, you two get in the back of the car and we'll see exactly what hap—"

A rock flew out from across the road and struck Officer Hoskel in the temple. Her right eye suddenly bulged from the impact. Her hand grabbed the pistol, but seemed unable to draw the weapon from its housing.

Bam!

A shot rang out from the holstered weapon and a spatter of muddy clay erupted in the soil by her feet.

Bam!

Another shot fired down, this time striking the officer in the foot.

Melinda stared at the fresh gunshot wound, expecting to see a fountain of blood fly up. None did.

Officer Hoskel staggered forward, trying to keep on her feet. A mask of confusion marred the woman's face as another rock flew out and struck her in the same spot. The eye burst free from its socket and offered the law woman a decidedly unnatural view down the side of her nose. Knees buckled and the Maine patrolwoman fell, twitching, onto the road.

Jason lowered his hands and ran to his wife's side. "C'mon!"

On queue, townsfolk emerged ahead and behind them, effectively blocking the road in both directions. The number of hayforks and lengths of wood reminded Melinda of a gathering of movie extras from an old *Frankenstein* film.

"Angry villagers," she whispered.

The people of Fellowship closed in around the two and the car, stepping carefully.

Jason shoved her towards the open driver's door. "In!"

Melinda dove into the front seat, jamming her pinky finger as she struck the center console. Jason piled in behind her, forcing her legs out of the way as he fell into the seat and slammed the door behind him. One knife split the passenger-side glass and severed the skin between Melinda's middle and ring finger. She jerked her hand away and screamed. A hayfork handled by a middle-aged man with jet-black hair thrust into the front driver's side tire. Jason pulled the lever into drive and stomped on the gas, the tire's momentum jerking the fork from the man's grasp and slamming it back to strike a woman's forearm with a bone-crunching thwack before continuing its journey and slapping against the ground.

The patrol car lurched forward, knocking into the angry mob, which parted rather than be mowed down. Rocks smashed against the glass, spider webbing them. A sickening grinding sound emanated from the car's left front. Men and women followed alongside the vehicle as it picked up speed, slapping whatever they carried, bare palms in the few cases where no weaponry was carried.

"Oh God, it hurts!" Melinda screamed, holding the split hand together.

Jason ignored the cry, "The pitchfork must still be in the tire." A second thwap came from the flattened tire and this time a clunk followed by constant metallic scraping screeched through the vehicle. The steering wheel jerked to the left and Jason fought it back to the right, fishtailing the car as he sped away from the psychotic foot traffic behind them. They rounded a curve and smashed through a logging gate. Steam started to billow from around the buckled hood.

"A gate? A friggin' gate on the highway?"

Melinda snaked around in the seat until she was upright. "This isn't the highway then."

"It's got to be the highway."

They slammed into something. Air bags released, snapping Melinda's head back painfully against the seat. Jason beat against the bag, trying to force the safety device aside. A handful of seconds later, all of the air bladders deflated and lay flaccid against their housings. The car's hood had buckled further, erasing what little could be seen through the shattered glass.

Opening the driver's door, Jason stepped out of the patrol car and placed both hands on its roof and rested his forehead against the exposed weather stripping. Melinda climbed across the seat and started to push past him.

"What's wrong with your door?"

Melinda looked at him a moment, then at the passenger side door before holding up her bloodied hand.

"Oh crap. Mel, what happened?"

"The mob...back at the car..." She corrected herself. "...back at where the car was."

He helped her out of the vehicle, lifting firmly on her good arm as she extricated herself.

"What in hell?"

Jason looked in the same direction she did. They'd slammed into a parked car...one of many parked cars...a veritable parking lot's worth of parked cars. The hilltop clearing had been filled with vehicles of all years and makes, though most didn't appear to be in junkyard condition. Granted, there was a lot of mud and rust on ones further back in the clearing, but most had more of an abandoned appearance—neatly positioned alongside others—all with windows rolled up and doors closed.

Yells came from the direction they'd retreated.

Jason, still holding onto her arm, jerked her along. "Move! Into the lot!"

Vehicles blurred by as they made their way further up the hill, kicking away whip-like weeds and escaped tire rims. Fords, Chevys and GMCs populated the portion of the lot they navigated. Melinda couldn't help but to glance in the windows as they passed. Long forgotten open cans of soda occupied holders; cars with CDs piled on the seat gave way to clusters of tapes occupying the same position in others. As they weaved past an F-150, the voices got louder.

"There they are!"

Melinda looked over her shoulder and ran into Jason, who'd stopped without warning.

"What're you doing?"

"End of the earth."

"What?" She looked around his shoulder.

A fifteen-foot high cinder block wall barred their way, going the width of the open lot in either direction and into the tree line. Directly in front of them were the words, 'END OF THE EARTH,' spray painted in Day-Glo orange. She looked along the wall's length. Where the tree line on their side met the wall, no trees mirrored them on the far side.

Jason stood, staring dumbfounded at the construction.

"Jason!" A thought struck Melinda. "The wall!" She grabbed him with her good hand and pointed as best she could with the other. "We can use the trees and get over the wall!" A single look over her shoulder at the closing group of people was enough for her to take the lead.

The statement seemed to shake Jason free of the surfacing shock and he followed her to the right. Trunks were navigated, a family of field mice displaced by the shifting of one vehicle they climbed across, and two rear windows on cars, which were more rust than paint, cracked under the sudden shifting from their combined weight.

Behind them, the townsfolk pursued, many choosing more dangerous paths of access to gain ground on the couple. Windshields smashed and boots met with car roofs, a few angry shouts came from those tearing clothes, or in some cases skin, on the rusting hulks. Each shout of pain was followed with a, "Praise him."

Neither one spoke as they navigated the next thirty cars, before coming to three pickups with campers parked tightly bumper to bumper and a newer RV backed up against the block work, creating a vehicular wall of its own. Jason looked down the four vehicles' length, gauging the distance from the farthest pickup and the ever-closing members of Fellowship.

Too close.

He grabbed the door handle to the RV and lifted.

Nothing happened.

Jason jerked on it a second time yielding the same results. He kicked at the door repeatedly and on the fifth strike the latch gave way, swinging the door and inner screen door open. Shoving Melinda inside he slammed the door closed and reset the lock, adding the ineffective chain lock as well. "Look for something!"

Melinda stumbled into the shifting vehicle's kitchen area and looked for a towel, finding none.

Something slammed into the RV's side.

Jason reached up and smacked the skylight, which doubled as the RV's emergency roof access. It popped free and he pulled himself up. Melinda looked up and through the square hole leading out as another series of smacks echoed through the mid-eighties recreational vehicle. She raised her hands, feeling blood trickle down her arm, tickling the inside of her elbow. Hands shot down and grabbed her forearms and she looked up into her husband's face as he hefted her up and through the ceiling. Breasts dragged painfully against the skylight's lip and then she was out as far as her waist, though still kicking the air inside with her legs. Then she was free and on the roof with him.

Men and women stood on either side of the vehicle, while still others arrived.

"Come down," the black-haired man, who'd stabbed the car's tire, said.

Jason turned to her. "Up on the wall, we can drop to the other side." He turned and took a running jump at the wall, catching the top and pulling himself up.

Melinda followed suit, jumping for all she was worth and grabbing onto the lip with both hands.

Jason sat there, straddling the wall and stared into the expanse on the far side. A confused expression marred his face, and he cocked his head like a dog that heard something unusual.

"J...J...Jason," she managed. Her grip started to slip.

Still he sat there, ignoring her, transfixed with whatever lay beyond the brick monstrosity they were navigating.

"J...Jason!"

Jason suddenly smiled broadly and laughed, putting his clenched fists in front of his eyes. Jerking his arms down for a second, he brought the right fist back up in a wicked arc, striking himself in the face, never looking from what lay beyond. His left followed suit, striking his nose with an audible crack. "Hallelujah!" He started a new volley of blows against himself. "Hallelujah!"

Melinda dug in with her sneakers and pushed up, getting her chin over the lip and using it to help keep what purchase she had. Her gaze shifted from Jason to what the wall hid and her eyes went wide.

Someone grabbed onto Melinda's foot and jerked her free of the wall. She fell, smashing through the bubble-like rear window of a Pacer. Pinpricks of glass sliced along her entire body. Something in her right leg, the leg she'd been grabbed by, gave way and felt somehow loose under the skin. She lay amongst the mouse-nested mass of what had once been packages of diapers and stared up at her husband, who still straddled the wall and had already beaten his face into a bloody pulp, which resembled a post-match boxer rather than that of the man she'd said, 'I do' to.

"The end," she managed. "The...end."

"Hah...yay...yuyah!" Jason cried out.

A man's voice outside her limited vision asked, "What about him?"

"Leave him," a woman's voice answered. "He's seen the Lord's plan." Julia stepped into view. "Now, what about you?"

"The...end," Melinda said, trying to convey what she'd seen. "The end." She held out her bloodied hand in a feeble attempt to hold off whatever assault they had planned, a wad of glass falling from the already injured palm.

Two men stepped in, each carrying a length of wood.

Julia's face went gaunt. "Stop!" She shoved past them and grabbed Melinda's hurt arm. "She's got the mark!" A sigh escaped from her. "Who will take this newest child of the Lord?"

No answer came.

Above them, Jason's self-pummeling had slowed, fists swelling in time with his face. "A...yay...yuya!" he cried out as best he could past broken teeth.

Melinda turned her own hands to see the mark the waitress had spoken of. The gash opening her hand had been sectioned by another slice, this time by the car's glass. The two together formed a crude representation of a cross.

"I," Julia said with pride, "will house you then."

"The...the end," Melinda stressed, tendrils of madness picking at what was left of her sanity.

The waitress leaned inside the car. "I know, sister, I know. I climbed a tree as a little girl once and glimpsed...." She brought up a pair of kitchen scissors and dragged them down the length of her scar. "I felt better once momma had done it. More worthy of *His* love."

"I...don't," Melinda screwed her face up and tried again.

"The...end."

"It's better this way," Julia continued, "if thine eye offends the, pluck it out. If thy tongue offends thee..."

Gargled screams echoed through the afternoon.

"A...yay...yu...ya."

THE END

SOMEDAY, IN HEAVEN
By A.L. King

Samson looked down the hill of clouds and felt a sense of euphoria as he watched the four-legged figure climbing toward him. He then became uneasy about feeling so good.

Excitement is to be expected in Heaven, he told himself. And this must be Heaven. There's nothing but clouds for miles.

The strange new dimension he found himself in seemed to wear only two colors: the white of the cloudy ground itself, and the blue of the sky, which appeared to shimmer like the waters of a crisp and clear pool on a sunny day.

As well as his instant happiness, and the beauty of his surroundings, Samson thought it was all pretty damn strange. He observed the form running his way and reflected on his time there so far.

After waking up on the semi-soft ground, he had wandered the landscape for what seemed like hours before deciding to climb the highest peak. What was it he'd expected to see? Signs of life? He already concluded he was dead, so that was laughable. He was even about to laugh out loud at the idea of spending an eternity there alone when curiosity replaced black humor. Something was beginning to stir in the ground below. Only, that observation was incorrect. The ground itself was moving, separating from itself, and becoming something else.

Continuing to take on its rightful shape, the shape climbing his way still partially resembled the same white fluff that spat it up. He tried pushing down a rising sense of elation, but the emotion was too strong. The form was that of a dog, and he knew it wasn't just any mongrel. It was his childhood companion, Sparky.

The clouds wisped into fur. Black and brown—colors other than the endless backdrop of blue and white—spilled into the little canine. It struck him as odd that his old companion had only seconds before been one with the earths of Heaven.

Am I made of clouds, too? Samson wondered, holding his seemingly real arms out before him. Maybe it's all an illusion? Even my own body…

He pushed those thoughts away. If he really were in Heaven, that line of thinking might be considered blasphemous and offend the almighty entity responsible for bringing him there. Besides, everything would be okay. The clouds that made up Sparky were continuing to bleed color, as well as further refining the shapes of his whiskers and nose and dopey canine smile.

He told himself to forget about the dog's transition from fluff to form. He would be happy with the company of an old friend, no matter how it had manifested within that divine dimension. Being put off by such a gift—now that would be truly blasphemous.

Would the clouds whip up his Grandma Zelda next? Perhaps his older sister Vivian, who died in a car accident when he was ten years old, might appear as her seventeen-year-old self, minus the lacerations that drained the life from her. Maybe Uncle Chuck would come strolling up the billowy hillside with a six-pack of Guinness in his hand, like the way he used to show up randomly at Samson's parents' house before he finally drank himself to death.

At any moment those family and friends who preceded him in death might spring out of the ground like white flowers and climb the soft, hilly crest to greet him. It was appropriate, he decided, that Sparky had arrived first. Sparky had been so loyal. Such a good friend.

"Come here, boy!" he called, and the dog's little legs beat the ground faster, sending up a trail of cloud-wisps. Its paws pedaled against the strange surface, giving off a quiet yet audible sound—thip-thip-thip—that reminded Samson of a rusty fan belt.

When the small mutt was close enough, it jumped into his arms—floated into his arms was more like it. He was surprised that a portion of the shapeshifting clouds had not twisted itself into wings and a halo for the dog. Then again, he supposed he should be more surprised that a dog even made it into Heaven. He had long accepted the widespread notion that animals were not graced with souls. And over the years, he had even come to view most human beings as animals.

I guess my mother was right, he considered, reflecting on her words following the burial of Sparky just beneath his treehouse.

"You'll see Sparky again… someday, in Heaven," she had said to console him.

But she didn't know his secret. He could never let her know.

What secret? he wondered.

The creature, which was cozied in his arms, tilted its head and licked his chin. He was relieved to feel the doggy saliva and find that Sparky felt of fur rather than the collective mist that had formed him.

Still, he tried to recall, What couldn't I let my mother know?

He decided that maybe the mysterious secret he couldn't remember would come back to him after he saw her. She would be there any second, he figured. More clouds had begun stirring below. Shapes would soon rise from the cyclones. Human shapes.

He lowered his four-legged friend to the ground. Then he slid down the fluffy hummock to where the white silhouettes had, as he predicted, started rising. The thought of descending such a high cliff might have frightened him during life, but he was in Heaven. What's the worst that could happen?

Sparky, who had just climbed to the top of the hill to see him, wasted no time following him down. In the days of yore, when he was young, the dog was practically glued to his side.

After the physical builds of the cloud folk had finished, the process paused. Samson walked among the white, blank beings, studying them. They reminded him of mannequins waiting to be dressed. He shuddered.

Heaven shouldn't be this eerie, his mind protested. These people should already be how they are!

The forms began filling with hue, starting from the tops of their heads. It was as if someone above were pouring a variety of paints into an invisible funnel that connected to each shape. The subtle shades of skin and hair filled in, appearing almost digital until the finished products displayed absolute, fleshy clarity.

Fleshy, he mused. Too fleshy. Too naked. Why would anyone want to see their friends and loved ones this way?

Except, he understood as he studied the bare cloud-makings before him, they were not his friends and family members. Most of the thirty-something people were women, and a few were men, but they were unrelated. Not his kin, although they did look hauntingly familiar. They did, however, have something in common. Him. Samson was the connecting factor.

They smiled, all of them at once. Their simultaneous grins stretched a bit too far, perhaps a grace provided by the malleable mists that made them up. For the most part, however, they resembled the shapes they used to have before Samson dismembered them.

A sensation stronger than fear ran through him. He could feel it in his veins, a lingering warmth flowing faster and faster until it became heat. The hotness even throbbed in his temples. It was becoming hard to think.

How could he have been so calm? He was dead!

A bit of fogginess from the chemical cocktail, he supposed. As the phrase suggested, the injections were lethal. They had carried him from one world to another and had yet to depart from his spirit. Instead, they swam through his soul, causing a painful friction that he could feel again, now that he knew it was there. Had Sparky not distracted him, he might have reached that realization—and felt the pain through his confusion—much sooner.

The hurting inside was almost too much for him to move. He barely managed to pivot and start up the soft hillside. He feared the clouds under his feet would become quicksand, holding him in place. Thankfully, their semi-firm state remained.

Sparing a glance backward at his victims—former victims, he understood, for he was now the one being pursued—Samson saw a series of small creatures shoot out from around their legs. More animals! Strays and pets and other little creatures unlucky enough to meet his wrath when he was young and still working his way up to people. They soon gained on him.

Try to remember that, underneath everything, they're just clouds, offered his frantic mind. Just clouds and nothing more!

Those just-clouds caught up and sunk their teeth into his ankles and most of his back. Part of him had hoped that the pain already swimming through his veins would cancel out the carnage those on the outside sought to inflict. He was wrong.

Samson fell headfirst, expecting a soft landing. However, there was far less give than he anticipated. A few fanciful billows shot in whimsical directions, but the ground that caught him felt like a pillowcase packed tightly with gravel. There was about as much give as the surface of a wrestling mat. He suddenly felt just how his opponents had during high school wrestling matches, where he allowed his sadism a little room to breathe in the open. He could have pinned most opponents in a matter of seconds, but he'd enjoyed the rough play.

Now he was the one being played. The animals he'd tortured and killed in his youth were biting into him as if trying to create a burrow. They dragged him back down the hill. Their claws and teeth ripped flesh and sent blood spraying until a circle of red formed on the white ground around him.

The clouds began shifting beneath his plasma. The sensation was like a tiny earthquake. He expected a fissure might run underneath him and open and swallow him into nothing but the strangely shimmering sky below. However, rather than breaking apart, the white ground started to bubble like boiling water. This sentient landscape, whatever it truly was, seemed to be cooking up something else.

It didn't take long for Samson to recognize the latest shapes spewed up by the ground. Hacksaws. The cloud folk eagerly raced forward and caught up with him and shooed the animals away. They then grabbed the handles of the sharp-toothed tools just as cold silver began creeping into the blades.

"Please don't!" he begged. "I've already paid for my sins with my life! That's why I'm here!"

Something like lightning flashed, and he saw a flicker of the lacerations he'd left in what constituted their flesh. Those scars traveled across their naked bodies, where limbs had rejoined. And then, as quickly as they appeared, the marks were gone.

He kick-crawled away, pleading further and offering up desperate attempts at an explanation despite the deeper hole he knew his mouth was digging.

"It was my sister's death that messed me up and made me who I am," he said through pathetic and, he hoped, pitiable moans. The tears burned as if every bit of the lethal injection were leaking from his eyes. "Who I was, I mean. You see… I was only te-te-ten when she died in a ca-ca-car crash. I loved her and I was numb after that. And then… later, when I found out about how cut into pieces she was, I fi-fi-fixated on it. That's why I chopped people up. Viv was taken so randomly, I wanted control over life and death."

Things were quiet for a moment, as the cloud folk appeared to consider. Then a single bark broke the silence. It was Sparky. With one, shrill syllable, the mutt sealed his fate. Maybe they would have seen through his half-assed excuse anyway. If he were being completely honest, knowing the details about the death of his sister was not why he murdered people; it was why he chose to murder people the way he did.

They lifted the hacksaws, stepped forward, and brought them down. Samson experienced every sharp lick in slow motion. Is that what the cloud folk felt before they became cloud folk, before he'd sent them there by sawing them apart, starting while they were still alive?

Several times he thought he might pass out, but losing consciousness seemed impossible, even when they cut most of the way through his neck and used their blood-covered hands to pull his head the rest of the way off, to a full break.

He was dead. He was awake. He was dissected. And he felt everything.

This isn't Heaven! he thought on a loop. This isn't Heaven! This isn't Heaven! This is—

Sparky appeared before him, wearing the same stupid

grin he'd been wearing just moments before Samson kicked the dog into the backyard pool. With only ladders and no steps to exit, the dog had swum itself to exhaustion before succumbing to the waters. Those waters, as he recalled, had been an awful lot like the strangely shimmering sky his severed head was now facing.

Mom doesn't know, he thought. His mind—now as fractured as his body—was going back to his youth. Mom can't know. I'll tell her he fell in and I didn't see it. She'll believe me.

But Sparky knew the truth. He had let the cloud folk know as well, with a single bark. Samson was eight when he kicked his dog into the water and watched with a curious grin as it drowned. That was almost two full years before a semi truck plowed through his sister Vivian's car and tore her to pieces.

The dog's dumb grin transformed, just as the mouths of the cloud folk—Samson's human victims—had widened moments ago. Sparky's jaw fell freakishly slack, almost detaching. Its teeth grew impossibly long and sank into Samson's temples.

Sparky carried him far, far away from the others, who were exchanging celebratory remarks following the task of detaching his limbs. It was an unusual sensation, for although the pieces of his body were left behind, he could still feel their portions of a collective pain.

Finally, Sparky stopped and dropped Samson's head. Facing the sky, which continued sparkling that brilliant blueness, he watched the shape of a tree sprouting upward like a magic beanstalk. Something started forming between the branches, and he realized in horror that it was a treehouse.

It's my childhood treehouse, he thought. My dad built it for me, but I barely played in it. We buried Sparky just beneath it.

It was now Sparky's turn to bury him. He could hear the

dog's paws, likely transformed like its mouth, digging in the clouds. Staring into the shimmering sky—a cloudless sky, haha—the executed man felt foolish for thinking that someone like him could ever make it to Heaven.

"This isn't Heaven!" Samson blurted through the tatters of his voice box. "This is Hell!"

The dog used its snout to nudge his severed head into the hole. It fell in such a way that the dead and decimated serial killer was looking up at his former pet. The monstrous maw had returned to that adorably infuriating grin, the same canine smirk that once upon a time drew out a young boy's murderous ire.

"Oh, you made it to Heaven, alright," Sparky said, a blood-infused string of saliva dripping onto Samson's forehead. "It just ain't your Heaven."

THE END

NO ORDINARY DISORDER
By J.J. Smith

The backup of mail had filled Mrs. Bagley's mailbox, leaving no room for any more letters or magazines, and that so worried Ernest Smallwood that he found himself slowly opening the front of the Bagley residence to check on the old lady. He was sure entering a client's home like this was against the duties of a Postal Service delivery carrier, but he did so anyway because he liked Mrs. Bagley. She always had a warm smile and hello when she came out of her home to collect her mail. But for the last week there hadn't been any sign of her, and the accumulation of mail in her letterbox led him to believe Mrs. Bagley might need help, and Ernest decided he wasn't going to wait for the police. Rather, he'd take a quick look inside and call the authorities if needed. That the front door was unlocked, allowing him easy access, both relieved and unnerved him. He was relieved because he didn't have to break a window, and unnerved because, despite her advanced age, Mrs. Bagley was still sharp enough to realize that an elderly woman who lived alone was a target, so she'd keep her doors locked.

Ernest waited until he crossed the threshold before shouting out her name. There was no reply. He then stepped through the foyer into the living area and was shocked to find the room was full of old and yellowed newspapers that were stacked from floor to ceiling, creating a real fire hazard. In addition to the newspapers, there were boxes and crates, as well as clothes and items ranging from old televisions to toys, to tools, to old computer parts and stereo equipment, all of which were peppered throughout the room in massive piles. To get around those piles, Mrs. Bagley apparently created pathways through the mountains of junk, which caused Ernest to be watchful for "stack collapse," a hazard the Postal Service warned carriers to be aware of. Letter carriers were trained to be prepared for unusual clients and houses on their routes, including houses in similar condition to Mrs. Bagley's. Plus, Ernest had experience with the disorder known as hoarding.

In addition to stack collapse, carriers are warned of other dangers lurking in such a house, including rats, squirrels and other rodents nesting among the debris, as well as roaches, silverfish and fleas, and just as dangerous as the vermin, there was the possibility of biohazards hidden under the trash. With all those perils, it is stressed that a carrier do everything possible to avoid entering such a dwelling, but if they had to enter, to know the locations of the exit nearest to them at any one time.

Ernest pondered leaving now and calling the police to let them check on Mrs. Bagley, but something stopped him. He didn't know why, but he needed to press on, certainly to find out what had happened to the woman who lived there, but just as important to Ernest, he needed to find out what was going on in this house, so he moved deeper into the trash dump Mrs. Bagley called home.

Ernest stepped onto a path that lead around a stack and into the dining room. Once there, he was faced with more of the same, but that's when he noticed something even stranger. The items seemed to be used to construct a network of smaller stacks that resembled walls, or dikes. He was amazed by the intricate detail of the structures, and thought, *Mrs. Bagley must be an architectural genius,* but he then recalled that at one time Mrs. Bagley had a husband. He found out that information when, not long after taking the route, he delivered a box containing the ashes of Mr. Bagley. Because they were human remains, the box had to be signed for. As Ernest held out the box, Mrs. Bagley said, "So that son-of-a-bitch is here." While her words were angry, her eyes became glazed with tears. As she signed for the package Mrs. Bagley related how her husband had been living out of state with another woman for the previous fifteen years. However, they never divorced so she was his next of kin. Therefore, all the decisions concerning his remains were made by Mrs. Bagley. *I suppose Mr. Bagley could have made these,* he thought, pondering the structures. *Or, they could have done them together, or maybe it's all her and that's why he left.* The only thing to do was continue to follow the dike-like structures and see if they led to Mrs. Bagley. He called out to her a few times, but there wasn't any reply. Ernest followed a structure into the kitchen, and that's where he found the opening to the tunnels. In the kitchen, the structure ran through the middle of the room where most homes would have a kitchen table and disappeared through a doorway. But as unusual as that was, what made it stranger still was there was an opening in the wall; Ernest investigated and saw the tunnel was split into two directions. He knew instantly that he had to check these tunnels for Mrs. Bagley, but he didn't have a flashlight, and looking in he found the section of the tunnel leading to the right was dark, but the section of the tunnel leading left was emanating light. So, the choice was made for him.

He dropped to his knees in front of the tunnel entrance and leaned forward so he was on all fours. He then crawled in the direction of the light, and after a few yards he wondered if his imagination was playing tricks on him, because the tunnel seemed longer than it should have been. He also thought, *I'm going TOWARD the light, which isn't usually considered a good thing.* The thought made him smile, and he then pressed on. As he noted earlier, the tunnel seemed longer, and while that couldn't be true, what was true was it took a lot longer to crawl the distance of the tunnel than to walk it. However endless the crawl seemed, it wasn't endless, and Ernest found himself at the entrance to a chamber that must have been the structure in the dining room. The interior of the chamber was larger than a pup tent, and able to hold at least two people comfortably, and in the chamber were two occupants, but neither looked comfortable.

One of the occupants was a woman: it was Mrs. Bagley, who, along with the second occupant, was nude, and she looked to be in distress if not dead. At that instant, Ernest discovered something even more surprising than finding out Mrs. Bagley was a hoarder who used trash to create an intricate network of structures and tunnels in which she likely died. The real surprise was finding out who her companion was. Ernest wasn't a religious man, and had never been so, but he recognized an angel when he saw one.

The angel was on its knees, slumped, as if tired or, more likely, depressed, and it cradled Mrs. Bagley's head on its lap and stroked her hair as tears rolled down its cheeks. Ernest was terrified, and his fear left him paralyzed. Nonetheless, he internally debated what to do next when he realized he was interrupting the angel's mourning period and was about to back out of the tunnel when the creature turned its head toward the letter carrier. Ernest froze and was going to scream, but the scream that had formed in his diaphragm was now stuck in his throat. Just as quickly, his fear evaporated, and while the angel didn't speak, Ernest knew that he was...welcome. Now sure that he didn't have anything to fear, Ernest relaxed and slowly entered the chamber to join them. He crawled to the opposite side of Mrs. Bagley and sat on his knees facing the angel. Ernest had seen angels depicted in everything from paintings to commemorative plates to comic books, and by marble sculptures and ceramic figurines, and they all shaped his imagination as to what such a creature would look like; the angel did not disappoint for it had a large set of white wings that dominated everything about him. *Is it right to call it 'him'?* Ernest wondered. *Does such a creature even have a gender?* To start with, the angel lacked telling genitals, and while it did have masculine features—its body was "V" shaped with broader shoulders, but its torso lacked nipples— its structure was both delicate and tough in a way Ernest had never seen in humans. The last time he could recall seeing such a structure on a living creature was on a Siamese cat. Other domestic cats mostly had thick, brutish legs, but not the Siamese; those felines had legs that seemed so delicate that their bone structure looked to be made of porcelain. However, the legs of those cats were very strong and tough, enabling the Siamese to run, jump and pounce as well as other kitties, and that porcelain strength seemed to exist within the angel, indicating that the creature could run, jump, and fly just as well as the rest of them. *But rest of who, and what was he doing here?* the postman asked himself.

While Ernest wondered about the angel, the creature's gaze remained fixed on Mrs. Bagley, but it then lifted its head and the letter carrier's vision was pulled to the angel's soft, sad eyes. After nearly a minute of silent staring, Ernest said, "Why are you here?"

The angel paused a few seconds and then its wings moved from behind the creature so that the tips gently caressed Ernest's face. At first the postal worker thought it was a gesture of friendship, the way humans shake hands, or hug each other, or give a kiss on the cheek, but he soon found out it was much more.

Ernest suddenly found himself in a cramped, dark place, and it increased his fear to the point that he was on the verge of panic; but, just as suddenly, some light flooded into the "enclosure," which was all he could think of to call whatever it was he was in. However, the introduction of light and the strong stink that invaded his nostrils made clear he was sitting on garbage, and further examination confirmed he was in a dumpster. If that wasn't surprising enough, the person who opened the dumpster's lid and was looking down at him was none other than Mrs. Bagley. She smiled and offered her hand, and the next "memory"—he called it that because that is what the visions felt like—was of being covered by a thick piece of cloth. Turned out it was her coat, and he was pushed down the sidewalk in a shopping cart. That memory was quickly replaced with one of being in Mrs. Bagley's living room and viewing the mountain of trash that wasn't in any type of order, but just thrown into piles. That was followed by images of the trash being organized into the series of structures and tunnels that Ernest had found, and was now kneeling in. Those images were then replaced with images of Mrs. Bagley spending many hours with her unusual houseguest, including bedtime when she would shed all her clothes and join the angel in the enclosure so she could sleep under the comfort of its wings. The visions revealed a Mrs. Bagley who was happy and joyful, with not the slightest bit of bitterness, and, in a surprise to Ernest, she called the angel "Bob," (*Was Bob short for Robert, the name that was on the box of remains that he delivered?* In another surprise, a voice said, "*Yes.*") But then those happy moments abruptly ended during a memory of Mrs. Bagley in which she had settled in next to Bob, and suddenly she was shaking, and moaning. Then, just as suddenly as they appeared, the visions were gone. Exhausted by them, Ernest slumped back onto his heels and looked at the angel, who never stopped stroking the woman's hair. That's when the postman noticed the not so subtle transformation of the angel's body. As beautiful as it was before, the angel was now gorgeous in a way that it sparked deep arousal in him. It was no longer masculine in nature, rather, its thighs had become plump, its slender frame had become smaller, with its wide shoulders considerably decreased in size, and nipple-less breasts had grown out of its chest. It had become feminine, but it didn't stop there; when it lifted its head, Ernest recognized its face as the face of a girl he had known decades before in high school, and whom he was attracted to. Her name was Partridge Denhart, and he hadn't seen her since graduation, but the unresolved feelings he had for her flooded through him causing him to ask, "Partridge?"

The face of Partridge Denhart smiled, and while Ernest was happy to see that smile, he knew it wasn't real, but at the same time he wanted to continue to see her smile at him, so he said, "You're aware that I have to report her death to the police. But because you've been hiding here, I don't think you want to be here when they come. So, if you want, you can come home with me." Partridge replied with a beautiful smile.

Ernest told Partridge they would have to wait until dark to sneak out of Mrs. Bagley's house, into his car, and to his home. He then departed the house and completed his route, returning to the dwelling that night. With him he carried a flashlight, a pair of sandals and a caftan. The street on which Mrs. Bagley's was located was a busy residential section, and the clutter of cars forced him to park a few houses past the deceased woman's home, a situation he didn't like, but had to endure. He was sure to leave the door open when he left the house hours earlier, and the flashlight provided enough illumination to quickly find the tunnel entrance, which he again crawled through to find Partridge still cradling Mrs. Bagley's head. Despite the darkness outside the enclosure, the area was filled with light. Ernest said, "I'm sorry to interrupt, but we have to go now to take advantage of the dark."

The angel seemed to understand, for it kissed Mrs. Bagley's forehead and gently set the deceased woman's head down. And then, in the blink of an eye, the angel passed by Ernest and was standing by the tunnel entrance when the letter carrier emerged. Partridge was already wearing the sandals and caftan and led Ernest to the front door before relinquishing the lead. Ernest then said, "I had to park my car a few houses down. I'll go first to make sure the street is clear." The angel stepped back, and Ernest exited the home. Once on the sidewalk, he looked up and down the street, and not seeing anyone, he turned and said, "We can go." Partridge then followed Ernest to his car, and they were soon speeding through the city.

* * *

The drive to Ernest's home was just under thirty minutes and ended with the postal worker parking in his driveway in front of the garage. Partridge waited in the car as Ernest checked the street to ensure no one was walking or driving on the block. It was empty, so he quickly led Partridge from the car into the house where he then gave a sigh of relief. After a brief pause, during which Partridge looked confused, Ernest led the angel through the house into the garage. He turned on a switch and light flooded the room revealing that the parking bay was full of undelivered mail, a mountain of it; Ernest estimated it weighed about two tons. While it was comprised of all different sorts of mail, it was mostly junk mail, but also bills, some personal letters (that he didn't read) and official letters from government agencies that he believed were better spent as part of his "collection." He didn't really want to call it "hoarded mail." He just knew it was his. Accumulating that much mail took years, and he didn't take all the mail from his route, just a few letters that caught his attention. The rest came out of the mail processing and distribution center where he worked. He often marveled at how easy it was to walk out of the center with mail that wasn't part of his route. Why did he do it? Why would he risk his job, public disgrace, and a possible prison sentence, for something as seemingly silly as stealing mail? That's a question he did not have an answer to, and probably would never be able to answer. But the look on Partridge's face as the angel examined the mountain of letters made the years of risks worth it. After a few moments, Partridge, who didn't speak, asked, *"This is for me?"*

"Yes, it's for you."

Again, without speaking, Partridge said, *"You are a rule breaker. That is an attractive quality. You are also my savior."*

A little embarrassed, Ernest dropped his eyes, and said, "You're welcome." He then knew it was time for him to go to bed, so he exited the garage, and as he did so, he heard Partridge transmit—if "transmitting" is what non-verbal communication is called—a phrase to sleep on. It was: *"Tomorrow night."*

It was no surprise to Ernest that sleep was elusive. He lay in bed and looked at the ceiling as he imagined what was occurring downstairs, and while he couldn't sleep, he did manage to control his desire to run to the garage to be with Partridge, whom he began to feel was less like an angel, and more like...dare he think it...a lover. He had that giddy feeling people get when they become infatuated with someone new, a situation that had never developed well for him, but he realized that had changed. So, when he got out of bed, he quickly went to the bathroom and carefully groomed himself before heading to the garage. When he entered the hangar, he was stunned by what greeted him. Partridge had been busy, for the purloined letters had been used as construction material to build a structure like the structure at Mrs. Bagley's house. Ernest then heard something pass over him, and not surprising, Partridge was behind him. He turned and looked at the angel and asked, "You built this?" A question that made him feel silly for asking because who else could have built it? Partridge further surprised him when the angel's wings quickly moved forward and enveloped him and filled him with pleasure, the likes of which he never knew existed. While Partridge's wings looked like ordinary feathers, they were anything but. They radiated a sensuality that sent an electric current through Ernest that both excited and relaxed him.

He closed his eyes, and his head filled with visions of a place that was more than beautiful. Words were inadequate, so the best he could describe the place was beauty and love and joy, and Ernest concluded that it must be Partridge's home, that it was Heaven. *"Not Heaven as you understand it,"* he heard, *"It's called Tartarus, and it is part of the cosmos."* Ernest then snapped out of the dream, or hallucination, or vision, he didn't know what to call it. As he regained full consciousness, Ernest saw he was in the processing room at work. He looked around and saw overturned bins with mail scattered all over the floor. In addition, from behind desks and overturned tables, both legs and arms were sticking out, and in his hands was a semi-automatic assault rifle.

"What!" he screamed as he dropped the weapon. *Just having such a weapon is a violation of the Postal Service's Violence and Behavior in the Workplace Standards*, he thought.

Suddenly Partridge's voice filled his head and said. *"Leave through the employees' entrance, the police haven't arrived yet, you can get away."* Ernest hesitated; he didn't know what happened, or what he had done, but he knew it wasn't good, and he didn't believe he should run. But then Partridge said, *"Come to me, I need you,"* and that was all Ernest needed to hear. He was off and soon found his car parked in the handicapped spot. He was a full block away before he saw several police cars converge on the postal facility.

As he drove, Ernest fought to recall anything. *The last thing I remember I was in the garage,* he thought, but after that he couldn't remember anything. Within minutes, he was home, and he quickly ran from his car into the house and headed straight for the garage.

The letter enclosure was still there. Relieved, he said, "I didn't hallucinate this!" He then found the entrance and crawled through a tunnel to the main area, *what would it be,* he silently asked himself, and just as quickly the word, *"Salvation"* filled his thoughts. "What do you mean?" he asked, making the last turn that led to the threshold of the center area.

"It is my salvation, and you made it possible," was the response.

Ernest was just about to ask how, when he saw into the main area and was shocked to see Partridge prone and no longer with wings. Rather, hundreds of feathers floated about the enclosure, with scores of them acting as quills, writing on pages of open letter after open letter. Factory-like in its organization, a feather would open an envelope, retract its contents while one would dip into Partridge's open mouth like it was an inkwell, and then write…write what? *"Read one if you like,"* Partridge said, and a feather deposited some papers before him.

Unable to contain himself, Ernest took hold of the papers and saw it was junk mail that advertised a time-share in Las Vegas. While that was what the text said, as he read more, the additional text…Partridge's text…made its way into his consciousness. That text proclaimed itself to be "CONFESSION OF A FRAUD" and said:

"The Gospels of Matthew, Mark, Luke, and John, on which the religion of Christianity is based, are actually plagiarized from much earlier religious beliefs that I adapted to fit the myth of Jesus, who never existed.

"The delusion to want to believe in a messiah made it easy to implant the myth of Egyptian and Greco-Roman gods into the thoughts of certain scribes, who, while never witnessing such events, actually believed them and proscribed them to a deity named Jesus. The beliefs pilfered from the stories of other gods include being born of a virgin mother, being born in a cave, heralding the birth with a star, having an angel announce the birth, and being worshiped by shepherds.

"Other aspects of the myths that I adapted to the Jesus myth are: When he was thiry years old, he was baptized in a river, and the baptizer was later beheaded. However, unlike the Jesus myth, other earthly gods had fewer disciples, but like the Jesus myth, they performed miracles, exorcized demons, walked on water, and restored life to the dead. Followers of the god-made-flesh called him 'Holy Child,' and a 'Sermon on the Mount' is alleged to have been delivered, which his followers chronicled, along with the rest of his life and his death by crucifixion. There are myths in which the gods were buried for three days in a tomb, and from which they emerged, having rose from the dead. The story of resurrection attracted followers who showered adoration on those gods calling whichever god they chose 'the True Way,' 'the Word made flesh,' the 'Messiah.'

"Of course, the ancients were wrong about this, and, as it turns out, so are Christians."

As Ernest read, the production of Partridge's "confession" never stopped, or even slowed down. The feathers continued to write causing the enclosure's walls to diminish until all that was left was a thin veneer that the postal worker could easily put his hand through. When he finished reading, Ernest felt exhausted, which caused him to slump into a heap to gather his thoughts. When he was ready, he said, "You can't let this get out!"

"Why not?"

"About a billion people believe in Jesus."

"At any given time, I can cite the exact figure, but no matter the number of worshipers, are you defending their gullibility? I must point out that others have willingly embellished the Jesus myth, willfully deceiving believers for increased power. I cite the Councils of Nicaea, and later, the King James translation."

"I…don't know. I just know it would shatter too many people's lives."

"Interesting, so you would rather they continue following a deception, that I am responsible for, rather than learn the truth."

"I wouldn't put it quite like that. I just know it'll hurt too many people."

"Do you mean the people who have turned worship of Jesus into an industry, or those who cite Jesus as justification for murder? While I do find that interesting, I do not believe it a reason to delay revealing the truth. Personally, I find it disgusting how so many believers in Jesus have been willing to commit atrocity after atrocity in the name of a non-existent deity. Do you not also find that disgusting?"

"Of course I do."

"Then I do not understand your resistance to the reveal."

"I don't know. This is all so crazy! I think I'm going crazy!"

"Despite those feelings, there is an opportunity here for you to work to end the pretense. Nonetheless, you should know that it will be remembered no matter what you choose."

"How?"

"Soon the authorities will come looking for you, they will enter this dwelling and find these stolen letters. In order to deflect their employment of a madman, the Postal Service will see to it that the letters are delivered to their rightful owners, who will open them out of curiosity, and not being

aware of it, will read my confession. Not knowing why, they will retain the letter and share its information with loved ones and friends, who will also want to share the information. It might take a century or more, but the news will spread, and I will be reprieved."

"But…why would the authorities come here?"

"Because you are a taker of life, but you did not do so in Jesus' name, so there are consequences." The fact that Partridge no longer had wings forced the angel to touch Ernest's face with a hand, and images flashed through the postman's mind. He saw Mrs. Bagley as he cut her throat, followed by Partridge clamping angelic lips over the wound to suck out the dying woman's blood like a vampire. That was followed by him entering the mail processing center and walking up to Emily, the district manager's secretary, and shooting her in the chest. In a blink, Partridge was on the dying woman and drank the life-sustaining fluid as it gushed from the wound.

Ernest then entered the district manager's office and found Dan Kane frozen in shock. Ernest took aim and dispatched the manager with the squeeze of a trigger. Just as with Mrs. Bagley and Emily, Partridge drank Mr. Kane's blood, not spilling a drop, or even letting any dribble away. On it went, Ernest hunting down colleague after colleague, shooting them despite cries and pleas for mercy. When the rampage was over, twenty-two postal workers lay dead, and Partridge had amassed enough ink to finish the project.

"I started with the blood from Mrs. Bagley, and I used what I gleaned from the woman to calculate how much I would need to write the confession on all of these letters; you did the rest."

"No! I couldn't have done that! I liked all those people! I loved them."

"That is false. Like with the followers of Jesus, the truth has been kept from you about Mrs. Bagley. I did so because I needed you to believe otherwise. You saw that Mr.

Bagley's cruelty was torturing the woman, and you resolved to put her out of her misery. Your subsequent action was truly motivated by mercy. However, the action you took with your coworkers was motivated by something else entirely. You resented and despised them. The fact is: you could only do what you did because you hated them."

"Take me with you."

"I'm afraid that is not possible. I plan on continuing my campaign, and you will soon be wanted for those murders. However, for your loyalty I will leave you with something," the angel said as it let the caftan it was wearing slip to the floor to reveal breasts with hard nipples, and a vagina with engorged lips.

"You're a woman," said the mesmerized man.

"No...not really, but I can sculpt what is needed. I will use it to provide you with the most intense pleasure possible. Come," said Partridge, taking Ernest's hand.

Once on his bed, Ernest kissed his angel, at the same time his mind thanking God for this moment. That's when the window exploded, sending glass everywhere, and before Ernest could react, strong hands pulled the lovers apart.

* * *

Everything happened in a blur. A group of individuals had burst into the bedroom through the two bedroom windows that overlooked the back of the house and attacked the pair. They did something that caused Ernest to black out, and when he awoke, he saw that Partridge was on her angelic knees, tightly constrained in a type of bondage and discipline restraint. It wasn't like anything Ernest had seen before. It was a golden substance, and it held Partridge's arms together in front of the angel. It locked the elbows together and banded upward, ending so her hands were frozen in forced prayer. In addition, to prevent running, each ankle was fused to the back of her thighs, thereby forcing

Partridge to kneel. Ernest tried to speak, but found he was unable to. That was when one of the intruders said, *"There is real sympathy for you because of your condition, but despite your madness, you had to know you would not be allowed to proceed with this campaign."* The speaker then turned to the others and said, *"Let us take our leave."* Two of the intruders then easily lifted the restraint that held Partridge, and exited the room.

The remaining intruders turned to follow, but one turned to the leader and said, *"What of him?"*

The leader looked at Ernest, and said, *"Unfortunately for him, Jesus has always been able to collect disciples."* Wings suddenly appeared behind the intruder, spreading up, one circled around to the front and reached out to touch the hapless postman.

* * *

Ernest awoke buried under a heavy pile. He tried to move, but the weight held him fast. He was very familiar with the substance that pinned him down: It was the stolen mail. And from his inability to move, they must have placed all the letters on top him. He was sure he would suffocate soon, but he suddenly realized that he wouldn't have the chance to do so because flames started to envelop him. Packed away in his own crematorium, Ernest never heard the police sirens through the sound of his own screams.

THE END

BAPTISMAL SCARS
By Nick Dinicola

Pastor Patrick sat in the front pew, far in the corner, watching his congregation mill about the entrance of their church. Each Sunday was like this: a slow, confused procession of mostly new faces wandering down the single aisle like it was a labyrinth, trying to sit in the back but pushed forwards by the friends or family who had brought them. Patrick smiled and nodded at each of these familiar faces, chuckling to himself as they fought with the new faces, insisting they all sit closer, as close as they could, until the second pew was filled, then the third, and so on. All the while the new faces glanced about, whispering questions, trying to square the majesty of the church as it had been described to them with the ramshackle church around them.

The church was just an old rectangular classroom portable. The entrance was on one short side, allowing for a nice long central aisle and several rows of pews. Big casement windows filled the other walls, letting in so much morning sunlight there was no need for any lamp. All the windows were cranked wide open to let in the fresh air, and to let out the smells that would soon take over.

The pews were really just metal folding chairs with no cushions, lined up eight to a row with the aisle splitting them in half. They were uncomfortable; Patrick knew this and sympathized with his flock, shifting his weight in his own seat, but he knew everyone would forget their discomfort once the service began. It wasn't a long service; Patrick didn't know much about this pastoring business and preferred to keep things short. He prided himself on not rambling overcomplicated sermons, on getting straight to the point with hard truths and then stepping away, letting the baptisms take over. That was what everyone really wanted to see, that's why they were all really here: to see the baptismal candidates give themselves to God and, hopefully, be rewarded.

The rest of the church was sparse. There was no pulpit. Patrick didn't want to hide when he spoke; he wanted everyone to see him, and everyone wanted to see him. There was no altar at the head of his church, no cross or any other religious symbol anywhere in the room. No incense, no candles, no statues, no chalice or cup or cruet, but there was a pink inflatable pool on the floor in front of all the pews. Patrick preferred blue, and he would go shopping for another pool before next Sunday, but for now the pink was the best he could find. It was the size of a well, with plenty of room for an adult to stand in, and plenty more room to catch any detritus that might fall off.

The entire back of the portable, the whole chancel, was covered with roll upon roll of plastic sheeting duct taped to the walls, ceiling, and floor. The plastic engulfed the pink pool, stopping just short of the first pew where a line of bricks created a lip—a poor man's rood screen.

Above the pool was the boss, the centerpiece of the church, the artifact that would change the world given enough time. A thin wood pane was screwed into the ceiling, on which Patrick had arranged a circle of stones, each the size of a fist, each scorched like it had fallen through the atmosphere, and each held in place by hooks and string and tape, anything Patrick could find to secure them without damaging them.

As the congregation filed in, no one sat in the front row with Patrick. Those seats were reserved for the baptismal candidates, and there were five of them this Sunday.

First up was Felix, the second oldest of the group, here for the third time. A man in his late fifties, who was happy to let his beard go gray, but still dyed his thinning hair a deep black. He wore a simple, traditional baptismal gown. The candidates were free to wear whatever they wanted, provided it could be easily removed. Most chose to bring bathrobes from home, but Felix was an old man hung up on old traditions, even when trying a new religion.

Suzanne was next, the oldest of the group, and another stickler for the appearance of tradition. Her gown was cruder though, likely homemade, cut from a bed sheet or curtain, showing a thriftiness that belied her rich fortunes. But her face exposed her wealth: skin powdered pale, pulled taught across her skull over multiple surgeries, each a little less effective than the one before. This was her sixth baptism.

Patrick had high hopes for Bernie, a dark-skinned, bespectacled, shy man who was here for the twelfth time. He was the most likely to become something better today, but the many baptisms had worn him down. Not even thirty and his hair was already graying, his face sagging, his shoulders slumping. Beneath his blue bathrobe his gut was growing, Patrick knew this from the last baptism. Bernie has long since stopped taking care of himself in anticipation of his divine reward.

Catharine, or Cath as she preferred to be called, was a young Asian woman whose round face exuded such gentleness that Patrick hoped the baptisms wouldn't grind her down like they had Bernie, even if they were all irrelevant in the end. This was only her second time; she had many more ahead. As the youngest candidate, she was lithe and attractive and very aware of it. In any other situation, the men in the room would have been excited to watch her slip off her cat paw patterned nightgown, but in this church only John seemed to care about her.

John was the newest candidate, here for the first time and thus made to go last, his usual jock swagger now gone, leg bouncing anxiously in an NFL branded robe. Cath clapped a hand on his leg, holding it down, and whispered something in his ear that seemed to calm him. He whispered something back, making her smile and peck him on the cheek with the comfortable affection of familiar lovers. She removed her hand and his leg started bouncing again, but neither of them noticed.

The congregation was now seated; incidental conversations created a white noise that made the place feel lively. Patrick was happy to see several back rows were empty. His church had room to grow. Soon, word would spread, those seats would fill, and they would have to find yet a larger venue, but for now their humble portable was enough.

Patrick stood from his corner seat and the conversations quieted. The familiar faces hushed themselves because they knew the service was about to start. The new faces were taken aback by the stunning man before them.

Patrick tried to hide his figure with jeans and a large formless polo shirt, but these left his arms exposed, and it was easy to extrapolate the lean swimmers body underneath from his smooth and muscled forearms. He walked to the head of the aisle, each step a dance, each movement flowing into the next with the grace of a practiced gymnast. He looked over his flock, all of them entranced by his deep blue eyes, glistening like sapphires in the morning light.

Beth and Sam came in from outside, closing the door but not locking it since some of the new faces were sure to run and Patrick didn't want them feeling trapped. His wife and son moved down the aisle with the same grace as their pastor, and then stepped aside to flank the pool.

Beth didn't hide her figure, showing off her chest in a tight tank top with no bra, and yoga pants that clung like a second skin. She was proud of what God had given her and reveled in the lustful stares from the new and familiar faces alike, exuding a glamour and glow that should have only been possible in fake photos.

Sam was fit beyond his age, stronger than most of the men in the room and more handsome too, even at just eight years old. His face expressed youthful innocence or wise maturity, depending on the light and angle. There were more girls in the audience today, and some older teens who probably didn't know his true age, likely convinced to come by a friend who couldn't stop talking about the cute boy at her church.

Some of the congregation were similarly beautiful, standing out like diamonds in dirt. Patrick knew some of his flock were only here to ogle—the weekly churchgoers who never asked to be baptized—and he was okay with that. His church needed the numbers and the new faces needed reasons to come back. Maybe there really was something holy about a poor church that could entice so many divinely attractive people.

"Welcome to our Church of the Holy Light," Patrick began. "Our *new* Church of the Holy Light. Those of you who have been with us since the beginning might remember me telling you that we would grow like a hermit crab, shedding one shell for a larger one. Well, we've upgraded."

He spread his arms wide, taking in the new space to scattered applause, then started his sermon.

He knew it by heart now. It was the same sermon he gave every week, for his was a simple message, one that didn't need study or interpretation or discussion. Those were the sorts of things people did when their faith failed them, and they needed an excuse to continue believing. A simple faith was a stronger faith, so he kept things simple.

"God is a creator. An inventor. A tinkerer." He stressed each word with a flourish of his hands, assigning each a divine grandiosity. "What He is not, is a manager." He shrunk his hands to his chest, emphasizing God's disdain for managerial duties. That's why He created us with the means to create more of ourselves." A gesture towards his family. "The truth is, God does not care about you."

Amens from the beautiful people.

"He doesn't care about your troubles, and He will not answer your prayers. He doesn't care about your faith, or your evangelism in His name. Those things have nothing to do with Him. They are all you, projecting yourself onto Him."

A new face stood, scooted to the aisle, and walked out, lips twisted in offense.

"He doesn't care what you do, but He cares what you are, for you are His creation, His invention. If you want to earn His love, you don't go out and create new things that will only pale in comparison to what He has already made; you give Him the means to create more. Let Him create, let Him invent, let Him tinker, using the only medium worthy of His holy touch: You."

Stronger applause, louder amens. Patrick walked back to his seat and grabbed a long stick from the floor. The new faces looked confused, whispering more questions, but the service was just getting started. Patrick was merely the introduction.

Using the stick, he reached up to the circle of stones on the ceiling and tapped the keystone into place. There wasn't anything special about the keystone; it was a rock like all the others, just offset slightly from the circle, but Patrick liked calling it the keystone because it added to the religiosity of the proceedings. When he tapped it into place, the rocks created a single unbroken chain, each scorched stone touching another, and opened a seal into heaven.

A pillar of white shone down from the circle onto the

pool. It appeared faster than light, faster than thought. It didn't even really *appear*, it was just there, like it had always been there, a permanent fixture of the room no one had noticed before. Seconds passed, then gasps and squeaks of shock rang out as the new faces realized what they were seeing, realized that the room had changed, and laughter erupted from the familiar faces remembering their own dumbfounded awe once upon a time.

The pillar wasn't light; it didn't fill the room and blind its audience. Its glow was entirely contained within straight edges. It looked solid, but Patrick lowered the stick behind it—a subtle move, but practiced and planned like a magician's show—to prove that it was actually transparent.

"That is why we are here today, to honor God by offering ourselves as clay for His molding. Felix, you have the honor of starting us."

Felix stood and pulled his gown over his head, revealing a hairy and tired body, worn down by years of physical labor, once dense muscles now oozing into fat. He stepped before the pillar, and Patrick clapped his hands on the candidate's shoulders, speaking into his ear loud enough for the rest of the room to hear.

"Now remember, our baptism is a process. Do not be dissuaded. Endure these tribulations." Patrick could sense the apprehension rising from the new faces, unsure what they were about to see, minds racing with possibilities and conjuring worst-case scenarios.

Felix stepped into the pool, into the pillar, and was lifted into the air. There were no gasps of surprise at this. After seeing the pillar appear, the new faces were at their most skeptical and this was an easy magic trick. They watched and waited, skepticism growing because they could only see Felix's back. They couldn't see the cut that opened on his sternum, couldn't see it draw down to his stomach, couldn't see his ribs distend from invisible hands, but they saw the bloody chunk that fell into the pool, sliding around the smooth plastic like a water balloon.

People stood, trying to get a better view of the chunk, confused and curious. Felix was lowered, and as God let him go, Beth and Sam were there to catch him, pulling him forwards, out of the pool to the back of the room.

The pain came fast. Felix fell to his knees, clutching the gash in his chest, moaning and heaving blood, struggling to breathe through one lung. He rolled over, leaned against the wall, facing the light and the congregation, and tried to smile but just sputtered all over himself.

This finally elicited cries of fear. New faces leapt to their feet while friends and family tried to calm them. Some stumbled into the aisle and moved towards Felix, so well intentioned, but Patrick blocked them, hands up like a traffic cop, meeting each of their eyes.

"All will be okay," he said. An absurd claim as Felix bled out directly behind him, but he was so handsome everyone wanted to believe him. So they hesitated.

Suzanne was already in the white. She had stripped her gown in the panic, taking advantage of the distraction to hide her naked body, embarrassed by her sagging and mottled skin but showing no such fear of the pillar. Her weightless limbs began to twist, arms and legs bent and contorted at impossible angles, her joints turned to rubber, head snapped backwards as her God tinkered away. Then her limbs straightened out and she fell.

Beth and Sam were ready, so practiced at this by now, and caught the woman, hooking their palms under her arms and tossing her forwards onto Felix, who sputtered more upon impact. Suzanne's head was still backwards, her paralyzed body flopping like a dead fish, eyes wide and fluttering with excitement, gurgling either screams or praise from shredded vocal cords. It was all incoherent at this point.

As Patrick expected, some new faces ran for the exit, bashing into the door, clearly expecting it to be locked or blocked. He smirked as they fell on top of each other, scrambling to escape the crazy killer cultists. He had seen all this before; the new faces were so predicable. Upon realizing they weren't being chased, their panic would wane, and they would tiptoe back, desperate for another glimpse of the supernatural.

Bernie was no longer embarrassed of his overweight body, waiting for calm before stripping. As he rose in the white, his skin rippled, muscles pulsing, bulging, bloating like a waterlogged corpse. Then the molding began: his flesh pounded with invisible chisels, each dent shaping him, little craters carving dimension into his body; his gut pushed in and folded upon itself, valleys of abs etched into it like knife wounds; his penis throbbed and thickened and grew; his jaw broke then reset, stronger, squarer; all of him violently beaten into dense muscle no human could ever achieve. When done, he was gently placed into the pool and immediately fell to his knees, praising his Lord for his new physique.

The congregation erupted in applause. Even some new faces joined in after seeing the true love of God and realizing this was no cult of masochists.

Beth had to tap Bernie's shoulder to break him from his beatitude and shoo him away. He stepped from the pool, standing beside it as a new parishioner, still naked and reveling in the respect and lust of his peers.

Cath stood and slipped off her nightgown slowly for she had nothing to be embarrassed about, eyeing Bernie up and down as he ignored her. Felix might have ogled but he was dead now, corpse bone-pale, gallons of his blood pooling on the plastic sheeting.

Cath winked at John and skipped into—and out of—the white.

It happened in a single, smooth motion. She was in, then she was out, curling into a fetal position, clutching what was left of her head. Long strips of her face and scalp, including most of her nose and part of an eye, hung in the air behind her before dropping into the pool. Bernie led the congregation in a polite applause while Cath screamed. The Good Lord was always so rough with the newbies.

Last and least was John. Patrick watched closely, intrigued what would happen to the first-timer. God was at His most inventive with those He hated.

John looked up into the white, clearly expecting to rise, but God only held those He respected, so John's feet remained locked to the floor of the pool. His arms jerked outwards, like Jesus on the cross, and were then divinely flayed: his skin sliced into ribbons and sheared away, muscle fibers frayed apart like withered rope, bones shattered over and over until their dust surrounded him—a fog of his own making. He had not yet earned any holy anesthesia, so he felt every rip, peel, and break, suffering in silence, his every scream interrupted by some new burst of pain, killing his breath.

Everyone knew it was over when blood began squirting from his shoulders. Sam was sprayed in the face, crying out like a kid tagged "It" on the playground. Beth and Bernie grabbed the walking torso, holding it straight so it wouldn't turn and spray the audience, leading it into a corner.

The baptisms were almost done. Patrick walked up and down the aisle clapping, commanding everyone to give the candidates their respect for showing such bravery. He noted the new faces hovering in the doorway, having returned from their initial retreat, still terrified but intrigued. Was this a show or a sacrifice?

"Bernie, would you help my wonderful wife? And Sam, we've got some towels in the car," Patrick said as he jangled a set of keys from his pocket and tossed them to his son. Sam ran outside, wiping his face and flicking his hands at the new faces in the doorway as he passed. They leapt away in terror and the boy laughed at them.

Bernie stood up straighter like a soldier called to

attention and nodded, proud to be of service. Working together, he and Beth dragged Suzanne off Felix, then dragged Felix back into the white and held him there while Patrick collected the robes and gowns from the floor.

Almost immediately, the gash in Felix's chest mended itself and the color returned to his skin. He came alive, gulping air into new lungs, legs kicking like a newborn, almost squishing his old lung slipping around the pool.

Patrick stepped before the candidate, arms full of discarded clothes, his mere presence enough to calm any confused wild animal.

"All will be okay," he said, handing Felix back his gown, still clean and dry, so unlike the man himself.

Felix muttered some holy praises, choking on the words, not used to his new lungs, and took his seat.

By the time he sat down, Suzanne was already in the white, her head cracking around into its proper place, spine and vocal cords and esophagus all mended. She shouted her holy praises, voice hoarse, then dressed quickly before sitting down.

Cath could still move on her own, so Beth and Bernie made no motion to help her. She crawled back slowly, swaying on weak arms, partly blind and oh so confused by the pain. She reminded Patrick of his own baptism, when he had set the stones in a circle in his backyard, thinking it a pleasant decoration, only to be hit in the face with God's judgment, flesh and bone and brain all burnt away, left flailing by himself in the hurtful dark, unable to scream for Beth, who had been inside, flailing about until accidentally flailing himself back into the white. Cath had it easy.

Her scalp and face were knitted back together, luscious hair sprouting up like a waterfall before falling around her, recreating the Birth of Venus. She didn't say anything as she took her robe and seat.

John was dead, and his lack of arms made him tough to carry. After some fumbling, Bernie grabbed his feet and

Beth grabbed his neck, lifting with an inhuman chokehold.

Once in the white, John's arms reformed from thin air. There were probably bits of his bones still floating above the pool, but Patrick knew none of that would be used in this recreation. That's what made the baptisms so special: They weren't just being remolded into better versions of themselves, they were being reforged.

Each resurrection was met with gentle applause from the familiar faces, the new faces too dumbstruck to do anything. When all the candidates were alive again, the applause became a standing ovation, a celebration of God—His wrath, His power, His grace—and those brave enough to endure each.

Eventually, the candidates stood and made their way out: a procession of God's anointed, led by a still-naked Bernie, his whole body a beautiful baptismal scar.

The rest of the congregation soon met them in the parking lot, lavishing them with attention and love no celebrity could ever hope to match. Patrick and Beth remained behind in the portable, air thick with gore seeping into their clothes but not their skin. The stench couldn't touch their skin. Then they embraced, Patrick kissed his wife and she kissed him back, long and deep. Today had been a good day, a good service. There had been more new faces this week than last, and there were sure to be more new faces next week. Their church would grow; it was too incredible not to grow.

Patrick broke from his wife and, still holding her hand, picked up the long stick and tapped the keystone out of place. The pillar vanished instantly, gone as if it had never really been there. Patrick dreamed of a day when the keystone would be unnecessary, when he would have a line of baptismal candidates out the door, so long he could open the ramshackle Gate of Heaven and let its white shine through all day, every day, remaking all of humanity.

But he was getting ahead of himself.

Sam returned with his arms full of towels.
Now, the portable needed cleaning.
Later, they would remake the world.

THE END

AND SATAN CAME WITH THEM
By Michael Martin Garrett

"I think a great deal about the Book of Job," announced Father Henry McCullers.

The priest stood before a workbench in the corner of a rotting shed, eyeing a selection of rusty implements. Pliers. Hacksaw. Screwdrivers. He ran his hand from item to item. A smile split his face like a wound.

"Compared to the Gospel of Matthew, for instance; but, of course, that's the New Testament..."

Drill. Nail gun. Arbor press.

"But even compared to Psalms, Isaiah, or Exodus..."

Angle grinder. Handsaw. Soldering iron.

"Job—the book, that is, not the man—teaches us values not explored so fully elsewhere in the Scripture..."

Hammers. Bleach. Assorted cleaners.

"Ask yourself: Where were we, pitiful creatures, when He laid the foundations of the earth?" He chuckled to himself. "Where were *you*?"

More exotic fare: Syringes, dripping clear solutions of sinister intents. Little silver silos of liquid nitrogen. Piano wire.

"You see, my point is, I suppose…" He turned around, sharp white teeth gleaming in the dark. "I fear Job's lessons are *undervalued*."

The Father turned. Before him, Allen Myers—an usher at St. Andrew the Apostle's and dairy farmer by trade, blessed in the worldly riches of land, beasts, and children—lay strapped to a table of darkly stained oak. Sweat beaded across his broad forehead. Tears leaked from bloodshot blue eyes. Tightly fastened leather straps bound his wrists to the table, rendering his fingertips the bluish-white of bloodless flesh. Saliva burbled around the ball gag between his teeth.

"Gahd, Gahd," he sobbed. "Wha' have I done to deserve thif?"

"Shhh, shhh." Father McCullers ran the bony spindles of his fingers across his face, gently wiping away his tears. "The wages of sin are *death*, my child."

The priest rested his thumb against Myers' right eye and pressed, feeling the vitreous mass depress as the man screamed against his gag. Father McCullers licked his lips as he drove deeper, savoring the gel-filled orb warping around his thumb, then released his eye and returned to the workbench.

"But perhaps you *do* deserve a more proper explanation. You're a man of faith, are you not? God-fearing? Rich in the blessings of the Lord?"

Myers nodded vigorously, sobbing, as if he might escape captivity on the virtue of his good works alone.

"Of course you are, my child. You're a *good* man. But is it for nothing that you are God-fearing? After all, the faith of 'good' men is a shallow faith indeed. Where is your faith in the face of pain? In the face of loss? When have you anointed yourself in ash in the depths of your sorrow, all your blessings reduced to dust, still faithful to He who takes away?"

Myers howled like a wounded animal.

"You see, this is my point about Job. We forget all too

often the *breadth* of *His* creations, I fear. The day, *and* the night. The dove, *and* the Leviathan. Good…" He picked up a pair of pliers, appraising it by the crimson light of the fire burning in its corner hearth. "And evil."

He turned, eyes invisible in the shifting shadows cast by the fire, save his irises gleaming like a cat's in the night. A wet, sobbing scream rolled up Myers' throat, muffled by the gag.

"Behold." The Father smiled, leaning in with the pliers. "You are vile. I will lay my hand upon thy mouth."

The man thrashed against his restraints.

* * *

Earlier that morning, Elizabeth Wilson, a stooped and grey-headed woman with tired eyes, took a seat for the first time in the backmost pew of St. Andrew the Apostle's, a spired temple of rust-colored bricks on Broad Street in Waynesboro. She'd arrived in town only the previous night. Her hands spasmed, not from age, but from a cold rush of adrenaline as she waited for the service to begin.

Fifteen years she'd already waited. Fifteen years since Malcolm had been stolen from her. The call to identify the body had been little more than a formality. The mass of mangled meat they showed her no longer resembled a man. At nights, visions of her husband haunted her, as he'd appeared when the police pulled the sheet away: fleshless, seeping, the details of the face burned away, the familiar curves of his nose and cheeks erased, replaced by a mask of charred, blistered muscle clinging to the skull. She'd vomited on the morgue floor.

After the initial shock, Elizabeth had attempted to adjust to a widow's life. Her mother had done it before her; now was her turn to bear the cross. Between the despair, the fatigue, and all the practical matters that needed attending, she barely even noticed that Father Henry McCullers, a humble homilist who'd joined the congregation not five years before, transferred to another church less than two weeks after her husband's death. Years passed. Her life approached something resembling a new normalcy.

Then, five years after Malcom's passing, a man in Fulton County was found mutilated almost beyond recognition. He'd been found in a shed of unknown construction or ownership, deep in the woods. Howard Bigler, 45, lumberyard owner, family man, devoted attendee at St. Stephen's in McConnellsburg. Then, four years after that, in Westmoreland County, Daniel Shindledecker, 62, CPA, father of four, grandfather of eight, and faithful parishioner at Our Lady of Grace in Greensburg, discovered in an abandoned mill off a closed road in an empty corner of the county. Elizabeth felt a profound disquiet, a still small voice whispering in her ear.

When Bigler had been discovered, she wondered if he'd been mutilated by the same hand that had tortured her husband, but she had forced the thought into the depths of her mind, where it festered like an abscess in her soul. By the time of Shindledecker's discovery, wonder blossomed into conviction, peace had devolved into obsession, and thought demanded to become deed.

In researching these killings, Elizabeth discovered something that stoked the flames smoldering in her breast: at each of the victim's churches, Father Henry McCullers had invariably arrived a few years before the murder, and left shortly thereafter. Just as he had come and gone from the church where she and Malcolm had been wed, now defiled by a darkness no light could ever illuminate.

By the time she made this discovery and tracked down the priest's whereabouts, he had already haunted St. Andrew the Apostle's for three years, more than enough time to have picked out a new victim. Mischief followed McCullers like a shadow, and the time had come for Elizabeth to give life for life, eye for eye, tooth for tooth, hand for hand, wound for wound, and burning for burning, so sayeth the Lord.

The familiar drawl of Father McCullers' voice ripped Elizabeth away from her thoughts as he took the podium to deliver the morning's homily. The sight of him—gaunt and hollow-cheeked, with eyes like two small coals burning in their sockets—provoked the taste of bile in her throat.

"One day," McCullers declared, his voice still, devoid of inflection, "there was a man, blameless and upright, who feared God and avoided evil. And on that day, the sons of God came to present themselves before the Lord. And Satan came with them."

Elizabeth recognized the sermon opening. It was the same one Father McCullers had delivered the morning before he had butchered her husband.

"And the Lord asked Satan, 'where do you come from?' And Satan answered the Lord, 'from roaming the earth, patrolling it'—as a master might patrol his fields, perhaps, overseeing the work of his servants."

Father McCullers paused to cast his gaze upon the crowd. Elizabeth looked away as the spotlight of his eyes passed over her pew.

"What an answer Satan dares to give the Lord! To suggest that while He controls the Heavens, the Adversary stalks His creations, sowing seeds of doubt and chaos in the hearts of men. And yet the Lord does not rebuke him, but instead *engages* him, asking if Satan has seen this blameless and upright man, most loyal of all His servants." The Father drummed his fingers against the pulpit, a twitch playing at the corners of his mouth.

"And sharp-tongued Satan dares again to question the Lord, to declare that this man is only loyal for God has blessed him! Were God to revoke these blessings, surely this man would blaspheme Him to His face!"

Elizabeth closed her eyes and took deep, shuddering breaths. She reached a hand into her red leather purse and wrapped her fingers around the handle of her recently purchased Smith & Wesson .38 Special. No. Not yet. Not here. Now was not the time.

"And, amazingly, again God does not rebuke him!" The priest slammed his hand against the podium. "No, instead, the Lord offers this man's life up to Satan's control. This man, upright and blameless, is delivered into Satan's hand by none other than the Lord himself. Why? Why! Why I ask you!"

Sweat shone on the priest's forehead, his breathing ragged with passion.

"But *who* are *we* to question the machinations of He who laid the foundations of the earth! He who shut the sea behind doors, who has shown the dawn its place so it might shake the wicked from the earth!"

Father McCullers paused, his voice still reverberating through the high-ceilinged hall. He scanned the room with his two burning coals, and they came to rest on Elizabeth.

"For what are we, what is our suffering, before His majesty, His knowledge, His infinite wisdom? Indeed, if the Lord sees fit to deliver us into Satan's hand, it is for reasons that are not ours to question." He smiled, and she raised her hand to her mouth, fighting back the vomit. "For the *fear* of the Lord is *wisdom*, and avoiding evil is *understanding*."

Elizabeth rose, stumbled to the doors, ran to the restroom, and released the contents of her stomach into nearest porcelain bowl. She lay against the cool tile of the bathroom floor until she could no longer hear Father McCullers' voice booming from the pulpit. The homily ended, she returned quietly to her pew and waited, her knee bouncing anxiously, until the time came for confession. She stood in line outside the ornate wooden coffin, silently mouthing familiar prayers for guidance. She clutched her purse to her chest as she crossed the threshold into the confessional and the door shut behind her. The outline of Father McCullers' face shifted behind the black lace of the confessional screen.

"Bless me Father," Elizabeth whispered, her voice shaking, "for I have sinned. It has been more than a year since my last confession."

"Speak, my child." The Father turned behind the screen. The lights of his eyes flashed in the darkness.

"I have carried hatred in my heart," Elizabeth said. Tears welled in the corners of her tired eyes and ran through the ravines carved into her wrinkled face. "For years, like a garden, I have tended to it, fed it, let it grow wild in my soul."

"Refrain from anger," the priest answered mechanically. "And turn from wrath; it leads only to evil."

"I have *already* let myself be led to evil," Elizabeth responded, her voice raw. She gripped the rosary beads around her neck that had once belonged to her husband. "I have desired vengeance, planned it, longed for it. Plotted foul deeds against one who has wronged me."

"Did you lay the foundations of the earth?" Father McCullers asked.

Elizabeth didn't answer, still gripping the rosary.

"No? Then vengeance does not belong to *you*. It is not for us to weigh the scales of justice. Vengeance belongs to the Lord. Trust in Him, for He tells us that the wicked will know He is the Lord thy God when He lays His vengeance upon them."

"Is it not possible," Elizabeth asked, removing her hand from the beads, "that mortal creatures, like you or I, might be the tools He uses to enact that vengeance?"

He laughed hollowly. "Who do you seek vengeance against, my child?"

Elizabeth slipped her hand into her purse. "A man who has wronged me, who has spilled innocent blood. A man who claims to be of the Lord, but acts in service of the Adversary."

Again she gripped the handle of her pistol, her hand trembling inside her bag.

"The Scripture tells us no blood is innocent, child. *All have sinned and fallen short of the glory of God*," the Father replied, his eyes burning holes through the screen between them. "Seek your vengeance, so that through your sinning grace may increase? Shall you accept only good from God, and not evil? Is it your place to return what God has seen fit to deliver you?"

The Father placed his hand against the screen and leaned in close, whispering like a breeze through desolate treetops.

"For perhaps you were delivered to the hands of this man who wronged you as Job was delivered to Satan—by the Lord himself." The white teeth of his smile shone behind the screen. "The faith of good men means nothing. The faith of the suffering means everything. Now, will you anoint yourself in ash, or will you curse God and die?"

Elizabeth didn't answer, her hand still wrapped around the gun.

"You will be forgiven for your sins of wrath. Say three Our Fathers so that you may grow in the virtue of temperance, and make an Act of Contrition."

Elizabeth took a shuddering breath, and released the gun. She repeated to herself the same message as before: Not yet. Not here.

"O my God, I am heartily sorry for having offended Thee," Elizabeth repeated, choking on her tears, "and I detest all my sins, because I dread the loss of heaven, and the pains of hell; but most of all because they offend Thee, my God, Who are good and deserving of all my love. I firmly resolve, with the help of Thy grace, to sin no more and avoid the near occasions of sin. Amen."

"Amen," Father McCullers repeated, retreating back into the shadows of the confessional. "Now go in peace."

* * *

That evening, Allen Myers howled in misery, now

eyeless and blind as Samson, as Father McCullers clamped his pliers around the soft and supple tongue. One of Myers arms was now free from his restraints, but it merely hung limply from the table, the bones pressed into dozens of useless fragments. Blood dripped from his fingertips where the nails had once been. A severed foot lay on the floor in a circle of bloody wire, the stump cauterized by liquid nitrogen, though crimson still dripped slowly through the blue and white charring.

The Father could feel the tissue beginning to tear as the fleshy cable that anchored the tongue to the bottom of the mouth protested against the pressure. Blood leaked from Myers' toothless mouth down his chin. The cable snapped and the tongue became untied, the rudder ripping free of the ship. The priest regarded the twitching pink and purple muscle between the pliers as Myers bellowed in inarticulable anguish, reduced to a quivering mass of suffering.

"Don't worry, my child," Father McCullers smiled, letting his tongue drop from the pliers to the dirt. "I've done you a great favor. The Scripture tells us the tongue is a world of evil that corrupts the whole body. And so I've removed it for you!" He laughed, caressing his victim's face. "And how your eyes caused you to sin! So I have plucked them for you!"

Myers shook his head back and forth, praying for the Lord to deliver him from this evil, praying for justice, but most of all, praying for death. His lips moved slowly in a pantomime of speech as he pleaded with a silent God.

Seeing this, Father McCullers chortled with glee.

"Praying, even now? Truly, what a blameless and upright man you are." He patted the side of the disfigured face, tsking his tongue.

So intently focused on his contorted and screeching victim was Father McCullers that he failed to hear tires rolling to a stop on the dirt outside.

From her car, which she had been driving lightless, painstakingly following the priest's tire tracks by the light of the moon, Elizabeth emerged and stood, upright and full of blame, holding the revolver tight in her bony fist. From the shack, she heard Myers weeping and shrieking, his voice stripped of its dignity and humanity. She wondered if Malcolm had sounded the same.

She crept toward the door, blood pounding in her ears, and slowly pushed it open. Father McCullers hovered over a man Elizabeth vaguely recognized as an usher from that morning's mass. The priest gripped Myers' face in his hand, staring intently into the twin voids where his eyes had once been.

"Shhh. Shhh," he said. "All of this can be over. Will you anoint yourself with ash? Or will you curse God and die?"

The man slowly nodded, blood gurgling from his mouth. Elizabeth raised the pistol, aiming through the shadow at the black-robed figure illuminated by the shifting flames.

"Yes, that's what you want? You blaspheme Him to His face?"

Elizabeth squeezed the trigger. Her gun spoke as if out of a whirlwind.

The bullet entered between Father McCullers' ribs and exited out the other side, bringing with it a spray of crimson that sizzled on the fire. He slipped from atop the table to the ground, clutching his wound. He turned to Elizabeth, recognition shining in his eyes.

"You?"

She fired again, spinning him round as the bullet caught his shoulder. Again, shattering his kneecap. Again, burying the metal slug deep in his gut. He lay on the ground, gasping for life as he watched Elizabeth above him.

"Still you have not learned your lesson!" The Father laughed, sending plumes of blood arcing from his mouth. "This is not your judgment to make! Where were you when He stilled the sea's proud waves? When the morning stars sang in chorus and all the sons of God shouted for joy?" He coughed a scarlet mass onto the front of his robes. "Where were you when He laid the foundations of the earth?"

Elizabeth stepped forward and pushed the barrel of the gun between his teeth.

"Where were *you*?"

She pulled the trigger.

The Father slumped to the dirt, the back of his head seeping into the earth. A single bullet still rested in the chamber. From the table, Myers trashed, his prayers answered, an angel of death delivered unto him.

But as Elizabeth appraised him, she found him broken beyond repair and past the point of saving, much like herself. But, unlike her, he would die on his own within the hour, and though he'd wished for death intensely this single evening, she had waited for its embrace for fifteen years. Fifteen excruciating years, and she could bear the waiting no longer.

"It is finished."

She turned away, bowed her head, and placed the barrel to her temple.

"O my God, I am heartily sorry for having offended Thee," Elizabeth whispered, filled by an emptiness deeper than the sources of the sea.

"I detest all my sins, because I dread the loss of heaven, and the pains of hell; but most of all because they offend Thee, my God, Who are good and deserving of all my love."

She could no longer hear Myers' cries, could feel nothing but the metal pressed against her head.

"I firmly resolve, with the help of Thy grace, to sin no more and avoid the near occasions of sin."

She was neither frightened nor dismayed. God would be with her, no matter where she went.

"Amen."

She pulled the trigger, and went in peace.

THE END

EUCHARIST
By Scot Carpenter

ather Ambrose approached the back door of the orphanage. He wore tan slacks and a flannel shirt, and carried an overcoat over his left arm. He shivered slightly as the night was cold for early spring. Sister Teresa answered his knock and stood in the dark doorway, holding the swaddled infant in her arms.

He stepped up to her and pulled a plastic baggy from his pants pocket. It held white powder. She passed the baby to him at the same time that he handed her the powder.

She looked at it, doubtfully. "It's not enough."

"Discipline, Sister. Discipline. You know how to get more if you need it."

The nun bowed her head and nodded, then silently turned and stepped through the door, closing it behind her. Father Ambrose looked down at the infant in his arms. Dark brown eyes stared up at him. It was, at most, a week old, perfect. He covered it with his coat and briskly walked away.

Father Graves sat in the dark blue Ford Taurus a block away, smoking his second cigarette. He anxiously watched for Ambrose and tossed the butt out of the open window when he saw him approach. Graves started the car while the other priest was still a quarter block away and drummed his fingers on the steering wheel as he waited.

Ambrose opened the door and slid into the seat beside Graves.

"Is it satisfactory?" Graves asked.

"It's perfect," he said, moving his coat to reveal the baby.

Graves carefully drove away, keeping exactly to the speed limit. The two priests didn't speak. He drove around to the back of the church and parked in Father Ambrose's designated spot, then got out and opened the car door for the older priest. Ambrose carefully stepped out while Graves opened the door to the rectory.

The two priests sitting inside rose as Father Ambrose walked in with the baby. The taller of the two, Father Leonard, appeared to be in his early 30's, as did Father Graves, while the other priest, Father Ocasio, was short, rotund and noticeably older. Graves followed Ambrose in and greeted the two priests while Ambrose carried the baby into the next room, then shortly returned.

He addressed the three other priests, "Would anyone like something to drink? I've just acquired a nice single malt."

Fathers Graves and Leonard nodded while Ocasio said, "Do you still have that cognac? I'd love a snifter." Ambrose left, shortly returned with the drinks and passed them around. He had just sat in his chair when the doorbell rang.

"Must be Horwitz," Leonard said. Ambrose opened the door and let in a man older than the others, medium height but slightly stooped.

"Welcome, Rabbi Horwitz," Ambrose said as the others stood. "Have a seat and tell me what you'd like to drink."

"Just a glass of water, thanks. It's a long drive home and I'd hate to get stopped with whisky on my breath."

The rabbi sat down and the others resumed their seats.

He looked around and smiled. "It's good to see us all together again. We should do this more often."

Ambrose chuckled. "Perhaps for Seder. I love the food."

"What's new with you, Rabbi?" asked Ocasio.

"Ah, a brand new Lexus, courtesy of an anonymous gift from the temple expansion fund. The congregation was quite moved that one of its members felt that their rabbi's old car should be replaced with something so nice."

"God bless a generous congregation," Ambrose solemnly intoned.

"Hear, hear," the others replied, raising their glasses.

Horwitz turned to Ocasio. "How is your little project coming along?"

Ocasio replied, "He's not coming yet and neither am I, but progress is being made. I'm tutoring him in Latin and he's bright as well as angelic. I believe he's gay, though it's hard to tell with an eleven-year-old, because he shows more interest in male nudes than females in the art books we look at. He was quite taken with some Indian erotic art and Japanese shunga prints. I showed him Donatello's David and said that I'd like to sketch him in that pose. He seemed quite enthusiastic. I'd better stop; I'm getting quite aroused thinking of it. The seduction adds so much to the actual conquest that I almost prefer it at this stage in life."

"It is nice to have a hobby," Horwitz said. "And what is the time?"

Ambrose said, "We have fifteen minutes until lunar zenith."

"Well, then. Shall we get started?" Horwitz asked, as he looked at the others.

They silently rose and walked into the next room where Ambrose had taken the infant. It was larger than the parlor they'd been in, square with a small fireplace centered on the wall adjacent to the door they'd passed through. The single window across from the door was shuttered and a closed door opposite the fireplace led to the kitchen. A simple altar topped with a marble slab sat against the wall next to the fireplace and tall candelabras stood in each corner of the room.

The infant lay in a small wooden box on a credence table next to the altar. Ambrose had swaddled it in a lambskin with the wool still attached. Arranged in the center of the altar were a bowl, a chalice and a tray, all of gold. A small knife with a golden handle and a wooden box sat on the right side of the altar.

Five hooks on the side wall held gray, ankle-length, long-sleeved woolen tunics. Each man donned one of the tunics over his clothes. Leonard and Graves began to light the seven candles on each candelabrum while Ocasio and Ambrose rolled up an Indian rug, revealing a large pentangle incised into the wooden floor. Horwitz arranged the items on the altar, then opened the wooden box and removed a scroll.

"Is it time, Ambrose?"

"We can begin now."

The four priests stood in a line with heads bowed as Horwitz spoke, "These are the true words from the Book of Genesis, revealing God's command to Abraham to sacrifice his son, Isaac."

Then he began translating from the scroll written in ancient Hebrew:

El olam appeared to Abraham and said, "Take your son, your only son Isaac, whom you love, and go to the land of Moria and offer him there as a burnt offering on one of the mountains of which I shall tell you."

So Abraham rose early in the morning, saddled his donkey, and took his son, Isaac. And he cut the wood for the burnt offering and arose and went to the place of which God had told him. And Abraham took the wood of the burnt offering and laid it on Isaac his son. So they went, both of them together.

And Isaac said to his father Abraham, "My father!"

And he said, "Here I am, my son."

Isaac said, "Behold, the fire and the wood, but where is the lamb for a burnt offering?"

Abraham said, "God will provide for Himself the lamb for a burnt offering, my son."

As they climbed, they saw a young woman coming down the mountain toward them. Her eyes were full of sorrow and she did not speak as they passed. When they came to the place of which God had told him, Abraham built the altar there and laid the wood in order and bound Isaac his son and laid him on the altar, on top of the wood. Then Abraham reached out his hand and took the knife to slaughter his son.

But the angel Ba'al appeared to Abraham, holding an infant swaddled in the skin of a lamb. He said, "Behold the Lamb of God, whom you shall sacrifice rather than your son, Isaac. El olam will surely bless you and will surely multiply your offspring as the stars of heaven and as the sand that is on the seashore. And your offspring shall possess the gate of his enemies, and in your offspring shall all the nations of the earth be blessed, because you have obeyed El olam's voice. As proof of his blessing, El olam commands you to drink the blood and eat the flesh of the Lamb, and you shall have life everlasting."

Abraham freed his son, Isaac, and then took the infant swaddled in lambskin from Ba'al and laid him on the altar he had prepared. Then he and Isaac partook of the blood and flesh of the Lamb and praised El olam for his beneficence. After Abraham burnt the offering, Ba'al spoke again.

He said, "All of your sons and sons of sons who perform this sacrifice at the height of the first full moon in Nisan, each at a point of the five cornered star of El olam, will also have eternal life. From this day forth, The Everlasting God shall be known as Yahweh and no other gods shall be worshipped in his stead."

Then Ba'al rose into the sky as smoke ascended to the

heavens. So Abraham and Isaac left the mountain and went to Beersheba. And Abraham lived at Beersheba.

Horwitz returned the scroll to the box and said, "Bring the Lamb."

Ambrose unwrapped the infant and stepped toward Horwitz.

Horwitz asked again, "Is it time?"

Ambrose looked at his watch. "In a minute."

Graves took the bowl from the altar and Horwitz picked up the knife. They waited until Ambrose said, "It is time," and held out the infant, holding it head down by the ankles. Graves moved the bowl under the infant as Horwitz held its head. The baby began to cry. The cry became a wail when Horwitz gently pushed the blade into the side of its neck. Blood poured out into the bowl Graves held. After a short while, the infant stopped wailing but blood continued to flow. When the last drops of blood had drained into the bowl, Ambrose held a cloth under the infant's neck as Horwitz turned and laid the body on the altar. He used the knife to slice five strips of skin from the body and lay them on the tray. Horwitz then held the chalice while Graves carefully filled it halfway from the bowl.

Horwitz stepped back from the altar and knelt, facing it as the other four knelt behind him. "Yahweh, may our humble sacrifice be blessed by you. We thank you for this gift of life and swear to uphold and obey you forevermore."

Horwitz, and then the others, rose. Horwitz placed the infant's body back into the wooden box on the credence table while Ambrose picked up the chalice, and Graves the tray. Horwitz carried the box containing the infant's body to the fireplace and placed it on the grate while Ambrose and Graves set the chalice and tray in the center of the pentangle.

The pentangle was oriented with one point facing the fireplace. The four priests prostrated themselves, facing inward at the other four points. Horwitz turned on the gas and lit the flame, then prostrated himself at the remaining point. As the fire began to consume the wooden box and its contents, the four priests closed their eyes and chanted in Latin while Horwitz joined them in Hebrew.

They continued chanting until a thunderclap shook the house and a light, bright enough to penetrate their eyelids, filled the room. They remained prostrate for a few moments, then slowly sat and finally stood up, remaining at their places around the pentangle.

Horwitz stepped forward, bent and picked up the chalice while Ambrose did the same with the tray. Horwitz said, "This is the body and the blood of the Lamb of God. He who partakes of it shall have life everlasting." He took a sip from the chalice and said, "Blessed be the blood," then passed the chalice to the man next to him.

Ambrose passed the tray to him and Horwitz took a strip of skin, saying, "Blessed be the body," before he ate it and passed the tray. After the chalice and tray had made the circle back to Ambrose, he carried them to the altar, and then returned to the group. The five held hands and prayed silently. When they had finished praying, they returned the tunics to their hooks and went back to the living room.

Horwitz spoke up, "A perfect Ritual. Thank you, gentlemen."

They all returned the compliment, and then Ambrose asked, "Would anyone like another drink?"

All but Ocasio demurred. Ambrose saw them to the door, then turned to Ocasio, "Another brandy?"

"Sounds lovely."

They sat silently for a moment, and then Ocasio said, "You know, this is the one constant in an ever-changing world. That stability comforts me amidst the chaos that the world is becoming. I remember centuries when nothing basically changed."

"It is hard to get used to," Ambrose agreed. "I thought that the Church would provide me a refuge from change, but even it's becoming something unfamiliar. But as long as we have the Liturgy, there will be a consistency in Catholicism. Though I do miss the Latin service. And allowing the Scriptures to be translated into English was a huge mistake. Inevitable, I suppose, though we both fought it tooth and nail."

"Damn that Martin Luther," Ocasio chuckled. "Those were the days. But I've gotten used to the lack of luxury and we still have our boys, though that is getting more difficult to hide."

"Do you ever think of the days before us, the time of Rome and the early Church?" Ambrose asked.

"From a historical perspective or more philosophically?"

"Philosophically, I suppose. I wonder what would have happened if Jesus' Pentad had not been betrayed and his remaining four hadn't written the Gospels and created the story of the Last Supper to hide the true nature of the Ritual. What would the world be like today if the Church hadn't come into being as a cover story for the Ritual?"

"Well, we'd not have had a job for hundreds of years," Ocasio said.

Ambrose chuckled. "True. But it's amazing to me that just one Pentad being exposed could cause such a change in the world. So many others have been found out and all that happened was that they were burned or hung."

"Witches make convenient scapegoats for all sorts of things. Lucky for us that every time a Pentad is found out, the world doesn't change."

Ambrose sat for a moment, and then asked, "What do you think of Graves?"

Ocasio hesitated. "His participation in the Ritual is certainly satisfactory but I have a sense that he's not entirely comfortable with it. Perhaps because it's so new to him. How old is he?"

"Fifty something. He's had over twenty Rituals. But I know what you mean. There seems to be some lingering doubt, perhaps even guilt. It's so hard to know how people will react in the long run. His confessions make me think that he'll be fine. When Father Johnson was killed in that car wreck, we had to find a fifth in a hurry."

Ocasio shook his head. "Amazing how much luck plays in it. When I think of some of the things we've survived... sometimes I think that God does favor us over others. I wonder if Abraham is still around. Hard to believe he could be, but who knows?"

"I wonder what he'd look like if he was. The world takes its toll on our appearance, however slowly. But I think we both look pretty good."

"Here's to a graceful old age." Ocasio raised his glass.

The next morning, Ambrose arose early as he always did after a Ritual. Its rejuvenating effects didn't extend to his mood. He stared at the mirror, critically looking at the lines in his face and the skin starting to sag under his chin. He lathered his face, picked up the straight razor, and wondered once again why go on. Ambrose sighed, put the razor to his throat and carefully began to shave.

THE END

WHEN HELL FREEZES OVER
By JL Shioshita

The light outside the window was dazzling, as the noonday sun shone down upon the white snow. Father Dreed closed his eyes against the radiance, but the afterimage still glowed, burned on his retinas like so many fireworks. After a deep breath, he reopened them and picked up the tattered Bible lying on the seat beside him, yet try as he might, he could not read one passage or even attempt his daily devotions. His mind was burdened, and his thoughts weighed heavily upon his soul like a heavy cloak. His beloved church was going to be shuttered unless he could find some way to pay off the many debts his small parish had accumulated over the years, and with attendance at an all-time low, the coffers were no longer full. They even had to use saltine crackers for communion, which the children didn't seem to mind, all three of them. *No,* Father Dreed thought. *I will not worry. Take your burdens to the Lord.* He closed his eyes to pray.

* * *

It was bright. Not a warm, cozy brightness, but a harsh, blinding, white light, the kind that illuminates public restrooms, revealing all faults and blemishes. The pain was intense, and as he started to move, his body cried out in agony, willing him to stop. He collapsed once more into the cold wet snow, a crumpled heap. He was alive. The thought struck him as inane and ironic, for though he had survived the malfunction of one of man's machines, he was destined to die, not by any human means, but by the unforgiving harshness of nature. He was dizzy, and his head hurt. It felt like he was swimming. He knew he wasn't in his right mind, and that understanding brought him little comfort. *I must have injured my head in the crash*, he thought. It was cold, so very cold. Father Dreed closed his eyes. He was so weak.

* * *

He awoke again, this time fully conscious. The harsh light was gone, replaced by an inky blackness. Not a star shone in the heavens above, yet a hidden moon seemed to cast an eerie glow over the surrounding, snowy landscape. As far as the eye could see, there was only snow. It encompassed all. All was white, white and so quiet. Slowly the memories began to creep back into Father Dreed's consciousness, the chain of events that had led to this current calamity. The horrible recollections flooded upon him, overwhelming him. *The train, it had derailed. It crashed*, Father Dreed remembered. *There had been something over the intercom and a nervous passenger pacing up and down the aisle; a child crying and a gruff voice silencing it…*

The memories seemed vague and fuzzy, like they belonged to someone else. Then, slowly, full realization dawned and Father Dreed understood the peril of his situation. "It's so cold, so cold," he said out loud, surprised by how faint his voice sounded. "I guess this it. This is the end." But with this understanding came no fear or anxiety.

For despite everything, he felt at peace. He closed his eyes and prayed, "Dear Lord, take me to paradise. I am ready, Lord. I am ready." And with that, Father Dreed prepared to die.

* * *

"Oh, so you finally decided to wake up, huh?"

"What?" Father Dreed replied.

"I thought you'd never wake up," the voice answered. "You've been out for quite a while."

The voice sounded raspy and high pitched, the kind of timbre that might belong to a mischievous imp or a gremlin.

All was black.

"I, I can't see," Father Dreed said.

"Oh, don't worry. Your vision will come. Like I said, you've been out for a while, and your eyes need time to readjust to seeing."

The speaker was right. Gradually Father Dreed's vision began to return. At first all he saw was a hazy blurriness, but slowly his surroundings came into focus—a cave, a dark cave with a large fire in the center. *A fire?* Father Dreed thought. *A cave?*

"I'm alive!" Father Dreed exclaimed.

"Yes, yes you are, my friend."

Father Dreed whirled around to face the voice. There, close to the entrance of the cave, hunched a short, squat figure. The figure was covered in dark rags, which smelled absolutely horrible, and as he turned to confront his apparent saviour, Father Dreed was forced to cover his nose and mouth with his hand, stifling the rising wave of nausea elicited as the putrid stench hit him full on. The ragged man—Father Dreed assumed it was a man—had a long face that came to a point at the chin, punctuated by a coarse, thin goatee. His skin was weathered and rough, like old leather worn from age, and he had two beady eyes like pieces of coal; yet, unlike coal, they glimmered and sparkled as if lit from some unseen fire within. A shifty hat adorned the man's pointy head, casting his face in shadow and giving him a somewhat devious look, while his dirty, unkempt hair spilled out from the dark folds of his hat like so many greasy worms. Father Dreed took an immediate disliking to him.

"And well, I might add," the dirty man continued.

Father Dreed didn't know what to think. "You saved me?" he asked, questioningly.

"Yes, yes I did, but don't be afraid. I'm not going to ask for payment or anything. I'm just glad to have been able to help. That frozen wasteland out there," he gestured toward the entrance to the cave. "It's dangerous. Many a man has died alone in that ice and snow."

"Well, I thank you for rescuing me," Father Dreed replied.

The peculiar man studied him for a moment before answering. "Think nothing of it. Now get some rest. Your body still needs to mend." And with that, the odd man closed his eyes and began to snore.

Father Dreed was dumbfounded. He didn't know what to think. Unanswered questions tugged at the back of his mind, seeking an answer that wasn't there. He began to study his surroundings once more, scrutinizing every minute detail. The cave was very plain. Father Dreed had never really been in a cave before, but this cave was just like how he imagined one would be. There was nothing singular or striking about it at all. He looked at the fire and watched the smoke drift upward toward the ceiling…but there was no ceiling. On closer observation, Father Dreed noticed that the smoke seemed to ascend into nothing. There was no rock above him, only a dark abyss. *It's probably just shadows playing tricks with my eyes*, Father Dreed thought. *I did just walk away from a train wreck after all.* He then refocused his attention on the strange man who had apparently saved his life. *What an odd man*, he pondered. *What's his game?* He was still studying his rescuer when the man spoke.

"Don't live backwards," the curious man declared.

"What?" Father Dreed stammered, but then noticed the man's eyes were still closed. *He must be talking in his sleep*, he thought.

The man's eyes suddenly snapped open. He immediately looked at Father Dreed and asked, "Why are you staring at me?"

"You were talking in your sleep," Father Dreed answered.

"Oh yeah, what did I say?"

"I'm not sure," Father Dreed replied.

The man seemed to ponder this in his head for a moment before replying, "Maybe it was a prophetic omen."

Maybe my rescuer is insane, Father Dreed wondered. But instead of voicing his opinion to the man, he calmly said, "I doubt it. You were just talking in your sleep. Probably something you ate."

"I guess you don't believe in premonitions or getting messages from dreams?" the weird man remarked.

Father Dreed looked him straight in those odd, black eyes, and with as strong a voice as he could muster, replied, "Of course not. That's all just rubbish, make believe."

"Is it now?" the man said, raising his arms up defensively. "Did you know that Hitler believed in dowsing and would send a dowser with his troops to the front lines to find water? He also believed in the theory that there was another world inside the Earth, one inhabited by a super race of human beings."

Father Dreed couldn't keep from chuckling. "Hitler was also a maniacal madman who tried to take over the world," he laughed.

The strange man rubbed his nose and started laughing as well.

Father Dreed stopped at this. The man's laugh was not a laugh that bespoke light-hearted humor or jest, but instead had a disturbing gravitas about it.

"You don't believe in ESP or telekinesis or the astral plane?" the man asked.

"No, I do not," Father Dreed replied. He was a bit shaken now. There was something about the way the man laughed and behaved that was unnatural, something off.

The eccentric man picked his nose, thoughtfully. His eyes narrowed as if studying Father Dreed, sizing him up like a predator. He flicked the refuse from his nose into the fire, cleared his throat and continued, "What about all the evidence to the contrary? What about the megaliths that dot Europe's landscape or the strange happenings that occur along ley lines? How can you explain these things?"

"I don't have to explain them," Father Dreed answered. "I know them to be false."

The unusual man sat back on his haunches, his eyes fixed on Father Dreed. His stare made Father Dreed very uncomfortable, made him feel as if he was in grade school again, being tested by an overly severe and critical teacher. He did not like the feeling.

The man seemed to sense Father Dreed's unease, which brought a crooked smile to his face. He cocked his head to one side, still staring in that unsettling way, and continued, "You don't believe in ghosts, monsters, spirits, poltergeists, psychic powers, or other unexplainable things, yet you proclaim yourself to be a godly man. God is unexplainable; some might even call H i m supernatural. He cannot be proven, and He is not of the natural world. I do believe that this would place God into the category that you so strongly deny exists."

Father Dreed stared at the bizarre man, shocked. "You know nothing," he stammered. "God is different from ghosts and goblins."

"But," the man interrupted, "there is more physical evidence supporting the existence of UFOs than there is supporting the existence of your God."

Father Dreed wrested his gaze from the disturbing man. It was all he could do not to reach out and strike him. Never had anyone so blatantly assaulted his faith like this before. He stammered and stuttered but could find nothing meaningful to say. The two of them sat in silence for what seemed like hours, the only noises the crackling fire in the middle of the cave and the ferocious wind blowing violently past the entrance to their cramped sanctuary. Eventually, Father Dreed mustered up enough courage to speak again, breaking the stillness. "How did you know I was religious?" he asked.

"I could tell," the creepy man replied.

Father Dreed now turned his back on his supposed rescuer. He refused to look at him a moment longer. This aberrant man seemed to be taunting him on purpose. The calm that had presided over Father Dreed's thoughts and actions become tumult. He felt doubt and anger towards the man for causing him to feel doubt. *I will confront him*, Father Dreed thought. He turned around with the full intention of putting the man in his place, but before he could utter one word, the horrible man spoke again.

"There's a blizzard raging right now, but it should break by noon tomorrow. There's a town about twenty miles north of here. We'll start out after the storm blows over. There we can part ways, and I won't defile you or your religion with my pagan remarks any longer," the man said, sarcastically. "Now get some rest." The man then lay down on his side, turning his back to Father Dreed, and went to sleep.

Father Dreed sat speechless but relieved. He could go. Get back to civilization, away from this crazy man and his crazy ideas.

As he sat on the cold, unforgiving floor staring at the sleeping form across from him, a form he had come to despise, Father Dreed noticed a bulky brown satchel that the man was using as a pillow. He had not noticed this bag before. It looked very old and very well used. There was a hole in the top of it, and through this hole, Father Dreed glimpsed a faint glimmer of green, which sparkled in a strange and unnatural manner. Curious, Father Dreed moved toward the disturbed man, who snored obnoxious and oblivious to the approach, in order to steal a better look at the contents of the mysterious bag. He carefully inched the makeshift pillow out from under the sleeping head of the foul-smelling man, amazed at his own brazenness, and upon success, retreated back to his corner of the cave.

What could a man like that be carrying with him? he thought.

He gingerly opened the dirty, brown bag, struggling to suppress the gag reflex that was tickling the back of his throat like a caged butterfly. The stench of the man seemed to have permeated the very fabric of the satchel, and the potency of the resulting odor was almost too much for Father Dreed to bear. Turning his face away, repulsed, he shot his hand into the rank depths, snatching up whatever lay inside, and then hurriedly hurled the empty satchel toward the far cave wall. It slumped empty against the rock like a limp, dead body. Fearing he had been too loud, Father Dreed glanced nervously at the sleeping man in the opposite end of the cave, but the form did not stir. His thievery had been successful. He held up his prize: a beautiful jade statue and multiple, thick stacks of hundred dollar bills.

Father Dreed was dumbstruck. The money itself must have totalled in the tens of thousands, but who knew how much the jade statue was worth? It definitely looked old and of high quality. His heart racing, he placed the stacks of cash behind him against the cave wall, out of sight, so that he could examine the statue in more detail. He took the strange, green figure in both of his hands and held it up to the glow of the firelight, positioning it carefully to keep it out of view of his sleeping companion.

It was fairly large, a little bit bigger than a man's fist, and quite heavy. As Father Dreed studied it, he noticed it was not just made out of jade. Rubies, sapphires, and emeralds adorned the intricate piece. He couldn't tell what it was supposed to represent. It was obviously humanoid, but other than that, was completely alien to his comprehension. It had a disturbing, twisted face, with two large diamonds for eyes and a large ruby embedded in the forehead. The craftsmanship was exquisite, with fine attention paid to every detail, and though Father Dreed could appreciate the artistry of the piece, it held a strange dread that enveloped the very core of his being. He dropped the figure and hurriedly moved away. It rolled along the cave floor before coming to a stop next to the fire, facing him, that twisted grin glowing against the flames.

Despite its unsettling nature, Father Dreed couldn't take his eyes off the figure. He stared at it for what seemed like an eternity, thoughtless and quiet, until a distant idea began to form in the back of his mind. The statue was evil, of that there was no doubt. More than likely demonic or satanic, and that meant the horrid man who kept it in his keep must have been just as sinister. The cash that Father Dreed found stashed with the statue must have been obtained through ill-gotten means and would only be used to further the forces of evil against good. Though he had no true evidence to support any of this, he knew in his heart of hearts that it must be true, and thusly he knew what he must do.

Father Dreed gently picked up the jade statue and tossed it into the fire to burn. He grabbed the stacks of cash and stuffed them into his pockets. He then shot one last bitter glance at the sleeping man in the far corner of the cave before rushing out of the entrance and into the swirling blizzard beyond.

* * *

Father Dreed pushed his way through the storm, pushed his way through the limits of his tired and beaten body. He didn't know how long he had been walking, but to his dismay, the blizzard showed no sign of stopping.

I've got to make it, he thought. *I've got to.*

He soldiered on. The snow swallowed up his legs to the knees, so cold and wet that he could no longer feel his feet; while the cutting wind sliced into his pale, exposed flesh, leaving it raw and ragged. And it wasn't only the storm that was taking its toll: Father Dreed found himself physically weighed down as if by some invisible burden. It felt like he had stones in his pockets, stones that got heavier with each step he took away from the cave, the statue, and the sinister man.

He tripped and fell, tumbling into the cold wet abyss, tired and exhausted. As he lay there in that swirling vortex, staring into an infinite canvas of white, a glimmer of hope appeared. He spied a collection of lights in the distance. He squinted his eyes and looked closer, relieved to discover they belonged to a town about a mile away. Overjoyed, Father Dreed attempted to rise, only to find that he could not. That invisible weight that seemed to grow heavier with each step was now insurmountable, those stones in his pockets, boulders. "No!" he cried out. "This can't be! I'm so close."

He struggled to rise from the snow, to pull himself up, to crawl toward the distant town, struggled until all of his strength had left him, left him with only his thoughts and the blurry promise of salvation twinkling in the snowy distance. He gazed at those lights longingly, the embodiment of hope, so close and yet so far away. Then, to his terror and astonishment, one by one they flickered out, disappeared until none remained and only white darkness filled the vacant void. And now a figure emerged from the void—a thin form approaching Father Dreed through the chaos of wind and snow, suddenly upon him, leaning over him. It had no face and no features, but spoke directly to Father Dreed's mind.

"He got you, huh? With his stupid test?"

Father Dreed answered without moving his frozen lips, "Please, help me."

The form crouched down, its hands on its knees, its empty face looking down upon the frozen man.

"Yeah, he doesn't play fair, does he? With all his tests and his trials, forcing you to constantly prove yourself through temptation and hardship. I could never stomach that. You know what I mean?"

The form let out a long sigh before continuing.

"No matter, I can help you now, now that you made your choice. Are you ready?"

Father Dreed thought he finally understood.

"And you are… God, right? You're here to take me to heaven?"

"Hell no, you already met him. I'm the Devil."

THE END

HOLY SHIT!
By Gerri R. Gray

Some men collect comic books and baseball cards; others collect postage stamps and coins. A man of means might collect classic European automobiles, big game trophies, fine art, or other items possessing great value. Louis IX, commonly known as Saint Louis, collected saints' relics and built temples for them. Napoleon Bonaparte collected countries.

Malcolm Thorndike, a man of vast wealth and questionable taste, also possessed a passion for collecting, although his was a peculiar one, to say the least. By the time he had reached the age of thirty, he had invested (some would say squandered) a large chunk of his sizable inheritance amassing an impressive and one-of-a-kind collection of rare stools from around the world. Not the kind of stools one would sit on, but rather the kind discharged from one's bowels after food has been digested.

Within his spacious Fifth Avenue mansion overlooking the wilds of Central Park, locked bookcases and lighted curio cabinets lined the walls of every room, their spotless shelves overflowing with the turds of celebrities, saints and sinners, as well as the dung of exotic animals and royalty—all proudly on display under clear glass domes that were polished three times a week by Malcolm's faithful Japanese houseboy, Motoshi. Smaller, albeit equally prized, specimens were housed in shadow boxes that dominated the stairwell and halls like exhibits in a SoHo art gallery. And in the center of the mansion's opulent and capacious paneled parlor, directly beneath a monstrous chandelier with hundreds of red crystals like drops of frozen blood, a fossilized pterodactyl dropping that set Malcolm's bank account back nearly five thousand dollars graced the top of an antique Chippendale desk. It pulled double duty as a paperweight and conversation-starter.

An icy drizzle blurred the windowpanes as, one by one, the guests arrived at the feces-filled mansion and gathered in the parlor like six of the seven deadly sins. There were R.J. Solomon—Chairman and Chief Executive of a multinational luxury goods conglomerate; Cromwell Mortimer—a British petrol-industrialist and founder of a major oil company; Giselle Delacroix—French socialite and heiress to one of the world's largest cosmetic companies; Gunther Vogel—German billionaire businessman and owner of an international pharmaceutical empire; billionaire shipping magnate, Jules Christos; and filthy rich (and filthy-minded) televangelist, Skyler Raines.

They were, without question, half a dozen of the world's wealthiest individuals. They had the best that money could afford—luxurious homes, luxurious cars, luxurious yachts, and the finest of everything. Yet, despite their extravagances and exorbitant toys, they still felt dissatisfied with their lives. However, their wealth and dissatisfaction were not the only things this group had in common: they each shared a burning desire for immortality... and were willing to pay any price to obtain it.

A low rumble of thunder echoed in the distance as the guests waited in jittery silence for their host to make his entrance. A cloud of shallow-breathed anticipation hung thick and heavy in the air. Giselle Delacroix lit one of her stubby French cigarettes, crossed her legs and eyed the German and the televangelist as the two men strolled about the room like art connoisseurs examining the unusual exhibits. Cromwell Mortimer, growing restless, cleared his throat and began tapping his fingertips on the arms of his chair. The others sat motionless, staring out into nothingness.

Lightning streaked past the rain-obscured window, dispatching a sharp finger stabbing toward the earth. Another rumble of thunder, louder than the previous one, growled overhead as if to herald the arrival of slow and rhythmic footsteps that echoed out in the hallway. They grew louder as they drew closer to the parlor.

A massive, carved oak pocket door slid open with an oil-thirsting squeak and Malcolm Thorndike stepped into the room. Motoshi immediately followed, wheeling a serving cart upon which rested a small, ornate tray of sterling silver and an ancient alabaster jar, which was sealed with a wooden plug covered in decaying black wax.

Malcolm took a quick gaze around the room. Satisfied to find all his guests present, he flashed a smile of rehearsed cordiality and greeted them. "Welcome! Welcome to my humble abode. I'm delighted that you've all chosen to accept my invitation!" He quickly turned and thanked his servant. "That will be all for now, Motoshi. I'll summon you when we're ready."

The Japanese houseboy bowed and departed the room.

No sooner had the squeaking pocket door slid shut, Malcolm popped the stopper from the alabaster jar and tilted it on its side until a shiny black log of petrified poop slid out of the ancient vessel and onto the ornate tray. A silvery-white aura faintly shimmered around the turd.

"Behold!" he trumpeted like an overacting thespian. "This is my latest acquisition! The crown jewel of my collection!"

Gunther Vogel wrinkled his bulbous nose in disgust and his upper lip curled upward to reveal a row of tobacco-stained teeth. "I did not travel all the way to the United States from Germany to look at a turd on a silver platter!" he remarked, his voice smoldering. "I came because I was told you had uncovered the secret of immortality!"

"An elixir that renders death obsolete, I believe," Jules Christos added.

R.J. Solomon cleared his throat. "A ten million dollar elixir to be exact. That's what we've all come here for." He turned to Malcolm. "Time is money, Thorndike, so let us get down to the business at hand. I have a plane to catch at ten."

"I wholeheartedly agree," said the televangelist, his high-pitched voice tinged with a southern accent. "Enough of this talk about turds."

"Ah, but the turd you see before you on this silver platter is no ordinary turd," the collector replied with a gleam in his eyes. "That I can assure you!" He gazed down lovingly at the excrement. "This is a turd so special, so venerated, so *sacred*, that it was kept under lock and key at the Vatican for centuries." Malcolm paused, grinned from ear to ear, and then continued. "Friends and colleagues, feast your soon-to-be-immortal eyes upon the holy shit of none other than the Son of God himself!"

A mixture of startled gasps and chortles filled the parlor.

"After Jesus died on the cross for our sins, he, to put it bluntly, shit himself—something a lot of dead people do as the muscles in their body relax. Mary Magdalene, who attended the crucifixion, gathered up the crap of Christ after the Roman guards had departed Golgotha and stored it in this alabaster jar."

Lightning illuminated the window and another rumble of thunder sounded as the guests exchanged hushed whispers among themselves.

"My friends," Malcolm continued as the thunder and

whispers died away, "I have promised each and every one of you everlasting life, and everlasting life is what you will have… tonight! I have gone to great lengths and expense to acquire this divine stool, for this is the stool of immortality! According to a lost scripture tucked away in the vaults of the Vatican, a life eternal—not in heaven, but right here on earth—is guaranteed to all who partake of the Christ turd!"

"This is blasphemy!" Skyler Raines declared, clutching the diamond-encrusted gold cross he wore around his neck. "But tell me more."

"Hold on a minute. Are you telling us we have to *eat* it?" Jules Christos asked, squinting his eyes in apparent puzzlement. His voice clearly rang with anxiety, which he seemed to make no effort to conceal.

Malcolm grinned, amused by the expression of alarm raging on the shipping magnate's face, and nodded his head. "Relax, Jules, old boy. A turd of antiquity possesses neither an unpleasant odor, nor taste."

"I'm not going to inquire as to how you've come to know that," the Greek man stated. "I will simply take your word for it."

Malcolm chuckled at his guest's remark and then explained to everyone, "Just one pinch of powdered Christ turd added to a goblet of wine will make you immune from the clutches of death. Or, if you prefer, you can snort a line of it like nose candy. The choice is up to you."

Giselle sensuously drew on her cigarette and exhaled the smoke ever so slowly before breaking her silence. Her lips, which matched the color of the Chateau Margaux in her crystal wine glass, parted, and in an impassive voice laden with a French accent, she inquired of her host, "Malcolm, darling, these things you tell us are, how do you say," she paused to find the right word in English, "extraordinary! But how can we be sure that the legend of this holy relic is rooted in fact, or even that it's safe for us to ingest it? After all, it doesn't appear that anyone has ever put it to the test."

Before Malcolm could string together the words to form a reply, the voice of an intruder bellowed from the pocket door that had slid open when no one was watching. It was a gruff-sounding voice, allocating dread and blazing with fury. It was a voice clad with familiarity.

"Everybody put your hands in the air! Now!" the intruder growled, his gaze darting around the room, his trigger finger ready to dispense death. "I want to see those goddamn hands!"

Without the necessity of turning around to look, Malcolm instantly knew the intruder's identity: It was a man by the name of John Butler—a master jewel thief to whom he had paid what one would call "a small fortune" for services rendered… services that included stealing the Christ turd from the Vatican and the killing of several Swiss Guards in the process. Malcolm had no delusions about the thief's motives. He knew he had come to rob him of the holy shit.

Giselle threw her head back in a defiant gesture, and the diamonds in her gold earrings caught the light of the massive, red chandelier above. "You have your nerve!" she blasted Butler, her painted lips curled in an insolent sneer. "Just what is the meaning of this *vulgarité*?"

"Shut your trap, lady, and get your hands up in the air like I told you!" the gunman shot back, the level of anger rising in his voice. He waved his gun recklessly in front of the woman's high-cheekboned face. "Do it, if you know what's good for you."

Giselle reluctantly did as ordered, all the while grumbling something in French.

Appeased by the woman's compliance, Butler turned his eyes to the other guests, whose faces reflected varying degrees of shock and dismay. Pointing his gun at random targets, he barked out more instructions. "Don't anybody try to be hero. I won't hesitate to blow a hole through your head if you so much as move a finger." His right eye began to twitch. "Just do as you're told, and nobody gets hurt. Got it?"

Heads nervously nodded in unison.

"Hello Butler." Malcolm said, flatly, his voice devoid of its usual good cheer. "So, we meet again, as they say in the movies."

"Hello shit collector," Butler replied, aiming his gun at Malcolm's chest.

"What do you want?" Malcolm inquired. "More money?"

Butler smiled, contemptuously. "You're a screwball, but you're not a stupid man, Thorndike. You know exactly what I want, and you know I won't hesitate to kill you and everyone else in this house to get it. Now, hand over that Christ turd!"

Malcolm placed his hand protectively over the stool on the silver tray. "For what possible reason could you want my Christ turd?"

"The Vatican hired me, of all people, to retrieve their precious turd. They had no idea I was the one who stole it in the first place!" A laugh escaped Butler's mouth. "They're paying me almost as much as you paid me to steal it. But when I found out its true value and *why* they wanted it back so desperately…"

"You decided it would be more advantageous for you to double-cross them," Malcolm said, finishing Butler's sentence.

"You're nothing but a blasphemer!" shouted the televangelist. His cheeks were flushed with rage and a pulsating, blue vein that traveled from the edge of his left eyebrow to his hairline made itself prominent. "There's a special place in hell for sinners like you!"

"Not if I become immortal," Butler snapped back.

"Thou shalt not steal!" Raines blurted out. His words did little but to arouse a look of amusement from the thief's face. "God shall judge and punish accordingly those who willfully break any of his Ten Commandments! You need to repent, my son. Let me save you."

Outraged by the T.V. preacher's blatant hypocrisy, Butler flew into a rage. "Shut up, you sanctimonious sleazeball! If God is going to give anyone a one-way ticket to hell, it'll be con artists like you who fill the heads of your weak-minded followers with lies and false hopes so you can milk their bank accounts in the name of religion!" He then pivoted and waved his gun before the trembling host. "The turd, Mister Thorndike… "

Unbeknown to John Butler, Motoshi had stealthily crept up behind him during his tirade, a heavy cast iron wok clenched tightly in his hands. Being the ever-loyal servant that he was, he raised the bowl-shaped frying pan above his head and then struck it against the back of Butler's head with all his might. The blow produced a loud cracking sound. Butler's eyes rolled up into his head, becoming ghost-white orbs. His body lurched forward in response to the impact, and he involuntarily squeezed the trigger of his gun. A shot rang out and a bullet darted across the room, ripping open a ragged gash in the throat of the Reverend Skyler Raines, before shattering one of the glass domes and imbedding itself in the oak paneling behind him.

Dropping her wine glass, Giselle erupted with a scream as Butler collapsed onto the floor before her feet, and the horrified preacher frantically clawed at his blood-spurting throat. From his bleeding mouth came a sickening gurgling sound in place of words. Raines began to stagger as though intoxicated and then fell forward into the antique Chippendale desk, knocking over the fossilized pterodactyl dropping. His legs gave out from underneath him and he sank to the floor, still clawing and gurgling.

Stricken with panic, Malcolm's guests leapt from their seats and bolted in the direction of the open pocket door. But, before they could escape from the feces-filled room and its metallic stench of blood, Malcolm blocked the exit, waving the holy shit in the air.

"My friends, please, you have no reason to panic!" he shouted, his eyes wild as the storm raging outside the mansion. "I implore you all to return to your seats! There's no need for anyone to leave. I have this situation well under control, as each and every one of you will soon bear witness to!"

The eyes of his rattled guests followed him as he calmly made his way over to the profusely bleeding televangelist and then grew wide with shock when he proceeded to insert the turd into the bullet hole in the man's throat. Within a matter of seconds, there emanated a loud sizzling sound from the wound, not unlike the hissing of bacon in a hot frying pan. He gently withdrew the turd from the wound and the river of blood that had turned Raine's white shirt the same color as the red leather interior of his brand new Rolls Royce Wraith ceased to flow. The room resonated with gasps of disbelief as all traces of red spillage mysteriously vanished and the ragged gash just as mysteriously mended itself. Malcolm then helped Raines to his feet.

The stunned televangelist brought his ring-adorned hand up to his throat and placed it over the spot where the bullet hole had been just moments ago. He then checked his hand for blood. There was none. Finding the wound completely healed and his neck as good as new, a look of astonishment spread over his face like an oil lick.

"It's a miracle! I've been healed!" he marveled. "Praise be to the divine turd of our Lord and Savior, Jesus Christ!"

Malcolm smiled at him and then turned to face the others. "Behold the miraculous powers of the Christ turd!" he exclaimed, holding the hallowed fecal matter high in the air for each of his astonished guests to feast their eyes upon.

The words that flowed from his lips ignited a blaze of cheers and applause from everyone in the room, with the exception, of course, being John Butler, who lay facedown on the floor, the graying hair at the back of his bashed-in head matted with dark and foul-smelling blood that was now congealing and mixed with bits of his shattered skull.

"If any of you had entertained even the slightest doubt about its life-giving power," he continued, "the spectacle you all just witnessed, here in this very room, with your very own eyes, should be more than enough to lay those doubts to rest."

The hand-clapping horde rose, almost in unison, from their seats, bestowing upon their host a standing ovation. Like an actor on a stage, Malcolm took a bow before his adoring audience.

"Who's ready for eternal life?" he asked, coyly.

The six immortality-craving guests immediately responded to his question by extracting bundles of cold, hard cash from purse and pockets and eagerly depositing them into his open hands, which he had cupped to receive them.

After stuffing his pockets to their brims with the money, he returned the turd to its alabaster jar and replaced the wooden plug. He then motioned for Motoshi with his hand and told him to take the turd to the kitchen and "prepare it," following to a tee the detailed instructions he had written down for him. However, before he could pass the jar to the young, obedient houseboy, he suddenly experienced the powerful grip of a hand around the ankle of his right leg, stopping him dead in his tracks. He instinctively looked down and saw that the hand belonged to Butler, who was, to his surprise, still alive. He attempted to kick his captured leg free, but was unable to do so. And then the sensation of sharp teeth sinking themselves deep into the tender flesh of his right calf muscle burned him to the core with excruciating pain. He lost his balance and fell to the blood-slicked floor, alongside John Butler, howling in agony.

The French woman let out another scream, springing from her seat and darting to the other side of the room in a fruitless attempt to find a spot where she might feel safer.

The unrelenting pain was bringing tears to Malcolm's eyes. He smashed the alabaster jar against Butler's forehead, again and again, until the Christ turd flew from the centuries-old vessel and landed on the floor. But still his assailant refused to release him from the death grip of his fingers and teeth, which now were stained red with Malcolm's still-warm blood. Fighting against his pain, he wrapped his fingers around the rock-hard turd, and with one mighty blow, plunged it into Butler's right eye, bloodying the gelatinous orb and bringing forth the spew of its milky-white contents like a geyser erupting into the air.

"If thine right eye offends thee, pluck it out and cast it from thee, so sayeth the Gospel of Matthew!" shouted the wild-eyed televangelist like a cheerleader at a sporting event. "For it is profitable for thee that one of my members should perish, and not that my whole body should be cast into hell!"

Butler shrieked, releasing his teeth from Malcolm's blood-drenched leg. In turn, Malcolm dislodged the turd from Butler's annihilated eyeball. Small, sticky blobs of stomach-churning matter clung to the fecal matter like chunks of red Jell-o. Butler covered what was left of his right eye with his hand, as if the action could bring relief of the savage pain and somehow restore his mashed eyeball to its former state.

Malcolm's mind was now racing with adrenaline-fueled madness. He jammed the turd into Butler's other eye and twisted it back and forth until the decimated orb spilled its gooey contents like a punctured, cream-filled, white-chocolate Easter egg. A sudden awareness that the wailing and thrashing of the man had stopped washed over him and his mania all at once subsided. He was sure that Butler was dead; comforted by the realization that a turd possessing the power to bring life could also bring death.

He withdrew the gore-covered turd and stumbled to return to his feet, despite the gnawing pain in his leg. He wasn't worried about his blood loss or risk of infection. He was confident that, after his partaking of the Christ turd, his physical wounds would immediately depart as the blessing of eternal life flowed through him. Looking down at John Butler, he was astonished, yet strangely satisfied, to observe the man's gore-filled eye sockets squirming with hundreds, if not thousands, of fat, little maggots. The legless fly larvae ate and ate, rapidly multiplying in their numbers, and feasted upon the eyeless corpse until a dark crimson puddle was all that was left of it. The puddle and the maggots slowly disappeared from sight until not a single trace of John Butler remained.

"Another miracle!" Malcolm exclaimed, his heart returning to a normal pace.

The preacher brought his palms together in prayer and raised his eyes to the ceiling. "We thank Thee, O Lord, for the gift of Thine divine defecation. Amen!"

A choir of "Amen" came from the others in the room.

Motoshi wrinkled his nose, unable to conceal his disgust, as he took the turd from his employer, placed it upon the ornate silver tray, and with it in hand, disappeared through the pocket door. Nearly half an hour passed before he returned to the parlor with the silver tray. Upon it now sat a decanter of expensive red wine, seven sterling silver goblets, and an eighteenth-century snuffbox, decorated with the Coat of Arms of the Thorndike family and filled with the pulverized remains of the coveted Christ turd. He emptied the powder from the snuffbox into the decanter and swished it around a few times, then poured some into each of the seven goblets.

One by one, Thorndike's guests reservedly took a goblet from the tray and stared, in silence, at the wine within its metallic confines. It was clear to Malcolm that they were all waiting for him to drink his portion first. He was unsure if it was due to politeness or cowardice, but nevertheless, he raised his goblet, offered up a toast to everlasting life, and then downed the wine. He licked the fragrant liquid that moistened his lips and smiled.

His guests followed his suit, each anxious to feel the blessing of immortality flow through their systems. With death no longer an encumbrance, they would be free to amass even greater wealth, even rule the world if they so desired. Nothing and nobody could ever stand in their ways again. They would be indestructible. Their collective euphoria overpowered any apprehension that dwelled within their hearts.

After an hour filled with idle chatter and the smoking of tobacco products, Malcolm's guests were growing agitated, waiting for something, anything, to happen. They had all expected a sign of something miraculous, an ineffable mystical experience, the phenomenon of religious ecstasy, or an epiphany. At this point, they would have even settled for a buzz, but they felt nothing. They were just as empty as they were before coming to the Thorndike Mansion. Some were entertaining doubts about Malcolm's immortality claims and began to feel they had been swindled out of their money.

"I think I speak for everyone in this room when I say we've waited long enough for a sign that a change in the status of our mortality has taken place," Mortimer Cromwell announced. He was normally a man of very few words; however, his rising anger was propelling his comments. "It's quite obvious to me that the Christ turd didn't possess the powers that you claimed it did."

The other guests agreed with him.

Cromwell then demanded that Malcolm return his money, and the others joined in, expressing their demands for a full refund.

"Everybody, please calm down," Malcolm begged, dreading the thought of parting with all that money that was weighing down his pockets like bricks. "These things require time to take effect," he said, hoping to stall for some time. "I think we should all wait and see what happens in twenty-four hours, or maybe give it three days—the time is took for Jesus' resurrection."

The raging anger burning in his guests' eyes scared him, but not enough to hand over the money. Visions of being torn limb from limb invaded his mind's eye. He contemplated how to make his escape.

Giselle retrieved Butler's gun from the floor near her chair and pointed it at Malcolm, aiming for between his eyes. "My money back, please, or I swear you'll be the first to have your immortality tested."

Malcolm panicked at the sight of the gun, but he tried to remain cool and collected. "Giselle, dear, please put down the gun. Don't do anything you'll regret later."

"I never regret killing men who steal my money," she replied.

"Motoshi!" Malcolm yelled, the sound of fear in his voice increasing. "Come here at once!"

Moments later, the Japanese houseboy entered the parlor through the pocket door. "Yes, Mister Thorndike?"

"Motoshi, did you prepare the Christ turd exactly the way I showed you?"

The servant nodded his head.

"And you performed the ritual of immortality without leaving anything out?"

Motoshi again nodded.

"I don't understand what could have gone wrong!" Malcolm's face was growing paler by the second.

"Say your prayers, Malcolm!" Giselle ordered, her finger anxious to pull the trigger.

With their voices rising up like an angry mob, the others began to shout for Giselle to fill their host with lead. As far as they were all concerned, he had fallen from grace and punishment by death was in order.

Malcolm fell to his knees, tears glistening in his terror-filled eyes, and begged, "Please, don't kill me. I don't want to die. All I ask for is a little bit of time."

"I'm afraid you're time has run out," Cromwell Mortimer observed.

The chant calling for Malcolm's murder grew in its intensity, prompting him to cover his ears with his hands. It rang throughout the mansion and was loud enough to drown out the sounds of the storm outside.

A deafening thunderclap suddenly shook the mansion like an earthquake as a hole ripped open in the ceiling of the parlor, and from it, a swirling column of blinding white light beamed down, illuminating the entire room. Cracks, like crooked lightning bolts, zigzagged down the walls, sending mirrors and artwork and turds on display crashing to the floor. Above, the chandelier swayed back and forth like a gibbeted man in a gale, its prisms of crystal tinkling. Doors banged with violent force as if trying to break free from their frames. Windows rattled and sprung cracks across their panes. Objects took flight from their places atop shelves and glossy table surfaces, as if thrown by invisible hands, pelting Malcolm and his screaming guests.

It was then that the venerated turd, which had, eons ago, made its way out of the holy bowels of the Son of God, rose out of Motoshi's pocket and floated across the room. Upon witnessing this, Malcolm realized that his manservant had double-crossed him, pretending to prepare the Christ turd in the prescribed manner, while intending to keep the holy relic for himself. Anger swam through his veins like piranhas. However, before he could do or say anything, the turd began to slowly rise up within the beam of white light.

"No!" Malcolm bellowed angrily, as he made a lunge for the ascending chunk of fecal matter. "That turd belongs to me, God damn it!"

A searing heat instantly engulfed his hands as he thrust them into the column of white light to grab his levitating prized turd before it could gain momentum on what he assumed was its heaven-bound journey. He cried out in agony as his flesh sizzled and peeled away from the bone. Unable to endure the blistering pain, he quickly withdrew his hands from the light, only to find two charred and smoldering stumps where his hands should have been.

Horror laced with adrenaline ripped at his gut. Choking on the greasy smoke escaping from his new stumps, Malcolm staggered on his heels like a drunkard after a nightlong drinking binge. He dropped to his knees, spasmed from shock, and then collapsed facedown on the floor. He prayed for God to deliver him unto the merciful hands of death; however, the god he prayed to was a cruel, bloodthirsty god, and had other plans for Malcolm and his guests.

All at once, they experienced a peculiar, warm tingling feeling racing through them, beginning at the tops of their heads and terminating at the tips of their big toes. They thought they could hear the trumpets of angels in between the claps of thunder. It aroused confusion, mixed with a strange elation, within their souls. They all knew something monumental was about to happen to them. They knew not what, but could feel it in their bones.

Motoshi watched, almost mesmerized, as the people in the room began to spin around like whirling dervishes. Faster and faster they spun until their legs could no longer support them, and, simultaneously, they plummeted to the floor, soaked from sweat, and lost in the intoxication of rapture.

But then something most horrible and quite unexpected occurred. Their skin began to take on a black, shiny appearance, and they could feel every one of their bones cracking and their internal organs painfully rearranging. Screams of unholy terror burst forth from their gaping mouths, which were now foaming with white froth like the mouths belonging to rabid beasts. Their bodies took on a round shape, formed a hard, protective cover, and began to shrink in size until they were no larger than two and a half inches. From their new bodies, six insect-like legs sprouted, followed by a pair of flying winds. From their heads a pair of horns emerged.

To their ultimate horror, they had physically transformed into dung beetles, and instinctively knew they were doomed to wander the earth, for all eternity, eating shit.

Motoshi, ever the efficient houseboy, swept the insects into a dustpan and deposited each one of them into the alabaster jar that had once belonged to Mary Magdalene. He sealed the top of the jar with the waxy wooden stopper and placed it on top of the antique Chippendale table, next to the pterodactyl dropping.

"Enjoy your immortality," he said, cheerfully, before turning off the light and locking the pocket door behind him.

THE END

ABOUT YOUR AUTHORS

Aron Beauregard was born in Central Falls, Rhode Island. He's been writing horror since the 6th grade when his parents discovered a short story titled "Zombie Child" wedged in the back pocket of his dirty acid-washed jeans. It was about a teenager who couldn't score the girl of his dreams in life so he decided to kill her and impregnate her corpse... You can imagine where it goes from there. Needless to say, his parents were not thrilled by this tale, and rather than acknowledging his creative genius, suspected he might be a budding serial killer.

Regardless of what he did in his life, horror always followed him. After pursuing careers (which ultimately failed) in music, filmmaking, and full-time drug use, he eventually circled back to his bloody bread and butter: writing highly disturbing and bizarre material that tends to explore the human potential for evil. After tooling around for decades, he's finally started publishing his work (to the applause of a handful of deranged perverts).

He also contributes to the Evil Examined Podcast, where he explores the strangest and most horrifying events in the history of humanity with his lady and friends. He emits a Manson-esque charm through the pathetic platform, peddling his works of smut and violence to any goon willing to listen. When you enter his realm, be prepared to embrace the ugly and FEEL THE SPLATTER!

* * *

George Bradley was born in London and grew up in Paris and Hong Kong; but, at its heart, his work comes from the American Midwest, where he now resides in Ohio with his wife Lisa, son Everett, daughter Evelyn and several odd pets. After moving to America in his early twenties, a casual interest in scribbling fiction became a love for possessing innocent minds through the potency of prose.

These days, George enjoys writing horror, science fiction, suspense, dark fantasy, the occasional bedtime ghost story (don't tell mom), and occasionally dabbles in screenwriting. Nevertheless, whether it be dark castles or decaying rust belt towns, the sticky seats of a county fairground or outer space, the common theme is always to explore the relationship between ordinary people and demons...both real and imaginary.

George is working on his debut novel, *Sowing Season*, aimed for release in mid-2020, as well as continuing to publish short stories.

* * *

Cardigan Broadmoor was raised in an old house by an even older New England family. During the day he works at a hole-in-the-wall bookstore in Providence, Rhode Island, and at night he reads and writes to pass the time. He has released several picture books including *The Bullywol Visitor* and *Dead Air*.

* * *

Scot Carpenter is a writer living in Arizona. His stories concern the darker side of humanity: crime, cruelty, perversion and unrepentant evil, and have appeared in the anthologies, *The Sharpened Quill*, *Southwest Noir* and *Switchblade Magazine*, among others.

* * *

Myna Chang writes flash and short stories. Her work has been featured in *Daily Science Fiction, Mad Scientist Journal, Twist in Time,* and *Dead Housekeeping*, among others. Read more at MynaChang.com or find her on

Twitter @MynaChang.

* * *

Clay McLeod Chapman writes books, children's books, comic books and film. Please visit him at: www.claymcleodchapman.com

* * *

Nick Dinicola saw *Candyman* way too young and couldn't sleep for days, thus beginning a lifelong obsession with horror. A Technical Writer by trade, when he's not trying to teach people how to use software, he's trying to scare the hell out of them.

* * *

Jude M. Eriksen was born and raised in Western Canada, and is a writer whose interests skew toward the uncanny places that lie just beyond the realm of possibility. When he isn't writing, Jude enjoys reading, hiking, photography, and fiddling with the unknown.

* * *

Michael Martin Garrett is an author, poet, and recovering journalist. He has broken courthouse corruption scandals, worked as the communications director of a U.S. Senate campaign, and played in a handful of shitty punk bands. His small-town crime and horror fiction has been published by Flame Tree Press, Close To The Bone Publishing, and Dark Alley Press. He lives with his two cats in Central Pennsylvania, where he spends his free time trying to remember to take his antidepressants. Follow him on Twitter @MichaelMGarrett.

* * *

Ken Goldman, former Philadelphia teacher of English and Film Studies, is an Active member of the Horror Writers Association. He has homes on the Main Line in Pennsylvania and at the Jersey shore. His stories have appeared in over 900 independent press publications in the U.S., Canada, the UK, and Australia with over thirty due for publication in 2019-2020. Since 1993 Ken's tales have received seven honorable mentions in The Year's Best Fantasy & Horror. He has written six books: three anthologies of short stories, *You Had Me at Arrgh!!* (Sam's Dot Publishers), *Donny Doesn't Live Here Anymore* (A/A Productions) and *Star-Crossed* (Vampires 2); and a novella, *Desiree* (Damnation Books in print and for Kindle, and for Kindle by eXcessica Publications.) His first novel, *Of a Feather* (Horrific Tales Publishing) was published in January 2014. His second novel, *Sinkhole* (Bloodshot Books) was published in August 2017.

* * *

Gerri R. Gray is an American novelist, short story writer, and a lifelong aficionado of horror, dark humor, and all things bizarre. She blames her twisted sense of humor on a wayward adolescence influenced by the likes of *Monty Python's Flying Circus*, Charles Addams, Frank Zappa, and John Waters.

Her debut novel, *The Amnesia Girl,* was published by HellBound Books in October of 2017, followed by *Gray Skies of Dismal Dreams* (a collection of dark poetry and prose), and *The Graveyard Girls* (an all-women anthology of horror.) Gerri has been writing since the 1970s, and her work has appeared in numerous anthologies and literary journals.

She lives in Upstate New York in an historic nineteenth-century house with her husband and a bevy of spirits. When she isn't busy creating strange worlds filled with even stranger characters, she can often be found rummaging through antique shops, exploring haunted houses, or traipsing through old cemeteries with her camera. For more information, please visit her official website at: http://gerrigray.webs.com

* * *

Christopher T. Hamel is an emerging writer whose work has appeared in *Massacre Magazine* (issues 11 and 12) and *Morpheus Tales* (eBooks #s 31 and 32). He and his wife, Alyssa, are facilitators for NAMI—known as the National Alliance On Mental Illness. Other than spending time with his wife, writing fiction, walking and reading—at the same time, and playing survival horror games like Resident Evil and Silent Hill, Christopher can usually be found being a weirdo with his friends and family.

* * *

Carlton Herzog is an Air Force Veteran. He is a graduate of both Rutgers College, *magna cum laude* and Rutgers Law School where he served as Articles Editor of the Rutgers Law Review. He has published both non-fiction—law review articles—and fiction—with six short stories coming out in 2019 under both the Horrified Press and HellBound Books imprints. He is currently employed with the U.S. Postal Service.

* * *

B.T. Joy is a British horror writer whose short fiction has appeared within the printed pages, Internet presences and podcasts of markets such as Static Movement, Surreal Grotesque, James Ward Kirk Fiction, Human Echoes, Flashes In The Dark, SQ Magazine, Forgotten Tomb Press, Chilling Tales For Dark Nights, Horrified Press and Pseudopod: The Horror Podcast, among others. His debut collection of horror stories, *Long Dead Before Dying*, was released in 2015. He has also published two collections of poems *Teaching Neruda* (2015) and *Body of Poetry* (2016) and, in what seems a previous incarnation now, he once thought of himself as a wandering haijin in the mould of Matsuo Bashō and has written two collections of haiku: *In The Arms of the Wind* (2010) and *The Reeds that Tilt the Sky* (2011). He later found that, although he'd covered enough physical ground in his travels, he was far too tangled in mundane illusions to make a serious fist at a truly ecstatic three line poem.

In addition to his writing, B.T. has worked in his home country, the USA, Italy and China in various fields. He is an educator and has taught in the primary, secondary and university sectors. He is currently working on his PhD at Glasgow University, where he his engaged in an examination of the onto-epistemological impulses of William Faulkner. B.T. can be reached through his website (http://btj0005uk.wix.com/btjoypoet) where readers are invited to contact him directly with thoughts, comments, requests and lists of their favorite episodes of *The Twilight Zone*.

* * *

A.L. King is an author of horror, fantasy, and science fiction. He proudly calls the town of Sistersville, West Virginia home.

* * *

Daryl Marcus is an IT professional and trained hacker working in Colorado. Despite all his technical certifications, he has found writing is the most fun he has ever had in front of a computer. He writes horror, thriller, crime, and science fiction, sometimes all at the same time. In his spare time, he enjoys finding and watching B-horror movies in the hope of discovering true gems the world has forgotten. He lives with his wife and an ever-growing menagerie of robotic pets. His writings can be found in various issues of *Under the Bed*, *Disturbed Digest*, *Cheapjack Pulp*, and *Tales from the Grinning Skull*.

* * *

Jeremy Megargee has always loved dark fiction. He cut his teeth on R.L Stine's *Goosebumps* series as a child and a fascination with Stephen King's work followed later in life. Jeremy weaves his tales of personal horror from Martinsburg, West Virginia with his cat Lazarus acting as his muse/familiar.

* * *

Donna J. W. Munro has spent the last twenty years teaching high school social studies. Her students inspire her every day. She has an MA in writing popular fiction from Seton Hill Writing University. Her pieces are published in *Dark Moon Digest* # 34, *Syntax and Salt*, *Sirens Call eZine*, *The Haunted Traveler*, *Flash Fiction Magazine*, *Astounding Outpost*, *Door=Jar*, *Spectators and Spooks Magazine*, *Nothing's Sacred Magazine* IV and V, *Graveyard Girls (2018)*, *Hazard Yet Forward* (2012), *Enter the Apocalypse* (2017), *Killing It Softly 2* (2017), *Beautiful Lies, Painful Truths II* (2018), *Terror Politico* (2019), and several Thirteen O'Clock Press anthologies. Contact her at https://www.donnajwmunro.com

* * *

Hari Navarro has one great fear in life: Writing in the third person. It scares the hell out of him and he worries that he is in fact dead or that perhaps Hari Navarro will one day try and contact him for the money he owes him. Hari has had work published at the very fine *365 Tomorrows*, *Breach* and *AntipodeanSF* magazines and numerous titles via Black Hare Press. Hari has also succeeded in once being in a film with Julia Roberts (she never calls) and being a New Zealander who now lives in Northern Italy with not one single cat. https://harinavarro.tumblr.com/

* * *

Trevor Newton works as a part-time farmhand, residing in a rural area outside of Raleigh, North Carolina. When he isn't up to his shoulders in complex grease or helping corral cows for auction, he enjoys consuming horror through both literature and film. In addition, he credits his interest in writing from a steady diet of Bentley Little, Richard Laymon and Edward Lee. He is working on multiple short stories and plans to have a fully polished novel completed by late 2020.

* * *

Drew Nicks has always been fascinated by horror. Continued viewings of *Jaws* and *Aliens* as a youth skewed his young mind. His work has been featured in *Dark Corner Books*, *Road Maps and Life Rafts*, *Oscillate Wildly Press*, *Pulp Dreadfuls*, and *The Lovecraft Lunatic Asylum*. He resides in Moose Jaw, Saskatchewan.

* * *

C. C. Parker lives on the fringes of the Cascadian/Seattle area where he continues to toil in the physical media underground while trying to stay sane. A metal obsessed, horror film, occult enthusiast who spends the bulk of his free time escaping into pockets of unreality (interior or peripheral) to stave off any lingering threat of apathy or contentment, deciding long ago these were unrealistic goals in an increasingly hostile world. A writer of dark/experimental prose/poetry for the past thirty years, having published much in small press horror mags during the mid-to-late 90s and 2000s: *Chimeraworld*, *Black Ink Horror*, *Bare Bone*, etc. Most recently, he's appeared in *Plinth*, *Massacre Magazine* and *Breaking Bizarro* (forthcoming). Favoring a dense, hermetic style with a heavily symbolist bent. Daring to push the boundaries of modern prose into something more akin to the decadent stylings of his forebears. C. C. Parker is a writer of both medieval & futuristic romances: a man out-of-time, yet very much a product of it.

* * *

Wolfgang Potterhouse is a prematurely gray, occasional vegetarian, high school teaching, non-native Texan. He has four children and a beautiful wife, all of whom think he is a pretty okay dude. He is a Cancer and is not afraid to tear up when someone gets voted off Master Chef. He has many stories published in an accordion file in his den; this is his fourth story to get legitimately published.

* * *

J.J. Smith is a writer living in the Washington, D.C. area. He's a veteran of HellBound Books with some of his stories published in the anthologies, *The Big Book of Bootleg Horror Volumes I and IV* and *Depraved Desires Volume I*. His stories have also been published in the anthologies, *Behind Glass Eyes: A Haunted Doll Anthology*; *Dark Magic: Witches, Hackers & Robots*; *Halloween Shrieks*; and *Tales from the Witch's Cauldron*, and in *Horror Bites Magazine*. J.J. has been a hard-news reporter for international news services and newspapers. After 16 years of reporting on the U.S. government, J.J. now spends his daylight hours writing summaries of House and Senate hearings.

* * *

Henry Snider has, for over two decades, dedicated his time to helping others tighten their writing through critique groups, classes, lectures, prison prose programs, and high school fiction contests. He co-founded Fiction Foundry (est. 2012) and the award-winning Colorado Springs Fiction Writers Group (1996-2013). Thirteen years to the month from founding the CSFWG, he retired from the presidency. After a much-needed vacation, he returned to the literary world. While still reserving enough time to pursue his own fiction aspirations, he continues to be active in the writing community through classes, editing services, and advice. Henry lives in Colorado with his wife, fellow author and editor Hollie Snider, son–poet Josh Snider and numerous neurotic animals, including, of course, Fizzgig, the token black cat.

* * *

J.B. Toner studied Literature at Thomas More College and holds a black belt in Ohana Kilohana Kenpo-Jujitsu. He has held many occupations, from altar boy to homeless person, but has always aspired to be a writer. His first novel,

Whisper Music, came out in 2019, and he hopes to release many more in the centuries to come.

* * *

Shawn Wood graduated from Central Connecticut State University with a BA in Anthropology. For the past couple years, he has been pursuing a Masters in English/Creative Writing from Southern New Hampshire University. He has been writing short fiction, including graphic novels, in multiple genres for the past several years. He currently lives in Western Maine.

Schlock! Horror!

An anthology of short stories based upon/inspired by and in loving homage to all of those great gorefest movies and books of the 1980's (not necessarily base in that era, although some do ride that wave of nostalgia!), the golden age when horror well and truly came kicking, screaming and spraying blood, gore & body parts out from the shadows...

This exemplary 80's themed/inspired tales of terror has been adjudicated and compiled by one Mr Bret McCormick, himself a writer, producer and director of many a schlock classic, including *Bio-Tech Warrior*, *Time Tracers*, *The Abomination*, *Ozone: The Attack of the Redneck Mutants* and the inimitable *Repligator*.

Featuring stories from: Todd Sullivan, Timothy C Hobbs, Mark Thomas, Andrew Post, James B. Pepe, Thomas Vaughn, Edward Karpp, Jaap Boekestein, Lisa Alfano, L. C. Holt, John Adam Gosham, Brandon Cracraft, M. Earl Smith, Sarah Cannavo, James Gardner, Bret McCormick, and James H. Longmore.

Graveyard Girls

Female authors + Horror = something spectacularly terrifying!

A delicious collection of horrific tales and darkest poetry from the cream of the crop, all lovingly compiled by the incomparable Gerri R Gray! Nestling between the covers of this formidable tome are twenty-five of the very best lady authors writing on the horror scene today! These tales of terror are guaranteed to chill your very soul and awaken you in the dead of the night with fear-sweat clinging to your every pore and your heart pounding hard and heavy in your labored breast…

Featuring superlative horror from: Xtina Marie, M. W. Brown, Rebecca Kolodziej, Anya Lee, Barbara Jacobson, Gerri R. Gray, Christina Bergling, Julia Benally, Olga Werby, Kelly Glover, Lee Franklin, Linda M. Crate, Vanessa Hawkins, P. Alanna Roethle, J Snow, Evelyn Eve, Serena Daniels, S. E. Davis, Sam Hill, J. C. Raye, Donna J. W. Munro, R. J. Murray, C. Bailey-Bacchus, Varonica Chaney, Marian Finch (Lady Marian).

Satanic Panic

An incredible homage to 1980's horror!

Satanic Panic, a mass hysteria created in the nineteen eighties, has returned to a small college town in the Midwest.

Ritualistic murders and the presence of the occult have bled below the surface of the town in the form of icy accidents and other coincidences.

And when three lifelong friends find themselves on the radar of a killer—and leader of a satanic cult—they must fight for what's good without being seduced by the evil that possesses their campus.

The Toilet Zone
RESTROOM READING AT ITS MOST FRIGHTENING!

Compiled and edited by the grand master of 80's schlock horror, Bret McCormick, each one of this collection of 32 terrifying tales is just the perfect length for a visit to the smallest room....

At the very boundaries of human imagination dwells one single, solitary place of solitude, of peace and quiet, a place in which your regular human being spends, on average, 10 to 15 minutes - at least once every single day of their lives.

Now, consider a typical, everyday reading speed of 200 to 250 words per minute - that means your average visitor has the time to read between 2,500 to 4,000 words, which makes each and every one of these 32 tales of terror - from some of the best contemporary independent authors - within this anthology of horror the perfect, meticulously calculated length. Dare you take a walk to the small room from where inky shadows creep out to smother the light and solitude's siren call beckons you?

Dare you take a quiet, lonely walk into… The Toilet Zone

Invasive Species

A monster has come to Maldus, Arkansas, and the residents of the small mountain town are too busy to notice. With the monster comes something even more terrifying and threatening than gnashing teeth or razor-sharp claws.

The monster has brought change.

The residents of the small mountain town are too busy to notice at first. Busy with things such as addiction, racism, work, or land deals. Unnoticed, the change the monster brings in its insidious wake spreads like wildfire.

Unnoticed, the town of Maldus falls prey to an Invasive Species.

An Unholy Trinity Volume 2

**FOUR HORRIFYING NOVELLAS,
FOUR EXCEPTIONAL AUTHORS,
ALL IN ONE PHENOMENAL BOOK!**

THE BLOODMOON EXPRESS - M.R. Wallace

Following a failed case in London three years before, Ian DeWitt finds himself on Le Train Bleu. The famous passenger train will ferry him to the warm shores of the Mediterranean for a much-needed rest. Ian soon finds that the horrors of the past have followed him, and the resplendent luxury train becomes the hunting ground for a monster all too familiar to the beleaguered Scotland Yard detective. Running out of time and woefully unequipped to combat such a beast, DeWitt must discover the identity of the creature and attempt to stop it before they are torn to shreds.

SAVAGES FOR REVENGE - Alex Marroquin

Failing as an artist, Derrick de Sousa travels to Argentina to recover his artistic inspiration after his college sweetheart invites him to reunite with her at Buenos Aires. Instead, he finds himself forced into a path of murder and cannibalism by a madman convinced that all humans must die in order to preserve the natural world for himself.

This mysterious killer, armed to the teeth for his 'war against humanity,' forces Derrick to follow in his bloody footsteps across Argentina. But with each life he takes, Derrick finds it harder to drop the weapon in his hand.

GARVEY'S EATS - Kenneth Seward

Deep in the backwoods of Texas sits a diner named Garvy's Eats, famous for its burger, the Garvy Special. Whitney and Tegan, best friends since Jr. High, are on a road trip to Mexico before college starts in the fall. After a thunderstorm forces the friends to take a detour, they end up at the diner where Roy Garvy wants the two girls for meat on the Garvy Special. Now with a monstrous, sick and twisted man known only as the Hellbilly hunting them down, the two girls must fight for their lives or risk ending up being served on a bun with a side of fries.

HellBound Books Publishing

**A HellBound Books LLC
Publication**

http://www.hellboundbookspublishing.com

Printed in the United States of America

9 781948 318853